Blood ran d[...]
leaped toward [...]
glinting bright sparks. She lifted, she plunged, and she saw
shock turn Barg's eyes glassy.

The steel slid softly into muscle, slipped between ribs.
The blade scraped bone. Barg's eyes went wide, and he
dropped away. The tavern swelled with voices as Knights
swore and cried murder.

Kerian shot for the door, hot blood on her hands.

The Age of Mortals Series

Conundrum
Jeff Crook

The Lioness
Nancy Varian Berberick

Dark Thane
Jeff Crook
(April 2003)

THE LIONESS

NANCY VARIAN BERBERICK

CHAPTER

I

Sir Chance Garoll looked ahead at his fellow Knights, five in all, and he the sixth. He looked behind him and sighted down the wide road, flattened earth, dun and sun dappled, straight as a shaft through the woodland. The overarching trees gave him the uncomfortable feeling of riding through a tunnel, one closing behind, opening ahead.

One of his fellows hawked and spat then looked over his shoulder at Chance. "Headsman," he called, "keep up!"

Headsman. The others laughed, one pulled hard on the reins, making his broad-shouldered mount snort and curvet. "What's the count, Chance?"

Sir Chance—Headsman Chance—hefted the sack hung from his saddle's pommel. Blood dripped, staining the ground. When he closed his eyes, Chance could see the killing ground, the sunny green swale in the forest where he and his companions had fallen upon a den of elf highwaymen. The Knights had run through the hapless robbers like death's own horsemen, swords flashing in whistling descent to swipe off heads.

Sometimes, Chance thought as he recalled the slaughter,

the death-scream had howled out of a rolling head's gaping mouth.

"A dozen," he said, settling the sack again. His tall mount's brown shoulder was black with blood. Blood etched a thin trail down the steed's foreleg. Trained to battle, inured to the scent of death, the great beast flung up his head at the thick, coppery scent, an eager light in his eyes.

Headsman, they had named him. He grinned. Not a bad name. He had not taken all the heads, but he'd taken most of them and collected them all. The orders from Lord Thagol had come to him directly; he considered it his duty to bring back the trophies. Chance shuddered, recalling how the brief moments in the Skull Knight's presence had seemed like hours. He'd have to spend time with Lord Thagol again, and here, far away from the Knight, he dared hope and wish it wouldn't be a long time.

Iron-shod hoofs fell heavily on the road. One of the Knights lifted his helm from his head and hung it on his saddle. The other five had a farther road to take than Sir Chance. With the Headsman, they would go down to Qualinost, then they would leave him and ride on to Miranost near the border between Qualinesti and the free land of Abanasinia.

Though the dragon Beryl held the elf kingdom in thrall, there were still ways past the borders of Qualinesti. The main roads had long been warded by Dark Knights who kept the elves in and intruders from any of the Free Realms out. Traders with the proper passes could cross the checkpoints, for these were a source of Qualinesti's wealth and so a resource for the greedy dragon who had her tribute from every steel coin earned. Other ways in and out of the elf land existed, all those that existed before the Dragon Purge and the coming of the great Green, Beryllinthranox.

Headsman Chance lifted in the stirrups, searching high ahead. He caught sight of a shimmer through the trees but decided that must be a glimpse of wishful thinking, for they were yet a three hour ride from the capital of the elf kingdom. No shining tower could be seen yet. He settled to ride, moving in unconscious rhythm with his mount's gait. It was a time before he noticed that in the wake of the passage of the dark Knights, silence flowed.

At the highest point of noon, no birds sang, squirrels did not dart and scold, rabbits did not leap aside and freeze in the bracken. In the sky, far above the arching green canopy of trees, hawks hung, wondering. Six humans armored in ebony steel rode through the Qualinesti Forest, Knights of an order once dedicated to a dark goddess now departed, warriors now in the pay of a dragon just as ruthless. Mail chiming, bridles and bits jingling, the six followed the south-running arm of the White-Rage River.

Though he had been posted to Qualinesti for five years now, Sir Chance had never experienced a silence on these roads like this today. A following silence, as though something he did not see—could never see—came after.

"Anyone hear that?" he said.

The tallest of his companions turned, Grig Gal from out of Neraka itself where lived great garrisons of Dark Knights, ogres, and fierce draconians. Grig sweated in his mail and breastplate, and his thick black gloves hung from his belt.

"Hear what?" he asked, and his voice held an edge like a blade's. Grig didn't like the forest, and he didn't like elves.

"The quiet," Chance answered, feeling foolish as soon as he did. How do you hear quiet?

Grig was not much of a wordsmith himself, not one to ponder the niceties of phrasing or meaning. "I don't hear nothing," he grunted.

3

The Knights now rode shoulder to shoulder, six in three pairs. Twice on the way, elf farmers with laden carts had to pull off the road. Once a load of fat grain sacks spilled and split, pouring golden wheat into ditches.

The elves cursed. Grig casually kicked one so hard his jaw shattered on the Knight's steel-toed boot. The elf had a voice like a banshee woman. His scream turned to high keening. To quiet the noise, Grig lopped off the unlucky one's head.

Chance watched it fall, and yes, he heard the wailing issue from the dead one's shattered jaw before the head finished rolling. The dead elf's fellows took to their heels, leaving spilled grain, harnessed horses, and the corpse. As blood mixed with the grain, the following silence swallowed the sounds of anger and pain. The Knights resumed their travels.

After a time, Chance looked back again, seeing only the shade and dappling sun. They rode now like thunder along roads where the greenwood gave ground to farm fields and orchards. Cows and goats grazed on the aftermath of a harvest, pigs ran at the edges of the wood in search of early fallen nuts and apples blown green from the last windy night. Farmers and their strong sons plowed on this last day of summer, preparing for the planting of winter crops. In the dooryards their wives and daughters shooed chickens into the coops. All of these, men and maids, heard the coming of the Knights as they would the coming of a storm. None, by glance or word, gave the dragon's Knights further reason to turn aside and bring them grief, not even the young elves who, by the look of them, would rather have ignored a father's command and pitched stones at the dark troop riding by.

The Knights desired no delay now. Past farms Chance and his companions rode, past a small village where it seemed word of their coming had flown ahead. Though the day was fine, no loungers were found in the yard of the tavern, no one walked on the streets, and in the stable yard not a horse was to be seen. They rode in silence until they came to the place where the forest fell utterly away before the deep gorge that surrounded the elven capital. Here, since ancient times, was the city's first line of defense, a gorge no mounted man could cross, one that men on foot would be mad to try. Two bridges spanned this gorge, and these were of fast burning wood. Elves had, in ancient times, died defending that bridge, had a time or two had reason to burn it and deny the crossing to foes.

Sir Chance wiped sweat from his face and thought the elves had done a good work when they'd planned that defense. Against all but a dragon, it would hold.

"Ay!" Sir Chance shouted. "On Lord Thagol's service! Let me in, and let my companions by!"

The guard at the wooden bridge called, "Say who you are!"

Chance shrugged and lifted the bloody sack. "You reckon you know who I am now?"

The guard laughed darkly. "Sir Chance, welcome!"

For form, the others gave their names. Sir Grig Gal, Sir Angan Heran, Sir Welane of the Hills of Blood, Sir Dern of Dimmin, and Sir Faelt Lagar. "On to the eastern border," Grig snarled. Before the guard could yea him or nay him, he snapped a curt order to his men, and the troop of them wheeled away from the gorge, leaving Sir Chance, thunder riding north.

Chance spurred his horse forward. Halfway across the wooden bridge, he pulled to a stop and looked back over his shoulder. Beyond the gorge, beyond the clearing, the forest shimmered, shifting before his eyes.

A heat mirage, he thought, wiping sweat again.

Chill touched him, turning sweat cold between his shoulders. Why did only the trees shimmer, the branches

5

waver as though he were drink-addled and his eyes unable to hold sight steady? Chance felt suddenly that eyes peered at him from the shadowy depths of the Qualinesti Forest, malevolent watchers.

"What?" said the guard, looking where Chance did. He looked, but plainly he did not see.

Chance shook his head. "Nothing. Just the heat."

Uneasiness followed Chance across the bridge and along the road as the four silver bridges spanning the city came into sight, the golden towers of Qualinost rising above in the late sunlight. In their bloody sack, the heads of thirteen elves, one bleeding fresher than its fellows, bounced against the horse's broad shoulder. Passing beneath the east-facing span of Qualinost's shining bridge, Sir Chance Garoll, Chance Headsman, looked up to the parapet running from watchtower to watchtower. North, south, and west, those parapets ran in clean, unbroken lines. This eastern one, though, bristled like a hound with its hackles up. Spears thrust up from the rampart, two dozen of them evenly spaced. Gleaming points winked at the sky. Here would rest the remains of one farmer and a dozen elf robbers killed like the worst criminals, beheaded with axe and sword. They were not more than luckless members of the scattered bands of ruffians and outlaws who had spent the summer harassing the green dragon's Knights. Chance and his fellows had harvested these heads from as far south as Ahlanost near the border between the elf kingdom and Thorbardin of the dwarves. The orders to rout and kill these marauders came from Lord Eamutt Thagol, himself commissioned by the great Marshal Medan, the dragon's own overlord and general, whose job it was to keep order in the elf kingdom.

A last chance for Lord Thagol, Chance thought grimly, this post to Qualinost. No one ever said it out loud, but Knights did whisper that Thagol had fallen afoul of his sponsoring lords in Neraka, had become a liability. It was Medan's faith in the man that kept Thagol from a worse posting than this one. They had once served together in the Chaos War, brothers in arms before the gods left Krynn and the world fell to the Dragon Purge.

It might be, said rumor, that Medan had his old friend posted to Qualinost, this relatively quiet place, because he'd seen or sensed the first shiverings of madness threatening the Skull Knight and wanted to get him out of the way of those who would judge him unfit to serve. Too long inside the minds of others, it was said of Eamutt Thagol, or it might be the Skull Knight had looked into the wrong skull, there in Neraka where the lord Knights of the order ruled.

When Marshall Medan heard a whisper or two in the forest, a tale in a tavern, a song newly minted about outlaw-heroes, he understood that this tinder needed only a spark for rebellion to flare, and only a man like Lord Thagol could curb such a rebellion.

The eastern bridge of Qualinost sprouted heads. Many more heads would join them as the robberies and outlawry continued. They were a stubborn and subtle people, the elves of Qualinesti, thought Headsman Chance.

Suddenly his belly clenched; his blood ran chill. He forced himself to think of something else. From Sir Eamutt Thagol few things remained long secret. Thagol Dream-walker, some named him, and such thoughts as those Chance had just entertained might well look like doubt, or worse, like insubordination. Such thoughts as these were best not framed in words, even inside the borders of his own skull.

CHAPTER

2

Soft, the girl with the spilling mane of honey hair slipped from her lover's bed. She smelled of exotic spices and foreign lands, for her soaps and oils and perfumes came to her from distant Tarsis. By merchant caravan, these toiletries came, traveling the green dragon's realm and brought to the royal residence, a king's gift for his beloved. Just then, Kerianseray's scented hair was her only covering, falling to her hips, thick and rippling down her back. On padding feet, she crossed the room, her footfalls making no sound on the soft thick rugs scattered around the high chamber. Woven in Silvanesti, a long time ago in the years before even the First Cataclysm, these rugs represented wealth on a scale that would have then fed a village of farmers for generations.

Kerian scooped up her clothing from the floor, the rose and purple blouse, the linen trousers, her small clothes. Lightest silk, the white camisole slid easily over her head. She stepped into silken trews of the kind that came only to above the knee and cinched the waist loosely with a drawstring of golden silk cord. In bed, the king stirred. Kerian glanced over her shoulder to see if he stirred to wake. He did not. Some dream moved him. She took a step closer, back to the bed, then another.

No sun shone in the window yet; the stars had only started to fade. Beneath a canopy of shadow, the elf king slept, and what light there was came in through the window to illuminate his face. His hair lay like gold on the pillow, his arm cradled his cheek. The son of Tanis Half-Elven, Gilthas would never have the beard his father had, for he had not the same measure of human blood in him. Still, in some lights he showed a downy cheek, the suggestion of a beard.

Again the king stirred. Kerian wondered whether he stirred in pleasant dream or in nightmare. With the latter, she had some familiarity. He was a haunted one, her lover. Outside, in corridors, voices ghosted by, whispering the day awake. Kerian turned from the king to continue dressing, crossing the room to the mirror, a long sheen of glass framed in scrolled silver. As she lifted her hair, she heard the king wake.

"Good morning," she said, smiling at Gilthas in the mirror as he sat up. He was a little taller than most elves, for he had a human grandfather, it was whispered, a man whose name no one knew. It was said that Tanis Half-Elven, the king's father, was a child of rape.

Gilthas gestured, one small motion of his hand, and Kerian turned, holding her hair ready to braid.

"Let me do that," said the king of the Qualinesti elves.

"Gil, no. I have to go. If I'm missed from my quarters—"

He gestured almost imperiously. His voice, though, was a lover's and so did not command. "Don't worry about Rashas. He's going to be hours dressing for the procession today. He won't miss one servant among all those in his hall."

So much was true. It took a king less time to prepare himself for the procession that traditionally welcomed the season of Autumn Harvest than this one proud senator. Rashas likely would not miss Kerian, a servant of the humblest station.

Kerian went to the king, holding back her hair as she sat on the end of the bed. He took the shining weight of it from her and combed it out with his fingers, separating it into three thick strands to braid. He worked gently, in silence, and bound up his work with a ribbon of rose-colored grosgrain. Finished, he gave the braid a gentle, playful tug. She turned, laughing, and he put his two hands on her shoulders, tenderly tracing the line of her collarbone with his thumbs. His forefinger outlined the tattoo on her neck, the twining vines winding round and round and down. That touch, the warming light in his eyes, she knew what these meant.

"No, Gil." She lifted his hands. "I have to go."

He knew it. She would go in secret, threading passages few but the king himself knew about. He had designed his residence, his forest palace built not in or of a grove of tall oaks, but as part of that grove, a many-chambered mansion that did not require the felling of ancient oaks but demanded that rooms and stairways, atria and sudden secret gardens, be built in such a way as to let the grove of trees guide the shaping. Because this royal residence had been dismissed as a moody boy-king's amusement, few had paid attention to the planning or the building. Few knew that, here and there, secret passages lay behind seemingly innocent walls, narrow ways to take a traveler hastily from certain chambers out into an innocent garden. One of these passages lay behind the eastern wall of the king's own bedchamber.

Reluctantly, Gilthas agreed. "You must go, for Rashas must never know about us." As one reciting a lesson, he spoke with a thread of sulky bitterness in his tone.

Not Rashas or another person more than those who

already did. Their secret was shared only by the ...
Mother, Gil's trusted servant Planchet, and Kerian's dearest friend in her master's hall, Zoe Greenbriar. That secret had been kept for thirty years, for political reasons, and it was for political reasons that, later today, the king would be obliged to attend a dreary Senate meeting.

Gilthas would attend the meeting of the Thalas-Enthia, ostensibly because Senator Rashas insisted that he do so. To Rashas, indeed to nearly everyone, Gilthas seemed a weak, vacillating youth who could not determine which color hose looked well with what tunic and so could be counted on not to interfere with any serious work the senate had before it.

"The lad—ah, the king—the king is a youth and he is learning," Rashas insisted to his fellow senators, the ladies and lords of the Thalas-Enthia. He insisted, but with seeming gentleness. "You see that our young lord is already showing wisdom in this terrible time, when the half of Krynn lives under the talons of dragons. He is showing the wisdom to wait, learn, and watch while older, wiser heads govern." Carefully, the senator would withhold his smile and maintain gravity. "We are blessed in our king."

Blessed in our king. Kerian knew the senator, in whose household she had been a servant for years. She knew the wily old elf's way of thinking. Blessed in our king, our malleable puppet king. Rashas might well think so, for early in his rule Gilthas had not made a reputation for himself as a strong-willed leader. Plagued by ill health in his childhood, in his youth he'd been haunted by the chill uncertainty that he could not ever be a son worthy of parents who had fought so bravely during the War of the Lance. Who could live up to the legacy of Princess Laurana, the Golden General? What son could stand free of the legend of the storied Hero of the Lance, Tanis Half-Elven? Early in his rule, Gilthas had, indeed, been a puppet king.

There came a time when he had stopped being the young man who brooded over uncertainties and filled up pages of parchment with grim poetry. In truth, he still composed his darkly moody poems. Kerian did not much care for these. For all but she and the Queen Mother he wore the persona of a young man who vacillated between a kind of depression and the vapidity of a spoiled royal son. To the two women who loved him and knew him best, however, Gilthas was more. Uncertainty still dogged him, and nightmare haunted his sleep, dark dreams that to the young king sometimes seemed like terrible prophecy, but these no longer debilitated him, these he fought to rise above.

There is the courage of the sword and the courage of the heart and soul. Gilthas had discovered the latter and for this Kerian loved him.

A lot of what Rashas thought he knew about his king was false, and a lot about his king Rashas didn't know at all. He did not know that a young Kagonesti woman in his service was beloved of the king. He did not know that much of what his servant heard made its way to Gilthas, dross to be sifted for grain. Rashas did not know—and if Gilthas and Kerian were careful, he would never know—that now and then, at a critical juncture, Gilthas found himself with just the kernel of information necessary to put him in a stronger position to bargain with his Senate than that august body might have expected.

In the last few years he'd put two governors into power in the eastern provinces, and these governors awaited their chance to prove themselves loyal. He'd granted favors to certain lords and ladies, knowing favors would be returned if needed. He hoped today to have another choice of his installed. He intended to set up the young Lord Firemane in the lord's late mother's position as governor of a northern province. Rashas had been, if not hoping for the old woman's death, ready to install a governor with no familial and sentimental ties to the royal family. Such positions were not hereditary among elves, but Gilthas was prepared to point out—correctly—that no other man or woman had the wealth or the personal regard among the people of that far province to rule well. There could be no other choice but young Firemane unless the senate was willing to fund the installation of an outsider. In these dragon-days, with so much tribute going to Beryl, few senators would be eager to underwrite a problematic candidate.

Wily as Rashas, Gilthas played a dangerous game. He pretended to dance to the will of his senate, a senate ruled by Rashas, while working in the shadows to help his mother in her struggle to free the elf homeland from the Dark Knights and dragon dominion.

Outside the bedchamber, Planchet's voice threaded among the others, the king's body servant calling the household to order. The Queen Mother, he told them, would not be joining the king for breakfast.

"Take the place setting away," Planchet said, following his command with a brisk clap of his hands.

Silent now for the sake of those outside, Kerian glanced at her lover.

"Mother received dispatches late last night."

Kerian raised an eyebrow, and Gilthas crooked a lean smile. "A note, delivered late while you slept, my love. She'll make her excuses and not attend the procession or the Senate session."

"The treaty?"

Gilthas nodded. Perhaps the dispatches were a packet of letters from Abanasinia, perhaps from one of the Plains-folk leaders; perhaps some word at last from the dwarves of Thorbardin, a sign that the High King and his thanes did, at last, thaw toward the idea of making a pact with the elves.

Who ever knew about dwarves, those long thinkers, age-long deliberators? In centuries past, the elves had been fast friends with elves, Pax Tharkas stood testimony to that. In these times, the dwarves had a decent regard for the woman who had played so large a part in the War of the Lance but not so much interest in coming out from their mountain fastness to join treaties. There had been war in the mountain in the years of the Chaos War, a civil war among the dwarven clans that, it was said, had left the kingdom in ruin. Upon the will of these wounded, erstwhile allies hung the fate of a treaty that might stand a chance of delivering the elves from their captivity.

Outside, the servants murmured to each other. Clothing was being laid out even as a breakfast tray settled on a carved ivory stand to await the royal pleasure.

"Time to go," Kerian whispered.

Out into the start of a day long beloved of the Qualinesti people. The elves would celebrate the change of the season and pretend not to notice the Dark Knights lurking. That was life in occupied Qualinost, but a much better life than in other Dragon Realms. Where blue Khellendros ruled, people starved; in the eastern parts of Krynn where Malystryx the Red reigned, the people wept blood. Here, in exchange for tribute, the elves had rags of freedom and full larders. It was the tenuous bargain.

Kerian brushed her lover's lips with a kiss.

Beneath her lips, she felt his rueful smile as Gilthas traced the line of her cheek with his finger. "Go, then. Come back again tonight."

This she promised, now as always, willingly. She kissed him again, and the king held her just a moment longer before he let her go.

In the fabled city of the elves, with towers gleaming and silvery bridges shining, the people went in the colors of Autumn Harvest. Men, young and old, dressed in nut-brown trousers, their shirts the russet of ripened apples, tawny barley, maples gone golden and dogwoods changed to the color of wine. The women, old and young and even the little girls, swirled in the streets and byways. They wore the same colors as their men, blue for asters in the fields, purple for the berries in the glades, gold, brown, and rose. In their hair they wove ribbons of silk, satin, and grosgrain. Around their waists they cinched sashes to match and the fringes hung down past the knee.

Men, women, and children, lord and lady, servant and tradesman, the people of Qualinost filled the streets. They went laughing from bake shop to wine shop, from weaver to jeweler; they gathered around the high-wheeled carts of apple sellers and nutmen and farmers in from the fields with the best of their harvest. In the horse fair, where traditionally elves met to buy and sell the fine beasts the kingdom was known for, folk watched the auctions of wide-chested dray horses and pretty palfreys for an elderly lady's evening ride. They observed the sale of sturdy mounts for long riding and little ponies that would delight a rich elf's child.

For this one day, dogs loped in the gardens and children ran and shouted, their wrists and ankles adorned with bracelets of shining silver bells. Pipers played at every corner, bards declaimed their verses, and young girls sat in scented bowers of wisteria and roses, listening to minstrels sing them songs commissioned by their admirers. Songs of tenderest love, of deepest passion, songs of loss, of gain, of hope, these songs brought tears to the eyes of the maidens and sly smiles to the lips of those who passed by.

The city rang with harvest joy, and through Qualinost, upon a route that might seem winding to a stranger, the elf king made his royal progress. He went in a fine litter canopied in tasseled green silk and borne by four strong young elves. These litter bearers were the handsome sons and lovely daughters of minor branches of House Royal. Privilege and place gave them the right to this honor.

All his Senate went with Gilthas, the whole of the Thalas-Enthia surrounding. Shining in silks and satins, glittering in jewels, the lords and ladies of Qualinost rode upon either side of the king. By their colors they were known, pennons borne like lances and mounted beside saddles as though they were, indeed, weapons. Satins sailed the scented air, and ribbons of proper color fluttered in the manes of their tall mounts, bands of silk braided into hair brushed soft as a woman's.

Only one rode before the king, and he was Rashas, resplendent in his purple robes, his rose-colored sash. The senator glittered in rubies and amethysts, and upon his silvered head he wore a wreath whose leaves were of beaten gold, each so thin, so delicately wrought that closest inspection would betray no sign of the hammer's blow.

Gilthas half-closed his eyes to shield them from the sunlight leaping in glints and gleams from each delicate leaf. He sighed, not discreetly, and wished he'd given the senator something less glaring as a Winter Night gift last year. The sigh caught the attention of Lady Evantha of House Cleric.

"It's a long route this year," Gilthas said, affecting to hide a yawn with a ring-glittering hand. He was not bored; he was not wearied. He was, in truth, edgy and eager and wishing he could leave the swaying litter and leap astride a horse as tall and fine as the shining bay Rashas rode.

Around them, the city shone, the people laughed, and someone cried out from the garden of the Bough and Blossom tavern, "Look! There! It's the king!"

Gilthas recognized a rustic accent, some farmer in from

the provinces with his harvest, determined to celebrate the festival in grand style. Perhaps he had gone to the horse fair, perhaps he had sold a good dray there or purchased one. He'd probably bought his wife a new gown in the Street of Tailors, his daughter some toys in Wonders Lane. Doubtless, the family would talk about this week through the winter to come, revisiting golden Qualinost in memory before the warming fires.

Gilthas looked out from his litter, parting the hangings a little to see. A young elf stood with his hand on the shoulder of a very small girl who looked to be his daughter. He pointed when he saw the king's hand on the silken hangings. The girl strained forward to see, and suddenly her father swung her high upon his shoulder.

"The king!" she cried, waving her hand. The belled bracelets on her wrist rang like silvery laughter on the air. "King! Hello, king! Happy harvests!"

People turned to smile at the child and her joyful, innocent greeting. Her father lifted her high over his head, and the little one squealed with laughter. Beside Gilthas, Lady Evantha sniffed and made a disdainful comment about how vulgar the folk had become in the provinces.

"Why, they are as uncouth as our own Kagonesti servants. No," she said, shaking her head in mime of careful consideration. "No, I misspeak. I think those provincials are worse. I think they live too close into the forest, and they forget how to comport themselves in cities. Whereas . . ." She nodded now, approving her conclusion before she spoke it. Sunlight glinted on her golden earrings; a warm breath of air gently lifted the filmy sleeve of her russet gown. "Whereas, I do believe, Your Majesty, that our servants are, indeed, gaining a certain noticeable—oh, can we say?—a certain degree of, well, if not grace, certainly refinement."

Gilthas nodded, and he pretended to consider her point

as he watched the farmer and his daughter turn away, back to their family, back to their celebrations. How marvelous the city must seem to them! How sweet the child's wonder and her impulsive, heartfelt greeting.

Happy harvests!

The greeting sat in his heart like wine sparkling as the procession wound through the streets. The esteemed leaders of the finest Houses of the Qualinesti riding in escort to their young king progressed through the city, past the fabled Tower of the Sun and Stars, out past homes humble and high, houses of the older style built among trees, magnificent houses of the newer fashion embracing the faces of the stone cliffs. The king and his court traveled at stately pace all through the winding avenues clogged with citizens of the city and elves come in from the provinces. Everywhere they went, people fell back to watch the king and his mighty senate, calling out greeting or blessing.

At the Mansion of the Moons, Gilthas bade the procession halt, for here were the quietest of all the gardens in the city. No one celebrated here; no one danced, sang, or laughed. The mansion, in truth a tall tower of gleaming white marble, stood starkly silent. Within, all knew, acolytes of vanished gods lived as though they were exiles, filling the days with prayer and the kind of hope only exiles have, long pared down to the thinnest edge, never given over. There was a time—in Gil's own living memory—when three moons had sailed the skies of Krynn, white Solinari, red Lunitari, and black Nuitari. There was a time when gods had walked upon the face of the world, when god-inspired magic existed that bore little likeness to the untrustworthy enchantments found in ancient relics and talismans. These days, not a deity among all the Houses of Gods spoke to any mortal, and mages were forced to move about in shabby gear with shabby hopes.

At the king's command, the procession rode on. Gilthas

went in silence now. He didn't look out at the city again until he heard Lady Elantha's snort of disdain. Gilthas parted the silk hangings to see what had caught her attention. They had come to the library district, that place of gardens and groves where the dominating buildings were the Library of Qualinost, far-famed and respected even in these days when Beryl's Knights kept most scholars out of the kingdom.

The king leaned a little forward to see a band of autumn dancers. Musicians, pipers and drummers shaped a wide circle in the garden, and within the circle dancers spun like leaves come down from autumn. His face softened, for among them he saw Kerian. They performed the Dance of the Year, a complex series of steps that took them round in spirals which closed tightly then grew wide again, intersecting so that those standing on the high balconies of the houses surrounding the library's garden would see the dancers as though they were patterns in a kaleidoscope. Variations of this dance went on in gardens all over the city, in parks and even in private gardens. This was a dance for the harvest, and elves who wanted to participate began practicing the complicated steps in the spring in order to be ready to perform in autumn. Kerian was an amateur dancer, perhaps not necessarily a gifted one, yet, what she lacked in precision or innate talent, she more than made up for in spark and spirit.

The music soared, the notes of pipes like a flight of birds. It came back to earth again, caught and held by the subtle drum beat that guided the steps of the dancers. Kerian sailed among them, lovely in her festival garb. She had abandoned the colors of Rashas's service in favor of harvest colors. She'd unbraided her hair and caught it loosely back in a shimmering scarf the color of corn silk. Her wide skirt swirled, golden as the oaks of autumn. Upon her wrists and the slim ankles of her brown naked feet, silvery bells rang. Sunlight warmed the day; she wore a thin silk blouse dyed the exact shade of the blue asters in the fields, the scalloped sleeves so short as to merely cover her lavishly tattooed shoulders.

Winding, Kerian's tattoos were like shadows upon her sun-burnished skin. Gil knew where each began and where each ended. He knew how they intersected and exactly where. Some of the Kagonesti covered their tattoos, either because a master decreed them uncouth or because they themselves had learned to feel ashamed of this unmistakable signing of the Wilder Elf heritage. Others covered the markings because they felt the tattoos were not for the casual observance of others. Kerian never covered her twining vines. She didn't care who noted the tattoos or how they felt about them.

"Ah, well," Lady Elantha murmured, watching Kerian dance. "I suppose not all the servants have learned grace."

"Indeed," said the king, smiling, because he must be seen to agree. He made a purposeful hesitation. "Yet she moves like shadows on the ground. Look, her feet barely touch the earth. That is a kind of grace, don't you think, my lady?"

Lady Elantha sniffed. "She is vulgar and half-clad, at that."

Not quite, Gilthas thought who knew this dancer clad and unclad, yet it was true that the silk of her blouse was so thin that she wore a camisole for modesty, and that was not of significantly more substance than the aster-blue blouse. The king saw the shadow of his lover's breasts as she danced, and Lady Elantha saw his hand move, a small restlessness he couldn't help. Gilthas then folded his hands as though casually, but he did not take his eyes from the dancers.

Shining, swinging from hand to hand in steps so complicated they looked like madness, Kerian flung back her head, honey hair tumbling in rippling waves from her kerchief.

The silk scarf caught a breeze and drifted toward a young man who stood watching the dance. He reached and caught the kerchief, holding it out to Kerian and teasing it back. Gilthas couldn't hear what was said, but he understood the man's gestures. He'd return the scarf for the fee of a kiss. Kerian's laughter rang like bells. Never missing a step, she took back her kerchief and lightly paid the fee as she passed round in the circle dance.

"Move on," the king commanded, his voice curt. He did not part the hangings again to look out until he discerned, by the receding sound of music and voices, that they'd come to a more utilitarian part of the city. They were in the Knights' quarter now. Not far from here, Gilthas knew, Lord Eamutt Thagol sat in his ugly barracks building, the Skull Knight issuing orders to his minions. This day, at the request of Rashas who was the Senate's liaison between the kingdom and the Knights, Thagol had agreed to keep his dark-armored patrols discreetly in the background of the festivities.

Gilthas folded his lips grimly as they neared the eastern bridge the way out of the city. The king parted the litter's hangings again, gazing eastward, feeling an aching and an emptiness. The bridge's silvery span lifted high above king and lords, high above the city itself. Connected to the other three bridges by a series of towers, no more than guard houses for the watch, there had been a time when this bridge was no different from the other three.

Recently, that had changed.

Gil's stomach turned, bitter bile rose into his throat. The eastern bridge bristled with spears like pikes. Upon the bloody points of those spears sat the fresh heads of elves. Above, high in the bright blue harvest sky, a darkness of ravens sailed. In the king's ears, the sounds of festivity seemed as the sound of a distant sea, barely heard, hardly recognized.

Out from the watch tower a stocky figure came, a Knight in black mail, high-booted, his hair cropped short as was the custom of all Knights. He carried with him a sack, and from the forest a murder of crows gathered over his head. The Knight pulled a head out of the sack by its long hair. Red hair it had been, and now it was matted with dark blood. The dead one had been a woman; Gil saw it by the delicacy of her features as the Knight took the head by the ears and thrust it hard down onto the steel tip of a spear. The dead woman's jaw dropped, as though to scream.

Beside the king, Lady Elantha seemed not to have noticed. Some of the senators murmured among themselves. One, behind the king's litter, made a choking sound of sickness. Horses that had never seen battle or smelled blood other than that of game, snorted and danced as the breeze from the forest brought them the stench of elf blood.

Only Rashas sat his mount calmly, in silence looking at the Knight on the wall as he walked back to the guard-house.

"My Lord King," he said, never turning to look at Gilthas, "you see there the expected issue of Lord Thagol's new orders. He fears the folk in the forest are becoming too ... obstreperous." The senator turned, his long eyes glittering cold, his face a waxen mask. "He doesn't want to see the robbers on the highway become a thing for a dragon to notice. Of course, you needn't distress yourself, Your Majesty. It's certain the robberies will stop now, the dragon's tribute will go by unmolested, for word will go from here, even today, of this display. Thagol only wants peace, My Lord King. He only wants order and compliance.

"As do we all, Your Majesty. The dragon, her overlord, your own most loyal Thalas-Enthia. Peace and order and—" Rashas moved his mouth in an imitation of smile. "—compliance."

In silence the senator said to the king: I will treat with this Knight, with our enemies. Not you, boy, and so let there be no more talk of Lord Firemane's governorship in further meetings of the Thalas-Enthia. From now on, let there be only your compliance with my wishes.

Sharp and cold, Rashas's command moved the procession along. Horses snorted, the clip of hooves quickened.

Gilthas let the silk hangings fall. After a certain amount of time had passed, he asked Lady Elantha to send word to Rashas that the king felt fatigued and wished the procession to come discreetly to an end near the royal residence. Once returned, he went to his chambers. He wanted quiet and a place to calm an anger he hadn't given Rashas the satisfaction of seeing, anger he wouldn't give him the pleasure of hearing about in gossip.

A newly laid fired crackled in the hearth, testimony to a servant's efficiency and acknowledgment that though the first day of autumn shone warmly outside, the night would come cool. Upon the marble-topped sideboard in the small dining chamber adjacent to both his library and his bed chamber, a silver tray sat, with two golden cups and a tall crystal carafe filled with ruby wine.

Gilthas had worn many rings that day, and now he removed all but one, a gleaming topaz whose fiery heart reminded him of a man long dead, his father the half-elf, Tanis, against whom he so often measured himself. What would his father have done, seeing the heads of elves decorating the silver bridge? Gil didn't know, couldn't ask. The man was long dead. He dropped the rings carelessly into the tray and saw propped against one of the cups a half-sheet of creamy parchment. Gilthas recognized the firm hand, the letters that looked as though they'd been formed by a general in the field. Even after all these years, his mother wrote dispatches, not letters.

The king poured a cup, tasted the sweetness, and

glanced toward his library. He had a burden of poetry in his heart, a grim, dark mood setting itself into verses that would look like raven's wings on paper and sound like the voices of murdered men when read. These he had, the words and the will to work them out.

Once in his library, the door closed behind him, and the scent of books and ink and rising sorrow surrounding, Gilthas would lose himself in words. He drew a long breath, hungry for that. He would change from his festival clothing and take these few hours before he must join his Senate in session.

Setting down the wine, he lifted the note from his mother.

Your Majesty,

I had thought we would have another guest at dinner, however as his health at the moment seems uncertain, I have advised the steward not to expect him.
L.

Gil's heart sank as he recognized the coded message. The guest, of course, was the treaty, its health at the moment uncertain. He read the note again and after the third scan took some hope from between the lines. Uncertain health was not a sentence of death, or so one could hope. Wearily, he tossed the note into the fire and went through to his bed chamber.

There he found Kerian, and he could hardly credit that a woman so shaken by sobbing could weep as silently as she did.

CHAPTER

3

K erian!"
Sobbing shook her; she did not lift her head or move in any way to acknowledge that she heard Gil's voice. The morning's bright dancer lay like a broken bird, hardly able to move.

"Kerian," the elf king whispered, lifting her gently into his arms. Gilthas barely caught the scent of the Tarsian perfume that had enchanted him in the morning. She smelled of the city, his city. Her perfumes were the richer scents of the horse fair, warm spice rolls from Baker's Way, a tang of mint from the garden in which she had danced.

Kerian looked up, her lips bitten to bleeding. She pushed her tangled hair from her face with shaking hands.

"Gil, she's one of those killed! Lania—she's been murdered!"

Through the window a breeze drifted, and it carried the sound of the celebrating city. The soft song of a mandolin twined with the laughter of children and the voices of their elders melding into a constant, pleasant hum that would not subside till dawn. The first whiff of wood smoke hung in the air. Tall fires would light the city tonight, a reminder in these genteel precincts of an earthier existence and a time when the elves who cleared spaces in the forest to farm lit up the sky with their hot, high fires to celebrate the seasons of light that had brought them health and harvest and to bid the long days of summer farewell.

Gil held her close. When he felt her calm, he let her go and went out quickly to pour a golden goblet full of ruby wine. She took a sip, then another. He took the goblet from her, and softly he said, "Who is Lania?"

Her tanned cheek flushed, her fists clenched, and the bitten lip bled again. "She was my cousin. Gil, did you see . . ." She wiped her lips with the back of her hand, blood and tears and wine. "Did you see on the eastern bridge?"

Feeling anger again, and shame, Gilthas said, "I did."

Cold, her voice, like wind from winter. "Did you see my cousin, my lord king? Did you see her with the ravens round her head?"

"Ah, Mishakal's mercy," he whispered, feeling powerless. "Kerian, I don't know how—she wasn't a robber, surely."

Color drained from her cheeks, golden tan turned ashen gray. The angry set of her jaw faltered and tears rose again in her eyes.

"No! She was . . . Lania was my brother's dearest friend. Gil . . ."

Gilthas had not seen Kerian's brother Iydahar in many years, not since before the Chaos War and the time of the disaster that resulted in the death of his mother's brother Porthios who had been, for a brief and blood-soaked moment, Speaker of the Sun and Stars, king of two elven nations. Upon his apparent death, Gilthas the puppet king had taken the throne.

Iydahar was, Gilthas knew, a proud man of the forest to whom even Qualinesti hunters seemed effete. He abhorred the status of his fellow Kagonesti, had no patience for the word "servant" when "slave" seemed, to him, closer to truth, yet fierce Iydahar had once embraced the cause Porthios had espoused, the dream that the two elven kingdoms, Qualinesti and Silvanesti, would be joined as one, that their Wilder Elf kin would be welcome in that broad and beautiful realm. Iydahar had believed with all his wild heart in this cause.

Iydahar had conceived no love for the boy-king who took the prince's place and turned over the kingdom to a dragon's Dark Knights. Porthios's wife, the Silvanesti queen Alhanna, and Silvanos their infant son, had fled Qualinesti. Exiles, they dwelt in wild lands now, forbidden to live in Qualinesti for their part in a failed rebellion, forbidden to return to Silvanesti by the foes they had made there. Gilthas had not seen his lover's kinsman since then.

Gilthas shuddered. Behind closed eyes he saw again the head of a red-haired woman, her mouth gaped wide, a dark veil of crows gathering round her bloody hair.

"Kerian," he said. "I'm sorry about your cousin. I know you're worried about your brother. I am too. I pray Lord Thagol is done now with his —"

Now she did move from him, only a little, but her eyes narrowed. "Done, my lord king?" Color flared in ashen cheeks. "He's done with Lania, surely."

She flung up from the bed, and the belled anklet made no sweet sound, only a tinny jangling. In one angry instant, Kerian reached down and yanked it from her ankle, flinging it across the room in almost the same gesture.

Calmly, the elf king said, "Kerian, I will send my men out into the forest to see what they can learn. I will speak to Rashas about Thagol."

With cool steadiness, Kerian said, "Do you think men of yours will be able to find a Wilder Elf if he doesn't want

27

to be found? We both know that Thagol has just begun to count heads."

She stilled. In that instant, standing upon an anciently woven carpet, in the bedchamber of a king who longed to make her his queen, Kerian looked like a wild creature, head up and testing the air. Wilder Elf! He had not seen her so in many years. Her tattoos enchanted him, his lips, his hands loved to trace the shape of them, but he didn't remember, or not often, that these twining vines signified that his Kerianseray had been born in Ergoth and lived in the upland forests on the foaming sea coasts, wilder places than ever he had visited. They marked her out as a member of the White Osprey Kagonesti, the daughter of the leader of that tribe, the sister of the man who surely led it now.

"Kerian," said the king, now firmly, "you underestimate my determination. I promise you my men won't come back till they've found safe word about your brother."

Kerian shook her head. "No matter how careful your men will be, Gil, Iydahar will know they're coming almost before they leave the city. No." Her jaw stiffened. "Iydahar is my brother. He is in danger. I must go myself."

"Kerian, you haven't seen Iydahar in years. You can't have any idea where he is."

Kerian looked at him long. "We know how to reach each other, Gil. There is a village, and there is a tavern. I can go there and leave the right word in the right ear. He will find me, or someone will show me the way to him."

She said no more, though he waited. At last, into his silence, she said, "My lord king, I will not give away Iydahar's secret."

He answered as her lover, the man who feared for her safety, who could no longer imagine how impoverished his life would be without her. Unfortunately, when he spoke, he sounded like her king.

"It's not only his, Kerian. It's yours. Tell me." Gilthas

rose, tall above her, and when he looked her deeply in the eye he trusted she would see his heart. "You might as well, because you know you cannot go yourself. There are brigands in the forest, outlaws and highwaymen. There are Knights who might well mistake you for any one of those things."

She swallowed hard but said nothing, the jut of her chin growing more stubborn.

"Kerian, if you go . . . if you go, you will be gone from Rashas's service without leave, and I won't be able to help you. You will be considered a runaway. You will be hunted." He stopped, caught suddenly as though by a cold hand out of nightmare. "Kerian . . . . if you go, if you are hunted, you will be branded a fugitive. You won't be able to come back."

He said no more. They were silent for a moment. "Tell me the name of the village and the tavern, and I will send men to learn if your brother is well. That is the end of the matter."

Kerian looked at him long, head up and suddenly cool. "It is the end of the matter, my lord king, if you, like Rashas, are ordering a servant." She did not add, as her brother might have, "or a slave." Still her sharp words hung between them, edged like steel.

In that silence they heard other voices in outer chambers, the king's dresser and the wardrobe master preparing his clothes for the senate meeting. Neither Kerian nor Gilthas spoke, and Kerian herself barely breathed. There could be no story to make seemly her presence, barefoot and weeping in the king's bedroom. Eyes on each other, like crossed swords, the king and his lover kept utterly still, completely silent.

The stubborn line of Kerian's jaw softened. She kissed the king tenderly. Her lips against his so that Gilthas did not so much hear her words as feel them, she said:

"He is my brother, Gil. If you want to stop me, you have only to call the guard."

She turned from him. He grabbed her wrist and caught her back. Eyes flashing, Kerian spun on her heel, angry words on her lips where a moment ago he'd felt regret.

The king held up his right hand. With his left, he removed the topaz ring from his forefinger. It was a lover's clasp, two circlets of gold each shaped as a hand. Worn together, each hand would hold the topaz. It had belonged to his faather and before that to some ancient elf king, a trinket worth a royal ransom in the times before the Cataclysm when kings might be ransomed for other than steel. In silence he gave one half of the lover's clasp to her; in silence she took it.

Outside, the dresser said to the wardrobe master, "Oh—look, there are his rings on the wine tray." A quiet gasp, then, low, "By all the vanished gods—! He's in his bedchamber."

Gilthas put the finger to his lips, the topaz ring into Kerian's hand. Barely mouthing the words, he said, "Go, my love. If you need me, leave this ring in the hollow of Gilean's Oak."

Gilean's Oak: the broad oak at the far western corner of Wide-Spreading, Gil's favorite hunting estate. The estate was named for the oaks that dominated the area. The tree itself was named for a discerning god because it was home to generations of owls, their nests admired by elf children. In days past, the owls had been courted by dreamers who believed the old legend that the man or woman who dreamed of seeing an owl there—in truth, the wise god himself—had the right to ask wisdom of him and expect it would be granted.

Kerian pressed the ring between her two hands, and then she took a golden chain from her neck, knotted it through the ring and slipped it over her head again. "Gil—"

Outside, the dresser said something to his companion.

The wardrobe master cried, "Good day, Your Majesty!" A woman's soft, gently modulated voice murmured a question; Laurana could be heard asking if either of the servants had seen the king. Quickly, the wardrobe master said, "I believe your son is sleeping within, Madam."

Gilthas took Kerian quickly into his arms. He kissed her, holding her as long as he dared as his mother's knock sounded on the bedchamber door. When he watched Kerian go, slipping on naked, silent feet through a passage so secret only he and the Queen Mother knew it existed, the elf king wasn't sure he would see his lover again.

In a quiet hour, when few walked the streets but Knights, two of those stood in purpling shadows, Headsman Chance and a man as pale and thin as the solitary sickle moon.

Sir Chance gestured upward to the shimmering span of the eastern bridge. Mist wraithed around the bases of the columns upholding the span, mist grown up from the ground, out from the forest. It drifted up toward the severed heads, pale fingers reaching.

The sickle-thin man looked up and smiled, a stingy pulling back of lips from teeth. They were like fangs, those teeth. Not in that they were sharp, they were only human teeth after all. Like fangs nonetheless, for they were startling to see, so white were they, and something about sight of them raised the hair on a person's flesh, as though he were seeing a wolf's deadly grin. Lord Thagol licked his lips.

"I think, my lord, there will be no more trouble with robbers," said Sir Chance.

The Lord Knight's white face shone like a scar. "Do you think so?" He licked his lips again.

"Well—I don't know that it'll stop all at once, but word of this . . ." He pointed upward with his thumb to the thirteen gaping new heads. A rat ran scurrying on the silvery bridge, another following. What the ravens hadn't tasted of dead flesh in the day, cheeks, eyes and tongues, the rats would sample tonight. "Word will go out into the countryside and the forest. Things will calm down, my lord."

The Lord Knight kept still, barely breathed, and his eyes had a strange sheen to them when they settled on Chance. The Headsman shivered again, drew breath to speak, explain something, assure his commander that all would, indeed, be calm now. In time, he let the breath go and said nothing. Lord Thagol was looking at him, but Chance didn't think the Skull Knight truly saw him. Chance believed that the strange Knight had in his mind already dismissed him. The Knight considered one thing, then another. Should he leave, taking the silence for dismissal?

"Go back out. Today."

"M-my lord?" The words startled the Headsman, just turning to leave.

"Go out again."

"But—" Chance cleared his throat and spoke more firmly. "Do you want more heads, my lord?"

Thagol's eyes grew suddenly sharp, his regard heavy and holding. Under the commander's gaze, Chance Headsman felt his heart shrink, contract as though squeezed by a hard hand. He gasped for breath, and felt his throat tighten. Pain flashed through his body, ripping across his chest, down his arm.

"My lord—!"

Sir Chance flung back his head, breathless and trying to scream. He saw the bridge, the severed heads and a rat swarming up the shaft of the nearest pike. Inside his own head a voice thundered, words flashing in his skull like lightning.

Never question me. Go. Into the forest. Now.

There was more, a command not framed by words, his lord's insistent will flowing into him, through him.

When he could see again, Lord Thagol was gone, walking away toward the low stone building that was his headquarters. Another figure walked beside the Knight, an elf by the slim build. Rashas of the Thalas-Enthia. The elf's voice drifted back on a small breeze, lifted in complaint. To Sir Chance, his head throbbing with pain, it sounded as though he were hearing a voice from underwater.

Sir Eamutt Thagol said nothing to the senator, never turned his head to look at or acknowledge him. He walked on, leaving the elf behind.

Sir Chance's mind, when it suddenly cleared, was filled with his lord's orders, with images of maps, rivers, roads. His lord's plans had been made clear to him.

He would gather up a force of good Knights. There must be watch stations within the kingdom now, guard posts on the Qualinost road. The stations would be manned, outposts of Lord Thagol's command. These would be established to be certain that those who traveled the road were indeed citizens of the kingdom about their normal business. Robbers would no longer find the good roads built by Knights a convenient place to hunt for prey. Tribute would go through, peace would be assured.

There will be order, Sir Chance thought, even as he knew the thought, the insistent certainty, wasn't his own, only the echo of Thagol's will.

Chance shivered in the rising mist. His head ached; when he closed his eyes, he imagined he smelled poison. He breathed deeply through his nose and exhaled through his mouth. He smelled and tasted nothing but misty Qualinesti air, yet the ground itself seemed shiver under his feet. Chance's blood chilled.

He would have to go out there again, today onto the roads where the Qualinesti Forest moved restlessly before the eye, and he would keep Lord Thagol's orders.

CHAPTER

4

Kerian slipped through the first shadows of day's end, a pretty serving girl with her hair tied back, dressed in clothing of a simple cut, rough cotton shirt, trews of a heavy, serviceable brown fabric, and black boots. But for the ribbon twined into her thick golden braid, she was unmarked by her master's colors.

The clothing she had from Zoe Greenbriar for a lie. "I'm going away with a party of the Senator's servants out into the wood to prepare his hunting lodge. The last time I rode in a skirt, thickets tore my skin and it's long pants for me!" She'd regretted the lie; she and Zoe didn't swear false to each other, but the Senator truly would depart for his lodge in a few days, and in a house as large as Rashas's, no one would miss her right away with Zoe's story as good cover.

The lordly part of the city slept, elves who had the luxury of leaving the debris of Autumn Harvest celebrations to their servants. Those, the Kagonesti in hall and house, cleaned garden and hall, laid firewood for the morning, lifted windows to the first scent of the season, the poignant mingling of settling dew, rich earth and fading leaves. Through the wealthy precincts of her lover's capital, Kerian went.

The streets and byways traced graceful curves, gentle windings round elf-made pond, round garden, past a shadow-draped and sudden house that only seemed to be a jutting of stone and tree from the side of a lofty cliff. Only servants did Kerian see and one or two dark-armored Knights on their rounds. Of those, one looked at her long and whistled low as she passed. Head high, she did not turn or ever acknowledge the man. He was human, lackey of a foreign occupier and dangerous. She had learned that the best way past these creatures of Neraka was to be always aware of where they were and never to make eye contact.

Gradually, the paths widened and became roads. The roads no longer went in wandering ways but became straighter as she came to the part of the city where tradesmen lived and worked. At the mouth of an alley running behind the frame buildings of Milliner's Row, she stopped and looked back. Down the long shadowy tunnel framed by shops and warehouses, she saw a brightness of late sunshine and the royal residence framed in the opening.

A small breeze drifted from behind, chill fingers tugging wisps of hair from the braid at the sides of her face.

Looking one last time at the royal residence Kerian's breath caught for a hard moment in her chest, then she turned away, lips tight. No man of the king's would ever find Iydahar, and if she did not leave her lover she would be abandoning her brother.

In all cities, in all lands, no one knows the ways in and out better than those who serve. Kerian had served for many years in Qualinost; she knew the city as well as all her Kagonesti kin and better than those who were her masters. In the late hour of the first festival day, with the sun slanting long to the west and shadows growing, Kerian made her way through the city unremarked, a servant with a leather wallet slung across her shoulder. Any who saw her thought that wallet held what it always did—missives from her master to one or another of his fellow senators, to the king himself, perhaps to Sir Eamutt Thagol in his grim, cold headquarters. It held nothing like that. In the wallet were a small sack of coins, among them three steel, and a smaller leather sack filled fat with hard cheese, bread and cold slices of lamb.

As she approached the eastern bridge, Kerian lifted her head, picking out a scent among all those of the city, one from beyond the shining bridge. Downwind, past the towers where Sir Eamutt's Knights walked, bristling with weapons, stinking like humans and clanking in their black armor, away past orchards and winding carter's roads, stealing into the sleeping city came a whisper of smoke, a thin suggestion of burning in the north.

In the next moment the wind shifted, as it does at day's end in autumn. It slid from the west and brought her the stench of rotted flesh on the severed heads piked upon the bridge.

Kerian hung for a moment in the darkness of shadow pooling around the eastern tower. She listened to the Knights talking above. They spoke in Common with a harsh Nerakan accent that made the utilitarian language known throughout Krynn sound guttural. They wondered when the watch would change, wondered if they would be paid.

Kerian took the ribbon from her hair, the braid bound by slim strips of soft, sueded leather. She did not want to be marked by her master's colors once she left the city. Should it be necessary, she'd prepared a tale that would leave any questioner believing she was but a servant from an outlying farm, gone to the city for the festival and on her way home again. She let the ribbon go, saw it caught by the wind and sent tumbling along the ground behind. One of the Knights spotted it and said to his fellows that he'd like to follow that bit of silk to the one who'd worn it.

"Ar," said another, spitting. "She ain't wearing it now, boy. Means she took it off for a reason that ain't got to do with you."

The Knights laughed, and carefully Kerian waited until the sound of their voices grew distant as they resumed their watch walk. When she knew them gone, she slipped right around the base of the tower, out from under the bridge and into the broad swathe of meadow grass that ran down to the peach orchards.

She ran low, bent over and barely ruffling the grasses, and she didn't stand straight again until she crossed the carter's road separating the meadow from the orchard. Baskets stood in stacks along the verge, left there from the harvest. Inside the orchard, leaves drooped, spent with the harvest, waiting to fall. Autumn breathed upon the rising mist, the scent of changing, of leaving.

Kerian shivered.

Once Iydahar had said to her, "You will hear it said the Kagonesti are savages. You will hear it said that Qualinesti did not steal us away. You will hear it said that others stole us, humans, minotaurs, ogres, or goblins looking for profit. Sometimes you will hear it said the Qualinesti rescued us from those creatures, but we know better. We will always hear the wailing of our kin. We will always remember the faces of those who stole us from our home. Stay in your city, Keri, but you stay at a cost. There will come a time, Turtle, when you find you can't remember how to be who you are."

Turtle. The old pet name didn't sting. It recalled her heart to another time, another place, and the brother who loved her no matter what befell. How would Iydahar feel about her if he knew her lover was a Qualinesti, and not only that, the king of the Qualinesti?

In the sky, crows shouted, raucous and sailing toward

the bridge. The scent of smoke vanished, then returned. Kerian ran swiftly, in and out the rows of peach trees, through the orchard, heading for the forest road and the way to Sliathnost.

At the edge of the orchard, where the ground sloped down into forest, Kerian halted and looked back. Over the gnarled branches of peach trees, four towers stood high. Silver spans of bridges gleamed. Kerian bade silent farewell to the bridges, the towers and the shining city. She ran down the hill and into the forest, that green and glossy realm which so much reminded her of the Ergothian wilds of her childhood. For a time, running, she was again the child, the girl who lived in a land of forest and seaside sky.

"Can't catch me, Keri! Keri can't catch me!"

Iydahar flung the old taunt, laughing. Kerianseray had known that scorn all her young life, and she had known its tempering love. What ran between them, brother and sister, was always a weaving of this, the scorn of the elder, the son whose place in the universe of his parents had been encroached upon by this unexpected girl, and the abiding affection he would never deny. She was, after all, and no matter how supremely annoying her very existence, his little sister.

"Turtle!"

In the sky, gray gulls echoed Iydahar as he ran ahead of her, long limbs shining in the sun, brown and powerful. Kerian struggled to keep up, sand like glue beneath her feet, her little legs pumping hard and seeming to take her nowhere. Iydahar sailed over reaching driftwood, and all the while his bright hair streamed out behind, the color of moonlight. His tattoos seemed like shadows on him, shadows on his back, his arms, his legs. Inordinately proud of those markings was Iydahar, her brother. They were now a year old, the pain of them long ago healed, and they denoted his lineage, his tribal heritage, the hopes his people had for him. Iydahar Runner, said the markings on his legs.

Kerian had not a mark on her except the bruises and scratches from her run through the forest and down to the beaches, from her stubborn insistence on keeping up with her fleet brother. She was still too young for marking, too young to bear the history of her people. This she resented deeply, believing herself to be every bit as worthy as her brother. Perhaps more so, for she was the unexpected girl, the child of parents who had no reason to look for a second, having been granted the gift of the first.

"Come on, turtle-girl!"

The child whose name meant Wing-Swift redoubled her efforts, and tripped over rock and fell flat on her face. The surf pounded the shore, the gulls shrieked, and Kerian lay stunned, the breath blasted from her lungs and little sparks of silver light jumping in her vision.

Iydahar's laughter skirled up to the sky—and fell suddenly silent. The sound of the gulls became strident, the drumming of the sea against the shore like thunder. Somewhere, far behind in the forest, a stag trumpeted, or seemed to. Kerian's heart hammered. No stag made that sound, not truly. It was a warning cry voiced by a Wilder Elf.

Spitting sand, Kerian tried to push herself up. Her head reeled, a line of blood trickled down her cheek. Feeling that, she felt sudden sharp pain where she'd torn her cheek. A shadow fell over her darkly. Two hands reached down—Iydahar's—and jerked her hard to her feet. The sight of his face, his expression tight with fear, stilled her angry protest. Past him, upon the sparkling blue water of the bay, she saw a tall ship, its sails black against the sky.

Iydahar, so much taller than she, bent down suddenly, like swooping. "Run!" he shouted, pushing her hard toward the forest.

Run! For those were slavers. Neither recognized the sails nor any flag, but they need not have. Someone in the forest had got word from someone else, around the curve of the bay, upland at some secret Kagonesti watch-post ... someone had seen the sails and known the ship. Word had passed, by runner, by drum, by cries such as that mimicking a stag's threat. Word had been passed all the way to here, this beach where the two children of Dallatar and Willowfawn ran, playing where they should not have been.

With all her heart and sore lungs, Kerian ran. She fell and scrambled up again. She ran, and she heard her sobbing breaths loud in her own ears. Iydahar didn't run ahead of her now, he ran behind, shouting: "Run, Keri! Run, or they'll catch us!"

She fell again, her brother grabbed her up, and this time he didn't let her go. Grasping her by the wrist, he ran, dragging her along with him, and in the sky the gulls shrieked. They gained the forest as the ship pulled into the bay. They scrambled into the shadows and kept running until they'd climbed up into the thickest part of the forest. Not until their lungs tasted the tang of pine did they stop.

Gasping, shuddering with exertion and fear, Kerian fell to the ground. Iydahar knelt beside her, waiting for her to catch her breath. Gasping, she could not slow her breathing. She thought her heart would race right out of her chest.

"Easy," he said, softly. He sounded like her father then, his tone gentle and a little amused. "Easy, Keri. You're all right." He gathered her into his arms. "We're all right. Easy, easy."

Over and again he said that, and she matched her breathing to the sound of his heart, the two slowing

41

together. Iydahar let her go and stood looking around, trying to see down to the ocean. Only a glitter showed between the trees. Looking higher, he saw that these trees offered no hold for climbing, or none that he could reach.

"Keri." He jerked his head at the tree and made a stirrup of his joined hands.

She understood at once. Hands on his shoulders, she climbed into his hands.

"Up!" her brother cried, and up she went, tossed high and reaching for the branch. She caught it, clung, and pulled herself up to straddle it. Scrambling, she climbed into the pine-scented heights, the long needles of the tree brushing her cheek, the sap clinging to hands and naked feet. The blood had dried on her cut cheek, but the brush of needles against the torn flesh stung. She kept climbing until she had the sky and a clear view of the bay.

"What do you see?" her brother called.

"Water—ship—people—" She stopped, her heart leaping suddenly into her throat. "People coming out of the forest—"

In a long line they came, men and women with children by the hand or on their hips. Kerian counted twenty. They were bound one to the other, and they went attended by weaponed guards. Sunlight ran along the edges of naked blades and pricked on the tips of steel-headed arrows.

"What, Keri? What do you see?"

Shaking, Kerian watched as four boats left the ship rowed by humans. Her stomach felt queasy; her throat went suddenly dry. The boats landed, the prisoners made to run. Up from the beach came the sound of children wailing. Kerian shivered, watching as the prisoners were loaded into the boats, some flung in, others made to move by the pricking of steel. One by one, the guards climbed in after and in short time the rowers had the boats out into the bay again.

"Keri!" Iydahar's voice held a note of impatience now. "What do you see?"

Tears pricked Kerian's eyes. She saw the boats return to the ship.

She saw that not all of those who had put the captured Wilder Elves into the hands of slavers had gone with the boats. Five—she counted them carefully—five turned and went back up the beach, into the forest. Five returned to their tribes, their filthy work done.

Years passed, and Kerian earned her tattoos, became known to all as Kerian Wing-Swift. One day she and her brother were caught and taken for "service" in Qualinost. On that day, the two huddled together in the hold of a ship very much like the one Kerian had seen in the waters off Ergoth from the top of a tall pine.

❧

Keri can't catch me!

The old taunt drifted up from memory and present need.

A swathe had been cut through the forest wide enough for a patrol of six Knights on broad battle chargers to ride abreast. Jagged stumps of killed trees lined the roadside, beyond lay the ruin of trees that the workmen had not had the decency to dry for firewood but left to rot. Tangles of trunks and branches loomed like a barrier between road and forest.

Kerian had a walk of several hours ahead if she wanted to reach the Hare and Hound before nightfall—and she did want that. She wanted to be well off this road with its dead trees like skeletons before dark.

High above, leaves whispered and, higher, crows called; from the middle terrace, softer notes of dove-song drifted down. Shadows gathered here in the wood. Kerian shifted

43

the broad leather strap and the weight of the leather wallet on her shoulder. The will to run like her brother gathered in heart, legs, and lungs.

Under her feet a storm of thunder gathered. The wounded earth groaned beneath the weight of steel shod war-horses.

Knights!

Kerian looked ahead and behind. Quickly, not choosing her direction, she bolted. She ran off the road, scrambling in the stony earth, slipping and sliding down the pitched edge. A rock turned under her foot, her ankle collapsed beneath her. Kerian tumbled to her knees and rolled. She didn't stop until she fetched up against the barrier of white birches. Hands scraped to bleeding, she pushed up to her feet. Her ankle throbbed, but it took her weight or would for a while. Braced against a white birch, bark peeling under her hand, Kerian stood still, trying to decide how to dare the barrier of broken trees.

On the road, the thunder of horses grew louder. A rough voice shouted something—one vile word in Common. Heart slamming in her chest, Kerian looked around wildly before plunging into the deadfall. Branches tore at her face, at her hair, ripped her shirt as she shouldered through the tangle. Her ankle gave way, she fell, and scrambled up again. On the road, the sound of riding grew, harsh voices shouted to each other. Damning her ankle, her bleeding face, Kerian shoved her way into the thicket of dead trees.

Almost through, the strap of her wallet snagged on the last branch. She pulled, she tried to twist away. On the road the Knights grew closer. Cursing in the language of her childhood, a word her parents had never taught, she yanked her little knife out of the belt sheath and severed the wallet by the strap. She reached for it as it fell—

"Ho!" cried a voice from the road. "Chance, what's that! Supper, eh?"

Supper: a deer in the thicket, a wild turkey, a covey of quails?

Kerian left the wallet, and heedless of the noise she made now, ran. Tripping, falling, and climbing up again, she put as much distance between herself and the road as she could. Headlong, she splashed through a shallow stream, soaking her boots. She slipped on stones, on patches of fallen leaves.

The last time she fell, she did not rise.

All around her, the forest seemed to waver. Her mouth ran dry; she tried to swallow and failed. The air seemed to press against her ears, against her temples. As from a great distance, she heard the Knights, their voices raised in sharp cries, yet she couldn't make out their words.

Kerian stood, unsure of her senses. She saw, but not clearly. Blood traced a thin red path down her forehead, her temple, her cheek. She hardly felt that. Most disconcerting, now Kerian heard nothing at all, not the Knights' faint voices, not even leaves rustling though she dimly saw them sway in the wind.

So it was, bereft of senses, Kerian had no warning before a hard hand grabbed her arm and jerked her down and back.

CHAPTER 5

Flung off her feet, Kerian hit the ground hard. She felt no pain but found herself gasping for breath. A hard hand clamped over her mouth.

Kerian looked up from the ground and right into the eyes of a dwarf. She had a swift impression of dark hair, a thick beard, and the kind of pale face they have who live under the mountains in Thorbardin. Sweat ran on his face, sliding into his black beard. He breathed hard. He had been running, too.

His eyes flashed, strange dark eyes with glinting blue flecks. He pressed harder, but with his free hand he gestured, away past the distant barrier of broken trees. He didn't jerk a thumb or point a finger; all the fingers of his free hand were oddly twisted, withered and useless, and so it looked like he was shaking his fist at the distant road.

Kerian tried to sit, but the dwarf shifted his grip and pressed her back, his elbow and all his weight behind it keeping her shoulders flat to the stony earth. She became aware, though dimly, of the sharpness of his elbow, the bite of a rough-edged rock between her shoulder blades.

The dwarf said something. Kerian knew he did because

she saw his lips move. She frowned; he jerked his chin. Kerian looked to the road again.

A troop of mounted Knights had stopped there, silent as ghosts in nightmare! Through branches and leaves, Kerian saw their black armor. One, the leader, threw back his visor and she recognized the stocky Knight named Sir Chance, he who had decorated the eastern bridge of Qualinost with ghoulish trophies of murder. Her heart jumped as one of the Knights pointed into the forest. The leader shook his head. He spurred his mount, and the others followed silent as phantasms, up the road and gone.

Kerian's eyes met the dwarf's. He sat back, letting her sit up. She rubbed the place between neck and shoulder where he'd pinned her. She'd just learned a thing about dwarves few realized—not so tall as elves or humans, still they were weightier than they seemed. As Kerian drew breath to speak, the dwarf shook his head. He pressed a finger to his lips. Then he touched his ear.

Listen!

Kerian did, and she realized that her ability to hear was becoming restored to her. She turned to the dwarf. With great relief, she said, "I can hear."

The dwarf seemed unimpressed. His voice pitched low, he said, "You can, and maybe yon Knights can't? Might be you're seeing better now, and they're not?" He snorted. "D'ye think, missy, you might want to be quiet a while yet, and a little bit still?"

I am not fond of this dwarf, Kerian thought.

Yet she had to admit he was right: The Knights were on the road, and they were not far away. She heard their voices now, some still pressing the point that they should have chased whatever had bolted into the forest. So close, they would hear her if she spoke too loudly, but they could not see her. There was too much of woodland between them. Stiffly, Kerian got to her feet. She dusted herself off,

picked dirt and brittle leaves out of her hair as best she
could.

"Who are you?" she said. She didn't whisper. As he
had, she simply pitched her voice low. Suspicion narrowed
her eyes. "What are you doing in the king's forest?"

The dwarf cocked his head. "The better question is,
what's happened to your king's forest?"

A chill skittered up Kerian's spine. She had thought of
the phenomenon that had confused her senses as a thing
that had happened to her, to the dwarf. She hadn't thought
of it as something that had happened to the forest itself,
but again, the dwarf was right.

"Didn't think of it like that, did you?" The dwarf
scowled.

Kerian said stiffly. "You haven't answered my question.
What are you doing here?"

The dwarf shrugged. "I could ask the same thing.
They're all kicking up their heels at the autumn party in
the city. Not you?" His lips twitched a little in his beard.
Not to smile, certainly not. "You don't look like a hunting
girl, and those pretty white hands never planted a field or
beat chaff from the grain."

Kerian raised her chin and lifted her hands to tuck
stray locks into her braid. She didn't know dwarves at all,
had not seen them but now and then in Qualinost, and
only from a distance in the years before the Chaos War
when hill dwarves came into the kingdom to trade their
goods.

Her voice cool, she said, "I haven't heard that of all the
dwarf clans, those in Thorbardin are the rudest. I am Kerianseray." She did not say, "of Qualinost" or "of the House
of Rashas." She did not say "a friend of the king himself,"
though she would like to have said all those things to this
arrogant dwarf. "You haven't answered my question."

He shrugged. "I'm here in the wood for the same reason

you are—not interested in having conversations with black-hearted Knights out of gods-blasted Neraka."

It was no answer, truly, but Kerian didn't press the point. She looked at him long. His beard was thick and glossy. His dark hair, shining silver at the temples, was cut rough and shaggy, long enough to fall over his shirt collar. The shirt itself was unremarkable, unbleached cotton and the wide-sleeved kind you'd see a taverner or shop-owner wearing. The same could be said for his breeches, made of brown, tough fabric.

Slantwise across his back hung a thick bedroll. Around his waist he wore a broad leather belt from which hung a throwing axe, a leather water bottle filled fat, a coil of rope and a knife. His boots were of fine sturdy leather, and he wore a single earring in his left ear, a bright silver ring to suggest he wasn't so humble of fortune as he might seem.

"Are y'finished lookin' now?" he asked when it seemed she was.

"You have my name, sir dwarf. What is yours?"

He shrugged. "I mean your king's kingdom no harm, girl. I'm only a traveler on the road, like y'self. Now and then, one of us dwarves slips us into the forest with wares to sell."

She made a softly disbelieving sound. "Fairly adventurous for the sake of a sale of goods."

The dwarf shrugged. "There are some venturesome sons among the clans yet." He reached into his shirt and took out a small leather pouch. It rang comfortably with the sound of coins. "All I'm here for is some selling—and I did a fine bit of that." His voice softened with sudden yearning, touched by a kind of gentleness she'd not expected. "I'm goin' home now, and I'll be glad to get there. I'm Stanach of Thorbardin. My family is Hammerfell; my clan is Hylar." He lifted his chin when he claimed his clan; his eyes flashed again, this time defiantly.

A Hylar. Well, Kerian knew her history, even the history of dwarves. There had been wars and wars in Krynn these thirty years past, wars of gods, mortals, and dragons. There had been, too, a war in Thorbardin, and that had been the worst kind of war. A civil war in which clan fought clan, often kinsman fought kinsman, and the balance of power did not simply shift, it shattered. The aristocratic Hylar, for long centuries the ruling clan, did not rule now. In the mountain kingdom the clans were still putting order back together again after a brutal war, still learning to trust each other and their new High King, Tarn Bellowgranite.

A civil war, Gil once said, is the kind of war that will break anyone's heart, and the kind that would wring the last drop of blood right out of a dwarf's, for after his forge god Reorx, a dwarf loves his kin best.

High up and far away, crows called, and Kerian shuddered, for those crows were not sailing west to Qualinost where they might be expected to find a feast of flesh on the eastern bridge. These flew east, right along the path of the road, crying their brothers to a feast.

"Ay well," said Stanach Hammerfell, "we're all properly introduced now, aren't we? You're clumsy for an elf in the home-wood, are y'not?" He looked pointedly at the ripped knees of her trews, her wet boots, scraped face, the torn flesh of her hands. When he marked her tattoos, the graceful vines twining, he shook his head. "You're one of those special elves besides. One of the Wilder Elves. Wilder than what—the hearth cat?"

Kerian's cheeks flamed. That from a surly dwarf who'd likely spent all his nigh two hundred years under the mountains and wouldn't know north from south if the sun were staring him blind!

Stanach ignored her reaction. "I reckon you don't know a better way to Sliathnost than yon road, do you?"

Stubborn, Kerian said nothing. She didn't know a better way, and she wasn't minded to confirm his guess at her ignorance.

Stanach snorted. "I figured."

She drew breath to say something, and then realized her leather wallet, with food and money pouch, hung somewhere on the branches of dead trees. She looked back, looked ahead. She thought, so what? She would figure something out when the time came.

"I am going to Sliathnost, too. They have a tavern there called—"

"The Hare and Hound, I know. All right then, you can come along with me if you like."

You know the way through the wood?"

"I can reckon it. Come along if you like."

Stanach walked away, heading north through the trees and somewhat east.

Keri can't catch me!

And you, one of those special elves ...

Perhaps it was as Iydahar had warned. Perhaps it was true, she had forgotten herself, forgotten how to be Kagonesti. She had lost herself in the city and the servitude that dressed her in fine silk.

She had lost herself, perhaps, even in the high bed of a king.

Ahead, Stanach stopped, and he looked back over his shoulder. Kerian ran to follow.

The way Stanach chose headed up, dappled in sun and shifting shade. Rocky and seemingly pathless, it wound between tall oaks whose wide stands soon gave way to fragrant pines growing closer together. Beneath Kerian's feet, oak leaves vanished to be replaced by years of brown pine straw, the fallen needles some as long as her forearm.

Kerian followed Stanach as closely as she could, slipping in the pine straw, picking herself up. No matter if she fell, cursed, and lingered over bruised knees and skinned palms, Stanach didn't stop. She imagined that if she'd tumbled right off the face of Krynn, he would not so much as look over his shoulder.

Kerian was growing no more fond of the dwarf.

Following, she never saw him consult the slant of shadow or the point of the sun in the sky for direction, yet he went faultlessly north and east, seeming to make his way by landmarks Kerian, versed in the winding ways of every street, path and wandering by-way of Qualinost, could not have recognized. The farther east they went, the more often they encountered great gray boulders thrusting up from the earth. Trees made way for the lichen-patched rocks as though, in some long ago fought-out treaty, they had agreed to cede a part of the forest to stone. There had been no treaty between forest and stone, of course. There had been, in fact, a kind of war, the great and terrible Cataclysm, many centuries before. All the face of Krynn had changed then, the world heaving and breaking, the very continents shifting. After the great upheaval, the land between elven kingdom and that of the mountain dwarves had become a wasteland of rising ground, gaping glens, and thrusting boulders.

Kerian, once a wild running child of upland Ergothian forests and shining sea strands, felt the strain of the climbing terrain. She had been too long in Qualinost, where she never endured any walk more difficult than the sweet curling path from the Library of Qualinost to the Temple of Paladine. Her muscles burned, her lungs seemed to shrink with every passing moment until own breathing was loud in her ears.

Seemingly unaware of her distress, Stanach kept a

steady pace through what Kerian saw as a trackless forest. Kerian remained dogged in her determination not to fall behind. Sweat rolled down her cheeks, made her blouse stick uncomfortably to her back. Her legs hurt, her ankles turned, and treacherous stones rolled beneath her feet.

Shadows now gathered darkly beneath the canopy of the forest. High up, the sky deepened. The air grew cool, damp with the day's end. Kerian's belly rumbled with hunger; her muscles began to tremble with more than exhaustion. She thought of the bread and cheese and meat in her lost wallet. Foxes must have found it by now, or rats or crows.

Kerian looked at the sky and realized it had a long time been strangely quiet. She and Stanach had traveled past what had interested the crows—or the crows had feasted full and gone on. When Kerian thought she couldn't take another step, that every muscle in her legs and back had turned to stone, Stanach stopped beside a tall boulder.

Kerian put her back to a rough skinned pine, resting her head against the trunk She wanted no more than to sink to the ground, and she dared not. She would not rise again, of that she was sure. She locked her knees, clenched her jaw, and she stood.

Not giving her so much as a glance, Stanach slipped the leather water bottle from his belt. He drank deeply, politely wiped the bottle's mouth, and handed it to her. Kerian's nose told her this was not water. She took the smallest sip of Dwarf Spirits. Her eyes watered immediately, streaming.

"Ah, that's enough now," the dwarf said, reclaiming the bottle. "You're staggering around enough as it is."

Stanach looked around again, as though looking for a landmark. How could he, a dwarf out of Thorbardin, know of forest landmarks deep in Qualinesti?

Dark-eyed Stanach saw her watching. "It's not the first time I've been here in your green forest, girl. First time, that was a long time ago and maybe your mam and your da were still looking at you in your cradle trying figure out a name for you. I came in from somewhere. This is true, eh? Do you think I didn't mark my way in so I could figure one or two ways back?"

Kerian pushed away from the tree. She wiped sweat from her face, tucked stray curls back onto the failing braid, and said, "I suppose I'm not thinking about it much at all. If you know your way back, I'm happy for you. If you'll point me in the direction of Sliathnost, I'll be happy for me."

He thumped the boulder with his right hand. "Then climb up."

Kerian eyed the tall boulder. "Why?"

Stanach shook his head as over a child's willfulness. "D'ye have a question for every occasion? Climb up."

Unwilling, still she did what he said, finding no foothold her wet-soled boots could use and laboriously pulling herself up the sloping shoulder of stone with only stingy handholds. The boulder was only twice her height, maybe a little more. After the exertions of the day, however, she felt as though she'd undertaken a bitter peak of the far Kharolis Mountains.

Once to the top, she looked down at the dwarf. "Well?"

"Well, what do you see?"

"Trees."

Stanach gestured to indicate she should turn around.

Carefully, uncertain of her footing, Kerian did. She looked to either side and back the way they came. Stanach muttered something about Reorx's forge and called:

"Would you look south and east, please?"

Kerian did and then saw a faint gray plume of smoke pointing down the breeze. Sliathnost! They had traveled in such a way that now they could enter the town from the north and not the south.

"Satisfied?" Stanach asked.

When Kerian said she was, he started walking away, down the hill toward little Sliathnost.

"Hey!"

Stanach looked up and around.

"Give me a hand—and don't argue, will you?"

He gave her his good left hand and did not argue. They walked down the slope together, they returned to the road shoulder to shoulder, and together, silently, they walked into the village, past little farms on the outskirts, past a small stone mill, and straight onto a main street lined by tidy houses of wood and stone.

Two large buildings dominated the town, one at either end. Coming in from the north, the blacksmith's forge and smithy stood strongly before a tall wide barn and livery stable. Behind that stretched a fenced enclosure where horses of various kinds grazed, a pair of little red ponies, a tall chestnut gelding, a neat-footed black mare and three thick-chested draft horses. Kerian looked quickly for signs of Knightly battle chargers and saw none.

At the opposite end of the village stood the tavern, the Hare and Hound. Stone from foundation to oak-shuttered windows, the walls were stout oak to the slate roof. Four chimneys rose from the roof. Smoke curled up from each, for here at the end of the afternoon, they were starting to cook in the kitchen. The Hare and Hound did a good custom, people traveling to and from Qualinost, tinkers and hunters, leathermen, sellers of furs. This season before winter was a traveling time; farmers had the yield of the fields and felt secure enough to spend a few coins on such luxuries as polished silver buttons and buckles, a scroll containing an illuminated text, a pretty blouse for a daughter who had been wearing homespun and home-sewn for the last few years. All these travelers stopped at the tavern and in this season people from the town often came to eat and drink and talk.

Kerian said, "Tell me, Stanach. What did you trade that you did so well on your foray into Qualinesti?"

He looked at her sidelong, his eyes narrowed. Then he shrugged and said he'd traded the wares of his cousin's metal shop. "Pots, pans, buckles, and bells."

"No wagon, no donkey?"

Stanach didn't miss his stride. "Donkey was killed, never did have a wagon. Me, I got lucky. Four bandits fell on me when I was nearly out of wares. They killed the donkey; I killed them." He was silent a moment, then he looked up at her, his smile cool as truth. "Guess you were lucky, too. Things turned out the other way, I might not have been around to lead you out of your backyard to safety and the road to the fine Hare and Hound, eh?"

Arrogant dwarf!

"Tell me, missy, how do you reckon you're going to pay for your fare inside?"

Kerian shook her head, not knowing how she'd pay for her supper, not willing to complain to him about her troubles. She would think of something, and perhaps Bueren Rose could be convinced to break the tavern's strict custom and trust her for the fee.

Coins rang, one against another. Stanach held out his hand, a small bronze piece glittering on his palm. "Go on. Take it."

After a moment's hesitation Kerian did, trying awkwardly to thank him. He walked past that thanks, and they said no more, going in silence again.

Kerian kept her eye on the tavern as they walked. Her heart rose with hope and filled with memories of her brother as he was the last time she saw him. Iydahar, tall, lean, and brown, lounging against the long oak bar, talking to the barman or flirting with the barman's pretty daughter, Bueren Rose. She would see her brother soon! She would see him soon and know at last that he was well.

Weary, tired of this dwarf's company, Kerian squared her shoulders and pushed on ahead. She was not going to go hobbling into the Hare and Hound behind this stranger.

As it happened, she didn't have to.

Stanach left her in the doorway of the tavern, where she had paused to adjust her eyes to the sudden dimness within. He did not say goodbye or even look over his shoulder. They might have been two strangers who'd never met.

Kerian lost all thought of the dwarf as she became aware of a creeping uneasiness. All the tavern had fallen still when the door opened. Near the fire, two hounds of indiscriminate parentage lounged. One pricked up its ears, the other snored loudly. That sleeping hound seemed to be the only creature in the place unaware of her. Everyone else's eyes narrowed, mouths in tight closed lines, staring at Kerian. Two plates of steaming food in her hands, even the barmaid, Bueren Rose, looked at her old friend as though at a dangerous stranger.

CHAPTER

6

Kerian's eyes met the barmaid's. She drew breath to speak, and felt Bueren Rose's unspoken warning like the jump of lightning across a summer sky. She looked around and saw that but for Stanach, all in the tavern were elves. Except for her, all were Qualinesti, farmers, hunters or folk from the city.

As though the silence were nothing to concern him, Stanach crossed the common room without looking back, making for a table near the fire where two rustically dressed elves, a man and a woman, greeted him with scant nods. At first glance, they looked like hunters, dressed in leathers and boots, each with a quiver fat with arrows slung across the back of a chair, a strung bow near to hand. Draped across a chair beside each hung a cloak of thick green wool. Beneath each cloak lay something hunter's don't carry: a sheathed short sword.

The woman gestured Stanach to sit. Her companion filled a tankard with foaming ale and pushed it toward him. In the moment she did, her eyes met Kerian's, and Kerian's mouth dried up.

She and the woman had encountered each other more

than once in the fine district that included the house where she lived as a senator's servant and the king's royal residence. She was Nayla Firethorn, and in the years before the coming of the dragon Beryl, her father and her brothers had been Forest Keepers, members of the king's royal army. Her father and brothers had fought in the cause of Prince Porthios, and all had died during that short, bloody revolution. When Nayla's companion turned to speak to one of the hounds, Kerian recognized this one as well. No matter the costume of the day, Haugh Dagger-hart was a carter, a provisioner for one of the finer taverns in Qualinost whose routes ran on every road between the eastern border and the capital city.

Their eyes met. Haugh's expression never changed, and when he looked away no one could imagine he had a thought for anything but what Nayla was saying to Stanach. Kerian took her cue and walked past the table without another glance.

These three knew her and pretended not to, while the rest of those in the tavern kept their sharp-eyed interest in her. It seemed that a mountain dwarf in the Hare and Hound was less remarkable than a Kagonesti woman. An elf by the far window stared at her narrowly. Two women at the next table put their heads together and whispered. In the center of the room a well-dressed elf, sitting at supper with his wife and two little girls glanced at her and then away.

One of the girls, her long golden braids hanging over her shoulders, pointed to Kerian. "Mama, what is a servant doing so far from home?"

Kerian flushed. By her imperious tone she knew the child to be the privileged daughter of a wealthy family of Qualinost. Stanach had his back to the room, but Kerian saw him lift his head to listen. So did others in the room, the old man, the village women, three elves at the bar.

The child's mother shushed her. She glanced at Kerian, then away, pushing a plate of untouched food closer to the girl.

The child began a pouting protest, her sister kicked her under the table, and her father glared. Objections fell to grumbling, then silence, as the girl tucked into the plate of venison and steamed carrots and potatoes.

Kerian glanced warily at Bueren Rose. The barmaid gestured slightly, only the barest tilt of the head, then called an order into the kitchen. From within, someone shouted back something that she couldn't hear; that was Jale, Bueren's father. Bueren opened the door to shout her order again, and out from the kitchen came a steamy warmth rich with the fragrance of roasting venison and steaming vegetables, of soup and stew and newly baked bread. Kerian's stomach clenched with hunger. That more than anything else propelled her forward.

One of the hounds at the hearth lifted its head and wagged a lazy greeting as she passed. Nayla and Haugh were careful to pay close attention to the food in front of them. Stanach had his nose in a mug of beer.

The three elves at the bar gave her sideways glances and edged away. These were, indeed, hunters with the spattered blood of recent kills on their leathers. One dropped some coins onto the bar and made a point of leaving. He headed for the side door that led to the privy. Kerian's cheek flushed now with anger. These two at the bar also knew her! Not well, surely, but in times past they'd greeted her in this very room fairly and passed the time with news of weather, crops and hunting. Now they treated her coldly.

"Hello Bueren," she said, low. "What's going on? If I were a kender I couldn't have gotten a less cheerful welcome here."

Bueren nodded. "If you were the lightest of light-fingered

kender, Keri, people might have been happier. Are you here looking for Iydahar?"

Kerian nodded.

"I figured." She wiped her perspiring face with the back of her hand, pushing rosy gold hair back into the red kerchief meant to keep it from her face. She drew a mug of ale and put it on the bar. "Look," she said, her voice dropping low. "People are getting strange around here lately. Things are getting strange. The forest is . . . unsettled.There've been Knights all over the road today. How have you managed to miss them?"

Ale froth on her lips, the rich taste warm in her mouth, Kerian chose her words carefully. "I saw some earlier, but it was only a patrol."

"There've been others, riding up and down the Qualinost road."

Near the hearth, the sleeping hound woke, sniffed his companion, and stood to stretch and bow. The second growled. Nayla Firethorn snapped her fingers. Instantly, the two settled. Bueren left the bar and came back with a laden tray, three plates piled high. Kerian's stomach growled again, painfully, as Bueren passed her to set the plates before Nayla, Haugh Daggerhart and Stanach.

"What are you doing here anyway, alone and dressed like that?"

Ignoring her question, Kerian took from her pocket the polished bronze coin Stanach had given her. She set it on the bar and nodded toward the three just fallen silent over their meals. "I'll have what they're having, all right?"

Bueren winked. "Put it back in your pocket, Keri. I'll fix you up."

"But—"

"Never mind. Sit." She ducked into the kitchen again and returned with another tray, this one host to a deep bowl of creamy dill and carrot soup, a plate of venison

smothered in spicy gravy, a crock of butter and a fat hunk
of brown oat bread. She unloaded the tray and whisked
utensils from behind the bar. "Eat. We'll talk later."

Kerian ate. The bar was suddenly quiet, empty of few
sounds other than the crackling fire in the hearth, the
indistinguishable murmur of conversation between the
dwarf and the two elves, the whisper of one of the little
girls to her parents, and the small noises Kerian's spoon,
fork, and knife made against the plate and bowl. Kerian felt
eyes upon her, the sense of being watched like a warning
itch between the shoulder blades.

In the silence and firelight, surrounded by the good
scents from the kitchen and the comfortable sounds of
Bueren Rose going about her work, Kerian applied herself
to Jale's delicious soup and then to the venison. She enjoyed
the ale; she layered the bread thickly with sweet cream
butter. Hunger abated quickly, and with that satisfaction
came a sudden realization of how very tired she was.

Her muscles ached, so did her head. She felt the bruise
of every fall, the sting of scraped knees and palms. The
muscles across her shoulders felt heavy and dull; those in
the small of her back complained at the least motion.
Kerian lifted her hands to brush away the tickling strands
of her hair and caught the scent of herself, sour with the
sweat of a day's hard travel.

As hunger had gnawed her belly, the sudden understanding of how far she'd come from home now ached in
Kerian's heart. In miles, she had not come far. In hours,
only a day's distance, yet here she sat, treated like a
stranger in a village she'd been used to entering freely, eyed
with suspicion in a tavern to which she'd always been welcomed warmly.

Kerian looked around her with small careful glances,
down the length of the oaken bar. For an instant her eyes
met that of one of the hunters who had so pointedly moved

away from her. From the shadows, he watched her. When their eyes met, he quickly looked away.

Bueren Rose went around the great room, igniting torches set in black iron brackets on the walls. *Abuerenalanthaylagaranlindal,* her parents had named the barmaid. Rose of Summer's Passing. She was a pretty girl, linsome and smiling, locks of her rosy gold hair curling around her temples and cheeks. Since childhood, friends called her Bueren Rose, deeming it a far better name. Summer Rose. One of the elves at the bar murmured something to her; his companion reached out and pulled her close. Bueren laughed, leaned in close and whispered something. Startled, he let her go, and she went about her work with a toss of her head and a knowing laugh.

Orange light chased shadows up the walls, and outside the windows night's darkness fell. The common room seemed to grow smaller.

In Qualinost Gilthas would be sitting at supper now, perhaps with the Queen Mother. Their table would be set with silver plate and golden candlesticks. They would be drinking delicate wines from crystal goblets, a new one for each course. In time, Gilthas would excuse himself and go to his chambers. He would sit in his library reading some ancient tome. He would take pen in hand, a fresh sheet of creamy white parchment from the stack always ready. All the questions, fears, hopes and challenges of his strange shadowy reign would change into poetry, sere sonnets, dark and sometimes bloody-minded. Were this another time—only the day before!—Gil would busily compose his sonnets until Kerian came slipping through the darkened passes of the secret ways.

Kerian steeled herself against regret and a sudden cold thread of fear. She had made her choice. She had come to find Iydahar, and she would do that. She would deal with after, after.

The kind of busy silence that attends those happy at their dining settled upon the tavern until, with a quiet word, the father of the two little girls let his family know the meal was finished. His wife wiped small chins and cheeks and told her children quietly to fold their napkins before they left the table. The father lifted one child from her seat, the mother took the hand of the other. Chattering like little squirrels, the children followed their parents to the staircase then went scampering up. When the father called one word in command, his daughters instantly regained their sense of decorum.

Bueren leaned her elbow on the bar, her chin on her hand. "Well?"

Kerian took a breath, dropped her voice. "Bueren, yesterday on the eastern bridge of Qualinost the Knights piked the heads of thirteen elves. Four were Qualinesti."

Bueren, herself Qualinesti, paled.

"The rest were Kagonesti. Like me. Word is they are outlaws, that they have been disrupting the roads and the free flow of wagons with supplies to the Knights and tribute to the dragon. Word is, more heads will foul the bridge if things don't get quiet here on the roads."

Bueren's eyes sparked with fear. "Merciful gods."

"Bueren, did you know—?"

Bueren Rose snorted. "Any one of the outlaws?" She wiped the bar with wide swipes. "Anyone doesn't stop in here to eat, I don't know them. Outlaws, I imagine, aren't much for socializing with village folk. No, but I don't hold with such . . . punishment." She pressed her lips together, considered and then decided. "Have you heard about the strange stories hunters are telling? You've been on the road today. Maybe you've noticed . . . what's happening in the forest."

"Yes."

"Yes. Those two down at the end of the bar, they said

they have felt something ...not right in the forest. It's a kind of—" She shook her head, at a loss for the right words.

"I know, Bueren. I've seen it or . . . felt it. No, it's not like that. Thing is, when it happened, I *didn't* see. I *didn't* feel or hear." She showed her friend the scraped and bruised flesh of her hands. "I fell—on hard rocks!—and never felt anything, yet look at my hands. While I was in the forest, Bueren, it was as if my senses were drained away. I couldn't see clearly, or hear, or even smell anything. Whatever it was, it came and went, all of a sudden. It stopped."

Almost she looked round at the dwarf Stanach to confirm her report.

"Bueren, I thought something had happened to me— that something dark had touched me in the forest. The more I think of it, though, the more I realize that something must be happening to the forest itself."

Bueren nodded. "People around here have been saying that for some time now. They used to think the Knights were causing it—or at least that Lord Thagol was—but the Knights don't know any more about it than we do or like it any better. Some people—" she lowered her eyes— "blame the Kagonesti."

Out the corner of her eye, Kerian saw one of the elf hunters rise and put a coin on the bar.

"Bueren Rose," he called, "I'll see you next trip."

Bueren called good night and wished the hunter luck. "Father's got a sackful of walnuts for stuffing, so we'll take all the grouse and pheasant you can bring us, Kaylt."

"Ay, well, it's the season, so start shelling." His glance fell on Kerian then slid away. "You take care while I'm gone, Rosie."

Kaylt and his companion left, a cool breeze ghosting into the tavern before the door shut. Torches flared, the hounds rose to sniff the night, then sidled up to Stanach's table where the dwarf put down plates for each. Tails wagging, they dropped muzzles to plate and lapped up gravy and bits of venison.

Bueren wiped crumbs from the bar and gathered up the supper plates. She looked past Kerian, to the windows and the darkness outside. "Keri, the Wilder Elves," she resumed, speaking softly. "We haven't seen your brother around here in nearly a year. We hardly see any Kagonesti these days. They aren't welcome in Sliathnost, because the people around here blame what's going on in the forest on the tribes."

The tribes. The phrase had a strange and distant sound to it.

Kerian shook her head, frowning. "The Kagonesti? How—"

Outside the tavern, rough voices, one growling, another snarling. A sharp order crackled, then silence. A breath of air on a quickening breeze slipped beneath the door. Kerian smelled horses. Hollow in the belly, suddenly she thought she smelled blood.

At the hearth, the older hound lifted its head. Tail curled tight, hackles high, it looked from Nayla Firethorn to the door. Nayla made sure of her short sword, while her companion spoke sharply to the hound.

A thud boomed through the tavern, the sound of a booted foot slamming into wood. The door flung opened. The hounds never moved, the older growled low.

Three Knights came into the tavern on a chill gust of wind. Behind them tattered leaves and golden bits of straw whirled around the feet of three of Eamutt Thagol's Knights. Armed, mailed in black, the Knights wore helms and kept the visors down. They drove a prisoner before them, a woman with hands bound in front, ankles hobbled. Her silvery hair hung in her face, matted with sweat and blood, She wore a hunter's gear, leathers and a shirt of bleached cotton. Cut loosely, meant to lace in the front, the shirt hung on her torn, rent nearly in half. She held the pieces together across her breast with bound hands. Cuts and bruises marred her lovely face, dirt and tears smeared her cheeks. She'd fought hard before her capture.

In the firelight and shadow, Kerian realized the woman was Kagonesti. Tattoos wound between the bruises and scratches on the sun-browned skin of her neck and throat, the creamier gold of shoulder and breast. The prisoner looked up, her glance skittering around the common room. Her eyes had a haunted, hunted look in them.

Bueren touched Kerian's arm. "Hush," she whispered. "If you do the wrong thing, or even say the wrong thing, you could get her killed. Her, yourself, or the rest of us."

Eyes on the Knights, the two hounds held their posts. The elf at the window and the two villagers shot glances at each other, looked away, and then quickly abandoned their tables with a skitter of coins. Like shadows, they slipped behind the Knights and their prisoner and out into the chilling night.

Bueren looked up, keeping her expression neutral, her voice level. "Sirs, can I get you food and drink?"

The tallest Knight flung back his visor and removed his helm. His bald pate glistened with sweat, and his scarred face was hardened by the habits of cruelty, eyes cold as stone and narrow, lips twisted in a sneer. He shoved his prisoner forward, so hard she fell to her knees. On elbows and knees, she stayed there, head hung, catching her breath. In her ragged breathing, Kerian heard low groaning.

Bueren gripped her arm, held her back.

The other Knights removed their helms, a dark-haired youth and a red-beard in his middle years. They wore merciless expressions. In another time, in the days before

67

the Chaos War, the Knights of Takhisis admitted only the sons and daughters of nobility to their ranks. Men such as these would not have been allowed to muck out the stables of a Knight's castle, let alone take a Knight's oath. The Dark Knights had been hard warriors in the cause of their Dark Queen, dauntless in pursuit of her Vision, but they were Knights, and they had prized honor and all the noble virtues. In these dragon days, these godless times, the Knights of Takhisis—now the Knights of Neraka—must fill their ranks however they could. It was rumored—though no one in Qualinesti could imagine the rumor true—that in some places even half-ogres wore the black armor.

"Sir Egil," Bueren said, striving to sound casual as she acknowledged the bald one. "I haven't seen you in a while. Won't you and your men take that large table in the middle there? I'll bring drinks—"

"Ale!" snapped the dark-haired one, his voice cracking.

"Dwarf spirit," growled the red-beard.

In the corner by the hearth, Stanach Hammerfell never budged, not even a twitch of his hand, but Kerian thought she saw the faintest flicker of scorn in his blue-flecked dark eyes.

Bueren jerked her chin at the woman on her knees. "What about her? You're not going to just leave her there, are you?"

Sir Egil shrugged. He strolled past the prisoner, kicking her absently. The dark-haired boy did the same, though kicking with more enthusiasm. Red-beard grabbed the woman by the rope binding her hands and dragged her to her feet. He shoved her ahead of him to a small table near the bar and tied her by the hobbles to the chair. His eyes were small and mean, like a pig's, when he narrowed them meaningfully at Bueren Rose.

"She don't get nothing, that Kagonesti bitch. No water,

no food. I won her, and she bit and cut me in the fight, so now I get to say. Ain't no one goes near her, hear?"

The younger Knight wiped his drooling mouth with the back of his hand. Kerian's belly shivered in disgust as he turned his gaze upon her.

Bueren poked her sharply. "You. Didn't you hear? They want food."

Kerian stared, Bueren gave her an impatient shove toward the kitchen. "Go on. Tell my father we have customers out here. Three plates, piled high."

Kerian nearly stumbled over Bueren's father as she went through the swinging door into the kitchen. She knew Jale as well as his daughter—a little deaf Jale claimed to be, but he heard most of what went on in his tavern. His face slick with sweat from laboring over the steam pots, spits and baking ovens, he handed her a laden tray.

"Out with you. Go feed them before there's trouble," he said in a low voice.

Kerian balanced the tray on her hands and turned back to the door.

"Wait!" Jale slipped her knife out of his belt, and threw a food-stained white towel over her shoulder—in all lands, dragon-held or free, the badge of a tavern waitress.

As she had seen Bueren do many times, Kerian managed the door with her hip, kept the burdened tray level, and returned to serve in the tavern. She put a plate of food before each of the Knights. Already boisterous with drink, the Knights filled the tavern with their shouted oaths and rough curses. Kerian bore the jostling and lewd comments. She managed to keep her temper when the red-beard's arms encircled her waist, his hands sliding swiftly up. Eyes low, she wrenched away, hoping he would think her cheeks colored with embarrassment rather than anger.

The one called Sir Egil rocked his chair back on two

legs, picking his teeth with his dagger. The dark-haired young man licked his lips.

"Come here, girl." Red-bearded Barg's eyes grew colder.

The boy snickered, rattling dice in the pouch. Spittle glistened on his lips, and he licked it away. Sir Egil yawned.

"Don't," groaned the prisoner.

Kerian turned.

Barg shouted, "Shut up, you!" in the instant before an empty pewter wine pitcher hit the floor with a clanging thud.

Swift as a rabbit out of the snare, Kerian leaped to retrieve the pitcher. Her fingers closed round the handle, and Stanach held up his right hand, showing broken fingers in the firelight.

"Damn thing just fell out of my hand," the dwarf said, snorting in disgust. He glanced at two gravy-stained napkins piled on the table. His voice louder, his tone suddenly irritated, he said, "Clear this mess off the table, will you, girl?"

Kerian picked up the napkins, nearly dropped the long-bladed knife tucked between them. With wide eyes she made what she hoped were convincing apologies for neglecting the dwarf and his companions. "If I can bring you anything else—"

Stanach just turned away as though she weren't there. Haugh leaned across the table to say something to him about how he was tired and would be going upstairs.

Kerian didn't hear the rest and didn't try to. In her hands now she held a weapon, at the back of the kitchen, she knew, was a door that promised escape. In their furtive way, the dwarf and his companions had told her they were with her, whatever happened next. Pitcher in hand, knife hidden, she now passed the prisoner, the bruised Kagonesti woman. She glanced at Bueren Rose. Her friend's eyes widened slightly.

Like petals falling from her hand, Kerian let one of the napkins drop. She bent to retrieve it, and her cheek was right beside the prisoner's knee. "Be still. Follow."

Kerian grabbed the prisoner by the wrist and yanked her to her feet.

"Hey!" shouted Barg.

The woman's knees went out from under her. Kerian pulled her up again as Sir Egil cursed and the dark-haired boy howled high, like a wolf. "Hey! Barg! Get 'em!"

Steel flashed, silver glints and red, and chairs clattered, tumbling over as the Knights jumped to their feet.

Gripping the prisoner's wrist, Kerian bolted for the side door. She sidestepped Nayla, a dog, and a startled Bueren Rose. A hand grabbed Kerian's shoulder, hard enough to leave bruises. Barg pulled her back, a long knife in his hand. Flashing, his blade came up, ripping the sleeve of her blouse as she jerked away, scoring the flesh of her right arm.

The Knight growled low in his throat and grabbed at her again. Hard around the waist he held her, his mailed arm digging into her flesh. She smelled blood, her and his, and the crimsoned blade pressed against her throat.

Bueren screamed. Her father, entering the room, shouted, and the youngest of the Knights darted in close. "She's mine! Give her over!"

Barg laughed. Kerian kept perfectly still. Against her throat pressed a blade with the taste of her blood still on it. In her hands, unseen and covered by gravy-stained napkins, she gripped another. Without moving, she tried to see the Kagonesti prisoner, spotted her sagging on the floor, looking worse than she had when she'd come in. Long elf eyes met, flashing. The woman had been beaten, surely worse, but she remained undaunted.

Kerian's blood sparked. Swiftly she squirmed in the Knight's grip, flung back and jammed her knee into his crotch.

Barg howled. In the same moment, Kerian pulled away. She grabbed the prisoner by the wrist, yanked her hard. The woman came up groaning, but she came up. On her feet, she stumbled, and Kerian pushed her toward the side door leading out to the privy.

A mailed hand dug into Kerian's shoulder. She felt breath hot on her cheek as Barg dragged her back, a long knife in his hand.

"No!" the prisoner cried.

Kerian ducked and turned, trying to free herself. The Knight's grip dug into her flesh.

Blood ran down her arm. Roaring her pain, Kerian leaped toward her captor, her knife suddenly alive and glinting bright sparks. She lifted, she plunged, and she saw shock turn Barg's eyes glassy.

The steel slid softly into muscle, slipped between ribs. The blade scraped bone. Barg's eyes went wide, and he dropped away. The tavern swelled with voices as Knights swore and cried murder.

Kerian shot for the door, hot blood on her hands, and grabbing the gaping prisoner.

CHAPTER
7

The woman's name was Ayensha, "Of Eagle Flight," she said, gasping the information as they ran out into the yard.

Ayensha pointed up the hill. "The forest."

Kerian cursed under her breath. In moments she was lost, blind in the night and falling over rocks. Ayensha slipped ahead of her, still groaning to breathe. Behind, the night filled with outraged shouts, with torchlight and the sound of horses stamping and bridles ringing.

"North!" cried the dark-haired boy, his voice high with skittery laughter.

"No, south!" shouted Sir Egil.

Kerian tripped. Ayensha of Eagle Flight pulled her up. Over their shoulders, down the hill, they saw torches like little red stars. Furious voices carried up the hill.

"Keep running!" Ayensha pushed Kerian ahead. "Use your hands, use your eyes." Her voice dropped low. She pulled her torn shirt together, shivering in the chill breeze.

They ran the climbing forest in darkness. Kerian tripped over stones. Often she stumbled into trees; brush snared her, and tangling roots. Cold air stung her cuts and scratches. Her right arm stiffened, throbbing with the pain of a knife cut. Behind them and below, the lights of torches ran along the road, swift in the night. Sir Egil and his men searched south, then turned to search north.

"Look," said Ayensha, pointing. The lights stood still, bright and sharp. The Knights had returned to the Hare and Hound, unable to find their quarry on the road. Small in the night, the tavern's windows showed as orange gleams. "We have to put distance between us and them."

Panting, Kerian said, "Why? They don't dare follow us. Their horses won't be able to take this slope in the dark."

"No," said Ayensha, leaning against a tree. She wrapped her arms loosely around her middle. Sweat ran on her face, plastered her hair to her forehead, her neck and cheeks.

More than sweat, Kerian thought. Silver tears traced through the dirt and blood and bruises on Ayensha's face. She seemed unaware of that.

Like fire, the woman's eyes shone fierce and desperate. She shoved away from the tree. "Let's go."

Kerian hated the darkness as though it were her enemy. She hated it with each step she took, despised it each time she fell, each time she staggered up again. A woman of the city, she was used to kinder nights and darkness tamed by hot, high, warming fires on streets outside the taverns, the cheerful flames of torchbearers leading a lord or lady's litter through the streets, the glow from windows of houses high and humble. Here night was complete, blinding.

Ayensha was not troubled. Kerian began to think the woman had the eyes of a cat. Night-eyes, the Wilder Elves called that. Kerian herself used to have the same skill, a long time ago in Ergoth. She fell again, this time so hard the breath left her lungs in a loud whoosh. Fiery pain shot up her right arm, blood sprang from the knife wound again.

"Up," Ayensha ordered between clenched teeth.

Kerian rose, and they traveled on. When she stumbled, she righted herself. When she hurt, she closed her lips tight to cage the groan. Once she fell and did not rise quickly, and saw Ayensha watching. In the woman's eyes, pity.

"Come on, you've got to keep going," she insisted.

Kerian followed Ayensha, running, falling, and climbing up again till all the night became an aching repetition of pain and anger and finally the simple numbness of exhaustion. It was then, with surprise, that she saw a glint of silver through the tops of the trees, a small shining. Her weary mind could not think what that shining was or imagine the cause.

"The moon," Ayensha whispered. She turned her face to the silver, her bruises and cuts showing black in the stark light. "Ah, gods, wherever you are, thank you."

Kerian watched the half-moon rise, and she watched the world around appear as though by magic. They had come far, and indeed, high. Around them now was more stone than tree, and the stones soared past her height. Some stood so close together they formed little shelters. Against one of these boulders, Ayensha leaned, but very carefully. The woman's face shone white as bone in the moonlight, her lips pressed into a thin line against pain.

"Sit," Kerian said, by habit still whispering.

Ayensha looked around, numbly. Kerian took her arm and helped her to a seat on a broad flat stone, helped her put her back to another. Sighing, the woman leaned her head against the rock and closed her eyes.

Listening to the weary rhythm of her heart beating, Kerian pressed her own back against a tall broad pine, the tangy scent of sap filling her, tickling awake old memories of the dark upland forest of Ergoth. Her breath staggered in her lungs, hitching. Muscles of her arms and legs twitched with exhaustion.

"Ayensha, where are we headed?"

Eyes still closed, Ayensha said, "Nowhere. Not now. We're finished running for the night." She took a careful breath and pushed away from the boulder. "We hide here, in the rocks, till morning, then see how things are and go on when we can."

An owl cried, not the mournful hooting reported in minstrel's songs and poet's verse, but the startling, rattling cackle of a raptor hunting. Wide-winged, the owl swooped out of a nearby pine, tail spread as it sailed low. Behind her, Kerian heard the sudden dash of something small through the brush, then a high, despairing scream. The owl rose, a rabbit caught in its talons, the corpse swinging. The sight caught Kerian hard by the throat.

"Come on," Ayensha said. It seemed she hadn't marked the small death at all. She pushed up from her seat, looked around, and pointed to a stand of three tall boulders. "There. Help me."

Kerian put Ayensha's arm around her shoulders. Though they did not walk more than a dozen yards, to Kerian it felt like miles the distance growing with the weight on her shoulders. The two tallest boulders leaned together, their tops almost touching, the gap between an entrance like a doorway without a door. It seemed wide enough for two to pass through. Kerian shifted Ayensha's weight and started through. She had not taken two steps before the woman hissed, "Stop!"

Startled, Kerian did stop, looking at her companion. Again, she saw pity in the woman's eyes.

From between clenched teeth, Ayensha said, "Check *inside*. There could be a fox denning there or a lynx or bear." She pulled away from Kerian and balanced with her hand against one of the tall stones.

Kerian didn't think any of those things were true, but she put her hand to the knife at her belt—the knife slipped to her by the unpleasant dwarf, she suddenly remembered, wondering briefly what happened to him and his two companions in all the commotion—cold fingers gripping the bone handle as she slipped the weapon from the sheath.

"Wait here," Kerian said, firmly as though the idea of looking were her own. She snatched up a handful of stones from the ground and pitched in one, then another. She stopped to listen, heard only the wind, and tossed in a third.

They peered into the darkness, the little cave smelling of ancient leaves and ancient earth. Faint and far, moonlight drifted through the cracks between the leaning stones, not sharp beams but a pale diffusion. Kerian took a moment to let her eyes adjust, then helped Ayensha to sit. She went outside, by moonlight found fallen boughs of fragrant pine to make a soft bed, and helped Ayensha to lie down. So weary was the woman now, so filled with pain, that she could not speak to say whether that helped her or to agree that it was good to be out of the wind or to say whether she felt a little warmer. She lay in silence, hunched over in pain. Once her breath caught in a small sob.

Kerian sat silent, her right arm throbbing, her hand on Ayensha's shoulder. In the quiet, she heard wind, again the cackle of a hunting owl, again the sudden scream of a rabbit's death. Shuddering, she held her breath and listened more closely to the night. As her heart quieted, she heard what he had hoped for—the faint, musical trickle of water sliding down stone.

"Ayensha," she whispered.

Ayensha groaned.

"Lie still, I'll be right back."

Kerian found water behind the little shelter, a trickle shining with the light of the half-moon, like silver running.

She washed her wound clean of blood, washed her hands and dried them on her shirt. She had only her cupped hands to carry the water, icy and tasting like stone. Still, with two trips, she managed to soothe Ayensha's thirst. She checked the woman's injuries and knew at least one of her ribs was broken, maybe more. She could only hope that organs had not been damaged. Across Ayensha's ribs Kerian saw the distinct print, in black bruising, of a hard boot's heel.

"Brutes," she muttered, helping Ayensha to lay straight.

"Worse," Ayensha whispered, "and I'm glad you killed that bastard Barg."

Yes, I killed him, thought Kerian, shocked that she had done it so easily and now felt so little regret.

Ayensha didn't say more. She closed her eyes, and in the instant of closing, fell asleep.

A long time Kerian sat beside the sleeping woman. It seemed to her, there in the misty moonlight and the cold little cave, that she'd been gone from Qualinost for weeks. All her muscles turned to water from weariness.

I will never be able to go home again.

She had killed a Knight, and here in this cave she still smelled his blood on her hands, warm and spilling over the bone handle of the dwarf's knife.

Kerian rose and sat near the opening of their shelter, the little doorway. Wind slid around the stones, small creatures with night habits rustled through the bracken. Kerian sat very still, listening to the tiny sounds of a fox lapping moisture. To test her ability for silence, she slipped her knife from the sheath. The prick-eared fox bolted, slashing away into the dark.

Kerian reached for the golden chain hanging from her neck. She pulled it out, moonlight gleamed on gold, on the topaz of Gil's ring. Without warning, tears spilled down

Kerian's cheeks, warm when all else was cold. She closed her eyes and saw tossing seas, whitecaps like bent-winged gulls, gulls like the peaks of whitecaps, each reflecting the other. In her ears, the forest breeze changed and became the sound of the sea. The piney scents changed into the achingly beautiful fragrance of home.

A long time ago, his arm around her, holding his little sister close as the sea grew dark and slaty, immense between the fleeing ship and the thinning line of Ergoth's shore, Iydahar had said, "Turtle, we'll never be able to go home again, but there will always be you and me. Always."

Yet Iydahar had gone to the mountains and forests to fight for a prince who had lost his crown, she to live in the city. To be a servant, Dar sneered, to lords who handed over their kingdom piece by piece to a dragon's Knights. Dar did not know her lover was the king, and grimly, almost with satisfaction, she thought, "Dar! What would you think of me if you knew that?"

She wished she could ask him now, to his face, but Bueren Rose said no one had seen him in a long while. Where was her brother? She wondered, was he well?

———◆◆◆———

Late, an hour past moonset, Ayensha woke and pushed herself to sit. Breathing hard, she asked for water. As she drank it slowly, she asked Kerian about herself. Kerian gave some detail about the life she had left behind, though by no means all. Finally Ayensha, her back resting against a stone, said, "Well, and here we are. I thank you for that. What are you going to do now, Kerian?"

Kerian sat a long time silent, listening to the night. "I've come out of Qualinost to find my brother. He is Iydahar of the White Osprey Kagonesti, or so we were called when we lived on Ergoth. Perhaps we—they—perhaps we are still called that."

Ayensha said she had not heard of the White Osprey tribe. "Nobody knows all the Kagonesti there are. Is he a servant, like you, your brother?"

"No. He never was. He and my parents have always lived wild. Our father is Dallatar. He and my brother fought for Prince Porthios."

Ayensha moved to find more comfort against cold stone. "You should go back to the city, Kerian. It's harder out here."

Kerian looked at her long through narrowed eyes. "It is fair hard in the city these days." Owls hunted the opportune night. Kerian closed her eyes. In private darkness, she said, "In Qualinost there are four bridges round the city. We have always loved them, for Forest Keepers used to walk watch on the silver spans and cry the hours from the watchtowers: All is well in the East! All is safe in the South! We are watchful in the West! We see all that moves in the North!" She breathed deeply, then opened her eyes. Ayensha's face was a pale oval an arm's length away. "All is not well in the east now. Upon the eastern bridge Lord Eamutt Thagol has piked the heads of elves killed by his Knights —"

Again, Ayensha shifted, still trying to find ease, still failing.

"One of the heads piked up on the bridge was that of our cousin. She was Ylania of the White Osprey."

Ayensha's breath caught, a hissing of pain as she moved. "Well, I don't know your brother, and I didn't know this woman Ylania."

An owl sailed past the opening of the shelter.

"Perhaps someone of your own tribe does." Kerian lifted her head, met the woman's eyes coolly. "For the sake of what I did for you, I ask that you take me to your people so I can ask. "

Ayensha laughed, a low, bitter sound. "All right. I'll take you into the forest and you can ask your questions, but don't blame me if you get an answer you don't like."

Ayensha lay down again. Kerian sat the night out, watching owls.

———◆———

Gilthas dripped honey onto both halves of the steaming apricot muffin on his breakfast plate. He took a long slow breath of the scent of the honey, of the apricots and minted tea in his cup. A wealth of strawberries filled the bowl at his elbow, waiting to be dressed in thick cream. From beyond the open doors, twinned and paned in dimpled glass, the scent of his mother's garden drifted into the small breakfast room. Rich green scents of her herb garden, and the ancient perfume of autumn as leaves changed from green to gold.

It was the autumn he thought of: leaving, going, changing. Kerian shaped his mood and all his thoughts.

Stubborn woman! He shouldn't have let her go. He should have held her, kept her. He was not only her lover, he was her king!

His mother filled a crystal goblet with icy water poured from a crystal carafe. The two chimed, one against the other, a perfect note.

Stubborn woman . . . he should have forbidden Kerian to leave, ordered her to abandon her fool's errand. Iydahar was nothing if not capable of taking care of himself.

"If you had ordered Kerian to stay," said Laurana, picking a peach muffin from the covered basket, "if you had, my son, you would have lost her as surely as though you'd commanded her into exile."

His mother's words, dropping right into his thoughts, no longer startled Gilthas. They did, as at times like this, often annoy him, but they didn't startle. Laurana had had the skill of reading her son's thoughts from the first moment he had thoughts, or so it seemed to him. She smiled her golden smile, and went on buttering her muffin.

Her tone had, he thought, contained just a note of the acerbic. The Queen Mother had a true liking for Kerian but also the kind of respect that could sometimes appear cautious.

"Mother," Gilthas said, seeking to turn Laurana's thoughts from his. "I've had all the news Rashas is willing to give this morning, which is news hardly worth having. The watch was kept calmly through the night. There was only a minor altercation at a tavern near the western bridge where the Knights go to drink. The festival will move out into the countryside today, people will light bonfires in the fields. Rashas isn't as happy about that as the people themselves."

Laurana looked up, only a small glance. Morning breeze ruffled her golden hair, nothing seemed to ruffle her composure. It was always that way with her, Gilthas thought.

"Mother—"

"Listen," said Laurana, she who in lands beyond Qualinesti was yet known as the Golden General. She held up a hand to still her son. She placed a finger to her lips.

In the garden beyond the open doors, birds sang. The whisper of voices washing in from the city lay under those songs, and the sound of the gardener speaking with her apprentice, ordering the final clipping of the roses for the season.

Gilthas frowned, his mother mouthed the word again. *Listen.*

He did, and in the next breath he heard the click of nails on the marble floor of the patio beyond the doors. He saw the hounds before he saw the elf woman, two long-legged beasts trotting across the patio with perfect confidence. They cast shadows behind them, and it seemed the woman appeared from those very shadows, the substance of her rising from the darkness. Gil caught his breath, startled. Here was Nayla Firethorn, a woman of his mother's household. Times were when the woman would be gone from the city for days, even months. Sometimes she would come and go alone, sometimes with Haugh Daggerhart, a man said to be her lover. These two, and others like them, were the voice and will of the Queen Mother beyond Qualinesti's borders, her trusted warrior-heralds.

"Nayla," said the Queen Mother.

Laurana lifted her hand and Nayla dismissed her hounds, sending them in to the garden before she came forward to the open door. A beautiful woman, Nayla wore her golden hair in a thick braid hanging as far down as the small of her back. Gilthas imagined that, unbound, the woman's hair would cover her like a shimmering cloak.

Nayla saw Gilthas and swept him a courtier's bow, a flourish of the arm, a bending of the knee.

"Good morning, Your Majesty," she said, rising. One flickering glance she gave to Laurana—it was not lost on Gilthas!—then, having received some signal indiscernible to the king, she seemed to relax. She stepped into the room and stood before Laurana. "Your Highness, I have returned early, leaving the completion of the task to Haugh. All will be well."

Clear as water on a windless lake, Laurana's expression never changed. "I see you have come back by unusual means, Nayla. You felt the need for secret haste?"

Nayla reached into her shirt and withdrew a small leather pouch. She spilled the contents into her hand, a gleaming emerald shaped like a leaf half-furled. This she

83

put into Laurana's hand. "I have, Madam, and I thank you for the use of the talisman. As magical talismans work these days, it served well enough."

She hesitated, then, when she spoke, she spoke directly to Gil.

"I've come with unexpected news for you, Your Majesty. I hope you will understand that although I might not understand the full weight and import of what I saw last night, I give you news of it with the best will possible."

Puzzled, Gilthas frowned. "Please speak freely."

She drew a breath, and she stood tall, trusting her instinct better than she trusted the king to hear her news calmly. "Sir, while I was upon my errand for your mother, I chanced to witness an incident at the Hare and Hound—"

Gil's heart jumped.

"—Haugh and I had sat down to supper when an elf-woman came into the tavern." Her glance jumped from Gilthas to the Queen Mother. "Madam, the rumors we've been hearing are true. There's something . . ." She shrugged. "Something *wrong* in the forest."

Gil leaned forward. "Wrong? What do you mean?"

"Your Majesty, it's as though something bewitches one's senses in there, in the deepest parts of the wood. On the road, one may be fine. Farther in—and with no regularity of pattern to discern—a kind of . . . it feels like magic takes hold, and all the senses are muffled. In the villages and towns, they mutter about the Kagonesti and say the Wilder Kin have something to do with it. I don't know about the cause, sir. I only know the effect." She paused. "It is the elf-woman I want to talk about, Kagonesti."

"At the Hare and Hound." Gil's voice was unsteady. If his mother or Nayla noticed, neither acknowledged it.

"She is Kerianseray, Your Majesty, servant in the household of Senator Rashas. I believe you know her, and

I believe you will not welcome the news I bring of her."

"Tell me," said the king, startled by the coldness of his voice.

"Your Majesty," said Nayla, "while we were there three Knights came in with a Kagonesti woman for a prisoner. She had been badly beaten. The leader of those Knights is Sir Egil Galaria, one of those beholden to Lord Thagol."

"Speak of Kerianseray."

"Sir, Your Majesty, there was a sudden altercation. Somehow she rescued the prisoner and fled the Hare and Hound with her."

A smile twitched at the corners of the king's lips. His heart swelled with sudden pride.

"She fled, sir, and on the way out, she killed a Knight. With luck, Lord Thagol doesn't know it yet, but when he does learn the news . . ."

She need not have finished the thought. Beyond Laurana's garden, past the grounds of her residence, the span of the eastern bridge shone in the morning sunlight, mist curling around its towers, wisping like ghostly tendrils of hair around the piked heads.

"Thank you, Nayla," said the king softly, after a long silence. "I appreciate your effort to bring me this news." He looked at her with faraway eyes. "I appreciate your discretion, as well, for you must have many thoughts on the subject of Senator Rashas's servant and reasons why I would be interested in her well-being."

Nayla bowed, again a courtier's sweep. When she stood, her green eyes were clear and bright. "I have no thoughts on the subject at all, my lord king. I hope you will trust me ever as your lady mother has. I hope you will know that in all matters, Haugh's heart and mine are as one."

He knew it. He had not known the Forest Keepers, that shining legion of warriors who had been the buckler and sword of a kingdom. Fate had commanded that he disband them, the breaking of that valiant army part of the fee to be paid for an uneasy peace that would keep his kingdom intact, his people alive. He saw in the eyes of this messenger the kind of loyalty few but kings would ever know.

Gilthas dismissed her with his gratitude and turned to his mother.

"My son," she murmured, "it seems your Kerian has become an enemy of your enemy."

"She has," Gil said, "and her head is no safer now than her brother's. She's a headlong fool, mother."

Laurana raised a brow. Her lips moved in a small smile, and Gil was reminded that the same had once been said about her by his father.

Laurana took a sip of water, another taste of the cooling peach muffin. "Let's give Nayla a chance to rest and eat, then let's see if we can find Kerian before Thagol does."

The glint in her eye, sudden and keen, was like that of sunlight on dangerous steel.

On the misty plane where Skull Knights can roam, what was fresh news to the royal family of Qualinesti was old news to Thagol Dream Walker. He wandered the dangerous roads between consciousness and dreams, listening to the sounds of death—the scream, the whimper, the moan. He listened for the sigh, the bittersweet acceptance, and the final silence. In him, his dream, his heart, his chilly soul, were the strains of a dark, descending symphony.

He knew the very moment when Sir Barg died, the Knight who in better times, older days, would not have

been so much as a groom in the stable of the lowliest
Knight of Takhisis. He knew the murderer, who was a
slave in the house of Senator Rashas. It had often been she
who ran messages between the Lord Knight and the senator. Kerianseray, her name. Kerianseray. In his mind, he
tasted the Knight's death, knew all the bitterness of his
dying, felt the shock of it, the knife scraping on ribs, sliding
into the beating muscle that was his heart. Like ice, he felt
what rushed in as Barg's blood rushed out.

By the time Gilthas had begun his meeting with the elf
woman Nayla, Lord Thagol had left his dreamwalking and
completed a meeting of his own with Senator Rashas. The
two spoke only briefly, then the Lord General was standing
before his assembled garrison, dark-armored warriors like
pieces of night come to life.

In the minds of the men was only one thought—each
knew he must stand well before the Skull Knight, never
moving, his breathing hidden inside the shell of his armor,
his eyes straight ahead, hands still. They might wish the
sweat didn't run on them, the small motion of a salty bead
sliding down a cheek, something to draw the Lord Knight's
attention.

He had but two things to impart to his garrison, and
Lord Thagol did that swiftly. One was the command that
the elf woman Kerianseray be brought back to Qualinost
for killing. His thought leaped from his mind to theirs. In
their minds they saw the woman, the golden mane of her
hair, the tattoos that marked her as a Kagonesti. They saw
the killer as though in a flash of lightning. They saw a murdered Knight as though his body lay at their feet. With one
motion, ten Knights stepped forward to volunteer for the
work. Thagol wanted more Knights than those. He commanded that those ten take patrols of four and range the
roads of the elf kingdom, stopping in every town of note,
every waycross with a tavern.

The other thing Sir Eamutt Thagol told his men was that the watch rotations on the four bridges would double, and in short order no Knights would be required to keep post at the doors to his headquarters, the ugly stone building that so irritated the Qualinesti.

CHAPTER 8

Like a storm come out of season, Lord Thagol's Knights flashed along the roads of Qualinesti. The hard hooves of war-horses tore the earth, trampling. Their voices lifted in laughter and cursing, for these Knights had been too long away from battlegrounds, too long consigned to the backwater of the green dragon's conquered lands. Out upon the roads, each patrol like a dark-shining blade, they sang battle songs, they recounted deeds brave and terrible. Blood-lusty they rode, each patrol upon its mission, each with a leader who spoke words of proclamation before the doors of taverns, inns, and hostels, in the squares of villages, on the streets of towns. These words they'd gotten from Thagol himself, not from his lips but words graven into their own minds in flashing bolts. No one of the messenger Knights, speaking, changed so much as the rhythm of their lord's speech.

It is commanded! By order of my lord Sir Eamutt Thagol, he of Neraka and lately of the Monastery Bone . . .

Elves would stand in perfect stillness, some caught like rabbits in terror, most of them taking care to keep their truest feelings from these Knights. They were not stone, these farmers and shopkeepers, the gods had made them of flesh and bone, and they had true hearts that stirred at the darkness of Knights. They had learned over the years of occupation that an elf could die of a resentful glance, a perceived arrogance. They kept quiet, they kept still, and they listened as the war-horses snorted and danced and Knights laughed in scorn.

The Knights gone, the elves would gather and speak of anger. Some spoke resentment, and when they did the name of the outlawed woman sprang to their lips.

Who is this Kerianseray of Qualinost? Who is this woman who brings down a plague of Knights upon us?

They would argue among themselves, quietly as elves do, their passion seen only in the glinting of their eyes. They would remind themselves that they must not let the Knights change them, they must not let these dragon-days become the days of their undoing. They had never tolerated murderers among them. Should they now because the killer killed a Knight?

Some among them did not agree, and they were always the youngest, the farm lads, the girls who must hold themselves still under the leering eyes of a Knight. These, in the privacy of their hearts or souls, didn't consider the killing of one of the occupation force a murder.

On the morning of the first true day of autumn, four Knights of Takhisis sat their tall battle steeds in front of the place where the trouble began. Armed as for war, encased in mail and plate, faceless in their casques, each held a flaring torch. The light of their fire ran on the shining steel blades. It slid down the arcs of breastplates, on knee guards, glinted from bridles and bits and shone like blood in the fierce eyes of war-horses. The four ranged around a fifth, the Knight known among his fellows as Headsman Chance. Sir Chance sat the tallest of the steeds, and all the Knights stood darkly behind him against the gold and red of the falling season glowing warmly in the forest beyond the edges of the road.

From out of the morning mist came muffled cries, emanating from nearby, the village proper. Hearing those cries, Bueren Rose glanced at her father, thinking Jale looked like a ghost standing in the dooryard of his beloved tavern, his Hare and Hound. A small breeze wandered by, tugging at her red-gold hair. The sign above the tavern door swung wearily, bolts creaking. Beside her, her father Jale looked terrified. She thought—a stray thought, like a stray curling of mist—that her father had run this tavern all his life. When he was only a child, he'd started out as a potboy in the tavern, his duties no more than those of young Firthing who held that job now, a scrubber of pots and dishes, emptier of slops from the guest chambers. In time he became the cook's boy, learning how to prepare dishes he'd become known for along road from Sliathnost to Qualinost. He'd been taught to cook by his mother. From his father, an old Forest Keeper retired from service after too many wounds, Jale had learned how to tend bar and toss out troublemakers. Since before the coming of green Beryl with her fangs and her Knights, there had been the Hare and Hound. Since before the Chaos War, this tavern had stood.

The breath of Sir Chance's horse steamed in the cold morning air. Bridle and bit jingling, the battle-beast tossed his head. Bueren thought the horse's eyes looked wild, red and eager. Worse, though, his rider's eyes shone winter-gray and cold.

Shivering, she slipped her hand into the crook of her father's arm. Upon the road, emerging from the mist, figures came walking toward them, men, women, and children herded to the tavern by two more of Chance Headsman's Knights. With rough laughter, the Knights urged the villagers to speed by the pricking of swords, the bruising nudges of lances. A child cried out and fell. Her father grabbed her up swiftly and held her in his arms, away from the iron-shod hooves of a charger. One or two of the younger elves showed the marks of resistance, blackened eyes, bloody heads, a broken wrist swelling.

Chance Headsman threw back his visor, his glance alighting on each elf as the Knights drove them to stand in the tavern yard, a huddle of frightened women, angry men, sobbing children. Not one of them had a weapon, not even the small belt knife every villager carried as part of his daily gear. The Headsman looked at all those gathered, men, women, and little children clinging, as though he knew something about each of them. Last his eyes touched Jale. Bueren Rose held her father's arm tighter.

Shouting, as though on a battleground raging with screaming and war cries, the Headsman cried, *"It is commanded!"*

At their mothers' skirts, children stirred and whimpered. In her father's arms, the girl who had fallen buried her face in his shoulder. Overhead, a crow called.

"By order of my lord Sir Eamutt Thagol," bawled the Headsman, "he of Neraka and lately of the Monastery Bone, for crimes of murder and insurrection, the woman Kerianseray, a Kagonesti servant late of the household of Senator Rashas of Qualinost, is declared outside the law.

"By Sir Eamutt's order, such decree renders her a person deprived of any consideration under the laws of her king. Neither will she receive the grace nor benefit of the laws of green Beryl, the dragon who rules here.

"All who see this woman are commanded to refuse her succor, denying her aid of food or weapon or shelter. All who see her are ordered to capture her by any means necessary and to bring her alive to Lord Thagol in Qualinost.

There, she will be beheaded, her head piked upon the eastern bridge. This sentence shall be executed within the sight of the citizenry of the city.

"All who are so foolish as to aid her will share in her crime and so in her sentence. *It is commanded!*"

Howling, their voices like demons, the five Knights then spurred their chargers, torches whirling over their heads. Hooves tearing up the ground, the largest of the horses, that of the Headsman, sprang directly toward Bueren. She screamed, clutching her father. The great beast plunged between them, breaking her hold, flinging both aside. A sword flashed like lightning. Sir Chance spurred past them, and Bueren scrambled for her father, for the old elf was lying still upon the ground. The cries of the villagers became distant to her; they had no more voice than a breeze in the trees as Bueren lifted her father from the dusty dooryard. Blood ran in a thin line on his neck, all the way from ear to ear.

"Father," she whispered. She lifted him, and her scream rang in the tavern yard, louder than the pounding of hooves, louder than the yowling of Knights. Her father's head rolled from his shoulders and fell bloody into the dust. Her wails of woe were heard over the crackling of flames, the roar of fire as Chance Headsman's men proceeded to put the Hare and Hound to the torch.

Firthing, the potboy, dropped to his knees beside Bueren. White in the face, his eyes glittering like polished stone, he took her hard by the shoulders. Thin, not half-grown into manhood, still he was strong, and his grip hurt. In her ear his voice grated.

"Come away, Bueren Rose. Come away!"

All around her, people panicked, Knights yelled, horses thundered. Villagers cried out, children wailed, and somewhere in the sky, ravens gathered. Firthing pulled at her now, on his feet, urgent. He jerked her to her feet.

93

She followed Firthing, running out of the dooryard, away from the fire, the screams and her dead father.

⬥⬥⬥

On the third morning since her flight from the Hare and Hound, after two days of hiding in the little cave to allow Ayensha to rest in stillness and begin to heal, Kerian went walking in the forest to check her snares. These she'd set using skills she only half-recalled from childhood, but the best hunters last night had been owls. Her snares were empty this morning. She sighed, hungry, and began a search for pinecones to free of their nuts. These she found in plenty, and a good stout branch to strip of twigs. She gave this to Ayensha for walking. She gave her most of the pine nuts, too, sweet and rich with oil.

"It isn't much," she said, "but I'll find a way to feed us better soon."

Leaning upon the sap-scented staff, Ayensha accepted the food and hobbled round the shelter to take water for herself. It was clear to both women that Ayensha would not lead today.

"Tell me the way," Kerian said. "Speak the map."

Ayensha lifted an eyebrow. "So. You remember the old phrase."

Kerian said stiffly, "Yes, I remember things, Ayensha. Speak the map."

In a voice small with pain, Ayensha did, with words painting a map upon which hills ran crowned by tall piles of stone, of pine marching on eastern ridges, and a narrow river in a deep chasm running south and then veering suddenly east. In all lands and at all times, this was the manner in which Kagonesti relayed information, be it a message carried upon the lips from one tribe to another, a tale as ancient as the time before the Cataclysm, or the safest path to a meeting site. Ayensha spoke the way to the eastern border of the Qualinesti forest, where the Stonelands lay between the kingdom of the elves and fabled Thorbardin, the hidden realm of dwarves.

They made their way through the stony forest. Though Ayensha directed and Kerian led, Kerian did not imagine them safe. They traveled deep into the wood, far from the road, and the Qualinesti Forest seemed as well behaved as it ever had.

"I think we've come away from whatever it was that affected the forest," she said to Ayensha.

Ayensha shrugged. "Do you think so?"

Despite her rescue from Lord Thagol's Knights, Ayensha evidently didn't trust Kerian nor seem to think much of her, but the woman knew something about the oddity of the forest's behavior or suspected a truth she was not willing to share. Of that much, Kerian felt certain.

On the afternoon of the third day walking, the lay of the land changed. No longer did they find the tall oaks like the wood near Qualinost. Here, the trees were all of the same clan, the fir, pine, and spruce. The land became a place of ridges and deep glens where water ran freely and caves studded the walls. Some of the caves ran far back into the earth, others were cracks in stone, a gathering place for shadows. Kerian and Ayensha did not lack for shelter in the night or for water. In these generous places woodland creatures came to drink, and here Kerian trapped or fished with growing ease. It seemed to her that all her senses were becoming honed, keen and bright. One night, sitting in the darkness at the mouth of a snug cave, as she and Ayensha ate the cold meat of hares roasted at the previous day's camp, they heard the crash and slash of heavy-footed creatures in the forest. All her nerves tingling, Kerian smelled the sulfurous reek of draconian on the wind. Unless the draconians turned from the path they were on, the reptilian beastmen would be near soon.

"Into the cave," she whispered to Ayensha, pointing into the deeper darkness.

Ayensha, sniffing the foulness too, lifted her head to speak. Kerian cut her short.

"I am no warrior, and you are too weak to make up for what I lack. Into the cave, and we'll trust ourselves to luck."

Plainly, Ayensha didn't like the idea of trusting herself to a servant girl from the capital and her idea of luck. Just as plainly, she understood the need. She slipped into the cave, keeping still in the shadows, so quiet Kerian couldn't hear her breathing.

Swiftly, her heart racing, Kerian cleaned the area before the cave of bones and any track they had made. They'd had no fire this night, there was no ash or cinder or smoking wood to betray them. She brushed the dirt with pine boughs, scattered forest debris before the entrance. She could do no more, and she sat just inside the cave's dark mouth, hidden and watching.

They came, four of them, skin the green of tarnished copper, wings wide.

"Kapak," Ayensha muttered.

The draconians marched upon the lip of the glen, their harsh voices echoing from one stony wall to the other. They spoke in roughly accented Common, each word coming out of thick throats like a curse. Their laughter raked Kerian's ears like claws. Not one of them stood less than six feet tall, and starlight glinted on their fangs, on their talons.

One, the largest, turned and spread its wings wide, roaring. The bellow lifted the hair on the back of her neck. The roar echoed from wall to wall. Kerian's fingers tightened round the bone grip of her knife. Her only weapon, it would do her no good if these creatures came her way. In a world where magic leaked away like water from a sieve, Kerian wished for a talisman, a charm, something to make her and her companion invisible.

Not moving, not breathing, she saw the sudden flash of steel, heard a high, rageful death-scream. The smallest of the draconians fell, tumbling over the edge of the gorge, hitting the side, hitting stone, dead of a sword in the gut before it ever hit the ground.

None of the luckless creature's savage companions even looked twice. One wiped a sword on the ragged hem of a tunic and absently sheathed it, the blade's work done. Another laughed, a third snarled, and the three were gone while dark blood poured out of their companion. The blood changed to acid, and soon the corpse itself melted into a dark and deadly pool.

"Let's move," Ayensha said, low.

"Where—?"

Ayensha snorted. "To a safe enough place, for now. You can follow me, or not. That's up to you."

"But my brother—"

Ayensha pulled a humorless smile. "Your brother has managed without you this long."

The reek of acid fouled the air, stinging their eyes, burning their nostrils and throats. Kerian didn't argue further, and they left the cave to find another place to pass the night.

The two elves traveled in the opposite direction from the draconians, back tracking and confident that the Kapaks would not do the same. Walking, Kerian breathed the night, the cleaner air. She listened to the hush and sigh of pines over head. When they found another cave, a quieter place, she turned the watch over to Ayensha and settled to sleep. Drifting in the place between waking and sleeping she felt a great satisfaction, for her weary muscles again knew how to find rest upon beds made of fragrant boughs and leaves whose perfume was that of eternal autumn.

They slept only until the sky began to grow light. Outside the cave, Ayensha leaned on her staff, more from comfortable habit now than from need. Four days into their travels, she'd begun to regain strength. Since they had left the Hare and Hound, she'd eaten well of what Kerian snared and the fishes she caught in the streams. She drank the cold, clear water and slept long and deeply at night. Sun had warmed the pallor from her cheek.

Over hours of walking, Ayensha brought them into a maze of gorges, winding and zigzagged, and all the while the walls grew higher. In some places they could not go dry-shod for there was room only for water, and they had to hold on to the damp stony sides for balance. A deep, distant roaring came to them from ahead.

The walls of the gorge grew closer, stone reaching for them, and the sides grew higher as the floor dropped. The two women came to the font of the water running through the gorge, a sudden spring burbling up from a crack in the stony floor.

Ayensha dipped up a handful of water and then another. "A river racing below the ground." She wiped her mouth with the back of her hand. "I've never seen it, but it's said there are places in part of the forest where there is more water below than above."

"Is that what we hear?"

Ayensha shook her head. "Lightning's voice. A waterfall."

Listening to Lightning, they walked until the passage became so narrow Kerian had to turn sideways simply to fit through. The rumbling became louder, the sky more distant, the gorge darker, the passage but a slit. Kerian's muscles cried for rest. She had none. They ate walking, following the brightness in the distance that seemed never to come closer.

At last, the voice of the falls grew louder again, deeper. Above, the slit of blue that had been the sky suddenly widened. The brightness made Kerian squint.

"Noon-bright," Ayensha said.

Only noon!

"Now put your back into it. We're almost—"

The gorge turned, daylight opened up ahead. With startling suddenness, they stood at the mouth of the gorge, practically at the stony lip of a shining lake.

"—there."

The falls known to elves as Lightning for its flash, to dwarves as Thunder for the roar of its voice, sped from such a height as to seem poured out of the sky. Silvery sheets of water flung over a cliff, headlong and heedless as a madman running. Thunder! Its voice bellowed so loudly that it pressed against Kerian's ears as a physical weight. In the presence of the cascading brightness and the furious roar, she found it difficult to breathe.

"There," said Ayensha, again smiling. "Nearly where we want to be."

Blinking, Kerian said, "Where? All I see is water falling."

Ayensha nodded. She set out around the edge of the lake, Kerian following. Little grew on that shore, only tufts of tough grass between the cracks in the stone.

"Years past count," Ayensha said, "the world erupted in volcanoes, fire spewing up from the belly of the world. The earth cracked, and the ground dropped down right here, so hard the river that runs must fall into this pool. Under the water, there is a vast bowl of stone made from the hot lava that hardened."

"The Cataclysm," Kerian said, her eyes on the falling water.

"No. This was before then, before anyone started naming ages or gods had much to do with Krynn. My people—" She slid Kerian a sidelong glance. "Our people have had this legend for as long as we have been."

Water fell roaring, and no conversation now was possible as Kerian followed Ayensha to the far edge of the lake. In silence, filled with awe before this wonder of the forest, the two stood beside the bellowing falls, soaked in mist and spray. Ayensha pointed downward, Kerian saw the rock dipping into shallow levels, like stairs. Water had done that, and water had done more. Behind the falling water she saw a depth, a passage running between the thunderous curtain of water and face of the cliff over which it raced.

Ayensha gestured. Kerian took her meaning and followed carefully down the steps, around through a cloud of spray and into sudden darkness broken by silvery bending of light through water.

Spray made the stony way slick as though it were iced. It rose by a narrow path, requiring that they hold tight to rough cracks in the stone, sometimes pulling themselves up, sometimes obliged to press themselves tight to the wall and inch along. Kerian looked once over her shoulder and froze. They were perhaps a third of the way to the cliff's height. Below the water hit stone in a madness of splash and foam.

Firmly, she turned back to the climb and saw Ayensha standing above. The woman did not cling to stone but stood at perfect ease within a dark crevice carved into the face of the cliff. Laughing, she beckoned. Kerian leaned her forehead against the rock wall, breathed as well as she could, gathered wit and strength, and climbed again. Ayensha caught her by the wrist and pulled her quickly inside to bellowing darkness.

Kerian sensed walls and ceiling, depth and height.

Behind her, Lightning fell with the voice of Thunder, shining silver ribbons twined in the darkness of shadow. She put her back to a rough, wet stone wall, every muscle in every limb complaining with weariness. Shivering, she closed her eyes just as a golden light flared behind her lids.

Ayensha held up a fat pillar candle that had been set on a flat of stone, held in place by its own wax. She handed it to Kerian and by its light folded stiff lengths of oiled sailcloth. These she tucked into a square coffer, one lidded like a case. Every seam was thickly tarred, and the case itself was lined with oily cloth. In there nestled a small pouch containing flint and steel. Beside this, a fatter pouch lay. By the shape, Kerian knew it held other candles of varying sizes. Ayensha snapped the lid shut and tucked the whole thing far back into shadows.

"Now, come!" she called, her voice drowned out, the shape of the words only seen on her lips.

Through a wide, high passage they went, candlelight bounding from slick stone walls. Kerian's right arm throbbed with pain, but she said nothing, for she would not appear weak before this woman. The deeper in they went, the thinner the mist, the more muffled the voice of the falls until, at last, Kerian saw pale daylight shining.

Something tall and dark came to fill the void and conceal the light.

Kerian gasped, but Ayensha's breath sighed out of her, shuddering with relief. She blew out the candle and set it high in a notch on the wall.

Kerian heard only the distant voice of the falls, the whispering of the torch. Then, low, a man's rough and ragged voice said, "Ayensha, my girl, we thought you were dead."

He held out his arms. Staggering with weariness, her breath still shuddering, Ayensha went to him. He folded her to him, bending low to hear what she whispered.

Kerian heard the man groan, a terrible deep sound of grief. She saw him hold Ayensha long and close and finally turn her and take her out into the light.

Alone, ignored, Kerian followed.

CHAPTER
9

Nayla and Haugh, with their hounds beside, went in stealth, keeping beneath the crests of the forest ridges, and when they could, they ran, bounding over stone, leaping over blow-downs. They headed for a smith whose forge stood beside the Silver Tresses River, a branch of the White-Rage River that reached into the forest farther east than Sliathnost. He was a friend of theirs, a good man and trusty, and in the days before he knew Nayla, Haugh had been, for a long sweet summer, much closer friends with the forgeman's daughter than with the smith himself. Frealle was her name. Nayla still wondered about Frealle and how it was that after all the years between that sweet summer and now he knew the way to the miller's house well as though he were walking on Baker's Lane in Qualinost, looking for a good place to buy muffins.

Haugh had, in the course of his life, more lovers than most. He watched now as Nayla slipped up to the crest of the ridge, one of the hounds in her wake. The Silver Tresses was a mere shine of a thread in the east, as Nayla paused beside a tall boulder, marking how far they'd come. Wrestle, the hound, stood close. Haugh waited to see if he should follow or if she were only checking the landmark. Wind came softly from the east, smelling a bit like snow off the Kharolis Mountains.

The second hound, Pounce, pushed her nose up under Haugh's hand. Absently, he scratched her chin. He cocked an eye at the sky. The sun slid down the noonday sky. Pounce growled, her ears flat against her head. Haugh looked to Nayla and saw nothing different than a moment before, yet the hound continued to growl, and Haugh never discounted the reactions of these beasts who had been Nayla's from the litter. He called her name. Nayla did not move. He looked left and right, up hill as far as he could see, and down.

"Nayla," he whispered.

She turned, and her face shone white.

Haugh ran up the hill, Wrestle behind him, and looked toward Sliathnost. It looked as though a dragon had run through. Where there used to be houses and shops, the livery at one end, the tavern at the other, was only a dark scar from which small tendrils of smoke rose.

"In the name of all gods," he whispered.

Nayla's eyes glittered. "In the name of the gods-cursed dragon. In the name of the damned Skull Knight." Her voice dropped low. "The damned dwarf," she said, grinding her words. "All he had to do was keep still, but no—he gave the stupid girl a knife."

She looked back to the burning, down the hill. Haugh heard her breath shiver, a sob kept at bay.

Haugh put a hand on her shoulder, let it slip down her arm to hold hers. With a low moan she pulled away from him. Loping down the hill, Wrestle at her side, she never looked back. Haugh followed, and by the time he caught her up, they stood at the edge of the town before the ruin of the Hare and Hound. Nothing stood now but burnt stone. Two of the chimneys had been toppled, and charred wood and blackened beams lay just as they had fallen from walls and upper stories.

"Nayla."

He didn't say more, for she left him and went into the ruin. She stood there in the center where the common room used to be. She looked around while Pounce and Wrestle poked among the debris. Watching her, Haugh heard nothing, not even crows in the sky. He thought that was strange. It couldn't have been two days since the fires were set, the burning done. Embers still glowed beneath the collapsed walls like malevolent eyes, red and glaring, yet no crow or raven came, no wolf hunted the empty streets or the fallen houses.

He wondered why, how the carrion eaters could be turned from the will of their nature. The place should be hung with crows, dangerous with wolves. Only wind moved and not much of it.

"Nayla, I don't like—"

She held up her hand, hissed him to silence.

Out from behind a pile of stone that had once been two chimneys a tall figure stepped. Brown as summer, his silver hair on his shoulders, the newcomer seemed like a spirit of the forest itself. He wore tattoos upon his arms, across his chest. He had the eyes that always chilled Haugh to the heart—the eyes of a Kagonesti in the wild.

Nayla's hand slipped to the knife in her belt, a broad-bladed glinting knife good for skinning a deer or killing a foe. The Wilder Elf didn't so much as quirk a brow.

"You," Haugh demanded. "Who are you and what are you doing here in this ruin?"

The accents of Qualinost, cultured tones no rough garb could disguise, did not impress the Wilder Elf. He looked past Haugh, up the road to the savaged village. When he had completed his survey—a leisurely one, Haugh thought—he looked at Haugh again.

"The same thing you are doing," he said. "I'm looking."

Nayla was in no mood. "We've been hearing things about the goings on in the forest, Kagonesti. We've been hearing about magic and hearing it might have to do with your kind."

The Kagonesti shrugged and looked away. In his eyes Haugh saw a sly light, a baiting gleam. "Qualinesti," the Wilder Elf said, "does your woman speak as loudly in the halls of your family as she does in the halls of the forest?"

Something like lightning crackled in the air between the three.

"Kagonesti," Haugh replied, striving to keep his voice level. "Many of our people have died here, and many of those were our friends. We don't know who lives, we don't know who is dead. We've come into the forest searching for a friend, a young Wilder Elf woman."

"A Kagonesti? A friend of yours, eh?" The Wilder Elf spoke as though in disbelief. "You seek her out, and yet you think that maybe Kagonesti had to do with this great burning?"

"No." Haugh looked around the ruin, the wreckage of homes and hopes where nothing moved but sniffing dogs. Crows called from the forest, from high up the hill. "We think the Nerakan Knights did this."

The Kagonesti nodded. "You think well. We saw them." He spat into ash. "They are wolves."

We saw them.

We . . .

"Kagonesti," Nayla snarled, "you saw this happen?"

He nodded. "I have said so."

"And you did nothing?"

"To prevent? No, we did not. We were only a band of four. We do not have armies, woman. We do not interfere in the business of the city elves and the Knights they allow in their kingdom."

She flared, filled with grief for deaths, filled with rage. "Kagonesti, you want a better tone with your betters."

A small smile twitched the corners of the Wilder Elf's lips. It had nothing at all to do with amusement. "Woman, you want a more courteous tone with anyone."

Two strides put Haugh between the Kagonesti and Nayla. His hand was out, away from his weapons. The Kagonesti turned.

In the instant, sunlight slipped like fire along Nayla's blade.

The Kagonesti shouted, "No!" Then again, "No!"

Haugh felt the shock of an arrow in his back. He fell among ashes of the Hare and Hound, stunned by pain and watching his blood run out of him. All the world erupted in storm-wind and thunder, his pulse rushing blood from his body, pounding in his ears. Through the storm of his dying, he heard the roar of a hound—Pounce? was it Pounce?—cut off by its own death-scream.

A hand touched his shoulder, gently. "Hold still," the Kagonesti said. "Hold still."

Haugh heard voices now, a man's, a woman's, another man's. The Kagonesti said something to one of them, his voice like an angry whip crack. What he said, Haugh couldn't tell. His words were simply sounds. In his mind, in his heart he heard other words, those of his king, Gilthas who had said, "Find her, Haugh. Show her the way to me. . . ."

Haugh said, "Listen—"

The Kagonesti leaned close.

"The woman—Kerianseray—"

The Kagonesti leaned closer, and Haugh heard his breathing roughen.

"My pouch—get me my—"

The Kagonesti took the pouch from within Haugh's shirt. He opened it and spilled its contents into Haugh's twitching hand, the golden half of a royal ring. "It is the king's. Find the match—the girl—she will—know what it means—"

The air on his skin felt cold, cold. He felt the tide of his life withdraw, taking all warmth and will. His lips formed a word, shaped a name.

Nayla.

He could give the word no voice and he knew, in the gasping last breath, it wouldn't have mattered. She would not have heard, his Nayla lying dead in the ashes.

───◆───

Kerian squinted. When her vision settled, she saw before her a stony clearing, a space in which four small campfires made a semicircle around a larger one, a clearing like a stone basin. Beyond the clearing rose a wall of climbing ground, all boulders and pines. She felt no more breeze here than she had in the narrow cave, the passage behind the falls. The place was well sheltered, and the only way in was through the passage she and Ayensha had just taken, or down the sides of the hill. All around her, the distant thunder of the falls seemed to flow into the whispering of the wind.

"Who are you, girl?" A man glared at her, his eyes hard and cold. He had silver-streaked hair that might once have been the color of bright chestnuts, once brown and shining with red-gold. He was past his middle years, and though his features were elven, his ears canted, his eyes slightly almond-shaped, the shape of his face showed an alien stamp, a coarsening line of his jaw, a roughness of hair on his cheek and chin, and that thickness in the neck seen in humans and half-elves. The man must have a human parent.

Around him, shadowy voices whispered: Who are you? Who is she? How did she get here?

A spy!

The hissing word sent fear through Kerian's belly, sharp as knives, and the half-elf said, "Are y'that, then? A spy?"

The hair raised up on the back of Kerian's neck. She wanted to look around to find the shadowy speakers but dared not take her eyes from those of the half-elf. Ayensha, though she might have, said nothing. She had brought Kerian here, and now she seemed inclined to leave her to what fate might find her.

In a firm and clear voice Kerian said, "I'm not a spy, and whatever it is you're keeping to yourself, you can have. I came here with Ayensha and—"

The half-elf snapped, "Name your name, girl."

Kerian's cheek flushed. Girl, he called her, as the dwarf had called her missy, as Dar used to name her Turtle.

Eyes narrow, voice cool, she said, "I am Kerianseray of White Osprey Kagonesti. My parents were Dallatar and Willowfawn, and Dallatar was a chieftain among my people. Willowfawn bore him two children, a son and a daughter, and all elves know that is great wealth. With my brother Iydahar my people lived here in this forest in the time before the coming of the dragon Beryl, even before then, in the years of the lost prince."

Kerian lifted her head, not ashamed to speak the next words. "Though my kin have not, I have spent time in Qualinost. Now tell me, what is your name?"

Ayensha stood away from the half-elf. She murmured a word to him that sounded, if not kindly spoken, at least reassuring. The man grunted. His arms closing round her again, he looked at Kerian long. His eyes narrowed as he reckoned her.

"Killed a Knight, did you?"

"Yes, I killed a Knight." Remembering Ayensha's injuries and the haunted, hunted look in her eyes when she'd come hobbled and bound into the Hare and Hound, she added, "I killed a pig of a Knight." She narrowed her own eyes in a show of defiance. "It's a good thing, I think, or you'd be weeping over a corpse now instead of hugging this woman."

The half-elf raised an eyebrow. A little, the corner of his lips quirked.

"Now it's time for your name, half-elf."

The epithet didn't sting him, it only twisted his mouth into a sneer. "Jeratt," he said, "Jeratt Trueflight." He looked around him, at the hills and the passage into the stone of the world behind her. He removed his arm from Ayensha, gently let her go, and he said, "I am of this place."

"Jeratt Trueflight, I haven't come here to harm anyone or spy on you. I left Qualinost to find my brother who . . ." She hesitated, in no hurry to give this man too much information about Iydahar. "I thought my brother might be in trouble, although in five days' time I find myself in more trouble that I'd imagined he could be in."

Jeratt snorted. "It gets like that, girl—"

"I told you: my name is Kerianseray." She took a square stance. "If you like, you can call me Kerian, but if you call me 'girl' again, I'll kick you a good one."

Jeratt's eyes widened as though he would suddenly laugh. He held the laughter, though, and cocked his head. "*You* kick *me* a good one? How good, girl?"

Swift, hardly thinking, Kerian swept out her leg, caught him with her foot hooked behind the knee and toppled him hard to the ground. His breath whooshed out of him, and she moved again, her heel upon his belly, right over a kidney.

Jeratt laughed then. Right there on the ground, he let go a good-natured bellow. He reached up a hand as if to ask for help up.

Kerian shook her head, not falling for the ruse. She stepped back, gesturing as a courtier. Wryly, she said, "Please, do rise."

On his feet, the half elf twisted another smile. "Besides Knights on your trail, what brings you here, Kerianseray?"

Kerian relaxed her stance, but not her guard. "Ayensha brought me here . . . in order to lose the Knights that were chasing us."

A moment's silence hung between them, then he turned to Ayensha.

"Knights on her trail, and you brought her here, did you?"

Ayensha moved away from the half-elf to sit upon a flat stone near the tallest fire. She bowed her head, her tangled, dirty hair hanging like a tattered curtain to hide her face. "I had to go somewhere, Jeratt. There's no one following. You know how careful I am."

When Ayensha groaned, Kerian took a step toward her.

Jeratt held up his hand, his eyes gone suddenly hard again. "Leave her alone. She's here now. I'll take care of her."

Who was he, her father? She didn't think so. They hadn't the look of each other. Kerian wondered, is he her lover then or her husband?

The silence between Kerian and Jeratt deepened, seeping out into the shadows. A small breeze kicked up, sighing low around the boulders and the trees.

"So here you are," Jeratt said. "In the heart of a place you don't know, far from anyone you do know, all so you can find—"

"Kill her!"

A woman's voice screeched, high and ragged and shrill, seeming to come from everywhere and nowhere, behind and before and around. The hair on Kerian's neck lifted, hackles rising at the sting of a primitive nerve. It was all she could do not to bolt and run.

"Killer!"

Kerian's heart slammed against her ribs; her hand

dropped to the knife at her belt. Jeratt's eyes widened, his own hand lifted to warn.

"Don't move—"

"Kill her!" screeched the banshee voice.

With an odd kind of gentle scorn, Jeratt said, "Don't worry. No one's killing anyone. At least not yet. Take your hand off your knife, Kerianseray." When she hesitated, "Do it now, or I'll give you to the old woman."

Kerian dropped her hand from the bone-gripped knife, and as she did, a cold grin changed Jeratt's expression to dangerous.

"Come to think of it, I'll give you to the old woman anyhow."

Shadows shifted. All around the basin the shadows gathered and seemed to coalesce as elves. Men and women came from three directions. Rough-dressed in leathers and buckskins, in oft-mended shirts, in boots they cobbled themselves, they drifted down the slopes.

Though they appeared to be folk who took their livelihood from the forest, they were not Kagonesti, for none showed tattoos. One or two wore bits of armor, a breastplate polished to shining, a leg-guard, a gorget.

As these revealed themselves, Kerian saw one shade-shape among them, a shadow that moved more slowly. The elves around it moved off. Like warriors they took posts around the basin, leaving Kerian and Jeratt and Ayensha alone in the center as the shadow advanced.

Kerian's mouth dried.

The shadow stopped, standing outside the small ring of fires. In the space of a breath, it began to change shape.

"Elder," Jeratt said, his voice colored by wariness, by respect and—Kerian felt it—humility. "Here she is."

She whom Jeratt addressed as Elder looked neither right nor left. She did not look up, and she did not look around. She was not breathing. Not even the least flutter

passed her lips or caused her bony breast to rise and fall.
She sat like a creature born of the earth, still as stone, her
eyes strange and unchancy as wind in the mad season
between winter and spring.

"So here she is," said Elder, her voice cracked as
ancient parchment. Her glance never shifted. Kerian wondered whether she were blind, but she saw no milkiness of
eye, no scar, no wounding at all. The woman simply looked
into some middle distance, some place into which no one
else could glimpse. "I see you, child."

Killer. I see you.

Kill her . . . killer!

"No!"

She tried to say more, but the old woman's intrusion into
her mind, her soul, had addled her wits and left her feeling
like all her words had been scrambled, her tongue changed
into something unwieldy as leather. She could not see
clearly. She could hardly hear. The sounds around her were
muffled as by distance or as though she were under water.

*You will kill again. Men will die because of you, women
will die, and children will weep. Because of you!*

Around her, Kerian felt the world grow cold. She heard
a hard wind howling, though she felt no wind on her skin,
none in her hair. The voice of the wind became the throaty
roar of flames, and before the fire she stood, screaming,
killer and victim.

A hard hand grabbed her, then two, holding her back
from a fall. In the moment she realized it, Kerian's knees
sagged, her belly went suddenly tight, and bile rushed like
fire up her throat.

Kerian's gut wrenched, the pain doubling her over.
Jeratt let her go as everything she'd eaten since daybreak
came spewing out. Her belly spasmed again, and falling to
her hands and knees, she gagged. The golden chain round
her neck slid and slipped, Gil's ring falling outside her shirt.

Light glinted sharply off the facets of the topaz. Sweat cold and thin slid down her neck. Confused, her head spinning, she looked around and saw but a forest of legs.

A hand reached down, big and brown. It took her wrist, not roughly, not gently.

"Up," said a deep voice, a voice not Jeratt's.

The word rang in her head painfully, like a clapper in a bell. Kerian winced. She tried to pull away from the hand but had no strength for resistance. The man's hand slipped down her wrist.

"There can't be much more left in you, so on your feet, Kerianseray of Qualinost."

She knew him then. In the scornful twist of his voice, in the subtle insult of the naming, she knew him. He pulled, she rose, and Kerian looked into the eyes of her brother, Iydahar.

CHAPTER 10

Kerian stood before her brother, but she didn't know him. She knew the shape of his face, the cut of his shoulders, the way he held his head. She recognized him, but not the hardness of his eyes, or the way he looked at her as though across a gulf of distance and time.

"Dar," she said.

His eyes grew colder.

Elves in their rough gear stood still. The little shadow that had been a screech-voiced old woman was gone.

"Brother," she said.

Iydahar turned from her. Silently, he held out his hand to Ayensha. "Ayensha," he said, and in all the years she'd known him, Kerian had never heard such tenderness in her brother's voice. "Wife," he said to the woman Kerian had rescued, "where have you been?"

Wife! Kerian drew breath to speak, to give words to her wonder. She fell silent, the words unshaped, for one tear, perfect and silver, slid down Ayensha's cheek, making a shining trail through the grime of days.

"Husband," Ayensha whispered. "Ah, I have been on hard roads."

Kerian saw again the haunted, hunted woman jerked into the Hare and Hound, hobbled and hands bound. She watched in silence, breathless, as her brother took in Ayensha's words and the meaning Kerian only guessed.

Iydahar opened his arms, gathered his wife to him, and held her gently.

A hand closed round Kerian's arm. Gruff, his voice like gravel in his throat, Jeratt said, "Give 'em peace, Kerianseray."

Jeratt led her away, across the basin to the foot of the hill. Someone came and brought her water. Kerian drank without tasting. All the elves who had been hidden in shadow stood now in the light of day, and there were at least a dozen of them. By design or instinct, they ranged themselves so that their backs were to the two weeping in each other's arms, so that they formed a wall of privacy for the wounded pair.

Kerian did not see or speak with her brother for a week after her arrival at the outlaw camp. Iydahar and Ayensha kept to themselves. That her brother was angry, she did not doubt. No sign of it did she see, but she felt it. At night sometimes, sitting beside a fire at meal, sitting alone and looking high to the glittering sky, she felt Iydahar's anger.

"Man's planning," Jeratt said to her, one evening when all slept around them. He poked at the fire, sending a plume of sparks dancing up. "Man's planning. You can see it on him."

Kerian could see very little to recognize in her brother. His eyes were cold when he looked at her, his expression stony, and that had nothing to do with his grief or his anger.

She thought about it often, awake in the nights, often alone. She paced the perimeter of the basin, silent-footed, careful not to disturb sleepers. They did not post watches here, Kerian marveled at that. They all slept the nights through, secure in the embrace of a warding none doubted.

"The old woman," Jeratt told Kerian on the first night. "You don't always see her, the woman's half-crazy, but you can count on the ward."

Kerian had seen that they all did, going about the nights and days as though they were safe within walls. And so she paced, and sometimes went up the hill and sat on high ground, thinking.

This band were outlaws in the eyes of Lord Thagol, hunted by his Knights and gleeful disrupters of his peace. They hated him, some with passion, some with private cause.

"Saw him once," Jeratt said. "Pickin' around the wreck of a supply train we tore up. Cold as winter, him. Nah, you see the mark of how mad he is on his Knights, the poor bastards he sends out to collar us and kill us. Them's the ones look like ghosts, for all you hear about him being the spooky one. Them's the ones." He shook his head, spat, and pulled his lips back in a feral grin. "The Skull Knight, he does something to their minds when he ain't happy. Fills 'em up with nightmares and such."

Her voice thin as a blade's edge, Kerian said, "On the parapet of the eastern bridge in Qualinost, Thagol pikes the heads of those his Knights catch and kill."

He scratched his chin. "Aye, but he can't pike all of us. We're all over the hills, Kerianseray. Here in the east, out in the western part of the kingdom. Not so many of us up in the north by the White-Rage, but a few in the south, too. Some's just outlaws, robbers and killers, but a lot of us ain't that. A lot of us're just drifters, not fittin' anywhere but places like here."

Kerian began to see that Jeratt wasn't so bad, and she thought that there were worse places to be than in the basin among the outlaws. They were cordial, if not friendly. This, for Iydahar's sake and for the sake of what she'd done for Ayensha.

"Ayensha is my niece," Jeratt said gently. "Her mother was my own mother's sister. I love the girl well, and I thank you for the saving of her."

"Are Iydahar and Ayensha part of your . . . band?"

He twisted a wry smile. "She is, he ain't."

Dar held a kind of sway over them, though. They looked to him; they heeded him. The mystery of that was not one Jeratt was willing to unfold, and Dar himself never came into the light of the fires to share the truth of it.

The days changed, nights brought warning of winter, and sometimes frost sparkled on the stones in the morning. Perhaps Kerian could have moved on, but she still hoped to speak with her brother. Most days there was no glimpse of him. Truth to tell, she didn't feel much like leaving this safe place.

On one of those frosty mornings, Kerian said, "Jeratt, am I a prisoner?"

Jeratt shrugged. "I don't know about that. Maybe you're a guest. You sit here among the fires, eat our food and use our blankets to keep you warm, and no one's stopping you from using the privy places, but you walk up the hill too far—" He shook his head. "Yeah. Maybe you are a prisoner, something like that. You walk too far, you don't get anywhere fast."

Kerian knew what he meant. She'd twice before felt the distortion of her senses and the lost feeling brought on by the forest. She had no interest in feeling that again.

Jeratt chewed on a strip of tough venison, working his jaws until it was soft enough to swallow. He offered her some. She chewed for a while and drank icy water to wash it down.

Into the gilded bedchamber of the elf king came news of death. Word came several nights after he'd seen Nayla and Haugh return to the wood with his order to find Kerian, his token to give to her. He had watched for their return, for Kerian's return. He had gone to sleep nights waiting, hoping. No word had come.

Now, this night, when he had no court function to attend, no meeting with his mother, no claim at all upon his time or attention to distract him from worry, the king sat reading in his library. He sat warm before a high fire, listening to the sounds of Planchet in the bedchamber, his servant muttering to himself, talking to others, ordering the rest of the night for his master.

Gilthas smiled, hearing his servant's voice. Planchet had been the first to know how things stood between the king and the pretty servant of Senator Rashas, the Kagonesti woman Kerianseray. He had been the first enrolled in the secret of their love and the secrets that had grown from it. Gil imagined his trusty man now, going around the bedchamber, his hands full of the clothing the king had discarded throughout the day—the morning robe, the robes of state for the afternoon's session with the Senate, a riding costume, for he'd hunted in the Royal Forest in hours after that. When Planchet knocked, he was not prepared to see what he did see, the white face, the darkening eyes as Planchet stood in the doorway between the bedchamber and the library.

"My lord king," he said. He held no armful of clothing, and he didn't seem to know what to do with his hands. They hung, empty by his sides. "They are killed, sir."

Gilthas closed his book, his heart loud in his ears. The breath of the fire in the hearth was a roaring. The red glow of the tame flames made Planchet's face shine whiter.

NANCY VARIAN BERBERICK

"Nayla Firethorn and Haugh Daggerhart. Dead in the ashes of a burnt tavern. The burning, it was the work of Sir Eamutt's men. The killing of your mother's folk . . ." Planchet's eyes glittered. "My lord king, that was the work of others. Kagonesti, they say."

"Kerian—"

"The burning was of the Hare and Hound in Sliathnost, and many houses in Sliathnost were also burnt. In payment for a Knight's life, they say. Two other taverns have been burnt, one at Ealanost, another ten miles south at the waycross where the north-south road from Ealanost meets the road to Qualinost. In all cases, it is said by survivors that Knights have come to demand that Kerian be hunted and captured and brought to Qualinost for—" he stopped, then swallowed hard— "for beheading, my lord king."

Planchet, faithful servant, winced to see his king take each word in, winced to see his poet king's eyes fill with dread.

"Find her," said the king, his voice grating, hoarse and thin. "Send more men to find her."

Gilthas turned his back on the library, on his servant then leaving to do his king's bidding. He opened the glass-paned doors to the balcony and stepped into the night.

Upon the bridges of the elven capital, the silvery spans that had stood to ward a fabled kingdom for centuries, the king saw that no guard walked. Beneath the starred sky, the moon just rising, no black armored Knight marched. The towers stood dark, no light of brazier gleaming from slitted windows, yet in the misty moonlight, he imagined he saw subtle motion, drifting images of ancient Forest Keepers. He imagined—it seemed so clear to him!—that he heard the tread of their booted feet, the rattle of their armor.

Gilthas shook himself, banishing the fantasy.

Behind him, Gilthas was aware of Planchet returning to the library, the chime of a crystal carafe against a crystal goblet. The king did not turn but remained looking out to the bridges. The severed heads of elves perched upon the eastern bridge. His belly turned as he smelled the stench of rotting flesh brought to him on an unkind breeze. He wondered where Thagol's Knights were, the ever-present patrols used to marching above the captured city.

Across the city, a tall dark figure walked out from the unlighted eastern tower, illumined by starlight and the new-risen moon. The elf king's eyes narrowed. The figure stood at the inner parapet, leaning upon the wall with a hand on either side of a severed head. He didn't seem to notice them or care that he breathed the stench of decay. The night breeze caught the figure's cloak and tugged it back from his shoulders, flaring like wings. In the starlight, the man's face shone white as a scar.

The king's face flushed with anger, his pulse thundered hard, high in his throat. He formed the Knight's name in thought—*Eamutt Thagol!*—and the man turned, as though he heard himself called.

Gilthas blinked. Behind his eyes, fire flashed, torches and flames, and smoke roiled up to the sky, blotting out stars. In his ears were the voices of elves screaming, men and women. He heard a child shriek, and the shriek suddenly cut off, as though by a knife.

Anger became mounting fear as Gil saw the evil in the eyes of Sir Eamutt Thagol. For a moment, his stomach lurched. The elf king drew a settling breath then heard the thunder of a draconian march. The air filled with the clank of steel and mail, the hissing laughter like poison on the air. The puppet king and the Skull Knight stood eye to eye across the distance, and when they broke, it was the elf king who broke first. Head high, Gilthas nodded, once, curtly as to dismiss. He turned and went into his library. In his ears still rang the sound of draconian feet. He thought of Kerian, his heart heavy with fear for her.

He called, "Planchet, I have changed my mind. Recall what men you sent after Kerian."

Planchet reappeared, his eyes widening a little in surprise. "My lord king?"

"Recall them. We will not pursue her; we will not seek her." He looked back into the night at the Skull Knight in his wind-caught cloak. "We will not lead Thagol to her."

We will leave her to her fate, thought the king. Bitterly, he thought, we must leave her and hope some god finds her.

———————◆———————

Time passed, and in this season, more quickly than in others, for autumn is short-lived. At the end of Kerian's second week among the outlaws, she smelled cruel frost on the morning air. In the morning, watching hunters come down the slopes with braces of hares and fat quails, Kerian poked the central fire awake, scooting close for warmth as she slipped her knife from its sheath. She was not permitted to go out with the hunters, not even to set or check traps. She was, however, expected to clean and prepare their catch.

"Workin' fer your supper," Jeratt said, twisting a smile. She had grown used to his companionable jibes.

One after another, trappers and hunters dropped their catch beside her. This cold morning, Kerian scented snow in the winds crossing the Stonelands to the east. That morning and all the day she sensed change. Later, sunlight fading before purple shadows, the outcasts, all the folk who sheltered in the rocky fastness behind Lightning Falls gathered round the old woman they named Elder.

One other came to the council circle with them, and sight of her filled Kerian with astonishment. She was Bueren Rose, white as a winter moon. In her eyes shone a light like funeral fires ablaze. Kerian drew breath to call her name, moved to take a step toward her old friend, to ask how she had come to be there. Jeratt's hard hand held her.

"No," he said. "Be still, Kerianseray. Let her be."

The sky above grew deeply blue and a thin crescent moon, ghostly yet, rose early over the trees. Bueren didn't look around or try to see the people she stood among. She did not seem to care about more than whatever consumed her.

Kerian kept to the outside of the circle. If Bueren saw her, all the better, for she imagined the taverner's daughter would like to see a friendly face in this strange place. Elder lifted her hand.

Iydahar left his wife's side and parted the circle. He did not stand before the old woman. Rather, he kept his back to her. Head high, he looked into a middle distance, some place no one else could see.

"Hear!" Iydahar's voice started Kerian. Strong and deep, the one word was weighty as stone. Those gathered grew even more still, and it seemed to Kerian that no one breathed. "Hear, for a thing has been said, and a thing has been done, and all must know."

Kerian stood still. Around her the outlaws did the same, attentive.

"It is commanded!"

In the sky, a red tailed hawk sailed, its shadow rounding on the stone.

In a voice his own and not, Iydahar said, "By order of the invader, my lord Sir Eamutt Thagol, he of Neraka and lately of the Monastery Bone, for crimes of murder and insurrection, the woman Kerianseray, a Kagonesti servant late of the household of Senator Rashas of Qualinost, is declared outside the law."

Those in the circle murmured, their voices like small echoes of the thundering falls beyond their shelter.

"By the invader's order," Iydahar intoned, "with Senator Rashas's agreement, such decree renders her a person deprived of any consideration under the laws of her king. Neither will she receive the grace or benefit of the laws of green Beryl, the dragon who rules here."

Someone snorted, commentary on the benefit of the laws of green Beryl.

"All who see this woman are commanded to refuse her succor, refusing her aid of food or weapon or shelter. All who see her are ordered to capture her by any means necessary, and to bring her alive to Lord Thagol in Qualinost. There she will be beheaded, this sentence to be executed in the sight of the citizenry of city.

"All who are so foolish as to aid her will share in her crime and so in her sentence.

"*It is commanded!*"

A shocked Kerian stood still as stone as Bueren Rose stepped forward to speak. She spoke of the death of her father and other luckless citizens of her village.

Her voice strained, as though freezing to ice, she said, "My father fell to a Knight's beheading sword."

The news struck Kerian hard. A woman near Kerian sighed. Bueren flung back her head, wailed to the deepening sky, "By Thagol's command, my father was murdered by a Knight his fellows named the Headsman!"

Jeratt's voice cut like a blade. "The bastard! Ah, Rosie—"

Bueren Rose looked up, her tears flowing. Her lips moved, but Kerian couldn't catch the words.

Voices rose in outrage, thunder rolling around the stony

basin, up the hill and rumbling down like storm coming. Elder shouted high, keening and bitter anger. Men and women reached for weapons. The hair lifted on the back of Kerian's neck. She felt ashamed of the trouble she had caused. Worse, Kerianseray of Qualinost, the runaway servant of Senator Rashas, was to be hunted and brought back for public execution.

She looked around, her hand on the dwarf-given knife, fingers curling round the bone grip of the little weapon that had both saved Ayensha and made an orphan of Bueren Rose. In the purpling light, she saw neither sympathy nor lack of it on the faces of the gathered outlaws.

"You," said Iydahar, pointing across the circle to her. "Come here."

Almost she thought, That isn't my brother! So fierce his eyes, so hard his expression, she did not recognize even the shape of his features.

Narrow-eyed, angry, she lifted her head and the breath she drew cut sharply into the silence. Before she could speak, a finger poked her ribs, hard, and Jeratt growled, "Go, Kerianseray. Don't argue."

She saw, behind her brother, Bueren Rose's face, wet with tears. Ayensha took Bueren into her arms, hushed her, and held her

Her voice even and cool, Kerian said, "'Brother, do you wish to speak with me?"

His expression did not soften, and he spilled into his hand something shining from the little pouch at his belt. Gil's ring! In her brother's hand lay the half of the topaz ring the king had retained.

Dar spoke, and the flintiness of his voice caused her to shiver. "Two elves of Qualinost are dead, and they should not have been killed, but feelings are high in the forest now. I wish it hadn't happened. You, too, might regret their deaths, sister. They came to tell you your master calls."

Master!

The word stung like a slap. Once out of Iydahar's mouth, it ran round the circle, growling, until, again, Kerian flung up her head. She spoke now, and not as her brother's small sister, not as a child or even a woman he knew.

"You speak, brother, without knowing what you're talking about. You make assumptions about things you don't understand. If you wish to talk with me, find a place apart and we will talk."

The circle shifted, men and women looked at each other, wondering what Iydahar, so clearly used to deference, would say to his sister's reply.

"Sister," Iydahar said, haughty, "I'm not used to begging."

"Neither, does it seem, are you much used to courtesy."

The breeze off the hill shifted, growing cold. Kerian saw the shadow of the hawk whirling, spinning round and round across the stone of the secret fastness, and it seemed to overlay another shadow, that of a wolf running. Startled, Kerian looked away. Her eyes now held by the keen gaze of Elder. In her heart she heard words no other did.

Killer! You have killed, and the Invader has killed. Each of you will kill again. For what will the deaths you make count, Kerianseray of Qualinost?

Frowning, Kerian lifted her chin, firmed her shoulders. The red-tail screeched across the sky, its whirling shadow vanished, taking with it the phantom of the wolf. She turned from Elder and met her brother, eye to eye. Her hands were fists. She lifted one and opened it.

"Give me the other half of my ring, Dar."

He snorted. "This ring you got from your master, the puppet king?" His fingers closed over the glittering gold and the topaz. "Will you go running back to him now, Kerian? Will you scurry home safe to your lover's bed?"

Her eyes narrowed at the insult. Murmuring rose up from all those gathered, questions, and again the cry, "Spy!"

Kerian ignored the suspicion turning suddenly threatening. She spoke to Dar alone and felt the eyes of Elder on her. "You are a fool, brother, but one I loved well enough to leave the city and come to find because I saw our cousin dead and thought you might be in need. It is true I killed a Knight and caused this sorrow to fall on Bueren Rose. It is also true that I rescued Ayensha and took chances with my own fate. I see now that you are not in any danger and have no need of me. I see that you have plenty of friends for yourself."

She glanced at Bueren Rose, swiftly, then back.

"Give me what is mine, Dar." She lifted her head, and from her lips came words to startle her brother, the outlaws gathered, and most strongly—herself. "Never again in my presence refer to Gilthas as a puppet. He is *our* king, Iydahar—he is mine, and he is your king and lord of all these here as long you feed and clothe yourselves on the fat game of his forests."

She said no more. She walked out of the circle and felt the eyes of all upon her. Most keenly, she felt the eyes of Elder. Surprised, she knew it in her bones that the ancient elf woman was pleased.

———◆———

That night winter came, and it was a night filled with snow falling, kissing the cold cheeks of sleepers. Kerian, sitting before the highest fire, that in the center of the stony basin, watched the flakes fall. She did not watch them gather upon stone or cluster upon the boughs of pine trees. She had eyes only for those spinning madly down into the flames. Dar had left, Ayensha and Bueren Rose with him. Kerian had not heard their departure or said farewell. She did not know where they'd gone, into the forest alone or to some hidden camp of Kagonesti. Now she knew that she had a decision to make: go or stay. Her brother no longer mattered. She'd learned what she came to find out, that he was alive.

Kerian sat a long time in silence before the fire until she looked up to see Jeratt sitting outside the light.

She said, "What?"

He came closer and sat across the fire from her. For a moment he watched the snow as closely as she. Then, "This king of yours, Kerianseray of Qualinost, is he worth anything?"

"Plenty."

"Is he worth your brother? Because Iydahar didn't leave happy."

Kerian shrugged. "We come and go, Dar and me. I didn't trade him for the king; I'll see him again."

"So. That king?"

She drew closer to the hissing fire. " He walks a tightrope, balancing between a dragon and a Senate that spends all its time and mind trying to reckon how to stay comfortable and alive rather than how to take back an ancient kingdom from the . . . invader."

Jeratt edged closer. "Your king, he's got a sackful of trouble." He looked around at the sleeping outlaws. Many, Kerian had learned, were one-time Forest Keepers dismissed from service under an edict Gilthas had been loath to sign; some were Wildrunners from Silvanesti, come out with Porthios in his noble-hearted and ultimately doomed quest to unite the elven nations. "Trouble your king's got, but he's got no army."

"No," she admitted. "He doesn't have an army."

No army yet. The thought startled her.

As winter came down, locking the eastern part of the forest into a cold season and Kerian into her decision to seek shelter among the outlaws, the startling thought stayed with her and became, through familiarity, less and less startling.

CHAPTER

11

"Practice with borrowed bow and targets drawn on trees," Jerrate ordered her, "but you're not gonna step a foot out to hunt until y've made your own bow, strung it with your own string, and fletched your own arrows. Till then, y'sit and clean the catch."

So over the weeks of winter Kerian practiced, savaging the trunks of trees with skill that grew from both practice and the return of memories of her Kagonesti childhood. Those memories, it seemed, resided in muscle and bone, in the sure understanding how to draw a bow, how to sight a target. She remembered how to account for even the slightest breeze when preparing to loose her arrow, how to sight only a little bit higher than one would imagine must be correct. With delight, she knew again the swift satisfaction of seeing her arrows hit where she sent them, and if this required yet another set of muscles to become used to long-forgotten work, she stretched these sore muscles with the contentment of one who has earned the right to grin and groan.

All the while, she strove to make her own bow, a thing she'd at first thought impossible without the tools available to even the poorest bowyer in Qualinost. With Jeratt's guidance, she'd found a fine yew tree, assured herself of the goodness of the wood by testing both its strength and its ability to yield. Under Jeratt's direction, with borrowed tools crudely made but well kept, Kerian freed the heart of the wood, the strong dark center.

"No one around here uses anything else but yew-heart for bow-wood," he'd said. Then he'd laughed, as though over a fine joke. "Unless we can get a bow for free." Stolen bows, reclaimed arrows, a sword taken from the hand of one it had failed to defend—these were free weapons not always the most trusted. "We like the yews from our own hands better."

Kerian had accepted that for the sake of learning but wondered why a bow crafted in the forest would be better than one made by an elf who had learned his craft from his father. Jeratt had only told her that in time she'd know the difference.

Kerian planed the wood until it became a stave, one long enough for her reach. She bound a stop onto the stave in the middle, a piece of wood no thicker than her finger, only enough for an arrow to rest before flight. This she placed just a bit higher than the exact center of the belly of the bow. In the making of the bow, she learned the names of all the parts.

"Know your weapon," the half-elf told her, "the way you know a lover. You'll be counting on it like a lover."

In the making, Kerian learned to twine gut and make a strong bowstring. No one had to tell her how to keep her bow polished and clean and dry. Memory of things like this came back to her with dawning delight. Over the weeks of winter, she studied the craft of arrow making until she began to know it for an art—the making of the slender shaft, the crafting of the deadly point. She learned to survey closely the small bodies of the fowl she had to clean and to salvage especially the feathers of geese for fletching her arrows.

A drop of blood sprang from her finger, splashing onto the white snow. With all she had learned, and that had been much, Kerian had not managed to learn the art of fletching.

"It's because you're slitting the arrow too wide," Jeratt told her scornfully, around a mouthful of breakfast. "Y'got no patience here, Kerian. Here's where you need it." Swiftly he reached across the fire and snatched the failed arrow from her hand. He tossed it into the fire and handed her another naked shaft. "The arrow's always going to bite your finger when you try to fletch into slits too wide. Try again."

The stink of burning feathers stung her nose. Kerian took out a small-bladed knife and began the work of etching the slits the feathers would sit in. Too narrow, the feathers would fail to settle, too wide . . . well, she knew about that already.

Around them, outlaws came and went, men and women going about the business of hunting, fishing, and trapping. Some had other missions, and now and then one would call Jeratt aside. These conversations were short, out of Kerian's hearing. They always resulted in a handful of outlaws drifting out of the basin, up the hill and away from the falls.

Once, when they came back, she'd noted their flush of victory. A ringing pouch of steel coin hung at a hip, an ornately decorated sword over the back of another, and two pairs of gleaming leather boots roped and slung round the neck of a third. Later she learned that two Dark Knights lay dead in the forest, ambushed and killed by these outlawed elves.

A black cock feather slipped neatly into the top slit; Kerian did not stop to rejoice. She settled in the two gray hen feathers on either side. As though casually, she lifted the arrow to inspect it. Jeratt watched a moment, then snatched it from her hand.

"What?" she demanded. "It's perfect!"

"Maybe for someone else." He held it close to the snapping fire. "But shouldn't Kagonesti choose white feathers in winter?"

Kerian lunged and grabbed back her arrow. She jerked her chin at the feathers and said, "I'll do that when your hunters fetch me white geese."

Jeratt's laughter rang around the stony basin. Here and there, outlaws looked up to see what amused him.

"All right then, Kerianseray of Qualinost. The snowy geese are gone away to warmer places now, but you go fletch yerself a full quiver of arrows, and day after tomorrow we'll go see if we can find something else to take down and make you a hunter."

Wind blew a scattering of old snow across the stony distance between Kerian and Jeratt. The wind bit her cheeks, stung the tips of her ears red. She wore a tight-sleeved, long-cuffed bleached woolen shirt, which she had got from one of the smaller men in exchange for first cut of whatever she brought down this day. Her coat of tanned elk hide, warmly lined with the beast's own fur, came from an end of autumn raid on a trader's cart headed into Qualinost. Had they been outlanders or Knights, the traders would have fared hard, but the man and his two sons were elves, and so Jeratt's outlaws left them roughed up and bruised, one a little cut, and all angry.

"Ought to know better than to bring that kind of thing through here," Jeratt had laughed, displaying the plunder. "Outlaws all over the Qualinost road. Didn't the fools know that? Nice of 'em, though, to come by with supplies."

Warmly outfitted, still Kerian shivered and longed to slip her stiffening fingers into the sleeves of her coat for warmth, but she did not. A silver ribbon of water streamed between her and Jeratt, leaping over rocks and lapping the dark lines of mud at either side. The mud on both sides of the water was churned by tracks, the marks of a deer's passage, Kerian had said upon spotting them. Jeratt had nodded agreement and positioned her deep in shadow on one side of the stream, himself concealed on the other, and said no more.

Wind-whipped, Kerian watched the stream. A blue kingfisher darted down and came up with a flash of silver in its beak. In the forest, a jackdaw called, its raucous voice drowning out smaller birds, and another answered. Kerian did not so much as glance in the direction of the sounds. She was held in aching stillness by the thought of Jeratt's mockery, his own jackdaw laughter should she so much as shift her weight from one foot to another.

"Dancey-footed folk go hungry," he'd snarled the first time he'd seen her do that. "Find your place and stay." He sounded like Dar when he said that. She could almost conjure up a memory of the ancient days when he let her come along while he hunted. She had not hunted to kill then—in those days she was just learning her bow skills—but here, in this place far from home, she heard an echo of Dar's gruff tones and frustration with her impatience.

It felt like a week of waiting, listening to the wind in the forest, the stream purling over stone, the rustlings of small animals in the fern brakes. She had a boulder at her back, one upon which she could sit with some ease. Even so, it seemed to Kerian that every muscle rebelled at stillness. Her left leg cramped, her right foot itched. . . .

She shifted her gaze from the half-elf to the forest beyond. She thought she saw something move in the green darkness, then the illusion vanished as the wind dropped. Very slightly, Jeratt lifted his head, for all the world like an old dog sniffing the air. He sniffed again, then resumed his stillness, his back against an old high pine, his bow strung loosely, heel on the ground, head against his hip. Kerian kept stone still.

The iron sky shifted, clouds parting, and she squinted as Jeratt seemed to vanish in a sudden flash of sunlight, then reappear when the clouds shifted again. In the after-glare, Kerian widened her eyes to adjust her vision to the change of light. Above, the sky resumed its lowering, clouds growing thicker. Now she smelled what Jeratt must have, the sharpening of the air that heralded the coming of snow.

The forest grew quiet, birds stilled, squirrels fell silent. Kerian looked to Jeratt, but he, as she, heard only the stilling, not the cause.

She lifted her head in question: What?

He lifted a hand to signal silence. In the same gesture, he took up his bow.

Kerian slipped an arrow from the quiver at her hip, nocked it neatly to the bowstring. Along her shoulder, down her arm, her muscles quivered with excitement. She drew a calming breath.

Behind her, the forest erupted in the crashing sounds of something heavy and swift tearing through the under-brush.

In one flashing instant, Kerian saw Jeratt lift his bow, an arrow ready to fly. She turned, heart crashing against her ribs, and saw a low, thick body coming toward her.

Wolf!

She lifted her own bow, pulled, and saw what came behind the headlong beast—a boy.

"Ulf!" the boy called, his cry ringing through the forest.

Kerian shouted, "Jeratt, no!"

An arrow wasped past Kerian's cheek just as she shouted, "Boy! Down!"

Whether he dropped or stumbled, Kerian wasn't sure. Relief washed through her to see him go down, to hear the *thock!* of Jeratt's arrow hitting the pine just above him.

Jeratt cursed, the dog shot past Kerian, fangs white and glistening. She heard the hiss of another arrow coming from Jeratt's quiver.

"Boy!"

From the ground, his face covered in blood and dirt, the boy screamed, "Ulf! Drop! *Drop!*"

The dog fell, a bright splash of blood on the stone beneath him.

Leaping to his feet, the boy cursed. He flung himself past Kerian and past the dog itself. Startled, Kerian realized he was heading for Jeratt and that the half-elf had another arrow in hand. She reached to grab the boy's shoulder and jerked him hard behind her.

"Jeratt—"

"Get back," he snapped.

"He's a boy. Look—he's no threat."

Out the corner of her eye, she saw the boy draw a gleaming knife from his belt. Whirling, she grabbed his wrist, twisted it until the knife fell ringing onto stone. She kicked it away, cursing.

Jeratt snatched up the knife, the boy snarled a curse, and Kerian jerked hard on his wrist. She saw now he was not so much a boy as she'd first thought. Still gangly with youth, dressed in warm clothes and high leather boots only a little down at the heel, he looked like a villager's son. Half-grown, he couldn't have had more than sixty years.

"Where you from?" Jeratt demanded.

The young elf glared without answering. In the still-ness, the dog whimpered, struggling to rise. The elf turned, alarmed.

Kerian increased pressure on his wrist. "It's not all decided yet, boy. Where are you from?"

The dog's fate weighed heavier than his own. His eyes on Ulf, the boy said, "Down west in the valley."

"Bailnost?"

He nodded sullenly.

"Your name?"

The boy didn't answer, watching as the dog staggered to its feet and moved stiffly toward him. Jeratt's arrow had scored a painful path across the dog's shoulder, but luckily the dog was not hurt badly.

Ulf put his head under his master's hand, and the boy said, "My name is Ander. I'm the miller's son." His long eyes narrowed, taking in their rough clothing, patched and mismatched. "You'd better let me go or I'll be telling my father and all who'll listen about the outlaws up here."

Jeratt's laughter rang out, harsh and unfeeling. "Boy, you ain't going to be alive long enough."

Ander's face paled, his bravado flown.

"Stop," said Kerian, to Jeratt and to Ander. She looked from one to the other. "Ander didn't offer us any harm. We injured his dog and almost killed the boy himself. Let it go now."

Jeratt frowned. Before he could speak, she turned to the boy. "Go on. Your dog should make it home."

Ander eyed her narrowly, then nodded. He muttered something that sounded like thanks and turned his back on them, walking away.

"Addle-headed fool," Jeratt growled.

Kerian shook her head. "Why, just because he—?"

Jeratt snorted. "Not him. You. That boy knows we're from no village around here, he knows what we look like—

we're either ragged outlaws hunting dinner. Or trouble." He looked up at the sky, the lowering clouds. "It's worse than that. He knows what you look like, and there's Knights around would pay him to learn where you are, Kerianseray. You know for sure he's off home and not off to settle a score with us and get him a handful of steel coins to boot?"

She didn't know that. Cold wind whirled snow on the ground, and now snow began to sift down from the darkening sky. Dry in the mouth, Kerian said, "What should we do, Jeratt?"

"Go kill him. Throw him down the hill, make it look like an accident. Kill the dog too, make it look like whatever you like."

She stared.

He spat. "Still a little squeamish from your last killing?"

" I—he's a *child!*"

"Child could be the death of you. Of all of us if he gets to talking." In the cold and the darkening day, he looked older.

"He won't find us, Jeratt. The Knights won't." She looked around, at the forest and the ways down the west side of the hill. "He saw us here; we could be miles from where we normally are for all he knows. By the time he tells this story to anyone, we *will* be miles away."

He looked at her long, but said only that they'd missed their chance for first cuts at a good supper tonight and that it was time they moved on. "Ain't goin' back empty-handed," he muttered. Then, darkly, "Ain't leading no Knights or nosy villagers to the falls, either."

They followed the silver stream through the rising forest to a place just below the tree line where tall boulders and embracing trees would shelter them from the wind. The stream ran swift and wide here, and Kerian took out nets from her pack and caught enough pink-sided trout to feed them well. They sat in silence while they cleaned and cooked her catch, in silence while they ate. Kerian took the first watch, keeping the fire hot and high while snow spat down fitfully. To her surprise, she slept deeply when Jeratt relieved her watch.

When she woke in the night from a chilling dream of the half-elf's steely eyes, cold as blades when he'd said he'd have killed the boy if it were his to do, Kerian found she was alone. The moon had set. Between the tops of tall trees she saw night fading from the sky. Kerian waited a moment, building up the fire, to see if Jeratt had gone into the forest for good reason. She did not hear him moving around. Breath held, heart hammering in her chest, she listened. She heard an owl, the cry of a killed rabbit, and nothing more.

Jerratt had deserted his watch for some purpose she couldn't fathom.

Kerian hung between concern and anger. Finally, anger won, burning her cheek with memory of her dream and of his determination that he'd have killed the boy to protect himself. She rose quickly, felt the knife in her hand that had killed a Knight.

Behind her, a footfall.

Kerian whirled. Firelight glinted in tiny spears of light from the honed edge of her knife, ran like ghosty blood on the polished flat.

"Nah, nah," Jeratt said. "Put it up, Kerianseray."

She frowned, not understanding. One long stride put him between her and the low flames and embers. Swiftly, he kicked up the dirt, covering the fire.

"What are you doing? Jeratt, you didn't kill—?"

"That boy?" He hefted his pack and slung it across his shoulder; he kicked hers toward her. "Should have, I told you. We should have killed him. The whole damn valley is up and hunting. Moon's down, night's goin'—and the place is filled with torches. You tell me, what do you think

139

is goin' on down there?" He sneered. "You think it just might be that a whole village is tryin' to find you and buy a little peace from the Knights?"

Kerian slung the pack over her shoulder, picked up her bow and quiver, and said more evenly than she felt, "Right. It's probably a good idea to split up. You go one way, I'll go another. Go back to the falls when you think it's safe, but I won't. I'll lead them elsewhere."

He snorted. "Where will you go?"

"I don't know."

He laughed to hear that, and some of the steel had gone from his voice.

"We'll split up—that does make good sense. We'll meet at King's Haunting, on the edge of the Stonelands. You know where that is?"

She'd heard of it, and she'd seen it from a distance, a staggered line of stony hills east beyond the ravines that scored the earth down the length of the border between Qualinesti and the barren land that lay between the kingdom of the elves and Thorbardin.

"Get there as best you can, and drop south but try to keep going east. I'll see you there when the moon is dark."

Four days.

"And the others? At the falls?"

"Fine time to worry about them now," he growled. "Leave it to me. You just get going, and keep away from the roads."

That much he didn't have to tell her.

"Jeratt—"

"Get going," he snapped. "No need to die for stupidity, Kerianseray, not yet anyway. You've got plenty of time for that if you make it out of this."

Kerian left him with no word for luck and no word of apology. No matter what occurred because of her deed, she would not apologize for sparing a child's life. With no backward glance, she faded into the dawning day, trying to remember where the road lay so she could take care to keep away from it.

———————◆———————

Cold wind chased her through the woodland, nipping at her heels, moaning in her ears. She had nothing to eat the first day, for she dared not take time to hunt and could make no fire for cooking if lean winter hares had leaped into her hands. Along the way, she kept an eye out for what she could forage, but there wasn't much. The finest nuts of autumn had been gathered by squirrels and the few farmers and villagers who ventured into the forest. What she found was broken shells, the nutmeats gone. She gathered pine cones and could not carry many. She took to stripping them of their small nuts, eating some and putting the rest in a small pouch. All the while, she longed for something more substantial.

On the second morning, Kerian woke in her cold camp, sheltered from the wind by three rising boulders. She went to drink from the rushing stream, and in the soft earth beside the water she saw boot prints. The marks indicated someone had knelt here to drink in the night. Suddenly afraid, she looked around her, listening. She heard only the wind. She glanced over her shoulder at the cluster of boulders that had sheltered her sleep. From here, one might not be able to see that a traveler had made camp, but one would surely see signs at the water's edge that she had been here to drink.

Kerian drew a steadying breath. If the visitor to the stream had meant her harm, the harm would have been attempted. If he had moved on, she'd have seen signs of that. She slipped her knife from her belt, regretting the weapons left at the campsite. Arrows and bow sat snugly beside her pack. She made to rise slowly, silently, then caught sight of the prints again.

The boot prints showed sign of wear at the outside of the heels. It was the young elf Ander. Kerian looked again but saw no sign of his dog, not any print or droppings or the telltale tufts of fur a thick-coated animal leaves clinging to brush or tree.

Interesting, she thought.

Neither did she see tracks to indicate that Ander had gone north or south along the stream. He hadn't crossed the water, and she saw no trail of broken branches or crushed vines to indicate that he'd slipped farther into the trees.

Quickly, Kerian made up her mind. Where she had slept cold and hungry last night, this morning she gathered kindling and wood, struck flint to steel, and had a fire among the sheltering boulders. From her pack she took her fishing line and a hook and cut a supple wand from a sapling for a rod. She found a sunny spot on the stream's bank and settled to wait for breakfast. The morning warmed slightly, Kerian watched the forest across the stream and listened to the woods behind her. She heard only the waking birds, the purling water, and once the sudden rustle of a fox who'd come upon her from upwind and darted away.

Kerian caught three fat trout. By the time the rich scent of cooking began to waft across the stream, her patience had its reward. Ander trudged out of the forest and stood on the far side of the stream, and now she saw that he'd been in some scrapes since last they'd met. Bruises discolored his face, and his lower lip was split and swollen.

"Are you hungry?" she asked, nodding to the trout baking on the flat stone heated in the embers of her fire.

Ander stared at her. "Aren't you worried I've brought half the village with me?

She laughed and gestured for him to cross the water.

"I'm supposed to believe all those people waited in silence through the night till I could catch them breakfast?"

Ander flushed, looking down at his scuffed boots.

Kerian poked the trout, releasing the mouthwatering scent of them into the air again. "Come and eat." She gave him a long, level look. "Tell me where your dog is."

He crossed the stream in one long-legged leap.

Ander had a ball of hard cheese the size of his fist and a hunk of dark bread going dry and stale to add to their breakfast, "The last of what I came out with." He showed her the tangle of his snares and told her ruefully that he hadn't had much luck trying to catch food at night. The rabbits all seemed to hear him coming.

"You're a miller's son," Kerian said, remembering what he'd told her when they'd first met.

"Well, the stepson of a miller." His widowed mother had married soon after his father's death. Ander thought about the word "death" for a moment, chewing a mouthful of the dry bread, then added, "My father's murder."

His eyes glittered. Startled, Kerian saw an expression hard as any she'd seen on the face of the bitterest exile in Jeratt's camp.

"Who murdered him?"

Among any answer he could have given was surely an accusation against outlaws, robbers, or bandits. Very suddenly, all her senses grew sharp. Had she invited a vengeance-seeker to share her fire? Kerian didn't move, but she knew right where her knife was, how quickly she could reach it should she have to defend herself.

"A Knight. A Knight murdered him."

Kerian didn't relax. "I'm sorry."

Ander grunted. "I hate them." He took another bite of

trout, then looked up. "I know who you are. They went around in winter telling everyone about you, telling everyone how they wanted to kill you."

She kept still.

"They said you killed a Knight in Sliathnost." He looked up, long eyes flashing. "Did you?"

"Yes. He needed killing."

"Are you an outlaw?"

"I don't know." Kerian poked at the fire, encouraging its warmth. "I certainly am a fugitive, aren't I? I am outside the dragon's law now."

"And the king's."

Kerian considered that ruefully. "Yes, I suppose I'm outside the king's law, too."

"Because he lets the Knights do what they want."

Kerian shrugged. "I don't know much about kings."

The fire hissed, the embers getting low. The scent of baked trout hung in the air, fading. Ander said, "What about him, the other one? That half-elf."

"You mean Jeratt?"

"The one who wanted to kill me."

Surprised, she could only say, "You heard that?"

"I'm not deaf. Where is he now? Did he leave you because you wouldn't let him kill me?"

That amused Kerian. "We'll meet up again. We just thought it was safer to give your neighbors two sets of tracks to follow."

In the silence between them, the sounds of the forest seemed loud. They heard the call of a raven, the sudden trumpeting of a stag from far up the hill. Kerian rose and began to break camp; Ander wasn't long in helping. They buried what was left of the trout, only bones and heads, tails and a few strips of skin. They killed the fire, and when they'd done all that, Ander asked her whether she still wanted to know what happened to his dog.

"Yes, I do." Kerian checked her pack, tied it closed, and leaned against one of the boulders that had made her shelter snug.

"He's dead." He stopped, looking down at his feet, then swiftly up at her. "They wanted me to tell them where you were. In the village, some of them wanted to find you and turn you in to the Knights. I wouldn't tell them. You could have killed me. The other one, that Jeratt, he wanted to, but you wouldn't let him. I couldn't tell them where you were after that, and they—" He fingered his split lip. "They tried to make me tell, and Ulf . . ."

Ulf had gone to the defense of his master, and he'd paid the ultimate price for his loyalty.

"Do you have any place to go, Ander?"

He shook his head. "I came to warn you, but . . . now there's nowhere to go."

Kerian made her decision quickly.

"Go get your pack," she said, nodding toward the fire. "I have a place to go, and you can come along with me as far as you like."

CHAPTER
12

"Can we go back?" Kerian asked, sitting across a dwindling fire from Jeratt.

Outside, beyond the sheltering hills known as King's Haunting, the wind moaned, sounding like ghosts to give the place a name. Legends told of dead kings slipping in and out of the shadows of these hills, kings of elves, kings of dwarves, even a goblin king or two . . . or whatever passed for a king among the goblins who roamed in the Stonelands. The wind made good stories with the night, but pretty much everyone knew where their kings were buried and where they haunted. Behind Kerian and Jeratt, in the shelter of the smallest hill's stony shoulder, Ander slept, or pretended to. Kerian cocked an eye at him. The boy kept very still beneath his blankets.

Jeratt didn't look where she did. He seldom looked at the boy and neither spoke to the other unless he must.

"Ah, Kerian," he said, "you do seem to be a woman who makes a habit of getting thrown out the door, don't you?" He poked at the fading fire with the stick they'd used to spit the lean hares that had been their supper. "I think we can go back. Sooner or later. Right now the camp behind the falls is gone, broken up and scattered across the forest. They heard about the hunt for you even before I got back to tell 'em."

"Who did you tell then?"

He pulled a lean smile. "Elder. Old woman don't run fast, so she don't run at all. She was there, sitting by her fire and taking care of herself. I don't expect anyone will find the way to her if she doesn't want them to, do you?"

Kerian didn't. "Why did the others leave?"

"They left because they wouldn't be confined, even by Elder's magic. She let 'em. She's no jailer. They'll be back, once they feel it's safe to run there again."

They were like animals, Kerian thought, a band of outlaws who didn't fight for ground, didn't hold land. Threatened, they cleared out until they could return to the good hunting ground again. Like shadows, they lived outside the society of the kingdom.

"They ain't got no grudge against you, Kerianseray," Jeratt said "It happens. You get found, you have to run. You come back if you can."

She looked at him levelly. "And you? It seems you don't feel quite the same way."

"Me?" Jeratt shrugged. "I'm here, ain't I? Told you I would be."

He looked around at the enclosing darkness, up to the starred sky between the hills. "We have to say away from the others for a while. We need to figure where to go next. Elder says the hunt for you has spread beyond Sliathnost again. They know you're nearby, those Knights." He spat. "If yon boy didn't turn them on you, one of his fine friends or neighbors did. They're swarming all over the hills."

He coughed softly, and jerked his head in a northerly direction, toward Qualinost. "You ever see any maps of the kingdom while you were chattin' with him—your king?"

She hid a smile at his attempt at delicacy. "A few. You want me to speak a map or draw one?"

"Ach, don't speak it. That's a pretty thing you Wilder Elves do, but I've not much use for that way of mappin'. Put it right out on the ground so I can see it, will you?"

Kerian took the spit, the tip dark as charcoal now, and began to sketch a map on the clear ground. She showed the several streams running away from Lightning Falls, some flowing due south, others wandering away west to fill little lakes in the foothills of the Kharolis Mountains.

"Here," she said, drawing a large, ragged oval well below Qualinost and west of the city. "This is a lake whose feeder streams run out through the densest part of the forest, all the way to where the mountains wrap around north again. Past that spur of mountain is even more forest, far more than on the eastern side. After that, the sea. Ever been there?"

Jeratt shook his head. Behind them, the sound of Ander waking, the first long breath, the stirring beneath his rough blanket.

"I have."

Kerian glanced over Jeratt's shoulder.

"When?" she asked, as though she didn't see Jeratt's scowl.

"A few years ago." Ander sat up. "Not to the sea, not past the mountains, but almost to them. My father was from Lindalenost, a little town near that lake. It's called Linden Lake because it's all edged with linden trees. They look like mist, the trunks are so gray. When he was murdered . . . well, we went there with his body so his family could lay him to rest among his kin."

Kerian considered this. Then she said, "We've heard there are Knights deployed in the south and draconians with them."

Ander nodded.

"We've heard they pretty much own the roads," Jeratt

said, his voice hard with suspicion. "What do you know, boy?"

"Not much, except I heard about the Knights and draconians." He twisted a wry grin. "But that I heard from a traveler at the mill."

"Could we go there for a time?" Kerian asked.

Again, Ander shook his head. "The village is right on the Qualinost Road. We'd be seen by Knights and draconians, but we could go into the forest, deep. They have small settlements here and there, sometimes just a few houses gathered around a tavern and a river ford. The Knights won't go far into the forest—"

Jeratt rose. "Because of that weird slipping of your senses." He scuffed away the map. "Shouldn't be a problem that far down there, or did your kinfolk say it is?"

Ander looked from Kerian to the half-elf. "I told you, I haven't heard from them since my father's funeral."

Jeratt looked up at the sky again. Kerian followed his glance and saw the stars fading before the gray light of dawn. "Okay, let's go. Deeper into the forest."

The three companions ranged far from territory any of them knew. Kerian felt the excitement of strange places when she turned her face to the winds coming down from the northern arm of the Elfstream, there known as the White-Rage, the border between Qualinesti and haunted Darken Wood in Abanasinia. Through the pale winter days, gray with threat and white with snow, Ander ran beside them, an eager boy who sometimes looked back. He had not in all his life been so far from home; he had never tasted water from the Elfstream or hunted fat quail so far north as this watery border between the kingdom of the elves and the lands of the humans. These far reaches of the kingdom overflowed with wonder for him. The young elf shone brighter the farther they traveled.

"I don't think he had a very good life back home," Kerian said to Jeratt, one night when they two sat watch.

Jeratt didn't answer at once. He'd become reconciled to the idea that Kerian had dropped this village lad into their hands, but only grudgingly. He stubbornly didn't trust the boy, who stubbornly did not trust him. Mostly, and this he'd made clear to her, he didn't like it that Kerian had brought Ander to their rendezvous at King's Haunting. He didn't like being forced into a choice he would not have made.

Jeratt spat into the fire, making the embers hiss. "Thinkin' about stepfathers and old nursery stories, are you? Don't be a fool, Kerianseray."

She considered asking him what senseless thing she'd done or said this time to have earned the name of fool. She did not. Kerian was growing weary of Jeratt's scorn.

When she said nothing, he looked at her sourly. "Have y'not considered that the boy's a little in love?"

Kerian laughed, genuinely surprised. "No. I've considered that he lived among people who would beat him and kill his dog." Her voice growing lower, she said, "I've considered that you must be a hard and unwelcoming sort in his eyes."

They said little more, and for a long while the subject didn't come up again.

They hunted and they trapped. Ander didn't have much skill at hunting large game, or even small, but he was a good hand at the preservation of what Kerian and Jeratt brought down. He knew how to smoke even fish so they were palatable days later. Their wallets were never empty of food, even when the territory they roamed might be.

Like wolves, they stayed long enough in good hunting territory to rest and eat and left when signs showed that game was moving or that elves or even Knights were near.

The latter didn't happen often. They kept to the deep woods and all through the rest of winter saw only a few lone elves hunting, and once, chanced to see two dark-armored Knights meeting at a fording place. Kerian had been all for staying, concealed, to listen. Jeratt had slipped a callused palm over her mouth to quell protest, glared lightning at Ander, silently commanding that he follow, and hustled her away.

Later, his eyes ablaze, he'd grabbed her, a hand on each side of her head and said, "What in the name of all gone gods do you care what Thagol's vermin has to say?" He'd gripped hard. "You want to keep this pretty head on your shoulders, Kerianseray, all you care about is how to stay out of their sight."

Wide-eyed, Ander watched the two quarrel, and that night, when he thought her sleeping, he ventured a question of the half-elf.

"Who is she, Jeratt?" Though he'd seen no sign of it— and an admirer would look hard—he ventured what he imagined was a man's question. "Is she your lover?"

The half-elf laughed. "Not her. She's the friend of an old friend who has a high regard for her."

Kerian lay in the dark, eyes shut and thinking about what she had overheard. At first she thought Jeratt referred in some oblique way to the king, but soon she realized that wasn't it. Her brother? No, they never spoke of her brother, and it had been months since she had word of Iydahar. The last person Jeratt had spoken with at the falls was Elder. Elder, who'd named her Killer and made a prediction that she'd earn that name over and again.

Puzzled, Kerian realized that the old woman must have charged Jeratt with her safety.

Even in this mildest of winters the three had to pour all their energies into securing food and shelter. She no longer required Jeratt to tell her such things as what creatures came to water near their sheltering cave. Now it was she who showed Ander the difference between the mark of a hare and a rabbit, the print of a wolf and that of a dog.

"They run feral," Kerian instructed him about dogs, "then they are as dangerous as wolves, for they remember how it is their far grandfathers lived or how they died. If they are not feral, still they are dangerous, for they slip out from a town, away from a farm, and then you want to be as careful because that means there are elves about."

"How about the draconians—how will we know when they are about?" Ander inched closer to the fire, the light and the warmth. "Will they pursue us into the forest?"

When she said nothing, Ander looked to Jeratt, who shrugged. "We won't likely find them roaming the forest, but I don't doubt they are quartered around here. They keep on the move, like us, but," he said with a grin, "we will smell them before they smell us."

At the end of winter, the three drifted south and followed the Elfstream along its westernmost banks. They continued to avoid roads and fed themselves from the bounty of the land. They gradually approached the legendary Forest of Wayreth. Here they came across signs of Knights more often than anywhere they'd been. Kerian was eager to understand why Lord Thagol's men were so thickly clustered here, why they saw the main roads widened and scarred, looking much like the Qualinost Road near the capital.

"Usual reason," Jeratt said.

They sat on a treed hill, a bluff over hanging a road. Piles of newly raised earth lined the raw edges, trees killed for being in the way made fanged barriers into the forest. Beyond, across the road and into the forest, lay a town of some size. The smoke of many chimneys made an orderly climb to the sky.

"Roads here are widened to let tribute wagons pass. Knights are stationed in the larger towns to make sure all goes well on the roads, and more Knights come to sweep out into the countryside to make sure everything gets safely through the roads." He pointed to a place north of the town to where a blacker, thicker smoke rose. "Forge there, and it don't look like a small one. See—there's water. You just see the silver through the trees. Might be that's an armorer or a swordsmith. Dragon likes that stuff as much as she like gold and jewels."

Somewhere, not far, surely, a tavern quartered Lord Thagol's Knights or fed them or endured them. Another barmaid tried to elude a rough grab, another serving boy was kicked hard to get him moving faster. These things were happening nearby, or they would be soon, for that was the vile illness spreading over the Qualinesti kingdom.

The Elfstream became their road, the river winding from the foothills of the easternmost reaches of the curving spur of the Kharolis Mountains up across the northern border of the kingdom where a branch became the Dark-water River, the waters spilling to Darken Wood. Another, mightier trunk became the swift White-Rage and defined the borders between a free land and a captive kingdom. Kerian wanted to go there, all the way north, and breathe the air of a Free Realm. Jeratt had no objection, and faithful Ander would have followed anywhere. They found that they must keep to the deeper forest not only to hunt but to keep out of the sight of regular Knightly patrols.

"Ain't like in the home-wood," Jeratt said. "There they

didn't like to come in too far. Here—" He spat. "Ain't like in the home-wood."

Kerian thought of that word, "home-wood," and she wondered whether Jeratt was ready to return to the eastern part of the forest, back the falls and his friends. She didn't ask him, not then, for if he was feeling ready, she was not. She reveled in the new paths, in encountering places she'd never seen nor even imagined. The foothills of the Kharolis Mountains lay snug between the arms of the rising hills. Here they occasionally encountered elves who made Kerian wonder why her brother considered the Qualinesti effete. Farmers in their narrow dales, these were folk who had never traveled so far as the capital for a festival day, who lived their lives by clock of the sun and the calendar of the seasons. They were not wealthy, unless in the good rich soil they farmed.

"Aye, and in peace," said one, a young farm wife whose husband had come across the travelers at a narrow stream at the edge of the wood and invited them to share the evening meal.

Her husband, Felan, eyed Kerian's tattoos, the weathered faces and rough dress of all three. "Knights all over the place, but we know how to recognize them. Meantime—" he slid a basket of bread and rolls across the table to Ander as his pretty wife refilled their mugs with beer "—we have a tradition of hospitality in these dales, and no Knight's going to break that."

"Do they trouble you much?" Kerian asked. She plucked a roll from the breadbasket, broke it open, and covered it in both honey and butter.

The elf shrugged. "We never forget they're there, them and their beast-men, but they don't bother us much. We're not worth the trouble."

Kerian raised a skeptical eyebrow, for this seemed like a wealthy enough farmstead, and laughed. Felan motioned for her to rise and follow him. Curious, she did. He opened the door to the fading light of day and stepped into his dooryard.

"Look," he said, pointing. "This farm lies in a very narrow dale, and the way in—as you saw—is hard." He pointed behind the house to the stony hills rising up on all side. "The way out is harder still. We're not easy pickings. It's like that all over these dales."

The sky hung in deepening darkness over the farmhouse. The sounds of night creatures drifted from field and forest. Kerian heard an owl, and the silvery song of the stream at the edge of the newly planted cornfield.

"Will you stay the night?" he asked. "You and your companions?"

They were good folk, these farmers. Kerian found herself sitting up late into the night talking, listening to their stories of farm life, their hopes for the newly planted crop. The tales turned to rumors heard about the Knights and how they had, indeed, set up outposts in the larger towns. A little farther east, "between here and poor Qualinost," no one passed on the roads without first having to beg a Knight's grace. "Now you never heard about that kind of thing here in this part of the kingdom. Not till lately," Felan said.

According to him, restrictions in the capital had grown tighter since autumn. Kerian thought of Gil, of the Queen Mother, and wondered whether this meant their cherished plans for a treaty between elves, humans, and dwarves had fallen to ruin.

Moving north along the foothills, keeping far from the chance of running into Knights or draconians, Kerian and her companions found that most farmers in the dales were of the same mind as the farmer and his wife. They were genuinely pleased to welcome travelers, especially hunters who arrived with a brace of quail at the belt or a string of fat fish to offer to the evening meal. These folk were generous with food and fire and news.

Kerian learned that the foothills farther north weren't so softly green as those in the south, and the soil was stony and stingy, not the kind a farmer likes. She was warned that she wouldn't find much hospitality from the mountain outlaws. From the sound of them, these were not the type of men and women she'd encountered near Qualinost. These belonged to no king, to no land, and had lived unchecked for generations uncounted.

"Keep away from them," warned Bayel, a farmer's young son. "They have no interest in anything but what they can take from you, starting with your life."

"Do they trouble the Knights much?"

He shrugged. "They mostly run on the west side of the mountains and a little down into the forest there. The Knights don't go that far, not yet. They're set up in the towns east of the spur. For now."

Bayel sounded like a keen-thinker, like one who knew how to listen and see how things might go. Kerian asked if he'd heard anything about Lord Thagol himself.

The farmer shrugged. "He's been glimpsed here and there. I've never seen him, but I heard from someone in a tavern that he looks like a ghost, pale and dark-eyed. You get the feeling of ghosts, so my friend said. It's all cold around him."

Jeratt snorted. "Aye, well, that'd be him. Face like a fire-scar, thinkin' all the time about killing. Out east, I saw him more than once, saw him with his Knights. He's a Skull Knight, and them's the worst. They say he can get right into an enemy's head and next thing you know you're having nightmares you never had before. I don't know about that, but Kerian'll tell you, he's the one ordered the killing of elves—Kagonesti and Qualinesti—in the eastern part of the kingdom. Bastard's pikin' heads on the bridge in Qualinost."

"Draconians are helping 'em." Bayel took a long breath and let it out again. In the room beyond the hearth-room the voices of his parents murmured. "One killed my cousin," he said low. "Killed him for traveling without a permit. He was leaving his own farm, out by Lindalenost, heading down the road to visit a kinsman. Who thought you'd need permission for that, eh?" The boy's eyes glittered dangerously. "Not me, and I don't see how that's right."

Silence drifted into the room. The farmer poked his fire again. He leaned toward Kerian from out of the shadows, his face bright in the fading light. "Stay with us," he said, urging and eager. He looked past her to Ander and Jeratt. "All of you, of course."

Ander moved restlessly. Jeratt saw that and elbowed him still.

"We're not staying," Kerian said gently. "We have to keep moving."

The young man's eyes lighted with interest. "I'd like to be doing that myself," he said. He looked right and left, as though someone might be concealed in the deepening shadows of the falling hearth fire. "I'd like to pay back one of them Knights. Or a draconian."

It should have been all that was said, that night before the dying fire, but Kerian said one thing more: "Do others feel the way you do?"

"Plenty. Lots of talk goes on in the kitchens of farmhouses, but not much gets done."

Kerian took those words with her as she and Jeratt and Ander left in the morning. They traveled north that day and steered wide of the unwelcoming places where bandits roamed or Knights were known to pass through. That night they made the first camp they'd had out of doors in several weeks, welcoming the starry roof, the embracing fragrance of the forest. Kerian took the first watch, and Jeratt sent Ander off to sleep, warning that the last watch would be his. They sat quietly for a while, neither speaking, each listening to the night song. The moon rose, climbing the trees and hanging high above the boughs.

"Tell me what you're thinkin', Kerian."

She glanced at him and nodded. She poked the fire, gathered up her thoughts.

"They're good folk here in the dales, Jeratt. I've spent most of my life in the city." She stirred the fire and made the flames flare. "In the service of a senator and . . ." Sparks sailed up to the sky. "And in the confidence of a king. I'll tell you, Jeratt—the king watches the Knights rule his city, hears how they treat his kingdom." She shook her head. "If he saw what I've seen since autumn, if he heard what I've heard—"

"What would he do?"

The scornful sneer, the sudden anger flashing in Jeratt's eyes irritated Kerian. "He would do anything and everything, if he could. He is a king with no court, the ruler of a Senate that holds all the power—"

"—and hands it over to Thagol."

"He is powerless, I tell you." Kerian shook her head, frowning. "As long as he has no army, Gilthas is tied, just like you say, hand and foot, but if he had an army . . ." She leaned forward. "One no one could say was his, but one he would know is his. If he had a fast-striking army—warriors who weren't quartered anywhere, who couldn't be tracked . . ."

Jeratt's eyes lighted. "One that ran like ghosts, striking hard and fast and vanishing into the night."

She smiled. "You sound like you're ahead of me."

He nodded. "Long years ago, with the prince, we had such an army. I came up with him from Silvanesti and got kind of good at forest fighting." He laughed grimly. "Hit those city elves and ran, hit and ran, us and the Kagonesti. Would've won, too if it hadn't been for dragons and bad,

bad luck. Would've been one kingdom then, a kingdom for all elves."

Kerian listened to the night, the rising wind that smelled of rain. She looked past Jeratt to Ander, beyond him, south to the dales where farmers still remembered how to greet travelers well and where the people were beginning to resent the mail-fisted Knights. In the wind and the hissing of the fire she heard words from an old woman she hadn't seen in nearly a year.

Killer!

"I'm thinking," she said, "that here is where to start."

Jeratt laughed, startling Ander awake. "You know what to do with them once you flush them out of the dales, the woods, and the hills?"

Again, Kerian's long, slow smile. "No, I don't, but you do. Don't you, Jeratt?"

CHAPTER 13

"Look! Damn Knights."

Ander slipped closer to Kerian, his breath warm on her cheek. In his throat, his pulse jumped. Sweat glistened on his cheeks, and in that he was not so different from Kerian or Jeratt. The sun of late summer shone down hot and the canopy of the forest provided shade but did nothing to cool the air. That certainly accounted for some of the sweat. The rest . . . the boy was coming close to what Jeratt called "first blood," his first battle. Today, or another day soon, Ander would do his best to kill another.

"First blood," Jeratt had said to Ander when they began to draw together resolve and make plans. He drew upon the earth, as he liked to do, sketching maps real and imagined, laying out the strategy of the forest-fighter whose best plan is to use the wood for cover, to dart out and kill and dart back again. In this, he found that Ander had a keen mind, a quick wit for understanding and for seeing how such plans worked. Between the two, the half-elf and the boy, growing respect began to replace grudging acceptance.

Though he spoke most often of tactics, most forcefully, Jeratt also spoke to Kerian and Ander, the untried warriors, of risk. "You spill someone else's, or he spills yours."

Ander pointed to the road again, a thin winding branch of the broader Qualinost Road. Kerian nodded to let him know she saw what he did. The narrow road ran beside a broad stream. The jingling of bridles and bits hung in the air, two Knights riding side by side. Behind came a heavily laden cart drawn by two mules. An elf drove the cart, man or woman Kerian couldn't tell from where she crouched. It was as, only the day before, Felan had told them it would be: two Knights and a cart full of swords, battle-axes, and daggers.

"Sometimes it's that, got from the smithies in this part of the country, made to Thagol's order to arm his men, here and in the city. Sometimes it's gold or jewels taken at the border from traders, hill dwarves from down southern ways who take their pay at our border and don't set a step into the kingdom. Other times, in season, it's harvest, most of it going to feed the Knights in the capital." Bitterly, he said, "We keep enough to seed the next year, barely enough to feed ourselves through winter, no more, and nothing to trade for pots and pans, plough shares, and belt buckles. We don't trade much for wine now, not for cloth, wool, or boots."

It was beginning to be here as it was in the eastern part of the kingdom—the elves were made to arm and feed their oppressors while they themselves plunged deeper into poverty. Felan, Bayel, and other dalemen bitterly felt this insult. It hadn't been difficult to convince them to keep an eye out, an ear to the ground, for the purpose of letting Kerian know when a Knights' cart or wagon would set out on the road to Acris.

"Listen," Jeratt told her, "and learn, but keep hold of patience, Kerian."

So Kerian watched patiently as carts and wagons

wound the river road. She stopped counting how much tribute was passing and learned to count how many Knights were deployed for a cart, how many for a wagon. She saw that—cart or wagon—the ones most keenly guarded were those bearing weapons. She learned that once on the Qualinost Road, the escort met draconians that saw every load of tribute on to Acris, the crossroads town some miles distant. From there, Felan said, a stronger force of Knights with more draconians escorted small trains of carts and wagons all the way to the capital.

"Acris," Felan told them, "is where you'll find Lord Thagol. His Knights are quartered all over in this part of the country, in villages and taverns, but the Lord Knight stays where he is, right in his den and keeping watch over all."

Felan and Bayel had sworn to find a dozen elves to join them, young men and women who had for more than a year now been chafing under the oppression of the foreign Knights. "We'll scour the countryside of 'em," he'd said. "Drive 'em right back to Qualinost."

Kerian refused at once, and Jeratt wholeheartedly agreed.

"That's your pride talkin', " he said. "Not a bad thing, unless it kills you. Ain't no twelve of you going to send Thagol and his Knights anywhere but to sharpen their swords, but Kerian, me, and Ander, we have a fair bit of experience keepin' out of trouble. You get to learnin' that, travelin' as we do. We got no wives or children, no farms to tend."

Faran had paled at that, and Bayel stayed silent.

"You let us do what we plan," Jeratt said gently, "and just keep an eye open now and then for a bit of news you might think we'd like. Later—" He shrugged. "Later, things could change and then we can talk again."

Later they might be looking around for good men and women to add to their number.

"Look," said Ander again. "Damn Knights. They ride through as if they own the place."

Kerian nodded. Behind her, Jeratt slipped out of the deeper gloom. "Three of them ugly draconians ahead on the Qualinost Road," he said. "Waitin'."

Kerian pointed to the Knights. Jeratt grunted.

"Tidy little package," he said.

Ander nodded. "Two Knights and an elf who'll flee or join in our side."

"Can't count on him not siding with the Knights."

The Knights came closer. Now Kerian heard the deep thud of hoofs on the road, human voices speaking roughly in Common. The cartwheels creaked, the mule snorted and pulled a little at the reins when the wheels hit a rut. The cart's burden sang, steel chiming faintly against steel.

"A cowardly elf and two Knights," Ander said stubbornly. "We could take them." Ander glanced from one to the other, in his eyes an eager light.

"Now easy, boy," Jeratt said. He glanced past Ander to Kerian. "Listen."

"For what?"

Jeratt pulled a predator's grin. "For me to tell you when to go."

Sunlight and shadow swam on the road. The willows hung so close to the ground their boughs brushed the earth. Horses snorted, a Knight cursed and looked back over his shoulder at the elf and the cart. The driver slapped the reins hard against the mule's rump, but the cart didn't move. The mule spread its forelegs and lowered its head.

Ah, Kerian thought, now slap those reins one more time. . . .

Which the elf obligingly did.

The mule brayed, and the crash of hoofs against the

front of the cart boomed through the forest. The Knights swore in unison as the elf slapped the reins again.

The mule kicked a second time, then a third. The cart wobbled, and the front of it broke away. The driver jumped free, as the cart crashed onto its side, spilling shining weapons all over the road.

"Now," said Jeratt, nudging Ander.

The boy leaped up, Jeratt beside him. Two arrows flew, and a heart's beat later, a third. Someone screamed high; a Knight tumbled from his horse, the horse itself bellowing in pain. Kerian's arrow had pierced its neck. Jeratt let fly a second arrow, taking down the second Knight. Behind him Kerian shot another. The Knight on the road was trying to stand, two arrows in his thigh. Ander, breaking the plan, let go his own second shaft. It struck nothing, not even the horse writhing and squealing in agony.

Jeratt grabbed him hard, shaking him. "No! Do what I told you!" He shoved him toward the slope. He turned to glare at Kerian, shouting "Go!"

She ran, scrambling down the hill to the road, slipping on old leaves and grass, righting herself every time. Heart slamming hard against her ribs, she bolted for the screaming horse. In one swift motion, she slit its throat. Blood spurted from the severed artery, rising like a crimson fountain, splashing Kerian's hands, her face. Beside the beast lay its master, the Knight with two arrows in his thigh. Kerian saw his eyes wide and white in the shadows across the road. Helpless, he lifted a hand to the blood-soaked elf woman standing over him, to plead for mercy or to ward off a killing stroke.

"Do it!" Jeratt shouted. "Now!"

Now, or the draconians would hear the commotion and come to investigate.

Kerian gripped the bone handle, and as she did something hit her from behind, a hard weight driving her to the ground. She lost her knife, the dwarf-given weapon flung from her hand. A voiced cursed her in Qualinesti as the driver of the cart jammed his knee into her back, crushing air from her lungs. The elf grabbed a handful of her hair.

There was her knife, flashing in the sunlight, across her field of vision, down toward her own throat. Her cry of fear and protest sounded like strangling.

Someone thundered, "No!" and the elf strangling her jerked once, then again.

He toppled, the release of his weight as painful as the weight itself.

Kerian tried to gain her feet and fell back. A hard hand grabbed her and dragged her up. Jeratt's bearded face came close to hers.

"Go," he shouted. "One of the horses bolted—they'll see it on the road. Go!"

Go . . . where? Strip the Knights of weapons and whatever gear they could use. Sink the tribute into the stream, let the fine steel rust and rot, useless to Thagol or the dragon.

Kerian ran, seeing the elf who'd tried to kill her out of the corner of her eye. He'd died of two arrows in the back, Jeratt's and Ander's. From the look of them, they'd struck at the same instant.

Jeratt and Ander sank the tribute, hauling the sacks of weapons to the stream, shoving those blades that had spilled out back among their brethren and letting the weight of steel hold the weapons under the water. While they worked, Kerian took the boots of the Knight with the smallest feet. She grabbed the swords of each and their scabbards and belts. Before her companions had returned, she stripped off the black mail shirts and left the Knights face up and staring at the overhanging willows from dead eyes.

She didn't stop to give in to the sickness roiling in her

belly until she, Jeratt, and Ander had fled the scene of the killing. Then she vomited, quietly, violently in a thicket so far from the road that the sounds of furious draconian discovery never reached her.

"You killed one of us," Kerian said, the sour taste of bile in her mouth hours later. "You killed that Qualinesti. That's not what we're supposed to be doing. We're supposed to be fighting the Knights and—"

"Just about anyone who's trying to kill us," Jeratt drawled, "and that elf was trying to kill you."

Kerian snorted. "He didn't know who we were or whether he was in danger—" She shook her head, trying to dispel the memory of the elf's body flung away by the force of two arrows. "You could have hit him, pulled him off me. You didn't have to kill him."

"There wasn't time!" spat Jerratt.

Silence stood between them, Kerian on one side of the campfire, Jeratt and Ander on the other. They had no hare on a spit over the flames, and no one had gone to catch trout from the nearby stream. Jeratt was eating a hunk of cheese and chewing on a small loaf of hard bread, which they had gotten from Felan's wife the night before. Chewing, Jeratt jerked his head at Ander, who slipped a hand into the pouch at his belt. Kerian heard the crackle of stiff parchment as Ander unfolded it.

Jeratt jerked his head again, Ander handed the paper across the fire. Little sparks jumped up, Kerian took it quickly.

"Read," Jeratt said.

She did, her eye leaping along the few short lines of a terse message. It commended the bearer to "the most esteemed Lord Eamutt Thagol of Qualinost and late of

Monastery Bone," and it urged the Lord Knight to reward the bearer according to the measure of his merit.

"Found this on the dead driver," Jeratt said around the last bite of cheese.

Kerian stared at the message.

"You're welcome," Jeratt said dryly.

She looked up, almost absently. "Thank you."

Ander leaned closer to the fire. "He'd have killed you, Kerian. He was *trying* to kill you."

The fire hissed over green wood. "I know the elf was trying to kill me," she said curtly, then, softer, "I was there."

Kerian balled up the parchment. "A collaborator! A cowardly collaborator working with the Dark Knights." She made to throw the balled sheet into the fire—then caught herself in time. She held it a little above the flame, then took it back and smoothed it across her knee.

"What?" said Jeratt, looking from her to the wrinkled page.

Kerian shook her head as she folded the parchment neatly along the original lines. "Nothing. Yet." She leaned forward. "We need to let Felan and Bayel know. Anyone they speak to could be working for Thagol—they're taking more of a risk than we guessed, helping us."

Jeratt snorted. "We aren't going to stay here and make a career out of kicking Thagol."

Their plan was to make short, sharp strikes in this part of the kingdom then slip away back home, let Thagol puzzle over things here for a while, then take up their campaign against his Knights from Lightning Falls. Jeratt had traveled back there twice, speaking to Elder, speaking with Ayensha, Bueren Rose, and the others.

"Right," Kerian said, "but they have to live here. I'm talking about setting down roots. Let's kick Thagol a few more times before we leave. Let him know trouble is brewing."

Jeratt nodded slowly in agreement, the grudging expression on his face saying he wondered just who was in charge sometimes, him or her.

She slapped her knee and looked around hungrily. "What's to eat?"

Jeratt laughed. "Used to be cheese and bread. Not much more now than a heel and a rind. Gotta get a better belly, Kerian." He jerked his chin at Ander. "You too, youngster. You're gonna see worse than you saw today. You'll do worse, too. Might as well not do it hungry, eh?"

Too late to hunt, too late to fish, Kerian and Ander went to sleep hungry. It surprised her, waking in the middle of the night to the sound of Jeratt tending the fire, that she could sleep at all. She glanced at Ander and saw him staring at the leafy canopy, eyes wide and nervous. He slid a glance her way. She saw him shudder and reach for the scabbarded sword lying near to his hand. They all had new weapons this day, looted from corpses. Ander's fingers didn't cringe to touch the pommel of a dead Knight's weapon.

In the morning, without consulting Jeratt, she told Ander to slip quietly through the forest first to Felan's farm and then Bayel's. "Tell them we know there was at least one collaborator among the elves here, that there might well be more. Tell them everything we discussed last night, offer them the honest choice—back out now, stay as they have been, or come to fight."

Ander nodded, eager to undertake the mission. Jeratt watched the two, eyes narrow, expression hard and unreadable.

"After you do that, don't come back here." She slipped a finger into the neck of her shirt and hooked the slender gold chain that held two halves of the king's ring. In a quick gesture, she removed one half and put it into Ander's hand. "Now, before you leave, speak with Jeratt—"

Jeratt, glaring at her now.

"—and he will tell you how to get to Lightning Falls. You must go carefully, because you're returning to the area where Knights have been searching for me and very likely now they are also searching for you. When you come near Lightning Falls, you will be challenged by folk who look like"—she laughed "—who look like us. They're outlaws like us, but answer the challenge humbly and quickly, no arrogance with these folk. Tell them you are from Jeratt and me, be quick, and show my ring. Tell whoever challenges you that seek a woman named simply 'Elder,' and tell her all that has happened here."

Ander took it all in silently, his eyes on her, lighting in excitement for the mission, shadowing in sadness for having to leave.

"After you tell her that, Ander, tell her Jeratt and I will be home before winter. Tell her things are changing in the kingdom now."

"I'll do it all, Kerian. I promise. Just the way you tell me."

"And you won't come back. The risk that you'd be followed isn't great, but it's a chance we can't take."

Reluctantly, he agreed.

"You're a fool," Jeratt growled when the boy was gone. "You're reckless. It's wrong to send the boy so far alone, with such a mission. He'll be lucky no one kills him before he gets to the falls. By all the gone gods, you're a fool, Kerian!"

She flared, hot and high and sudden. "Don't *ever* call me that again!"

He didn't step back; in the sudden silence of the forest, Jeratt held his ground, his face set and stubborn.

"You think you're not bein' foolish? Y'think the boy didn't just turn to fire for you? Kerian, he's in love with ya. He'll do anything you tell him, and he won't be thinkin' about anyone else but you." Jeratt shook his head, then spat. "That will get someone killed someday."

"Getting prescient, like Elder, are you?"

"Wonder why I say you're a fool, do you?"

She flared again, he laughed at that and tapped his chest.

"I have a year or two more on me than you, Kerian. I haven't lived in gilded palaces; I've lived in the hard world, the place where people die of stupidity, their own or someone else's. Happens all the time, and I ain't no seer, I just pay attention to what I see."

The falling fire lay between them, yet they might have been standing toe to toe.

Coldly, Kerian said, "You are welcome to your opinion, Jeratt. I don't know if you're right or wrong about Ander, and I can't undo a boy's heart, but I can use him where he can do the best work. He'll let the others know what we're doing, let them know to be ready for our return. And he'll be away from me for a while."

Jeratt's stance relaxed, his expression softened. "Y'did what y'could, I'll grant it." He stood in grudging silence for a moment longer. "The plan isn't all that foolish. I'll grant it, too."

"But—?"

He met her eyes. "But y' should have sent him on a long time ago."

By her silence, she agreed.

Between them embers breathed faintly. "I'll not name you 'fool' again, but I might be sayin' one day or another that y'could think something through a little harder. You have a good, keen mind, Kerian. Sharp as a dagger and bright. You learn, and that quickly."

"But girl," he continued, and she heard the affection in the naming, "y'came out of your king's palace and walked into the forest with no idea but to find a brother who didn't have the good sense to be happy about it. Now you're puttin' together a plan your king doesn't know he can dream of. Y'like to leap at the bright idea. Maybe that's good, but a lot of the time, it isn't."

Kerian kicked at the dirt, sending a fine spray of it onto the embers. Jeratt did the same. Between them, they smothered the fire. The half-elf winked.

"Well, even when I think you're bein', uh, not too sensible, I'm with you, Kerianseray of Qualinesti. I like the flash of your steel."

———◆———

Jeratt liked the flash of Kerian's steel, and Lord Eamutt Thagol learned to hate it. Through the end of summer and into the beginning of a late-coming autumn, he found himself having to increase the size of the escort of Knights who accompanied tribute wagons to Acris. What had seemed to be isolated incidents of brigandage began to look like more than that. Lone wagons, no matter the number of Knights, were raided with increasing frequence and efficiency, and survivors reported that they were struck by growing bands of elves who fought by no rules any Knight or soldier knew, who seemed to reinvent their tactics daily. Soon he sent to Qualinost for more draconians with the trains that went on to the capital.

Through the summer of hot days and steamy nights, the outlaws became four, and then five and then more. Bayel and Felan left their farms and joined them, and so did others from the dales, men and women who wanted to strike a blow. They never ran as a solid or identifiable group. Sometimes they were eight, nine, ten at a time. After a raid the dalemen would fade away, back to their lives as peaceable citizens of a bleeding kingdom. They came at call, they left when the work was done, and each knew the danger of collaborators, the invisible enemy. Each knew he must not speak with anyone who was not part of the group.

They came to be known as the Night People, for they struck most often at night and vanished into the darkness before they could be identified. They went with soot-blacked faces, their bright eyes the more fearsome. They moved like shadows, like darkness.

The Night People. Kerian spoke the name to her growing band of warriors gleefully, proudly as though it were the name of a renowned fighting order.

"They come out of the woods on all sides," one dying Knight reported to his lord.

The Skull Knight took the man's head in his two hands, leaned close so his eyes were the only thing the dying man saw. A great shudder went through the man, and blood spurted from the wound in his side. In his mind, he felt Thagol walking, prowling, searching for something.

He wanted a name. The Lord Knight desired to see a face, a form, to know his enemy. The dying man couldn't give him that, and in the end the agony of his death didn't have all that much to do with his wounds.

The Night People changed strategy. They stepped up their raids, killed as many Knights as they could, as quickly as possible, then fell back, drawing the infuriated survivors after them and into the mouth of a trap that had been well set—a wall of waiting elves who let through their compatriots and closed around the Knights, howling terrible war cries, curdling the blood with screams. They killed swiftly, and they left nothing alive behind, not Knights, not horses, not draconians. They stripped the dead of weapons and what equipment they wanted, then destroyed the rest, leaving nothing but corpses for Lord Thagol to claim.

Some of the Night People died too, but their bodies were always stolen away and hidden and buried, so that the occupying force no longer knew who to trust in the dale.

Sitting in the tavern at Acris, Lord Thagol ransacked the minds of his dying men. He sent word to every town and hamlet in the forest, every farmstead in every dale, that the elf who gave him what he needed to know, who brought to him the head of the outlaws, would be richly rewarded—but not even then was he able to learn the face of his enemy.

At last, though, he was able to learn of one strike before it was made.

CHAPTER

14

Felan stood before the lord Knight, his hand trembling slightly so that the parchment he held out rustled, whispering of his poorly suppressed fear. A line of sweat ran down the side of his face.

"M-my lord," he said.

Lord Thagol didn't look up. Before him lay spread a map of the countryside, wide and newly made. Upon the map Felan noted the Qualinost Road, that artery connecting this rural part of the kingdom to the capital and places beyond. Today a wagon of fat sacks filled with grain waited in a secluded place, guarded by draconians and Knights. Others would join it tomorrow and the next day until there were enough to escort to the capital. One would be filled with weapons and war supplies, another perhaps filled with the tribute the dragon loved—ancient treasure. In the south of the forest, where rich manors lay, lords and ladies were beginning to pay the dragon's tax with the family jewels.

Felan registered a series of small red marks on the map, like check marks ticking off a list. These were the sites of recent encounters between the Lord Knight's forces and the Night People. In none of these had Lord Thagol's men fared well, and in the last, the battle near a small creek known as Brightflow, fourteen Knights had died. Two of the outlaws had perished as well, one killed by a sword, the other gone screaming to his death in a pool of acid, the revenge of the kapak draconian he had killed.

Felan swallowed, wishing his hand would steady, wishing for a sip of white wine like that in the Knight's cup or simply a drink of water. At his hip hung a water flask, but he dared not move to reach for it. The draconian at the door had stripped him of every weapon. He'd endured the dry, cold touch of the creature's clawed hands, its reeking breath on his cheek as it grabbed away the knife at his belt, the bow and quiver across his back, even the small eating knife everyone in this part of the country carried as a matter of course. He felt that disgusting touch even now, even as, standing before the Knight's table, and he felt the draconian's reptilian eyes still on him. He didn't doubt that reaching for the flask would be a mistake.

He said again, "My lord."

At the bar, the taverner looked up, an old elf with thickening jowls and thinning silver hair. No one but these four, taverner, Knight, draconian, and Felan, occupied the large common room. Lord Thagol had taken up residence here and made it his command post for the region. If this were another Knight, Felan might have wondered whether the human missed the comforts of the capital, the glittering towers, the good food and quarters. This Knight out of Monastery Bone, though, bore the look of one used to the lack of comfort and the imposition of discipline. Here, in the Waycross, he looked like a man in his element, poring over maps and messages, waiting for the reports from soldiers. He'd been here all the summer long, the winter before, and back to the end of autumn. In all that time, the owner of the tavern hadn't had payment for the food and wine Lord Thagol demanded for his Knights and draconians, and no elf for miles around came to dine at his tables or drink at his bar. The poor taverner had the pinched, white-eyed look of a man who sees ruin ahead of him.

Felan waited, and Sir Eamutt Thagol put another check mark on the map, his face white in the flickering firelight and shadow. His lips compressed in a thin, hard line. Beside his hand the crystal inkpot looked like a small carafe of blood. Now he set aside the quill pen, moved the inkpot aside with the side of his little finger. When he finally looked up and met Felan's eyes, the elf's knees wobbled. His blood changed to ice, washing through him so that he thought the horrible cold would stop his heart.

"Remind me. Do I know you?" the Knight asked.

In his mind Felan heard a sound like footsteps so clearly he almost turned to see who'd come up behind him. He swallowed again, this time harder.

"I am Felan of the Northern Dales, my lord. I—I don't—we have never met. I have brought a letter—a paper."

Sweat ran on him now, soaking his shirt. In his mind, he heard the footsteps coming again. He looked over his shoulder, very carefully. No, the draconian stood at its post, a tall, reeking presence in the shadows by the door.

Felan held up the paper, in the dim light seeing the sweat stains on it. None of the ink had been smeared though. He'd taken care to preserve it in a condition to be read. When Thagol took the paper, his fingers brushed against Felan's.

"M-my lord," the elf gasped.

Lord Thagol read. The lines were few, the message clear. The bearer was to receive compensation according to the measure of his worth.

"What," the Knight asked, "shall I use to measure your worth?"

Felan regretted coming. He wanted to run, to risk that

bolting the room, flinging past the draconian and out the door. He held still. "I have valuable information, my lord."

Thagol looked up. Felan thought, as others before had thought, that the man's face was so pale it looked like a burn scar. The Knight's eyes seemed flat, dead, and empty. Felan had to lock his knees to stay standing in place. In his head the footsteps stopped, as though a searcher had come close to what he was looking for.

"And that information is . . . ?"

"The outlaws . . . the ones they call the Night People. I—I know about them."

The Knight remained silent, staring.

"I—I have entered their trust, my lord. I know how they work. I know—" He stopped and swallowed, trying to ease his parched throat. "I know that they sweep out of the forest and do their foul work, and I know they vanish into it again, invisible. They are not invisible, my lord, and they are not such an army. The leaders, at the core, are only four."

Lord Thagol raised a pale brow, interested now. "Four?"

"Only that, my lord. These four are the heart of the trouble in the forest. They plot, and they plan, and they are the ones who call for other men and women to fight and then send them all away again when the work is done." He looked around nervously. "I know where they are tonight, my lord, and I know they'll stay there for a day or two." Emboldened, he moved closer to the table and put a finger on the place a little north of the Brightflow. "There is a glade here, surrounded by tall pines. You wouldn't think to look for it. From any direction it looks like more forest with no clearing to see unless you stumble upon it. This is their hiding place for now. They will move again soon, either to gather a force to strike or simply to move. For now, they are there, planning. Hiding. Just the four."

Just the four. Cut off the head, and the twisty, slippery creature preying on this once-quiet corner of Beryl's captive kingdom would die. Lord Thagol smiled. Felan heard the hiss and sigh of the hearth fire. He glanced at the taverner who did not meet his eye.

"You know this," Thagol said, "because you have gained their trust? How?"

"I—I worked with them. For a time. For a while." He spoke hastily now. "Until I saw how wrong they are. Now I am here."

Lord Thagol tapped the parchment. "With this."

"I had it from one of your Knights, my lord. When I told him what I knew, he sped me on to you."

"Very wise of you both," Lord Thagol drawled. "You won't mind if I question you a bit more closely, will you?"

Felan opened his mouth to speak. The icy fear that had chilled him upon entering the Skull Knight's presence now clamped around his mind with terrible grinding claws. They spread each thought wide, as though each were a book. They plunged deep, the icy claws, tearing at his mind. Felan could not do anything but scream.

The draconian turned, barely interested. At the bar, the taverner shuddered and poured himself a drink. The bottle rattled against the glass. No one noticed, and Felan's scream went on and on, far past the point where his voice turned to rags and blood choked him.

An instant later, he fell to his knees, onto his face at the feet of the Skull Knight, voiceless and begging for mercy.

Like a glacier, the ice in his mind withdrew, and the elf Felan lay in the rushes on the tavern floor, blood trickling from the sides of his mouth, from his eyes, from his ears. His message had been delivered and accepted. Lord Thagol looked at the taverner and suppressed a yawn.

"I didn't really question him all that closely, you

know. All was as it seems, and he is a turncoat. But . . . "
He shrugged. "Well, it seems he was a bit weak-minded."

He jerked his chin and the elf came out from behind the
bar. He dragged the corpse across the floor, silently cursing
the blood trailing behind and grumbling about how he'd
have to go off to the well now and fill a bucket to clean the
floor.

The draconian stepped away from the door with laughter
that sounded like snarling. The door slammed shut, and
the elf dragged Felan's body all the way across the dusty
dooryard and behind the springhouse where cheeses hung
and jugs of milk cooled. He left it there and went to find
a shovel. He was all the rest of the day digging in the earth
behind the springhouse, far enough away from the
spring itself so that the water wouldn't undermine the mean
grave. No one bothered him or called him back to his
tavern. Lord Thagol had matters of his own to consider,
and he didn't care about the concerns of taverners or
turncoats. The taverner buried the dead in peace, and
when he was finished he covered the raw earth with
piled stones. Wolves didn't run often in this part of the
forest, but the elf wouldn't take the risk of the grave being
disturbed.

He murmured something at the end of his work, standing over the mound of earth and stone. It might have been
a groan for the hard work. It might have been a prayer. So
weary was he that even he didn't know.

At night, when the taverner lay down in his narrow
bed in the smallest room above the kitchen, he listened to
the sound of iron-shod hoofs thundering into the dooryard, and he lay a long time awake hearing the raucous
voices of a half dozen or more Knights feasting from his
larder and drinking his bar dry. He heard them leave
again, then there was only silence as the Lord Knight
retired, leaving one draconian on guard at the door.

Those vile creatures, the taverner thought, never seemed to need sleep.

Neither did the Skull Knight. Even sleeping, Lord Thagol did not sleep. Lying in the bed of the finest room in the Waycross, he dreamed and dreamed again the encounter he'd had with the elf Felan. There had been nothing in the turncoat's mind to suggest that everything he reported to Thagol was less than true. Nothing. Not the least shading of exaggeration, not the least shaving of the truth marred the tale. That was the problem. The elf's presentation of a truthful telling had been, well, *too* true.

Kerian watched the wink and flash of fireflies dancing between the straight tall pines. She sat barely breathing, not eating. Jeratt poked her with his elbow, and when she looked at him he nodded toward the cheese and bread and apples. Provisions from Felan's wife, the last he'd brought in the fat leather wallet they'd all come to look forward to seeing slung across the farmer's shoulder. That had been three days ago, a day before he had volunteered to be the one to take her carefully crafted message to the Lord Knight in Acris. He'd been a day gone, and no one expected to see him back here. They had expected to hear from Bayel, or one of the Night People drifting into camp, that he'd returned home to his farm.

What they'd heard was that Felan's wife had had no word of him.

"Eat," Jeratt said. "It's a bad habit, not eating before a fight."

Kerian nodded as though to agree, but she didn't eat. She liked her belly feeling light and empty before battle. She liked the edge that hunger gave her.

The Night People had begun to arrive into the glade like

shadows, like night. Farmers and hunters, they knew how to move though the forest so stealthily that they could come upon a doe drinking and get within touching distance. None knew the forest better than these young men and women of the farms and dales. None had a stronger will to fight. They hated Lord Thagol, and they hated the Knights. They loathed the draconians, and here, away from city and the politics of keeping a kingdom whole for as long as possible, they wanted nothing more than to fight, to rid themselves of those who would steal their goods and gains, who would rob them of the dignity they considered a birthright.

"Listen," Jeratt said into her musing. She looked up and saw he knew her thoughts. "He volunteered."

Kerian nodded, knowing he spoke of Felan.

"He helped shape the plan."

"Yes," she said. "He did."

"You didn't send him to his death." The word out, it hung between them. "You know him. You know why he insisted on going."

Felan's wife was childing, the news learned only weeks before. He had been, always, an enthusiastic rebel, happy to do anything for the cause or to pass along information from one farm to another, content to do whatever part came his way. The news of impending fatherhood, though, had fired him with passion. It was not a passion for the kingdom or a kindling at the flame of revenge. Felan wanted only to secure his child's birthright.

He'd said, "I want my child to be able to walk this land as I did growing up. I want him to know that the forest and all its bounty are his, that what comes of this farm I will leave him—all of it!—will feed him and his own children. I want him to know who he is—a free elf, not the slave of a thieving dragon's Knights. I'll go beard the Skull Knight in his own den, if that's what it takes."

One after another now, her Night People drifted in. None spoke, not even to greet each other. Kerian took the count of them. There were now thirteen in the glade. Bayel went among them, clasping a hand, slapping a back, wordless greetings. She saw him lean close to a young woman, listening to whispered words. He nodded once, curtly, and came to sit beside Jeratt. He ripped a chunk off the loaf of coarse brown bread the half-elf offered.

"He's dead." He looked from Jeratt to Kerian. "Wael at the Waycross saw him die."

"How?" Kerian asked, heart plummeting at the news.

"Skull Knight killed him." Bayel looked away, then back. "Felan delivered the word, however, just like we planned. The Skull Knight took it, and Wael says he swallowed the bait grinning."

"How?" Kerian said again. Her voice grew colder, harder.

Bayel shook his head, sad and sorry. "The Knight went in for a look, eh? Went into Felan's mind to see if all he said was true. Wael says Felan held out, showed the bastard nothing to make him suspect we're diverting his Knights into a trap while the most of us hit the wagons up the Qualinost Road. He let Thagol see nothing but what we wanted him to see."

That broke him, body and mind.

Kerian looked around the glade. More warriors had arrived. She counted again. Twenty-five—no, twenty-eight. "How many Knights are coming?" she asked, distracted.

"Wael says just the usual detachment that hangs around the Waycross, no more than six. Maybe a draconian or two. Easy pickings. Maybe the Lord Knight himself if he thinks he's going to cut off the head of us easy, eh?"

Maybe. Kerian hadn't counted on it, but she had considered it and would have gotten great pleasure to find

Thagol himself in her trap. She sat in silence for a while, thinking sadly of Felan's sacrifice. There would be thirty-five of her warriors here before long. She looked hard at Bayel. "Tell me again—do you think the Skull Knight suspects nothing?"

"Kerian," he said, gently. "You know Felan. He was a stout heart. He held out, for us, for his child, for the future of the kingdom. Six Knights, maybe a few draconians. They're going to hit here in the dark hour before dawn. They think they're going to take four heads back to Waycross and start there what they've been doing in the capital. They're ordering our heads piked so everyone around will know there is no point in resisting."

Even so silent, twenty-eight warriors made the glade whisper with their breathing, their small motions. Kerian listened as she cast a glance at the sky. The moon had set, the stars shone brightly, but so thick was the canopy of trees that their light did little to illuminate the world far below. The forest would be deadly dark tonight. She sat forward, feeling Jeratt and Bayel draw closer. Bayel's eyes shone in the firelight. Jeratt sat still as stone, a seasoned warrior preparing to do battle.

"Felan's dead, something's changed. I don't know how, I just know it. I smell it."

Bayel frowned, not understanding. Jeratt nodded, knowing well what she meant. You feel the danger, you heed the instinct, and you wonder what triggered it later. He winked at her and slapped her knee.

She said, "Thagol's not going to send a hunting party after us tonight. He'll send more."

She pointed to the earth before them, the smooth place where they had drawn their plans. Marks still remained, lines and circles and deep marks where Jeratt had stabbed a stick to emphasize some point.

"We'd planned two hits tonight—one here where

Thagol and his men are set to walk into our trap and one here where Jeratt and Bayel plan to hit the wagons camped on the Qualinost Road from north and south." With one sweep of her foot, Kerian erased the sketches. "Let the bastard Knight come. Let him bring as many Knights as he likes. He'll find the place empty, no one here but the ghosts of our fires."

"What are you gonna do, Kerian?" Jeratt asked.

She told him, and he said this would mean she'd not be able to stay long in this forest now.

"We didn't plan to stay forever, you know that. Ander's waiting at the falls. The others are waiting."

He knew this, and his approving grin flashed cold and bright. Bayel nodded, and he said he thought the idea was good. Kerian looked past them to the darkness where her Night People stood or sat, checking their weapons.

"It's time," she said. "Jeratt, take your warriors. Bayel, you and yours come with me. We'll meet back here when it's done." She looked keenly at one, then the other. "Any questions?"

These two, who with her and Felan had been the heart of the Night People, had no questions.

"Then go," Kerian said. "Remember who we do this for."

Once they were four. Now they were three. This was for Felan.

❖

They owned the forest, Kerian and her Night People. They knew every trail, each game path. They knew where the streams ran, where the deer gathered at dawn. They had run here as children, as youths hunting. They flowed through the forest this night like silent dreams, men and women with soot-black faces, warriors dressed in leathers like hunters, hung with the weapons of war. Jeratt divided his force, sending ten into hiding west and east of their camp. Seven went south with him, slipping between the trees, and they went so silently that the nine Knights riding by in the opposite direction never saw them. These were not the six Wael had predicted, but Jeratt considered them no threat. The elves knew the air as wolves do, and they kept downwind so the horses picking their way through the night forest didn't catch their scent. Jeratt watched them go.

Since the Knights rode by night, they did not go with visors down. They did not go armored, only mailed, for it seemed they wanted to be as quiet as possible. They had dismounted at the head of the trail, where the ground rose and grew stony. They'd led their horses then, with the beasts' noses wrapped in cloth or covered with a hand to muffle the sound of their snorting. They did not go by with a ringing of bridles and bits tonight. Those had been quieted, too, with slim leather casings on every metal piece that might chime.

Jeratt noted, too, that these were only human Knights. No draconians were with them, for those creatures had no skill at running quiet. The beast-men were gone to the highway or were perhaps still at the tavern.

When the Knights came closest, Jeratt marked the first rider and knew him by his white face and his dead eyes. The Knights went up the trail, and the forest settled back to its usual sounds, the rustle of small things in the brush, the sudden flight of an owl, the sound of something caught in sharp talons and dying. Jeratt looked south toward the crossroad and the little village where Lord Thagol had lately come to rule. He was a half-elf, and that meant he shared in much of the heritage of his elf parent. As could any elf, he was able to see the outline of a creature walking in darkness, the red glow of the heat of its body. Its life force, some said. In the full darkness of a forest night, Jeratt looked and smiled in satisfaction when he saw the distant flicker—only here and there—of a thin red glow, the outline of other elves. There was Kerian, and with her, her warriors, slipping silently, a force the size of his own running south to the crossroad. As he looked, he saw half their number break away, the light of their bodies gliding around to the west in such a way that the two groups would find themselves in position to attack their prey from front and behind.

"Good girl," Jeratt whispered.

One of his warriors looked up. He shook his head, and they all settled to silence, so still that the high shrill cry of a nightjar startled Jeratt.

"All right now," he whispered.

From the campsite came a harsh curse, sudden shouting. Jeratt held his people still with one gesture. Another cry, more cursing and the sounds of night creatures fleeing. The bright clash of steel, a sudden scream too loud to be human.

A horse down!

"Hush," Jeratt said to the restless warrior beside him. "Wait."

They saw the faint red flickers of men and women in combat. The forest filled with cries now, bellowing human rage and the eerie banshee cries of the Night People.

"Watch," Jeratt whispered, his lips close to the other elf's ear. "See."

See it all, the shape of the battle. Jeratt grinned coldly, and the woman warrior made a small, satisfied sound as, pursued, Thagol's Knights fled the campsite, all but one on foot. Eager now, Jeratt watched a handful of his men pretend to flight. Swiftly they came through the forest, leaping streamlets, blow downs, boulders, and leading the Knights onto rough ground. In this way, the hunt came crashing through the forest, tearing through the underbrush, the Knights believing themselves in pursuit of ambushing foes. Furious, driven by Thagol's cursing, the humans tore past Jeratt and the remainder of his warriors, and at the exact moment Thagol passed him, Jeratt sent another nightjar cry into the darkness.

His eager warriors burst from cover. Voices high and howling, in one swift maneuver they blocked the Knights' pursuit. Turning, the elves circled the five humans, a noose tightening. Afoot, four had no chance against the greater number. Three died at once, the fourth after a flashing steel struggle.

The fifth Knight, Thagol, was still mounted. He abandoned the field before the first Knight died.

———◆◆◆———

Kerian saw her people slip into position, half in the forest shadows beyond the tavern's dooryard and half in back, both exits covered. She looked for Bayel and found him coming around the back of the tavern. He dropped to a knee beside her at the overgrown verge of the tavern's wood lot, never rustling leaf or branch.

"Seven inside," he said. "The taverner, two Knights and four draconians."

She nodded then leaned close. "We're ready. Remember the taverner."

Bayel's eyes on the Waycross and the golden light shining out from the windows, front and back, he said, "It'll be done as you wish, Kerian."

Someone—or something—passed before the wide window looking into the tavern's front yard. Draconian by the shape, Kerian thought. It stood too tall to be an elf, the shape of it too grotesque to be either human or elf. The tavern door opened, and the wind shifted. Two draconians came out into the night. She smelled their dry reptilian stink, the bite of the acid reek of their breath. Here, outside the forest, stars shone brightly. The sky was awash with them. Their silvery light glinted from the harnesses of the draconians, metal buckles, polished leather, a bright length of steel as one unsheathed a long knife.

"Got it off that elf," the creature growled. It laughed, a ripping sound. "Right before his head exploded."

Bayel moved restlessly. Kerian clamped a hard hand on his arm.

"No," the other snarled. "Didn't explode, did it? Bone and brains all over?"

The first draconian shrugged. "Might as well have. Blood pouring out of it everywhere, mouth, ears, and eyes. That lord of ours—" It laughed again. "He's got a searching way about him, eh?"

They stood for a moment admiring the blade, arguing a little about whether it should have been given over to the Lord Knight and deciding that since Lord Thagol hadn't asked for it, there was no need to offer. Kerian watched them walk away from the Waycross toward the road. They'd take up guard posts there, she thought. Thagol was gone, probably most of his Knights with him. He was an arrogant bastard, but he wouldn't leave his headquarters unguarded.

She was right, and when she saw them settled, one at the north-south road and the other at the east-west, she nodded to Bayel.

An owl's rattling cry tore the night's silence. One of the draconians looked up, expecting to see the raptor bursting up from the woods, a struggling rabbit in its talons. It looked again then turned to its companion. The other shrugged.

"Bad luck," it said. "I guess—"

Four arrows wasped from the forest. The draconian

jerked as though yanked to attention. It screamed a curse and fell, dying and filling the night with the sting of acid. Four more arrows tore out of the wood. Two missed and one bounded off the second draconian's scaled hide. The missile fell into the pool of green acid that had been the body of the first, the wood hissing as the arrow died. The fourth took the draconian in the soft underside of its neck.

The draconian howled, clawing at the arrow in its throat. The front door slammed open, a human voice called a question.

Kerian slapped Bayel's shoulder as the clearing around the Waycross erupted in the high keening battle cries Lord Thagol's men had come to hate.

Kerian ran into the howling as her warriors converged on the tavern. She heard someone scream, a high shriek that was no battle cry, and she saw an elf die in the terrible embrace of the draconian he had killed. The stink of acid, of burning flesh, hung on the night, and soon the reek of blood joined it.

A Knight filled up the front door, golden firelight glaring behind him so that he was faceless. The light ran on his drawn sword, and Kerian leaped up the two stairs to the long porch, her own sword in hand. One downward stroke, and the man's blood spurted from a severed hand. His sword fell with a dull thud onto the wooden porch, Kerian kicked it aside, the hand still gripping. In horror, the Knight saw that and finally felt the agony. He howled, and Kerian lunged for him, thrusting. She felt bone scrape her steel, and swiftly she kicked the dead Knight off her blade.

Another scream came from behind the tavern. Knight

or elf, she couldn't tell and didn't stop to wonder. The swell of elf voices behind her merged with the shouts inside the tavern. Kerian plunged through the doorway, into the chaos of shouting and ringing steel.

"Elf bitch!"

She turned, sword high, and the jolt of a heavy blade striking hers rang all the way up her arm. Kerian fell back a step. The Knight pressed. She let him, moving step and step, maneuvering him until his back was to the door. Behind, she felt the sudden heat of fire, and out of the corner of her eye she saw she was near the hearth. Flames leaped up the walls from behind the bar, roaring and eating the thick oak boards. Even as she saw that, she saw the taverner Wael flee out the back.

The Knight brought his sword down. Again she felt the blow up to her shoulders. She fell back another step, but the Knight's sword held hers now, pressing her with all his strength. She did not try to match him. She seemed to yield, to weaken before his greater strength. His eyes lit with furious hatred. She stepped back again then swiftly turned, her sword describing a bright circle in the fiery light. Overbalanced by his thrust, the Knight stumbled, and Kerian came about so quickly she thought it likely he never felt her blade slip and turn between his ribs.

"Kerian!"

She turned to see Bayel, his eyes wide.

She turned again and saw a draconian rushing at her from the flames of the burning tavern. The last one, and she dared not engage it, for to kill this thing and be anywhere near it dying was to die herself.

"Get *down!*" Bayel shouted.

Kerian dropped, falling to her knees in the blood of the dead Knight.

An arrow screamed overhead, then another. Each missed, and she heard the sound of Bayel being flung to the floor. Kerian rolled and saw the sooted face of Thullea, a woman of the northern dales. A silver flash overhead, a dagger flew. The draconian screamed and fell, an elven blade through its eye.

Kerian scrambled to her feet and shoved Bayel out the door.

They found no chaos there, only the eerie silence after killing and two Knights surrounded by the Night People. Wael the taverner shivered in the chill dark as his tavern burned.

"Good," she said. "Now we'll settle down to wait."

They did not wait long. The stars had hardly moved in the sky before Kerian heard the approach of Jeratt and his men. He came with only thirteen, for three had been killed in battle. "We got the rest of 'em though. Caught 'em ragin' back when they knew they'd been fooled. "

He looked down at the dusty ground. "Didn't get the big one, though. Killed five of the Knights, left the others bleedin' in the forest . . . and Thagol, I don't know how, but he got away."

Kerian listened and didn't say anything for a long while. Fire leaped to the sky, her Night People reunited, and the two bands spoke amongst themselves of the deaths they'd suffered and the deaths they'd dealt. She'd wanted Thagol to see this burning, this ruin. She wanted to kill him here where he'd killed Felan. She wanted to settle that debt and all the debts the Skull Knight owed her from the moment he murdered her cousin and piked her head upon the bridge in Qualinost.

Fire roared, and the heat of it made her men drop back to the crossroad itself, taking their prisoners and poor Wael with them.

At last, Kerian looked up. "Kill them," she said to Jeratt, jerking her thumb toward the Knights. "Someone take Wael to a safe place."

Jeratt spat. "And the Skull Knight?"

"He can watch the burning from wherever he's hiding." She looked around, at her Night People and the fire. "We're not finished this night."

Jeratt understood. He and Bayel gathered half the warriors and sent them out into the forest, running silently through the forest and up the Qualinost Road. Kerian took the rest and paralleled their run across the highway, deep into the wood. Both halves of her force came upon the encampment of tribute wagons in the dark hour before dawn. Six Knights and four draconians heard the single piercing call of a nightjar. Some looked around for the bird, startled, others only heard it in their sleep in the instant before the Night People fell on them. Half the Knights died before they knew they were under attack. The draconians died instantly of arrows through the eye, their deaths causing the agonizing deaths of anyone else near. Kerian herself cut the dray horses loose and sent them into the forest. She, Bayel, and Jeratt handed out weapons from the little wagon filled with that treasure, and scooped up four pouches of coin from another. One she gave to an elf to deliver in secret to the taverner.

"The rest is for Felan's widow. Give her a good sword, and give her these pouches of steel. Tell her they are her child's inheritance from his father."

They fired the wagons, leaving behind nothing of use.

Before the smoke could travel far, they separated, two dozen and more warriors returning like shadows to their homes, some far-flung, others nearby. They would not come out to fight again; they would vanish into the population, become simple farmers and tradesfolk.

"For now," Kerian told them. "For now, until you hear otherwise."

For now . . . they murmured, all in agreement as she went among them, clasping hands, clasping arms.

"And you?" asked one, the eager young woman who had fought beside Jeratt in the forest.

Kerian grinned, bright and feral. "The next time the coward Thagol hears about us, he'll know that all this kingdom is our battleground."

CHAPTER

15

That winter, in the eastern part of the kingdom, there were glad greetings as Kerian and Jeratt returned to the Lightning Falls. "Or Thunder as the dwarves name it," Ander told Bayel. The young man had settled in well among the outlaws. Jeratt's welcome was one of shouts and laughter and back thumping. Bayel was introduced and accepted warmly and went easily among them for the sake of his reputation in the east as a harrier of Knights.

Kerian returned to them a different person than they had known. She had been Jeratt's student in the arts of living, the hunter he must coach, the fletcher who couldn't fletch, the Kagonesti servant of Qualinesti masters too far gone from her heritage.

"She is not that now," murmured Briar, a flame-haired elf woman, to the young man who shared her sleeping furs. "Look at her, all golden and tall and—" She shook her head. "Damn if the woman hasn't learned how to stride."

Kerian thought there might be some tension over Jeratt, once the leader of the band, now deferring to his student, but none resented that because the half-elf made it clear that he didn't mind.

"She's what she is," Jeratt said, quietly to his old friends while she lay sleeping. "I'm what I am. We're good enough, the two of us, for what's coming now."

Elder, that small huddle of an ancient elf woman, said nothing to either of them upon their return, but Jeratt knew her of old, and so he knew by the feel of the forest, the air, the very stones that made the basin behind the falls, that Elder was pleased. The two began a strange conversation.

Kerian didn't know for sure, but she imagined that Elder was a shaman of some sort, a sorceress who practiced the kind of earth magic the Qualinesti and their aristocratic kin the Silvanesti had long ago forgotten. In a world from which magic had vanished, where even talismans of legend sputtered into unreliability, Elder kept hold of something made of the ancient whispers of the land itself. Her conversations with Elder were never easy, sometimes as wrenching as tumbling into a maelstrom, for she spoke with a woman who smelled of magic in a world from which magic leaked like heart's blood from a wound. Yet painful as these conversations could be, confusing, often as terrifying as the very first one which had left her on her knees and vomiting, Kerian never came away from Elder without feeling that she could—here and far away—create a force of men and women who would stand against the Knights and for the elves, who might, one day, be useful to an embattled king.

They settled into winter, the rounds of hunting and trapping, of preparing food and seeing to weapons. Kerian forbade raids on hapless travelers and on Knights.

"Leave them alone, for now," she said. "Let the winter settle in peace. The Knights will know we're here when I'm ready."

Now and then, because he was not known to Knights here or to villagers, she sent Bayel to learn the news. He visited taverns, the forges at the river crossings where folk came and talked, he went among farmers as they used to do in the dales, a hunter come with bounty for the table in exchange for local gossip and a night by the fire. In this way Kerian learned that Headsman Chance still quartered his Knights in the taverns, that he had not forgotten the outlaw maid Kerianseray, and that he continued to hunt Kagonesti, who were seen less frequently now in the this part of the kingdom.

Kerian learned only one stubborn tribe remained, far away in the high forest, and Briar told her this was Dar and his White Osprey.

She learned, too, that the king was well in his palace. The mention of his name woke a longing to see him, to feel his arms around her again. Those longings she kept to herself and changed into dreams. She learned that the Queen Mother remained in health, and that the lords and ladies of the Senate were no different from seasons past. Surprisingly little had changed in Qualinesti politics. The highborn elves played a game of small losses, counting each day they hadn't lost all as a gain. It was not a difficult game right now, for Sir Eamutt Thagol had been keeping himself and his Knights and draconians in the eastern part of the kingdom where the snow fell thickly and few traveled on the roads or even gathered at taverns. In the cold season after his humiliation, there was scant news of the Skull Knight.

Kerian dropped the fat brace of hares to the ground, careful to keep it well away from the bloody snow and the four dead elves. She slipped her longbow over her shoulder as she bent to crouch over the largest of the scattered corpses, the armor-clad man from whose throat sprang six

arrows. Her breath hung on the icy air, gray plumes drifting over the carnage, weaving around the shafts of the
white-fletched arrows. Winter arrows of the Wilder Kin.

"Kagonesti must have got the Knight," Jeratt said. She
didn't look up or acknowledge the obvious, and he added,
"The Wilder Kin didn't get the others."

The others, three elves dressed in the leathers and furs
of hunters, had been sword-hacked. These were folk who
lived in winter on their wits, not villagers, not farmers, but
elves who supplied taverns and the tables of the wealthy.
Luckless, this time. One had bled out his life from a throbbing artery severed when his left leg had been hacked off.
It hung now from his flesh, a dark fat thread pulled to
unravel a life. All around him the snow carried a frozen
overlay of bright red blood. Another of the hunters had
died of a slit throat. The third had been trampled by steel-
shod hoofs, his neck broken, his skull shattered.

The Knight who had killed them . . . Kerian's lips
curled in a wolfish smile. He'd been made to pay the
blood-fee.

"Y'got a bad look on you, Kerianseray."

Kerian pointed to the frozen spread of blood. "Knights
are killing elves all over the hills, Jeratt. Qualinesti and
Kagonesti. How sweet should my expression be?"

Jeratt said nothing to that. He picked up her bow and
handed it to her.

She looked at him long, and whispering in the silence
between them were the ghosts of conversations past, arguments about politics, about the occupation, about knightly
abuses like that before them, and worse. The dragon's tribute,
thinly disguised as taxation, was bleeding a rich kingdom
like sickness. Over the winter, the cold nights and ice-
gleaming days, they all had talked of ancient hopes, the history of the elf kings right back to Silvanos himself who
united all elves in Silvanesti. They spoke of ancient glory

and ancient wars. They were elves and though they had lived outside the law, some for decades, they knew their history.

Their hearts and imaginations were enchanted by ancient tales. One thing remained unknown. Would all the outlaws fight the dark Knights when she asked them to? Would they lift their swords for a king they despised? Or had they come to be so comfortable in outlawry that in the end they cared for nothing but their own survival?

Count on them, Jeratt had told her each time she wondered.

Kerian snatched up the brace of fat hares. "Come on, Jeratt. You want to give these to the widow, or shall I go do it alone?"

Kerian started away down the hill, Jeratt following quickly. The crisp wind in their faces made breath stream out in wisps behind them. It scoured their faces until their cheeks shone red. At their feet it blew the snow into little dancing white devils. They went strongly, swiftly, each knowing the way over snow-covered ground. They knew the markers that had nothing to do with slender trails, a particular bend of a tree, a boulder where—if there were ground to see—the path would have split. At this boulder they went west and ran beneath the snow-laden boughs of pine trees until it seemed they went through a tunnel, so low did the trees hang with their burden. At the edge of it, in the place where the over-arching trees fell away, they stopped and stood to gaze down into the dale, where a sprawling stone house sat. It had once been the home of a prosperous farmer and his family. The farmer now was dead. He and his son had been killed in a hunting accident years before, leaving only Felyce, a widow who would not give up her homestead.

"Well, y'know," Jeratt had said, once in early winter when Kerian had asked how it was that Jeratt, such a strong hunter, came often back to camp with far fewer kills than might be expected, "I knew the son, and I knew the father. I'm not going to see the widow Felyce go starving."

Smoke rose up from the chimney closest to the front of the house. Chickens minced though the mud in the door-yard, dipping low to find the leftover corn from the morning's feeding. The outbuildings, a stone byre and a wooden hayrick, squatted at the edge of the clearing to the north of the house. Nothing moved near them, and no one seemed to be within.

Kerian looked for other signs of presence and saw none. She listened for the cow that must surely be in the byre by now, for Felyce did not like to go late abroad after her milker in this season when the night fell swift and sudden. Of the cow, they heard nothing. Jeratt came close, his breath warm on Kerian's cheek.

"Too quiet down there."

It was. The muscles between her shoulders tightened. Kerian dropped one shoulder, let her strung bow fall to hand. Jeratt's long knife hissed free of its sheath and whispered home again, tested. In his own hand, with the swiftness of long-gone magic, his own bow sprang.

The wind shifted, turning a little and coming to them from the forest behind. The tang of pine hung on that breeze, and the sudden musk of a deer. Kerian lifted her head, thinking she caught the thick odor of horse. The wind dropped then stilled. She smelled nothing. The sky darkened with a noisy wing of crows, and below a light sprang in the window beside the front door.

"All right," Jeratt said on an outgoing breath.

Kerian heard, *She's all right,* but hid her smile as she hung back. Jeratt loped ahead. Long-legged strides took him swiftly down the hill. Half-elven, his human parentage aged him well before an elf who bore the same years. In the last light his silvering beard shone, and his eagerness lent youthfulness to a face weathered by the forest and the seasons. Kerian followed, keeping a closer eye on their surroundings. She sniffed the wind, caught the scent of deer again but no whiff of the stable.

Neither did she catch the scent of cooking, of soup, stew, or roast that any farmwife would have simmering on the hob or sizzling over the fire at this darkening hour.

Kerian stopped, still and listening. The crows had long flown over; the sky hung empty of all by dying light. Again, she noted no sound of Felyce's milk cow, no comfortable lowing.

"Jeratt," she called, but low.

He heard and stopped to turn. Stopping, he saw her eyes widen in surprise as Felyce came out of her door. Even from this distance, Kerian noted the woman's pallor, the way her hands moved in restless wringing. Jeratt moved toward her, and Kerian leaped to hold him back.

"Wait," she whispered. "Something's wrong."

He moved again, spurred. She gripped hard. "Wait."

Jeratt quivered under her hand. Feigning a casualness she did not feel, Kerian called, "Good evening, Felyce!" Deliberately casting the lie, she said, "I know we're unexpected company. I hope we aren't intruding. We've been hunting and came by on the way home to share our take."

"Aye, who'd thought to see you, Mistress Gellis," Felyce said, improvising a name even as she yet wrung her hands. "I thought you'd gone to kin out by the sea long before now."

"The winter caught us," Kerian said, following Felyce's lead. "I'm here for the season, like it or not. Come spring though"—she elbowed Jeratt "—come spring I'm poking up my old father here, and we're bound for Lauranost and the sea."

Jeratt's eyes widened to hear himself described as Kerian's "old father," but he managed to keep still. He held out the brace of hares, and Felyce came close.

"Go," she whispered, white-faced, her eyes bright and glittering with fear. "There's a Knight inside. More are coming."

A dark shape crossed before the window. Kerian's blood ran quicker as Jeratt said, "Are you all right, Felyce?"

"Yes." She pushed a strand of hair from her cheek. "I'm all right. He's offered no harm, and he seems content to wait peaceably for his brother Knights."

"Why are they here?"

Felyce shook her head. "I don't know. He says little. I think they are scouts, Kerian, but the why of it doesn't matter. They hunt Kagonesti, these Knights, but they haven't forgotten what brought them here last year, the hunt for you."

Again, the whiff of the stable. Kerian slapped Jeratt's shoulder. "Let's go."

He hung on his heel, reluctant to leave.

"Go," Felyce said, and now she spoke only to the half-elf, her pale cheek tinged with a flush of rose. "For the game, my thanks. Go!"

They did, before Felyce's unwanted guest could come again to the window, curiosity growing, but they did not go far. Up the hill and around into the forest they found a place of concealment from which to watch. Neither spoke. Neither had to. They found a shelf of stone high above Felyce's little dell, above the low, running breeze, and wedged themselves into the stony shelter.

Night fell. Three of Lord Thagol's Knights came riding down the hill, following the same track Kerian and Jeratt had lately taken. They went in silence, no sound but the snorting of their horses, the clatter of hoofs on stone. The look of them, horses and men, spoke of a long ride. One pointed to the lights in the dell and rode swiftly down the hill to Felyce's stone house. The others spurred to follow.

Kerian watched them, narrow-eyed and thinking.

When they'd reached the dooryard, she leaned close to Jeratt and said, "They'll be there all night. I don't think they'll hurt Felyce. "

Jeratt growled and snatched up his bow. Kerian stopped him. "No. If we go in, they'll kill her right now. You can count on it. Go back to the camp."

There were, in all, but a dozen and a half outlaws there at this time, eighteen in all not counting Elder.

"Get me ten fighters and come back here." Her eyes on the Knights, on the stone house below, Kerian said, "Nothing will happen to Felyce while you're gone, and we have the bastards trapped."

Jeratt grinned. He took up his bow and with no word slipped away into the night. He was not long gone.

Kerian followed the flight of an owl drifting on the night, wings wide, silently sailing. Concealed from sight of anyone below, she listened to the sigh of wind in the trees. In the dell, every window of Felyce's house shone with light, orange glowing like eyes looking outward. Now and then a restless Knight would pass before one or another, upstairs or down.

"Like they've commandeered the place," Jeratt growled.

Kerian snorted. "They won't hurt her as long as they need her to cook and fetch for them."

They had three times seen Felyce walk out to the stream behind the house and return with laden buckets. By the light from her windows, they'd watched her lay the table in her front room and pile platters high with food.

"My hares," Jeratt muttered sourly

"Don't worry," Kerian said, gaze roaming the darkness. Somewhere in the forest, ranged round the lip of the dell, elf outlaws waited in utter silence. Their breaths did not make as soft a sigh as the wind. Kerian had asked for ten. Jeratt had found eight volunteers and challenged two vacillators into joining. Her plan was simple and quickly explained. Her order, only one: Not one of Lord Thagol's men would come out of the forest alive.

"They'll leave at gray morning," Jeratt said, not watching the forest but the dell. "They'll probably take the south-going road, back toward the Qualinost Road and whatever tavern the Headsman is squatting in now."

"Bayel says he's at The Green Lea."

Jeratt and Kerian sat in silence while stars wheeled across the sky, while the lonely silver moon set and the darkest hour came then died before the pale breath of dawnlight. He was first to see the stirring of dark forms in the widow Felyce's dooryard, the first to hear the impatient snort of a horse.

"Ready now," Jeratt said, soft.

Kerian fingered the golden chain round her neck, the slender necklace Gilthas had given her on the night she'd left him. Ander had returned the token, and now the ring was whole again, two hands clasped.

"Ready soon," she whispered, her lips close to Jeratt's ear. She scanned the rim of the dell and saw nothing moving. She had been with these outlawed men and women on hunts; she knew how still they could keep and for how long.

"Jeratt," she said, "one band should watch the north road, one the south. You take the north. There is only one signal: the movement of Knights. You know what to do."

They parted, slipping away until they occupied opposing sides of the high ground above the dell, each with a clear sight of the farm and the dooryard. Kerian had charge of a band of six. Even as she completed her orders, Ander came close and said, "They're leaving the farmhouse, Kerian."

She looked where he pointed and saw motion in the dooryard. The four humans wore faint outlines of light. Her elf eyes saw not only the flesh and bone shape of them, but the heat of their blood running, their life-force glimmering. They stood like red ghosts in the dooryard, and among them stood Felyce.

"She's all right," Ander said with a relieved breath.

Kerian stilled him with a gesture. Behind the sounds of the dawn, the first sleepy chirp of birds, a brook talking to itself, the wind rising then falling, she heard the voices of those in the dooryard. One Knight turned from speech with a fellow and nodded curtly to Felyce. Something small spun through the air between them, the first light winking on it. A coin dropped into the dooryard at Felyce's feet. The Knights kicked up their horses and rode out from the farmhouse yard, heading south. To the Green Lea, then, to Headsman Chance.

"Wait," Kerian said to Ander. "Wait, and soon we'll follow."

In the forest others moved, Jeratt and his band of six. They didn't move to join Kerian or pursue the Knights. Seven weaponed elves, outlaws and soldiers of an old, nearly forgotten cause, melted into the darkness of the wood and went by various ways to the Qualinost Road.

Kerian waited until she felt they must be well on their way. She smiled, thinking of a vise, and softly said, "Now Ander. Now we go."

Four Knights rode through the graying forest. One professed himself pleased to see the sun pinking the sky, one smiled to see the shadows fade. Another watched the day prick out glitter on the stream they rode beside. His fellows also watched the water. A dragon's enforcers, the strong arm of a Skull Knight, they went as though they were lords of the forest. One hawked and spat, the phlegm of a night of drinking from the widow's wine cellar. In the pines, a jay shouted. From across the purling stream, another answered. Behind, the water splashed, two Knights turned and saw nothing but morning mist rising on the banks. Two others turned right and left, expecting to see the forest shimmer. The trees remained still. Not even the long, thin needles of the pines stirred in the morning breeze.

A horse snorted. One Knight slipped a hand low, gripping the pommel of the sword at his hip. The gesture sent tension running among them. Other hands touched weapons, seats shifted for balance.

Now they realized they heard no other kind of bird, just a riot of jay voices as they went carefully downstream.

When it came at last, the wasping of an arrow flown, it sounded like thunder in the ear of the man it passed, felt like lightning in the eye of man it struck.

The forest erupted in howling, in war cries and fury.

Kerian ran before them all, one of seven elves pouring down the slopes of the forest.

"The horses!" she cried. "I told you—kill the damn *horses* first!"

Fire-haired Briar leaped to the fallen Knight and snatched up his sword. She gutted the horse of the Knight who turned to strike her. She swung upward and hacked the Knight's leg at the knee, severing it and unleashing the shower of blood that would be his death.

Screaming, two more horses went down. Blood

steamed in the cold air, the thick reek of it hanging. A Knight, caught beneath the bulk of his fallen steed, screamed as his beast writhed in its own agony. The screaming became a bubbling groan. Kerian shouted again, in Elvish, a language none of these Knights understood. Two of her outlaws lifted their voices in ululating cries. When the echo of those cries was gone, so were the elves.

In the eerie silence, now afoot, the two remaining Knights stood back to back, each with swords held high. Their breaths, panting, streamed out gray on the brightening air. One looked north, the other south. One looked west, his fellow east. They saw nothing. They heard nothing but the death struggle of the horses.

Silence fell upon the little glade, thick as a funeral pall.

"Where?" whispered one.

The other shook his head. He saw nothing, no one, only the dead and dying.

In shadows thick as night beneath dark pines, Kerian drew a silent breath. Beside her Ander crouched, an arrow knocked to bow. Kerian felt him quicken with excitement, the muscles of his shoulder close against hers quivering. Wind shifted.

"Wait," she said, the word only a motion of lips.

Ander breathed through his nose, silent.

"Wait," Kerian said again. Behind her, her outlaws had become as stone again.

The two Knights put the distance of a step between each other's back. They consulted in quiet voices. Knights with no foe to fight, no enemy upon whom to take revenge, they turned and left the glade. Their weapons glittered in the new light of day, but neither sword had tasted blood, and this was their disgrace.

Kerian gestured to her fighters, a simple command: Let them go.

This they did, but not happily. Still, they heeded, and they watched the two Knights walk out of the glade, south toward the Qualinost Road. They watched them return, not on their feet but dragged by the heels, corpses come to join their brothers.

"Now," said Kerian, "strip them all of weapons, even of eating knives. Leave nothing behind we can use."

She watched as they did so and forbade the looting of personal possessions. Let the rings stay upon the fingers, the talimans around the necks. Only one thing more did she command, and though most of those who heard her didn't understand, Jeratt did. He took Lea and Briar along to carry out Kerian's strange order. They were all day gone from their fellows but returned to the stony shelter behind Lightning Falls by dawn.

"Did you do it?" Kerian asked.

Jeratt assured her that he had, and she told him to come sit and eat some breakfast.

Upon the doorstep of the Green Lea four empty helms stood, hung on saplings stripped and changed into woodsy mockery of the pikes that desecrated the eastern bridge in Qualinost. Empty-eyed, like the sockets in the skulls of murdered elves, they stared at the tavern door. So well were they posted that these were the first things Chance Headsman saw when he walked out in the morning on his way to the midden.

His fury passed quickly. He ordered his men mounted and armed and followed a trail easy to see to the glade where his four missing men lay. They were not Kagonesti who had killed his Knights, for none of the arrows he found bore white fletching. Each man had been looted of his weapons and mail shirts and boots, and the horse of each had been killed, gutted or throat-slit. Anything of use to the killers was gone from the corpses; what couldn't be used had been systematically destroyed.

A chill crept up Sir Chance Headsman's spine, the kind that warns a man that he is about to fall.

CHAPTER
16

In the next week snow fell often, but no one believed
this was a last assault of winter for the sun shone
brightly and warm between the gray times, and snow
didn't last long on the roads or in the clear places. The
songs of birds changed from winter-weary dirges to
brighter airs. Spring came behind the snow, the changing
scent of the breezes said so, and Kerian began to think of
her brother. She hadn't seen him or heard word of Ayensha or even Bueren Rose since they'd left the outlaw camp
long ago. The time had come to go and speak with Dar, to
let him know that some things had changed in the kingdom and with her. She would ask him to consider a request
of hers, a bold demand made in behalf of a bold plan, but
first, something else had to be done and said.

"Jeratt," she said, sitting back on her heels, "I'm going
to take a small trip."

He sat closer to the fire, so the light sent shadows
curling around him from behind. She couldn't read his
expression, but she knew him now, and well. This was
news to him.

"I must see the king," she said.

He sat silent.

"Tell me what you're thinking, Jeratt."

He shook his head. "No. You tell me if you're coming back."

"I'm coming back."

Simply, he said, "Then you don't need to know what I'm thinking."

Wind soughed around the top of the rocky bowl. Campfires glowed pale in the thin winter sunlight. Elder slept near the hottest, highest one, and when Kerian looked at her an image ran though her mind—no, behind her eyes—of a huge misshapen beast running. Ice crackled up her spine, and her heart lurched as it did before battle. Voices and the rattle of stone distracted her. She wrenched her gaze away from Elder and saw two hunters coming down the stony slope, one with a small roe deer over his shoulder, another with a brace of quail and one of hares on his hip. She looked behind her and saw Briar going to relieve the watch at the entrance to the falls.

Jeratt said drily, "Give the king my regards."

She laughed, but the image of a loping beast still haunted her eyes, and her laughter sounded shaky in her own ears. "I'll see you at the rising of the moon. Here."

Two weeks. He nodded and reached out a hand. She took it in the hard warrior's clasp, and she got up and pulled together a kit for traveling—thick woolen trews, a woolen shirt and fine boots looted from a young Knight. Then she went into the forest. Ear to the ground, nose to the wind, she learned of the whereabouts of her lover before she came within sight of Qualinost. He and a contingent of servants, his lady mother, and a covey of senators had removed to his forest lodge, Wide Spreading, for two weeks of hunting. It was there she found Gilthas, and she did so by slipping past his nominal guard, his servants, his mother and her people, and into his bedchamber by starlight.

Kerian stood in the center of a bright square of starlight, silver shafting down from a high window in the ceiling of the royal bedchamber at Wide Spreading. The waking breath of one who had been deep asleep came softly. When the king's eyes opened and he saw her, he did not start.

"Kerian." Gilthas sat. "I dreamed of you coming here. I dreamed I heard your footsteps."

"You didn't dream, my lord king."

He opened his arms in invitation, Kerian covered the distance between his window and his bed with swift strides.

"Kerian," he said, whispering against the tangled gold of her hair. "Kerian, is it really you?"

"You dreamed," she said, almost laughing. "Now you doubt?"

As though to answer, the king wrapped her up in his arms. He smelled of soap, and clothing taken from scented drawers, and closets hung with sachets of shaved sandalwood. He shone, a king well tended, and held her as though the marks she left upon his faultless bed clothing—soot and grime and sweat stains—were not more than the faintest imprint of a perfumed body.

"Come," Gilthas said shortly, slipping out of bed. His night robe moved in silken grace around his body. "You look hungry, love, and thirsty. I'll find you something—"

Kerian shook her head, a gesture used to still men and women lately grown accustomed to heeding her. The brusque gesture surprised him, and she did not apologize.

"My lord king, I'm feeling suddenly in need of a bath."

He laughed, quietly for the sake of this secret arrival. "All this way for a bath? Well, then, let it be. I will summon Planchet. He will see that you have one and all else you wish. Sit. Here on the bed. It will be brought."

There were kettles of steaming water to warm the marble tub kept in the bathing apartment off the bed-chamber. With starlight glittering in through wide, tall windows, Kerian bathed long, and later she showed her king how much she had missed him. Afterward, by fading starlight, in her lover's arms, she looked carefully at him, his face in repose, and she touched the downy cheek inherited from the mysterious human who had fathered his own father, Tanis Half-Elven. He stirred to her touch, and she hushed him.

"I'm sorry to have waked you."

"I'm not sorry you did," the king said.

He reached for her, but she stopped him, a hand on his chest. "You think I have come home."

The bluntness of her statement startled him. Gilthas nodded.

"I haven't. You said I couldn't, my king. You said if I went away, I could not come home again. I went, and I have been to many places and done . . . many things I never thought I could or would. You were right: I am back now but not home. Let me tell you, love, how it has been with me."

She spoke past his doubts, she told the tale of her outlawry, of the first killing at the Hare and Hound, of the burning of the Waycross. She told of finding her brother and losing him. She did not—and this surprised her—speak of Elder, but she spoke well of the half-elf Jeratt, of his band of outlaws and young Ander whose silence on her behalf had made him one of them. She told the king of the elves of the dales, of Felan and his widowed wife, the child orphaned before it was born. She told him all this and more.

"We are outlaws all, my love, and yet, in truth, we should stop calling ourselves that. We must stop naming ourselves outlaws, for though others say so, we are not. We are more."

Gilthas sat forward, eager to hear what caught his imagination.

"We are some of us outlawed." Her smile twisted wryly. "All the gone gods know that I am, but many of us are Kagonesti, shunned for being who they are. Others are old soldiers, Gil, forgotten warriors of Silvanesti and of your own kingdom, who once served your Uncle Porthios."

Outside his chamber, Planchet spoke with a servant, and they heard footfalls come near and retreat as though a message had been given and sped.

"My lord king," she said, pride shining in her voice, "we are the ones who through the summer and autumn harried Lord Thagol's force of Knights in the western part of your kingdom, and we have fought not as brigands and outlaws. We have fought as warriors."

Planchet had long ago taken away her worn clothing to be washed and mended, but he had not touched her weapons, her bow and quiver, the dagger and the sword she had taken from a Knight after she'd killed him. She now slipped the blade from its sheath. The steel gleamed in the moonlight, sliver running on the edges.

"This sword, my king, I have brought you. This, and the fealty of my heart and the loyalty of men and women who have not forgotten the days when they were free."

His eyes shone, his poet's soul leaped with fire as he took her meaning. Outside the window, the sky grayed with the coming day. Gilthas let his glance dwell there for a time, and then, his kindling glance darkened.

"Things aren't going well for us, Kerian."

"The alliance?"

He nodded. "My mother has hung her hope on an alliance with the dwarves for as many years as I've been alive, Kerian. It's become more urgent now. The dragon is building her cache and her war trove. The Senate has been told the tribute in weapons must increase." He twisted a bitter smile. "Of course, the tribute in gold, silver, and gems must not decrease. We hear from friends outside the kingdom that the dragons are growing restless. Once Beryl gets all she needs of us, what will she do? We need a way out. All of us, Qualinesti and Kagonesti."

A way out!

Like the sudden glint of starlight on the sword's blade, Kerian knew her moment, the moment when something bright would be born.

"My king, my love, you need time. There is no way to truly end the dragon's hold on us or Thagol's grip. That isn't the goal anymore, is it? The goal must be to confound and confuse them until Thorbardin can make up its mind.

"I have come with the coin to buy you the time you need. I have come to bring you warriors. They are few now, but the Wilder Kin in the forest have reason to appreciate us. I think this force of warriors I offer can be as many as you desire."

Gilthas looked at her long, his face alight, his hope shining. "Who are you?" he whispered, and she thought she heard a note of superstitious wonder in his voice, as though some mage of old had cast a change-spell upon her.

Kerian took his hands in her own. "Why, I thought you knew. I am the King's Outlaw, my love. I am your weapon, I am your warrior, and I am your lover, my lord king. Never doubt it."

In the golden firelight he looked upon her as though upon something magical, powerful, and his.

There, in his bed, they began to speak of something no one else had ventured to discuss in all the years of the dragon's occupation, through all the depredations of her Knights. While Senator Rashas and his fellows enjoyed the hospitality of the king they professed to honor and yet in truth despised for a weakling, the king and his outlaw began to speak of resistance to all they had until now endured.

The King's Outlaw left Wide Spreading the next day, a freezing day of black and gray. She left with her breath pluming out before her, carried by the following wind. Gilthas had provided food and a pouch ringing with steel coins. A fat quiver of arrows hung at her hip, a fine long bow across her shoulders. In its sheath was the bone-handled knife she'd had from a dour dwarf, the sword she'd taken off a battleground.

Kerian went up into the forest with her hope rising. What she'd said to Gil about the Kagonesti having reason to be grateful to her and her fighters was true. She would try to rally them all, the elusive tribes, and ask if they would join her and make the elf king's cause their own. First, before all, however, she would try her brother, for these were kin.

She knew the way to Eagle Flight's encampment, though her brother had not told or shown her. She knew because Jeratt knew, for he came and went when times allowed, to see his niece Ayensha. He used to say to Kerian, "You know the way, but don't go unless you have to," and by that she knew that her brother would not have welcomed her. Now, this snow-threatening day, she decided she would go, and it wouldn't be up to Dar to decide whether she should come.

When she found him, she found him standing as one who trembled on the edge of the legendary Abyss.

Kerian's nostrils filled with the nauseating stench of burnt flesh and bone. Under an iron sky the earth Iydahar stood upon stretched out to a purling river, a great gaping blackness of ash and burning. He didn't see her, or if he did, he didn't care. He knelt before a pit still steaming from a great burning, grey tendrils ghosting up from the charnel pit and wolves lurking across the river, staring. He didn't care about wolves, for he carried no weapon, not even a knife at his belt. He dipped his hand into the pit, into sooty ash, and he stood.

Iydahar turned slowly. She saw that his hands were dark with soot, as he rose and came toward her. He moved as though stalking. She wasn't sure he recognized her. Kerian's hand drifted to her knife, then fell away. She did not challenge her brother but took a step away to let him know she was no threat.

"Sister," he hissed, "you've come to visit? Too bad, too late. Knights came before you did, with torches and swords. We stood as best we could, but . . ."

They were a dozen Knights with swords and maces. They were a dozen Knights and encased in armor like midnight. Their war-horses were weapons, steel-shod hoofs trampling any who resisted, and then any who got in the way. Old people, little children, they died under the steel shoes as warriors scrambled for arrows that in the end did little damaged to armor-cased Knights.

Dar gestured around the blackened ruin of what had once been the encampment of the small tribe of Wilder Elves, a winter home by the river. Looking at him standing in the ruin, Kerian heard, faint, the echoes of that killing, as though the cries of the slaughtered yet clung to the woodland and the hills beyond.

"There's no one here but me now."

Ayensha! Ah, gods! Bueren Rose!

"No," he said, understanding her frantic glances

around, but the sound was a growling, hardly a word. "They're not there. My wife survived the burning, and Bueren Rose. A few others, too. They are off and away, gone to be with your outlaws."

His hand shot out, grabbing her wrist with grinding strength. She did not pull away or force him to disengage. Dar bent. She watched, fascinated, as he ran his fingers through ash and soot like a painter's brush on a palette. He rose again, making one stroke and then another; he painted her face in patterns of soot.

Finger pressing the flesh of her face roughly, he made a mask of darkness on her, and he said, "Do you remember, Kerianseray? Or have you so far fallen that you've forgotten how the Wilder Folk mourn? Do you remember how to paint your sorrow on your face?"

He blackened her brow. Kerian let him. He smudged her temples. He ran a sooty thumb down her nose, and he smeared her chin with the heel of his hand. His teeth flashing in a terrible grin, he darkened her cheeks, and when he was done, he flung back his head and he raised his fists as though to threaten the sky.

"They are dead!" he shouted, to her, to the forest, to the sky where people used to turn their faces and imagine they could speak with gods. "They are dead! The children! The mothers! The fathers!"

As he turned, she saw that the strength had run out of him with the shouting. Kerian leaped. She caught him before his knees gave way. He bore them both to the ground, but she dropped first to her knees and so was able to lower him gently.

She knew how to mourn. Though she had not practiced the Wilder mourning in many long years, she had not forgotten how to grieve. They wept the grief-storm, brother and sister. They washed away all the colors of sorrow with their tears. One wept for all the people he knew, the other for all the people she would never know.

In the end, with night falling, they began to talk. Iydahar spoke of his rage, while Kerian spoke of her mission. He told her how well and deeply he hated the Knights, how little love he had for her king.

"The boy who sold his throne. For what? A year or two to play at being king?"

Anger rose in her, flushing her cheeks till then cool with sorrow. "No, Dar, don't speak of Gilthas that way. He's—"

His expression grew hard. It was as though a door had suddenly swung shut. "Ah, you, Keri. No one could miss the secret you hold, girl. It's all over you, all the time. So you keep his bed warm, do you? Aye, well," he growled bitterly, "good for the little king, then. If he doesn't get to rule or wield armies, he gets some of the privileges and rights of kings. "

Coldly, she said, "What are you going to call me now, Dar? The king's whore?"

Iydahar regarded her, hard from narrowed eyes. "No one's calling you his wife, are they? No one's looking at you in the streets and naming you his queen. Is he ashamed of his Wilder Elf woman?"

The loud crack of her palm across his face startled them both. He sat gaping. She leaped to her feet, cheeks flaming. The print of her hand showed white where Dar's grief-paint still clung, red on the naked flesh.

Though she had planned to tell her brother about her plans for a resistance, counted on it, Kerian realized she could not. She did not dare ask him to join a rebellion intended to buy time for a king he despised.

"Dar, is there anything I can do here?"

He shook his head. "I'm not staying."

"What about Ayensha?"

His eyes flashed, anger and pain. "She thinks she's found a cause." He sneered the word. "Go look for her with her uncle and your outlaws."

Kerian looked around at the scorched earth, the charnel pit, the wolves padding. Softly, night crept down, the bowl of the sky turned deeply blue and the pale sliver of the new moon showed in the east, high beyond the tops of the trees. Dar rose. He looked at her long, and she felt a hollowness in her heart, feeling his eyes on her, his distant gaze. He was already thinking about his path away from this black and burned place.

"You're going?" she asked.

"Away."

Kerian heard that in silence, then she said, "Don't go south, Dar. There are draconians there. Don't go west, they hold every road, and the Knights are with them."

He didn't thank her for her warning, and she didn't wait to hear more from him. She rose and left him. She did not expect to see him again.

CHAPTER
17

F ool!"
Fists clenching, Kerian looked around at the half
dozen fighters, three of them bleeding, two of those unable
to stand, and two dead. Flies buzzed over the wounds. The
coppery stench of blood hung in the dusty summer air.

One of the dead was Briar, a woman Kerian had first
met in the sheltered basin behind Lightning Falls. Autumn
had come and gone twice since then, and winter and
spring, and now summer grew old around her. Yet it
seemed she had known Briar for a score of years, certainly
for a score of battles. Briar had become notorious among
the Knights for her fierceness. Into every battle the tall elf
woman had worn the mail shirt that might, a long time
ago, have been made for a prince. Even princely mail
couldn't protect her against stupid mistakes.

Kerian looked at the overturned wagon, two wheels
still spinning. Two outlaws dead, three wounded, and one
Knight bleeding away the last of his life. The other Knight
of the two-man escort had abandoned his companion and
the driver of the wagon and fled through the forest to the
Qualinost Road. Already, Elder was sinking into that eerie

trance of hers to call up the confusion of senses. In moments, the Knight would find himself helpless on a road he'd traveled so often.

A thin line of pain etched between Kerian's eyes, as if a thumb were pressing hard on the bridge of her nose. Head up, she listened to her body, tracking the source of the pain until the tightened muscles of her jaws assured her that the headache was nothing more than the result of teeth clenched in anger. It could have had a more dangerous source.

In spring the Skull Knight Thagol had returned from the east of the kingdom, drawn by news of the Night People. Since then Kerian suffered headaches, and since then she understood that some headaches were the result of hunger, weariness, or injury, and others had no natural explanation. The touch of the mind of a Skull Knight caused these.

Thagol sought the leader of the Night People. Down the avenues of the night, he hunted her in dreams. The strange headaches had started after the first successful raid Kerian mounted against one of the border outposts. These were ugly structures of stone and wood built between the forest and the gorges that scored the earth between the elven kingdom and the Stonelands. Five Knights had died in the first raid, and four more perished when they arrived to relieve the watch. The four who died last imagined the three black-armored warriors they saw on duty were their knightly brethren and didn't discover until too late that they were five of the Night People in Knights' clothing. Kerian had ordered the dead stripped of anything useful then left the corpses to rot. This time that tactic, used for gaining weapons and depriving the enemy of steel, did not serve her well.

Soon after, on a dark-moon night, Kerian woke from a dream and sat up shaking, cold sweat running on her.

Shivering with her blankets wrapped around her, she looked up at the sky ablaze with stars too bright to long behold. Across the stony basin, in the night where embers of the outlaws' fires breathed faintly, she saw the old woman, Elder, whose voice was like prophecy. As though beckoned, she rose and went to the ancient. She sat down beside her. White hair like starlight, shining, Elder leaned close.

"He hunts," she whispered, her voice low. "He hunts you, Kerian of Qualinesti, on the roads of your dreams. If he catches you, he catches all, even your king."

"How does he do this? Can you help me?"

Elder didn't know, but she could help Kerian and did. She knew a way of magic to prevent her dreaming. She knew how to enchant and what spells would serve to protect.

Protected, Kerian also knew loss. She had met the king twice more since that first time in winter, met him in the forest in spring when he called her to warn that Thagol had returned, again at Wide Spreading in early summer. She didn't dream of him any more, for she carried a bloodstone from Elder, draining her of dreams and shielding her from Thagol's magic. Even so, the Lord Knight didn't give up his hunt, and though he could not stalk by night, he did well by day, catching psychic scent of her when one of his Knights died by her hand. Somehow he tracked her by the deaths of his warriors. Waking, she had no warning of his approach, his stalking, his nearness, only headache.

Flies buzzed on wounds; sun glared from a hard blue sky. Kerian again looked around her at her warriors. She pointed to one, a lanky Kagonesti youth who wore the tattoos proudly on neck and shoulders. The boy was named Patch, for the streak of shining white in his dark hair. It had grown there on the dire night he learned the news that the Eagle Flight tribe had been slaughtered. He was one of the handful to survive that killing.

"Patch," she said, "take Rale and go find and kill that Knight."

His eyes lighted like green fire, and he leaped to do as she bid.

Kerian kicked the wagon; she kicked the dirt. Patch had a lot of hate to lose, and she wondered whether it was right to use that for her own weapon. She didn't wonder long. Not all her weapons were as trusty as Patch, and she felt her anger rising hotter. Kerian glared around the clearing till she found her target sitting in the dust, bleeding.

"Rhyl, you're a *fool.*"

The word rang again, louder, through the forest. On his knees binding the bleeding arm of a wounded companion, Jeratt looked up, then went back to his work.

Rhyl stumbled to his feet, still wiping blood from a seeping head wound, still stunned from a blow he hadn't seen coming, the backstroke of the dead Knight's sword, the blow struck a moment before an arrow took the human through the throat. Rhyl looked around at his friends, living and dead. Wobbly, he put a hand on the wagon to steady himself. The bounty of the wagon lay all over the ground, bales of tanned pelts that would have gone to Qualinost, into the shops of leathermen, there to become boots and jerkins and sheaths for swords. Tribute to the dragon.

"Who are you calling a fool?" Rhyl snarled, wiping blood from his face. "One Knight's dead, and the other will be soon."

Kerian grabbed a fistful of the elf's shirt and jerked him closer until they were nearly nose to nose. "I told you we weren't hitting anything on this road until the supply wagons came down." She jerked her head at the little wagon. "That look to you like four wagons full of weapons, Rhyl?"

Rhyl spat in the dirt at her feet.

The others, wounded and hale, looked away, exhausted. Jeratt said nothing.

Kerian drew a purposeful breath. The wagon wheels creaked. In the sky the wind rose and sighed through the trees. Beside the broken wagon, the Knight groaned out the last of his blood. One of the wounded outlaws helped another to his feet. There would be ravens soon.

She said, "Getting hard for you, Rhyl, is it?"

He eyed her suspiciously.

"Hard not to just run down the hill and do a bit of thieving like in the good old days?"

He growled a yea or a nay or a leave-me-alone, and spat again.

The hand that had grabbed his shirt now moved to rest on his shoulder as though in friendly fashion.

"You agreed to be part of this, Rhyl. From the first night we talked about this, from the first moment you lifted a bow to kill a Knight, you agreed to take orders from me. You didn't do that today. You broke out on your own, hit this little wagon too soon, and now there's two of our comrades dead and if Patch doesn't kill that Knight there's going to be word in Qualinost about this. Maybe there will be anyway."

Rhyl shrugged and twisted a lip to show he was not intimidated, but he backed a step away when Kerian narrowed her eyes.

"Rhyl," she said, her voice like winter's ice. "I have to be able to count on you."

He snorted. "All this for your king," he said, sullenly. "We burn a few bridges, we plague a few Knights, we lurk around the taverns to pick up crumbs of news."

Before Kerian could reply, Jeratt's laughter rang harsh as a crow's. "Not hardly, Rhyl. You have a fat little coffer hidden in the passage through the falls, all yours and shining with booty. Didn't used to be more than a skinny crate with nothing but a few brass coins and mold growing in it."

The first ravens sailed the sky, circling the clearing. Kerian gripped Rhyl's shoulder and turned him round to see the wounded and the dead.

"Now I have to know—can I count on you?"

She glanced at Jeratt. The half-elf shook his head.

Above, ravens shouted, the mass of them darkening the sky. Kerian looked up to see a half dozen of them peel away from the rest. They sailed over the forest, westward above the Qualinost Road. A triumphant cry rang through the forest, high and eerie. The hair rose up on the back of Kerian's arms. Patch had found his kill, and he would be lopping the head from the Knight's neck even now, using the dead man's sword to do that.

"Jeratt," she said, not looking at Rhyl again. "Get things cleaned up here. Don't make a big job of it. Leave the Knight's corpse, and drag the wagon into the forest. Thagol's going to hear about this, so he might as well see some of our handiwork. Just haul the worst of it off the road so farmers can get by."

He cocked his head. "And you?"

"Well, I have to go talk to Bueren Rose, don't I?" Her voice had the edge of a blade. "There's word needs to be spread now."

He said nothing, frustrated as she. Neither did he look at Rhyl as he bent to the work of clearing the road. He nodded, and she did, understanding between them.

Kerian turned to leave and in the turning felt the return of the ache behind her eyes, the pressure against her temples, as though someone pressed that tender place with thumbs. She closed her eyes, at the same time holding her bloodstone amulet in her hand. The pain began to recede, but it did not vanish. When she opened her eyes again, it was to see Jeratt's keen glance, his hand reaching to steady her.

"I'm all right," she said.

He looked doubtful, his brows raised.

"See to this mess." She looked around. "And see to Rhyl."

Jeratt scratched his beard.

"He's out. Meet me when it's done."

———◆———

Gilthas stood in the doorway between his private library and his bedchamber. In the hour before bed, the hour of his poetry, this time when pen drank from the inkwell and his heart brooded on loss, he stood with a stack of tightly rolled scrolls in his right arm. He'd heard a sound, the soft scuff of a footfall, perhaps a whisper from beyond the far wall of the library.

Holding his breath, Gilthas let the scrolls slide out of his arm silently onto the brocaded seat of a delicately carved cherrywood chair. Moonlight spilled through the window in the bedroom behind, washing over the bed. The empty bed, he always named it, for no moon had seen Kerian there in many months.

The empty bed. Not so empty, after all. Nightmare joined him there, often now. Dark dreams that Kerian would know how to banish with a touch of her hand, brooding fears that she was able to soothe, these came to him now more nights than not. He used to dream of fire and death, of the breaking of his ancient kingdom. He used to dream that all he knew and loved would fall to a terror he had no name for, something born in the Abyss of a goddess long gone from the world. These nights only one dream haunted him, cold and fanged. These nights he dreamed he saw a head being freshly piked upon the parapet of the eastern bridge of his city. Honey hair thick with blood, mouth agape, eyes staring, Kerian's death scream followed him down all the roads of Qualinost.

There! Again, a sound from the secret passage few knew about but he and Laurana. Gil's heart rose with sudden hope. Only one other than they two knew of the narrow warren behind the walls of the king's residence. It must be Kerian. He listened closely. He heard nothing now. Outside his suite of chambers, servants murmured in the halls, someone dropped an object of crystal or glass. The shattering of it rang out and did not cover a dismayed cry. The king hardly wondered what had fallen, what had broken.

Behind the wall, he heard another footfall.

Kerian! Had he conjured her? With moonlight and memory and inked lines of longing, had he magicked her?

Even as he hoped, Gilthas knew there was no hope. Kerian was nowhere near the city. He had followed the tales of her, trying to reckon the gold from the dross, the truth from the fables. Easier, far, to reckon out her doings by noting where last Lord Thagol put up a newly fortified guard post.

Nor would she come to him without prior arrangement unless—no. Not even if she were in trouble, especially not then.

Gil's fingers closed round the silver handle of the knife he used to shave the points of the quills that were his pens. Even as he felt the slight weight of the little blade he thought wryly, against what little sprite or rabbit will this defend?

Soft, a tap. Louder, two more. Soft, a third and a quick fourth.

Gil relaxed, letting go a breath he hadn't known he'd been holding. What was his mother doing behind the wall?

She stood in a spill of torchlight, the Queen Mother like

a ghost with her golden hair down around her shoulders, a silvery silk robe loosely belted over a flowing blue bed gown.

"Mother," he said, "you're barefoot—"

The elf behind her, of middle years with the eyes of an ancient, stood bleeding from a poorly bandaged wound. He wavered, exhausted, and tried to bow. Gilthas caught him before he toppled, and the king and the Queen Mother helped him into the library.

No one cared that he bled on the brocaded chair, no one cared that his muddy boots left tracks on the tapestried carpet.

"Sir," he said, "I have come with word from the High King of the Eight Clans of Thorbardin." He gathered himself, wit and strength. "Your Majesty, the dwarf king thinks it best you come soon to defend your suit for alliance or send a champion to do that."

———◆———

Smoke rose lazily from Three Chimneys, a roughly built tavern that had, over the course of a long life, been first a roadhouse of doubtful repute, then a post house in the years before the coming of green Beryl. Through all its years, Three Chimneys had been a wayfare, a tavern for travelers to stop and find a good meal, perhaps a bed for the night in the common room or the barn. It was that now, and something more. Bueren Rose ran the place, purchased for a small pouch of steel from an elf who had been happy to sell, eager to leave the area.

"What with the outlaws and Knights and all, I'm going north, where they're saner and I have kin."

Kerian stood on the road, watching smoke rise from the stone chimneys that gave the place its name. The smoke hardly disturbed the purpling sunset sky. The tavern lay in a fold of an upland valley, one high above Lightning Falls and farther east. From the hills surrounding, one could see right out into the borderland between the kingdom of the elves and the land of the dwarves.

Bueren Rose walked round the corner of the tavern, a heavy yoke of filled water buckets across her shoulders. Three Chimneys had in its upper story a small, windowless room, a private place between two other chambers, from the outside undetectable. It was this secret room, much like the private passages in Gil's royal residence, that recommended the tavern to Kerian when she and Bueren Rose had gone looking for a place.

The upper room was a place where plans could be safely hatched. "Three Chimneys is not at a crossroad," Bueren Rose had said. "That would have been too likely and too dangerous, but it is near the borderland, and taverners know that the best news there is flows back and forth across borders with traders and thieves."

So Bueren Rose had taken possession of the tavern, purchased with steel robbed from a wagon bound for a dragon's hoard, and she set up business quietly. Her tavern gained a reputation for good food and good cheer, for clean places to sleep and reasonable rates. Her bar was stocked with drink from all parts of Krynn, again thanks to thieves who smuggled a keg of this, a tun of that, a few bottles of something exotic and potent from down around Tarsis.

"Keri!" Bueren stopped suddenly, the yoke rocking, the water sloshing from the buckets.

Kerian leaped to steady the yoke. Water splashed her feet, turned the dust to dark mud around her boots, "Sorry. I didn't mean to startle you."

Bueren shook her head, her rosy gold hair escaping from her kerchief, spiraling around her neck in loose curls. "I didn't expect you today. I thought—" Her expression darkened, and the skin around her eyes grew tight. She

229

looked behind her, around, and when she felt certain of safety, she spoke very low. "Is something wrong? Is the raid—?"

"The raid won't happen."

"But—"

"There's no time now. Send word to Releth Windrace at his farm. Tell him he has to send his own boys out to stop the others."

The two farmers down the valley and their sons and daughters, the miller's own boy, all the dozen others, quiet citizens of a hostage kingdom who could be called upon at need to strike a blow against the dragon of her Knights— word must get to all of these, mouth to mouth, farm to farm, casually and quietly so that no suspicion would fall on any of them.

"We've got to tell them all there will be no meeting at the mill tomorrow night." She clenched a fist, slammed it hard against her thigh. "Fool! That damn Rhyl's a fool. If he'd held his hand, left the wagon with the bales of skins alone . . . Thagol's been tracking me again. He's going to know what happened soon, if he doesn't know now that those Knights are dead.

"Damn it! Those wagons full of weapons are going to have to go by without us so much as being near to curse."

Bueren said nothing. She put down her buckets, hurried back to the wellspring, and called to the potboy, the orphaned son of one of the elf farmers in the valley whose wife had died of sickness in winter, who had followed her in grief in spring. The boy was no part of Kerian's conspiracy. He had no idea that Bueren was. Kerian knew Bueren would do as she always did, send the lad with a simple message to Releth. He would say, "Bueren Rose doesn't think she'll be able to join you for supper tomorrow evening." Releth would understand. Word would go out, whispering down the valley like ghosts.

When Bueren returned, the boy having sped off, Kerian was looking up at the sky. When she looked back at her friend, she had made a choice to speak what she had only lately decided.

"We have to do something about Rhyl, Bueren. He's dangerously stupid."

Behind her eyes, throbbing like the promise of storm on a blue bright day increased. She reached for her amulet, the bloodstone, and the pain settled back to a dull ache.

Bueren unhitched the buckets from the yoke and leaned it against the side of the building. She lifted one bucket.

"Keri," she said, "something has come."

In the act of reaching for a dripping bucket, Kerian stopped to look up. She didn't ask what had come. She didn't ask from whom.

"When?" she said, her voice that of idle curiosity. There were wayfarers in the common room, one coming around the corner of the building to find the privy.

"Last night."

Kerian nodded and picked up the bucket. They entered the kitchen like two old friends, talking and laughing for the sake of any who would observe. All the while Bueren Rose stuffed a leather wallet fat with food and poured a wineskin plump.

"Go," she said at the kitchen door only a short while later. "Take the path along the ridge. Knights have been riding the roads close to here. You'll see them in plenty of time to avoid them. What shall I tell Jeratt?"

Kerian embraced her friend and for her ears only said, "Tell him to go ahead with all that we've planned." She hitched up the wallet, checked the seat of her quiver on the hip, the sword at her side. "If you don't see me soon, listen for word."

231

Beneath the spreading branches of Gilean's Oak, upon a bed of moss and fern, Kerian lay in her lover's arms. Close, his skin warm against hers, his breath mingling with hers, it could be said there was nothing between them, yet there was.

He had asked her to carry out a mission for him, an embassy. She had agreed.

Kerian's breath hitched in her lungs. He stirred beside her, and she closed her eyes.

Gilthas, the Speaker of the Sun, the King of Qualinesti, had asked her something else, with his heart in his eyes, all his longing and determination. He'd asked her to marry him.

"Be my queen," he said, "Kerian, be the queen my people need. Be the wife I need."

Asking, seeing her draw breath to speak, he'd quickly put a finger on her lips, whispered her to wait, wait, and think about it this time.

"I have been too long without you, Kerianseray of Qualinesti. I've been too long with you gone from me, and I see it—" In her eyes he saw it, in her hands touching him he felt it, in her voice he heard it—"you have been too long without me."

Kerian lay half-waking, not really asleep, and so she saw a sudden darkness as an owl glided overhead, interrupting the moonlight.

Gil's finger stroked her cheek. He leaned to kiss her, and she lifted her face, hardly aware that she did. How long it had been since they'd lain like this!

"Gil," she said, looking up to the moonlight sifting through the leaves. "I have been having nightmares."

He moved, shifting so that he held her in both arms now. She put her head on his shoulder.

"I've had nightmares, Gil, and they are all about being hunted. An old gray wolf runs in them, and I know it is Thagol. He is trying to track me by the killing I do." She shuddered, and he held her closer. "I have an amulet." She reached for it, the talisman that never left her, not even now in this hour when only moonlight and shadow dressed her. "It used to work well. It used to protect me from him. Now—it works a little sometimes, but it's gone the way of all the magic of Krynn. It sputters, like a candle guttering. I can't count on it, and I can't . . ." She leaned up on her arm now, brushing her hair back from her face. He reached up to comb it free of leaves and little twigs.

The breeze of a late summer's night grew chill, slipping low along the ground. Kerian, robed in moonlight, shivered. Gilthas sat up and wrapped his shirt around her. He followed that with his cloak, green edged with gold. He found the rest of his clothing and dressed himself, reminded of cold now. He took back his cloak, slipping her own blouse over her head and tying it at the throat. He gave her the rough trews she'd come to him in, thick wool the color of chestnuts, torn and much mended.

Silence, then the owl's triumphant cry. Kerian hadn't heard the cry of the prey, but she saw it now in the owl's talons, a squirrel in its last twitching struggle.

The king said, "That will be us if this treaty between elves and humans and finally dwarves is not well made: dying, twitching in the talons of the dragon."

She knew it. It had been the reason she'd gone out into the woods to harry the tribute-bearers, the reason she'd killed Knights and seen her friends die. To buy time for this treaty, for dwarven deliberation. Now, it seemed, more must be done.

"Perhaps it will be good if you go away for a while," he said gently. "Let Thagol wonder. Let the nighmares subside. Live to fight another day, and—"

"I will go to Thorbardin for you, my love, but how will we know that Thagol won't follow my trail?"

"There's a way." Gilthas lifted the flap of his saddlebag and scooped out a small pouch. This he opened into her hand, spilling out an emerald pendant. Shaped like a leaf unfurling, it glinted in the moonlight. "Nayla and Haugh traveled on this magic when my mother's need sent them far outside the kingdom. The talismanic magic that protects your sleep, the magic in this relic, isn't so trusty as it used to be, but I'm told that if you keep your mind strongly focused on where it is you need to be, you'll surely get there.

He leaned closed and kissed her gently.

She lifted the pendant and watched the emerald leaf twirl as the golden chain spun straight. "How do I do it?"

Gil took the necklace and slipped it over her head. Again, he combed his fingers gently through her hair, waking the woodland scent clinging to the honey lengths. Oaks and autumn and cold mountain streams, earth and wind and the memories of old campfires, this was her perfume now. With a lover's hand, he smoothed the chain along her neck, settled the emerald upon her breast.

"It's a matter of concentration. Keep your mind focused on where you want to be. It doesn't matter that you've never seen Thorbardin—you know Thorbardin exists. That is the thought you must hold firmly."

The emerald warmed her skin. Kerian observed that it would be a good idea not to suddenly pop in on the high king while he was having his bath.

Gil smiled. He filled his hands with her hair, all the forest-scented locks spilling through his fingers. She went close to him, lifting her face to kiss him. Between them now was only the question she had not answered.

"My love," she said, "you've asked me another thing."

He put a finger on her lips, gently. "Hush," he said, his breath warm on her cheek.

It was in her mind to answer, to tell him no, to refuse the king's offer of marriage. She would be a lightning rod as his queen, a Kagonesti woman to sit beside him, a servant raised up, a lover led from his bed to his throne. Rashas would run wild with the notion, would discredit Gilthas in the first week of his marriage and use the indignation of the kingdom to wrench him from his throne

No, she meant to say. No, Gil. I can't, you know it wouldn't be the right thing.

She said nothing like that. She lifted the emerald from her breast and held it in her hands. She felt the gem tingling against her fingers, warming the flesh.

"Concentrate?"

His voice gentle, the king said, "Concentrate. Keep it firmly in your mind where you want to go."

Kerian took a breath, and the emerald throbbed against her fingers. She gripped it, its energy stung, and she loosed it again. Cradling it now, as though it might fly away or bite, she closed her eyes, trying to clear her mind of all thoughts. She slipped into her senses, smelling all the forest, the oaks, the stream rilling beyond the grove, the sweetness of the rich earth, and the ferns cut from the brakes that had made their woodland bed soft. She heard the whistle of a thrush, the whisper of wind, and on her skin she felt the sunlight. She thought of Thorbardin, the fabled city she had never seen. She thought of the legends she knew of the place, the tales she knew of Tarn Bellowgranite himself, the High King of the Eight Clans.

Around her, the world grew suddenly sharp, all her senses keen-edged. In the moment she realized it, she felt the oak grove fading, dissolving underfoot, around her.

"Thorbardin," Gil said, his voice level, firm. "Thorbardin, Kerian."

NANCY VARIAN BERBERICK

The word rang in her thoughts, chiming like a deep-throated bell.

She cried, "Gil!" as the whirlwind came roaring out from the forest, up from the ground, down from the sky. "Gil!"

Whatever he shouted, whatever word or cry, became lost, torn apart by the whirlwind, changed into a terrible roaring, a bellowing so deep, so loud it was as a storm with no beginning, no end.

From that storm came a voice, one lone voice speaking with unreasonable calmness about curses.

CHAPTER
18

"Ah, now y'know there's all kinds of curses," said the dwarf. "Man's a fool who doesn't reckon that."

Kerian fell out of the whirlwind to find herself on her knees, the echo of magic's bellowing still in her ears, her body feeling as though it had been hurled right across the Kharolis Mountains.

Kerian didn't see the speaker, down on the floor of what she knew to be a tavern by the smells of ale, dwarf spirits, and roasting meat, of sweat, smoke, and fire. She was, though, relieved to realize that the dwarf was using his native tongue, the rough-hewn language of Thorbardin.

All right, she thought, that's a good sign.

She tried to stand and failed.

The dwarf who spoke of curses continued to speak. His fellows continued to listen, eight or more dwarfs bellied up to the bar. Other than those drinkers, the tavern was empty. It had the feel of a place just opened, the regulars perhaps having been waiting at the door, the rest of the night's custom coming later.

"There's big curses and minor ones," said the dwarven

expert, "the curse of your mother-in-law and the curse of an unchancy god."

"No telling which of those is worse," said an old dwarf at the end of the bar. His fellows laughed, and one said he reckoned *he* knew.

Kerian's belly felt loose and dangerous, as though she might heave up the last fine meal she'd eaten, the pastries, wines, and thinly sliced fruit, the braised duck, the . . . She dared not think on that now. She tried to breathe slowly through her mouth and tasted the tang of metal, steel and slag. The odor of sweat drying on skin and wool stung her nose. Quietly, she groaned and wished she hadn't, yet no one seemed to notice her there on the floor.

Where in the name of all lost gods am I? She glanced right, she glanced left, and out of the corner of her eye she saw a doorway into a brighter place where people— dwarves—walked by, some alone, others in pairs or groups. Their voices washed in through the door and washed out again as they passed by.

"Eh, there's all kinds of curses," the dwarf said, now with the air of one who had just done with his subject.

Kerian tried to stand again and failed again. Ah, gods, her head hurt!

The dwarf's listeners at the bar variously laughed, grumbled, or questioned, and one youngster opined that he supposed this was how the tavern got its name. "Because it's cursed."

"Nay," said another, his voice tight with impatience. Kerian winced at the thud of something hitting wood, like a filled pitcher being set down heavily. "The tavern isn't cursed. Can y'not read, lad? Or did they shoo you right off to shovel coal for the forges thinking you didn't have the wit and a half needed for the skill and wouldn't want it there anyway?"

The youngster closed his mouth, and Kerian drew a

surprised breath. She knew the voice! She knew the speaker. She put one hand to the rush-covered floor and pushed herself to her feet, head still throbbing. A dwarf at the bar turned. He was not a handsome fellow. Illness had pocked the skin of his face, and his beard hung thinly from a slight chin and jaw. His eyes, set in pouches of flesh, went wide at the sight of an elf in the bar.

"By Reorx's beard," he said, "what's an elf doing here?"

Nine dwarves turned from the bar. The youngster who'd mistaken the name of the tavern closed his fingers round the grip of the knife at his belt. "Ain't no one lettin' elves or anyone else in at the gates that I know about."

Muttering ran around the bar.

Very carefully, Kerian said, "I'm looking for Stanach Hammerfell."

No one seemed appeased; no one liked the idea of a sudden elf. One dwarf then another stood, and the youngster said, "Someone call the watch. No one knows how she got in here." An inch of gleaming steel showed in the sheath at his belt, then a swiftness of blade.

Before Kerian could draw her own knife, a hard hand flashed out, a dwarf lurched over the bar and jerked the youngster so hard by the back of his shirt that he pulled him nearly off his feet.

"Idiot," Stanach said. His blue-flecked black eyes glinted dangerously. "Do you know I saw that girl kill a Dark Knight with that selfsame little knife of hers?"

The young dwarf's face lost some color.

"Nay, y'could not know that, I suppose, but this you do know, idiot Kern: Y'don't try to kill the customers in my bar, boy. It's a house rule I get tired of explaining to you." Growling, he roughed the boy, shaking him hard and shoving him away.

The curious stared at Kerian. They glanced at Stanach from the corners of their eyes, waiting to see what he'd do.

Most of them, though, were clearly waiting for the tale of the Dark Knight's death, for they did love tales, dwarves.

Stanach, however, was pleased to say nothing. He leaned his forearms on the bar, prepared to serve her silence until she spoke.

Kerian cocked her head. "You don't seem pleased to see me, sir."

Sir. The word murmured round the room. Sir, indeed!

"I wasn't expecting you, missy."

"What, then, Stanach? Are unexpected visits another prohibition in this bar of yours?"

Sly smiles replaced murmuring. Head throbbing, Kerian wavered again, and a strong hand slipped under her elbow. The gesture seemed to thaw Stanach who waved her to the bar and pointed to a stool.

"Sit. Y'look a bit wan."

She nodded and accepted a tall mug of water. The others crowded close, and even Kern sidled up to see what could be seen. Stanach waved them off and would hear none of their grumbling.

"Go shout into the kitchen," he said to Kern. "Tell whoever's cooking in there to bring out food. Y've all done enough drinking on empty bellies for now. I'm not going to be hearing from the guard about the rowdies coming out of here again tonight."

Kern did as he was bid, and when the hangers on at the bar migrated to tables in anticipation of food, Kerian found herself suddenly alone with the dwarf who had, a long time ago, given her a weapon and put her foot on an unexpected path. The last time she had seen Stanach Hammerfell, he'd been in company with two elves of the Queen Mother's household. This dwarf, this Stanach Hammerfell who drank with elves in Laurana's service, once claimed to be a trader and now seemed to be a barman—what was he? On the face of it, since she'd last seen him in company with

Laurana's own people, she would imagine him a friend.

Kerian dared not take that for granted.

"I didn't think I'd ever see you again," Stanach said. He took up a rag and wiped rings and spills from the polished wood of the bar, glossy golden oak. For this, his right hand had a use. The crooked fingers grasped a bar rag well enough.

"Never thought I'd see you again either," Kerian said. She took a drink of water, her stomach settling, her head still aching. "I thought you were a trader. Have you found a new line of work now, Stanach? Keeper of a cursed bar?"

His mouth moved in a smile almost bitter. "I'm a man of many parts, girl." He looked round the bar, at the patrons obviously his friends, at the rough paneled walls, the rushes thickly strewn on the floor. Spitoons gleamed, the brass polished brightly; on the walls torches flared in bronze cressets. "It's a common misconception that the bar is cursed. It isn't. The name of it is Stanach's Curse. Different thing."

"A different thing," she said, agreeing. "The bar's not cursed, you are."

"Well, we're not going to be all night talking about it." His eyes grew hard, and when he leaned across the bar the hair rose prickling on the back of Kerian's neck. "Now, tell me, missy, what are y'doing here?"

"Well, I—"

He lifted a finger, as though to a child. "Don't be shaping lies now. We like order here in Thorbardin, and there is a guard comes by here regularly. It wouldn't take but a shout to call them down." Again the smile but this time very cold. "Everyone in this place had his back to the door a little bit ago. Everyone but me. I saw you come in."

Her head pounded, and her hands shook. She wondered if she had failed in her mission not an hour into it. Kerian reached for the mug of water, but the dwarf's left hand closed over hers before she could lift it.

"Nay," he said, "you'll just spill it. Take a good breath, Mistress Kerianseray. Tell me your story." When she hesitated he said, "Or tell it to the guard on the way to the dungeons. I don't think you'll like the dungeons of Thorbardin. We tend to forget about the people down there, and when we do remember, it's not always in time."

Kerian gauged the threat, and she gauged the dwarf. She reckoned back along the months and seasons, back along events to the time she first saw him. She believed she knew who he was, this trader, this barman, and she slipped the emerald talisman from her shirt, the unfurling leaf he might well have seen Nayla or Haugh wear.

He had. She saw that in the sudden glint of his eyes, the way his head lifted.

"Tell me now, what are you doing here?"

Kerian's voice dropped low, soft for only the two of them to hear. "My king has sent me."

Stanach raised an eyebrow, then lifted the water jug in silent question. This, or better? When she nodded to her mug, he filled it again.

"I'm here to see your king." She slid him a sideways glance. "I'm hoping his ambassador will help me to an audience."

"I'm not his ambassador, girl." He shook his head. "I'm not anyone's anything. I did my thane a favor, that one who sits on the Council. I was in the Outland, a long time ago when your king's mother commanded dragonarmies." His eyes softened with remembered pain, the fingers of his ruined hand twitched on the bar rag. "Ah, a while ago. I know the ways of Outlanders, some. The thane, he said our king needed a man like that to go out to Qualinost to speak with the elves. No more than that, and I'm glad to be done with it." He wiped the bar, pushing the rag around with his useless hand. Softly he said, "It's no good thing to be gone from here. It's no good thing to leave."

The tavern rang with the clattering of plates and cutlery, the voices of hungry dwarves, those who'd been at the bar, new customers coming in. Kerian leaned across the bar.

"Will you take me to the king, to Tarn Bellowgranite?"

"D'ye think I can just go knocking on his door, girl? Do you think—"

"I think you are a man who can do pretty much whatever needs doing. Can you do this, Stanach Hammerfell?"

After a moment more of bar wiping, the dwarf said he supposed he could.

———————◆◆◆———————

Kerian waited, uncertain whether to go into the council chamber or to wait for an escort. Stanach was gone, slipped away through the gardens outside the great shining brass doors to the chamber. Those doors stood ajar now, not swung wide but not tight shut. From within came the rumble of deep dwarven voices. They sounded like distant thunder, a storm roaming a far mountaintop. Then, sharply, one rose in striking challenge. The thanes of the clans didn't seem minded to let their deliberations end easily. From her stance outside the door, she saw only a great cavernous hall beyond and had a sense of high ceilings and wide walls. Lights gleamed redly, in silver cressets torches flared, and tripod braziers stood at regular intervals. By their reaching light, Kerian saw thick marble columns marching upon each side of the hall, creating a broad aisle of bright marble leading to a dais.

Behind her, the city shone, a brightness of light. Thorbardin had sustained great damage during the wrenching civil war, but in this part of the city, high in the magnificent Life Tree of the Hylar, all seemed rebuilt and wondrous. Light poured in from the distant outer world, sliding into the city upon shafts of crystal. The gardens outside the Court of Thanes grew as richly as though they lay in an elven glade, but here, Kerian saw, gardens had only the seasons their gardeners wished them to have, for here light, temperature, and water were strictly under dwarven control. The crocus of winter grew happily beside the red rose of summer, and spring's yellow jonquil nodded at the foot of a tall wisteria.

Kerian found it strangely unsettling, this confusion of seasons. She couldn't imagine how they marked the passing of time beneath the mountain where the moon didn't shine and the sun didn't rise.

As she watched, the people of the vast underground city went forth and back, men, women, and scampering children about the business of their day. One child stopped, tugging at her mother's skirts and pointing.

"Mam!" she cried, brown eyes wide above plump ruddy cheeks. "Look at that, look! An elf at the door!"

The dwarf woman hastily shushed the child. She turned her quickly away but not before others passing by noted and murmured at the sight. An elf at the door to the Court of Thanes!

"No good coming of that," an elderly man muttered.

"Nothing but trouble, them elves," the gray dame beside him sniffed. "Look at her, dressed like a robber, all dusty and rough. Coming around looking for something. They always are, them elves."

Feeling like a beggar at the gate and keen enough to be amused by that, Kerian slipped inside the gleaming brass doors. Stepping into safer shadow, wryly she thought, now that's better. Thorbardin's day can progress undisturbed by the sight of me.

With those few steps, Kerian had walked from one world to another. Outside the doors, the world of dwarven life went on as it would in any city. Inside the doors, veiled in their shadows and separate from the murmuring thanes who did not see her, Kerian felt a seeping of homesickness for Qualinost. She once had a place there. She had been a servant in a senator's house, a laughing girl with time for the taverns, songs, and dancing. The song of the city beyond the doors was like a sigh from that past time, and suddenly she was lonely. They loved their city, the dwarves of Thorbardin. They loved it as the sustainer, the giver of air, of water, of food. They loved it as an elf loves her forest.

Quiet in shadow, straining to hear what she might catch, what drift of deliberation she could, Kerian stood very still. The dwarves argued as though they had been at it all night, some thanes speaking strongly against the elf king's proposal, others advising caution.

"Which doesn't mean shouting no, Dorrin," said a dwarf with an accent out of the south of the kingdom. "It just means you listen and think." Someone else laughed, a rich rolling sound, and the rumbling of discussion resumed.

They are divided, Kerian thought. They were divided into three camps: those who would not consider even the least part of Gil's request, those who thought they would be fools to ignore it, and those who wanted more time to listen and think. At the moment, as she counted, there were more in the last camp than in the other two. This, she thought, boded well—or at least, not ill.

From her concealment, she looked around the council chamber in the Court of Thanes. She stood beneath a high ceiling of marble, surrounded by walls of marble, her feet upon a cold marble floor. The place was a wonder of stonecraft, and the marble itself flowed like a tapestry, rose-veined, and gray-streaked, black upon the floor, snowy white stairs marching up to the dais where sat the high seats of all the thanes and the throne of the High King.

Into this hall over time had come men and women of all races, elves, dwarves, and humans, in friendship and in war, as supplicants and dispensers of favors. Kerian's heart thrilled. During the War of the Lance, Gil's own father, storied Tanis Half-Elven himself had come here in company with the Plainswoman Goldmoon who had carried for Krynn the blessing of a goddess, holy Mishakal. Looking like beggars, Tanis and Goldmoon had stood as heroes and pricked the conscience of a dwarven council whose dearest wish was to close the gates of Thorbardin and let all the world die of dragons if that's what would be.

A Hylar thane had ruled in those days, not a king but a steward, faithful and waiting for a sign that a king would return to the dwarves. Kerian remember the history of her lover's family, and she wondered whether the surly Hylar dwarf at the Hare and Hound, he who now presided over a bar in Stanach's Curse, had known that troubled steward.

She listened, breathing quietly, reckoning how the currents of contention shifted among the thanes.

Thorbardin. All of it smelled like a temple long deserted, the sight of faded glory like the last ghostly whiff of ancient incense. Everywhere her eye glanced, she saw the scars of a war not yet forgotten.

Behind her, a voice rough as gravel said, "Now, how was it our good old King Duncan put it? Ah yes: Let the stone remember, and may all our deliberations in this place be nourished."

Kerian turned, startled. Her hand dropped to the knife at her belt then fell when she saw the glint of amusement in the eys of the dwarf who'd stolen up behind her. Beard and hair were iron gray, but his eyes shone with a youthful light. He was not so old as he seemed. Older, she thought, than the count of his years.

"Pretty little knife y'got there, young woman. Dwarf-made, is it?"

She nodded, her eyes surveying the way behind him. Old habit, outlaw's habit. "A gift at the very moment I needed it. I've had better since, but none I like so well."

The dwarf considered the "better" and let it go. "You hear people say that about a weapon they trust, one that weighs nicely in the hand." A shrewd light shone in his eyes. "Maybe one they made a good kill with, eh?" He nodded past her, into the council chamber. "You won't need your knife in there, lass. Not everyone's going to agree with you, and you might not get what you want or need, but no one in there is looking to kill you, Mistress Kerianseray."

Kerian balanced between an intuitive liking for this dwarf and a strong instinct warning her to be careful. Speaking with cool courtesy, she murmured, "You know my name, sir. You have the advantage of me."

The dwarf nodded, genially agreeing. "Not for long, lass. I'm Tarn Bellowgranite, and I've heard you're looking for me."

Taken aback, Kerian, a creature of courts before ever she was an outlaw of the forest, bowed at once. "Your Majesty—"

He snorted. "Whose majesty? Never mind that. You're speaking for your king, so speak as your king. Him and me, we've not yet laid eye on each other, but I know the tale of Gilthas the son of Tanis Half-Elven. I know the tale of him and the tale of his kin. Your King Gilthas has had a judgment on him, eh? Since the day he lifted himself onto his dead uncle's throne he's been weighed and found wanting in the eyes of people who don't know what gets sacrificed so they can stand around in tavern and hall making grand opinions."

His eyes darkened and Kerian thought this king knew about sacrifice and the subtleties of what must be forsaken so others might live.

"Nay, speak proudly for your king, Mistress Kerianseray. In the best of all ways of being, that should be enough. As it is, you can do that and still hope all will be well."

Kerian's liking for this dwarf grew. She bowed again. "I will, sir, and I thank you for the grace."

Tarn laughed, a great booming roar. "Aye, rough looking as you are, your hair all running down your back, booted, belted, and bristling with knives—rough as that, nothin's scraped the elf out of you yet, eh?" He chuckled. "Well, well. I think those deliberants in there have been warming the air long enough, don't you? Let's see what ideas they've nourished in our old King Duncan's hall."

Honoring the tradition of hospitality, the High King of the Eight Clans of Thorbardin ushered the ambassador from the Court of the Speaker of the Sun the rest of the way into the hall.

This he did by putting his hand at the small of her back, giving her a none-too-gentle push as he said, "Get in there now, lass. Get it said, and let's get it moving, onward or done."

CHAPTER
19

Ah, you're everyone of you madmen!"

Ragnar Stonehigh's scornful judgment boomed through the high hall of the Council of Thanes like thunder, rolling round the high ceilings and raining down in echo upon Kerian. He was, this bristle-browed thane with the fierce Daewar eyes, the third of seven thanes to condemn her mission. Ebon Flame of the Theiwar had rejected it out of hand, and Skarr Forgebright of the Hylar refused to entertain the idea of combining with humans and elves in a treaty against dragons. His had been the most reasoned argument, the one Kerian would address if she could slip in a word between the Daewar's bluster.

"Why," Skarr had asked mildly, "should Thorbardin risk even a drop of dwarven blood or a bent copper of treasure for Outlanders? We don't need them, and their need could bring down a dragon's revenge upon us. No," he'd said, seeming to be genuinely regretful, "I can't sanction this alliance."

Shale Silverhand of the Klar had argued for the treaty but awkwardly. Donnal Firebane had come down in favor of it for the sake of old alliances. No one knew the opinion of the thane of the Aghar, the third Bluph the Third. He sat far back upon the throne of his clan, sucking the marrow from the bone of an old meal and cleaning his fingernails one with another.

Neither could Kerian reckon the feelings of Tarn Bellowgranite. The high king seemed content for now to watch his council shout it out. He was not, Kerian thought, inclined to suggest to anyone that the emissary from the elf king be given a chance to speak.

"She's a mewling girl," Ragnar sneered. "By Reorx's beard! Sent here—what?—to talk for her puppet king?" He looked around the vast hall, at all his brother thanes seated upon or standing near the thrones of their clans, at the High King himself upon the throne round which these ranged. Very pointedly, he did not look at Kerian. He threw back his head, his dark Daewar eyes flat as a snake's. "It's an insult! A damned elven insult! In the name of all Reorx has forged —"

Yawning, scratching his chin through his beard, Rhys Shatterstrike of the Neidar sat up straighter. "In the name of all Reorx has forged," he said in the drone of the bored, "it is an insult. It is tantamount to a declaration of war, so insulting is it that the elf-king—the dancing boy who gave away his kingdom for a chance to go about his golden city in jewels and furs—comes to ask our aid in the name of old friendship." He yawned again. "At the risk of insulting *you*, Ragnar—not a difficult thing to do—I ask you to offer new arguments and to stop repeating this weary old one."

In the moment of silence between them, flames licked at the darkness from the tripod braziers alight between each of the marching columns. They had been in this council chamber since day's end. No window graced the hall. What light there was came from torches and braziers. It was, through all hours of the day and night, a deliberative darkness.

In that gloom, Kerian's glance shifted from the thane of the Daewar to the thane of the Neidar. Shadows sculpted their faces, unfriendly masks. They did not love each other, those two. Rhys scratched his beard again. Ragnar bristled.

"You're a fool, Ragnar. You haven't even heard the girl's embassy. You don't know what she's been sent to say—"

"Hah! I know good and damn well what she's here for. She's here with her king's hand out, that's what. I'm telling you now—" He glared around the chamber, not sparing even the high king his disdain. "I'm telling you now, no good comes of it. None!"

Ragnar drew breath, filled up his lungs to pour out more objections. In that startling moment of silence, Kerian took a step forward.

"My lord thanes," she said. She spoke quietly, and two of the thanes leaned forward as though uncertain she had spoken at all.

"Ah, now what?" Ragnar snarled. "Look at this! The girl's got no manners, either. Interrupting a council—"

Tarn Bellowgranite shouted, "Enough!"

Ragnar's eyes went wide, and his face flushed. Ebon of the Theiwar sat forward, thin hands folded one over the other. These were, Kerian knew, the dangerous ones, the lords of dark-hearted clans.

"What wars they have in Thorbardin," Gil had said, "are generally started by Theiwar, soldiered by Daewar, and ended by Hylar."

Not this time, Kerian thought. This time Theiwar and Daewar find themselves shoulder to shoulder with a Hylar thane.

Donnal of the Daergar exchanged veiled glances with Shale of the Klar. In the corner of his high seat, the throne of a thane, the gully dwarf Bluph curled up, snoring with a cracked marrowbone tucked under his arm. Ten years this treaty had been in the making, the work of Tanis Half-Elven and Princess Laurana, the hope of their son's embattled kingdom.

By all the gone gods, Kerian thought, not sure if she would laugh at the irony, will it all hang upon a snoring gully dwarf and a high king who has so far remained undeclared?

"Enough," Tarn said, a note of weariness underlying the firmness of his voice. "We've gone around the hall and a dozen times back with this. For days and weeks, we've gone around. For longer than that, it's been in our minds. Enough now. There is a man with a pressing need. We've left him standing on one foot long enough."

"Too long," he said, darkly, "too long for honor."

The Daewar snorted, but not loudly. He was not chastened, not he, but to Kerian it seemed he was, indeed, warned.

Tarn rested his hands on the arms of his throne, his fingers curving gently over the smooth black obsidian. "My brother thanes, this young woman represents the reason for the council." He glared at Ragnar. "I bid her speak."

Speak! Kerian's heart rose to the chance to present her king's need. At last! She stood before them all in the very hall whose tapestried history was part of the legend of her own lover's family.

"My lord thanes," she began, no louder than before. Let them be quiet now to hear. Let them lean forward, yes, and cock their ears. "My lord thanes, I stand here in this hall, this storied chamber, and it won't surprise you to know how much of my king's own history is woven in the wondrous tale of this place.

"I won't tell you what you know or speak of ancient friendships and long-ago treaties. You have only lately honored one, the old pact that made a fortress rise up again to bestride the mountains. Pax Tharkas! It stands whole once more because you and the elves of Qualinesti remembered the pact made long ago." She smiled, a little. "A pact between dwarves, elves, and humans."

Ragnar snorted, the gully dwarf snored. Skarr of the Hylar sat a little forward.

"That pact stood you all in good stead, I'm told, firm friends, allies true. There was another time, wasn't there? There was a time when my king's own father stood here." Her eyes met those of the Hylar thane. "You will remember that, perhaps, many of you. It wasn't so long ago that Tanis Half-Elven and the lady Goldmoon herself—god-touched Goldmoon!—prevailed upon Thane Hornfel to grant asylum to human refugees from a dragon highlord's cruelty. This grace he granted from his heart, and his heart served him well."

She paused, listening to the fires breathe, to the rustling of old ghosts, old hopes and old fears. Clear-eyed warrior, canny outlaw, no one in the room was unimpressed by her speech.

In that breathing silence, the high king looked at her long. Quietly as she, he said, "Tell me, Mistress Kerianseray, why a Kagonesti woman stands here to champion the king of those who enslave her people."

A startled murmur rippled round the dais, and the Hylar's brows drew together in a dark and scornful vee above his hawkish nose. "Slaves," Skarr of the Hylar said, looking as though he wanted to spit. "They enslave their own kind, those elves."

So said her brother, Iydahar with whom she seldom agreed these days. That argument of his Kerian had never managed to refute. How could she? She knew what was said in the halls of elf lords about the relationship between her people and Gil's. She knew, too, how she'd come to Qualinesti.

Calmly, not rising to the bait, she nodded. "Your high

king is not mistaken. I am not Qualinesti, my lord thanes. You can see the truth of that on me—" She tossed her head proudly, exposing the tattoos on her neck. "I'm Kagonesti, and it isn't always easy for us in the land of the Qualinesti."

The Klar picked up his head, interested. He knew about hardship. They did not have a servitor class in Thorbardin, but they had the Klar, the Neidar who'd stayed within the gates of Thorbardin during the Dwarfgate War. They were not beloved of the mountain dwarves; they were not beloved of their hill dwarf kin. It was a Klar you saw fetching and carrying, a Klar doing char work, doing service.

"It is not easy to be a Wilder Elf in the elf kingdom, and it grows, in some ways, harder, but I will tell you this, my lord thanes, I am a Kagonesti here before you, championing the cause of the Qualinesti king because I know his cause is right. I'm not sure it is for me to try to convince you of that rightness. I don't know your hearts, and you don't know his, but I do know this . . ."

She stopped and looked at each of them in turn, from the high king himself twining his fingers thoughtfully in his iron beard right to the snoring gully dwarf.

"I know, my lord thanes, that if you say no to my king"—she lifted her voice now, not high to shout, but strongly to carry "—if you say no to the alliance, you assure the day of your own destruction."

The word rang like a war cry. Kerian didn't back down from it.

Ragnar bellowed. He leaped to his feet, pointing a long scarred finger not at Kerian but at Tarn. "Do you hear her, High King? She dares threaten us!"

Ebon the Theiwar, a long time silent, looked around at his brother thanes, all of whom seemed troubled now, to one degree or another made unhappy by Kerian's words. Seeing this, he sighed.

"I've always wondered whether wisdom or madness would be found in this foreign alliance. Now we see. She stands here and threatens us in the name of her king."

Tarn glanced at Kerian, who did not move or look away. She gave no credence to Ragnar or Ebon. "You know the portents, Your Majesty. You are a king. You know."

She declared this a matter for kings, and Tarn Bellowgranite accepted that. The hall filled with a grim, troubled silence of the living, and there were ghosts in the smoke, their voices almost heard in the embers settling in the braziers. Daewar, Theiwar, Hylar. Tarn looked to the Klar, the thanes of the Neidar, the Daergar, and the Aghar, the gully dwarf just then rolling over to scratch himself and settle back to sleep. There was an eighth kingdom in Thorbardin, an eighth clan. Its throne stood removed from those of the thanes of the other clans and that of the high king himself. At the back of the dais, draped in shadow, this dark throne had never felt the presence of a living dwarf, and it held the memory of all the dwarves who had ever lived, who had ever died.

His eyes warily on that throne, his own attention drawing the attention of all in the room to that place, Tarn Bellowgranite rose.

"Brother thanes, Kerianseray of Qualinesti does not threaten. She reminds. She knows what her king knows, what the humans in the Free Realms know." He looked at them all, drawing back their glances. "She knows what I know, and what you should know.

"The elf king cannot threaten us. You should know that. He cannot harm us; you should know that, too. A dragon holds his kingdom and bleeds it of its treasure. He has no army. If you don't know that, you are fools. A Skull Knight abuses his people—"

Skarr of the Hylar said, "He permits this."

Tarn turned to him, his eyes holding Skarr's. Glances

met, bright and keen as blades crossing. "He permits it, yes. He is a wise king. He knows his council of lords holds the power in his kingdom. He knows he cannot wrest it from them. He knows—" His voice rose, now for all to hear. "He knows that if he had all those shining lords behind him, all his men and women in arms again and willing to die for him, he might—*might!*—be able to defeat the Dark Knights. He would not defeat the dragon.

"I don't know about the boy. I've heard all you have about him, and the only good from his own mother and this Kagonesti warrior here, but I will tell you that while the most of you consider Gilthas a coward, I would consider him a fool if he threw himself against the dragon."

Like a whipcrack came his voice. "He is no king who sacrifices his people to his own vain bid for glory!"

Gently, "He is a good and courageous man who plans for a way to save his people. If we signed to this treaty, we would agree to be the route to safety for his people, a road out of the dragon's talons and on to the lands of the Plainsfolk. This treaty would give hope to a besieged people. I will tell you, brothers: if we turn away now, if all the kingdoms of Krynn fall to dragons and we are left—we are assured of our destruction. For we will be the last for a dragon to pluck, or we will die in the dark under the world, alone and unremembered."

One more time, he looked to the throne of the Eighth Kingdom, the kingdom of the dead.

"Brother thanes, you have made a good man beg for too long. Let us deliberate for the last time on this matter. Keep in mind that in all our considerations, the dead do listen. Among them are kings, and many of those kings would have stripped themselves flesh from bone for the sake of the clans."

To Kerian, in all courtesy, he bowed. "Mistress Kerianseray, I will know where to find you."

She knew herself dismissed, and when she walked from the hall, Kerian resisted all impulse to turn and look over her shoulder.

What would be now would be.

* * *

The High King of the Eight Clans of Thorbardin found Kerian in Stanach's Curse. She sat alone, mid-morning in an empty tavern drinking ale. Two weeks had passed since she'd stood before the dais in the Court of Thanes, making her king's case. In that time she had slept in an upper room of the tavern, eaten well from the kitchen, and had to drink from the bar. She could not pay for this fare and was told not to worry. Stanach reckoned kings would make it right. "Or not. Kings do what they will. All the rest of us hop when we're told to."

In the weeks of her stay, Kerian had come to know the regulars, and they knew her. They drank together at night and dined well, and she learned the intricacies of the dwarven dart game that asked more of a player than that he hit the board. He must, aiming for the squared marked brightly in runes, tell a tale. Sometimes in the afternoon she stood outside the doors trying to fathom the name of the tavern. She looked up at the sign, a board shaped not like the traditional shield but like an anvil. Upon the anvil lay a broken forge hammer. The words "Stanach's Curse" stood above the image, written in dwarven runes. No one was inclined to tell her the meaning of the tavern's name for the asking, and she was having no luck in the reckoning.

"We don't talk about it much," said Kern one day, the dwarf whom Stanach usually referred to as Idiot Kern, though Kerian didn't think the dwarf's wits were afflicted by more than youth.

Two weeks after the council meeting, passing beneath that sign, the High King of the Eight Clans of Thorbardin nodded curt greeting to her and entered the tavern. Tarn pulled up a stool at the bar, another for her, and ordered ale.

Stanach tapped a fresh keg and put a well-crowned mug before the king. He filled two more and put one before Kerian, the other a little out of his own reach.

"Mistress Kerianseray," said Tarn, "our council has made a decision."

Her heart pounded. At last! Kerian took care to show the high king only a mild expression of interest.

Tarn lifted his mug and took a long swig. He wiped his lips with the back of his hand. "They are a stubborn lot, those thanes of ours. They are all on your side but one, and that means none. We all agree, or none agree, and in this matter I will not ride rough-shod over the rights of the clans."

Ragnar, Kerian thought. Ragnar doomed it.

"Ah," said the high king after another swig of ale. "It's that stubborn Hylar, Skarr. He's rooted to stone on this matter, and he says he will not be happy unless someone goes out and comes back to give him the truth of your king."

Behind the bar, Stanach grunted. Kerian glanced from the king to Stanach and back again.

"King," said the barman, Stanach of the ruined hand. In his dark, blue-flecked eyes was a kind of pleading. "Don't."

"Nay," the king said, low. Kerian knew herself to be no longer part of the conversation. "Nay, Stanach, and if I don't ask you, whose word will Skarr accept?"

"Anyone Hylar."

"You. He wants you. He's your uncle, lad. Your da's own brother. He trusts you." The king laughed, but with little humor. "It's your curse, Stanach Hammerfell. You've a reputation for trustworthiness among those in power, and damn me if those in power insist on trusting you."

There is no resisting the power of a curse, this Kerian knew. Stanach didn't try harder and didn't argue. He drew the untasted mug of ale toward him and lifted it in silence to his king.

*   *   *

They went out from Thorbardin by secret ways, down to the lowest level, down to where the damage of the recent war showed in scarred stone walls, in broken battlements, in ruined streets and collapsed roofs. They went farther down than that until they stood upon the shores of the great underground body of water known as the Urkhan Sea.

Stanach pointed out across the black waters to a wall pocked with what seemed to be the mouths of caves. He told her to stand still and bade her listen. Beneath her feet, Kerian felt a soft, persistent vibration, a kind of humming in the rock.

"Worms," Stanach said.

She frowned. "How can that be? Worms can't eat through—"

"Y'know that for certain, do you?"

She glanced at him, then back to the gaps in the stone wall. The rumbling came closer, beneath her feet the stone vibrated, the vibration shuddering up her legs, to her belly, to her arms and shoulders. At the edges of the Urkhan Sea dark water lapped nervously against the stone. Out from one of the cave mouths came something large, something with two probing horns, like those seen on snails. Even from this distance, all the rippling black water between them, Kerian reckoned that the horns were as long as she was tall, perhaps as thick around as the width of her shoulders. The creature had no face, no eyes, no nose, only a constantly working mouth.

"Worms," she breathed.

"They eat stone. That's all they do. The earth back there, behind those walls, is riddled with tunnels. They bore out here to drink and go right back in again. Tame enough, the beasties. Mostly we leave them be."

He squinted across the water, then turned, saying it was time to go. "Let's don't use that pretty little emerald leaf of yours until we have to, aye? I wouldn't want to find myself lost in some Reorx-only-knows-where tunnel with no way out."

Kerian agreed, and she did not call upon the unchancy magic until they saw clear sky above them again.

CHAPTER

20

Magic did not set Kerian and Stanach down where they hoped, but at least it didn't drop them down in Tarsis or the Sirrion Sea. It put them down only a few miles from Qualinost, in the thickness of the oak forest north and west of the capital. They were reeling with dizziness. The dwarf's face showed green.

"Not a day's walk from here to Qualinost," Kerian said reassuringly to Stanach.

The dwarf was leaning his back against an oak, his eyes closed. He had the look of a man praying. He groaned something that sounded like a curse then, between clenched teeth, "Good."

Kerian waited for color to return to his cheeks and for her own stomach to settle. "That's not where we'll go. We'll be wanting to go first to Wide Spreading, the king's hunting lodge. There we'll find a trusty man who will take word to the king that you've come."

Stanach looked around at the oaken wood, the tall trees thickly growing. "We'll walk to where we're going, aye? Enough of the magic now."

Kerian agreed, counting herself lucky in the way the

talisman had treated them. She gave Stanach a little longer to settle while she calculated a route that would take them to Wide Spreading by forest paths known only to hunters and deer, then she led the dwarf along those barely seen game trails as though along the manicured paths of a garden in Qualinost. Stanach had nothing to say about that, and she was pleased to take his silence for appreciation.

They went until the sun had climbed past noon height. The season had turned in the short time Kerian was away. The taste of autumn hung on the wind, only the suggestion of it in the fading green of the forest, yet she saw no hunters. When they climbed the slope of a green vale and looked down, they saw no farmers at work in their fields. They saw only great swathes of black staining the golden crops, where the roofs of barns and houses gaped with holes.

Stanach's good left hand filled with his throwing axe.

"It's long done," Kerian said, bitterly. She pointed to the sky. "Look, empty. The crows have quarreled and had the best of the feast."

"You sound like you're used to this," said the dwarf.

She did sound so, and she couldn't help that. "I'm not used to it, Stanach. It's how things are."

Yet it seemed to her that something had changed. The depredations of Knights had, until now, taken place close to the towns or in villages. Elder's confusion of magic, and the swift-striking Night People who seemed to the Knights like forest ghosts, had kept them out of the woods and away from the smaller settlements and isolated farms.

Something had indeed changed.

Nor did they go alone through the forest. Behind them came the soft whisper of a footfall. To the side, the rattle of browning bracken so faint to the ear that one could be forgiven for doubting one's senses. Above, down the side of a tall, broad boulder, a shadow, slipping across the dapple of sun, soon gone.

"We're being followed," Stanach said, the first night as they sat before a small campfire. "You know that."

She did. "I know who follows. Leave him alone. He'll come out when he wants to or go away if he wills."

The dwarf considered this, then said, "You don't think him a danger?"

Kerian looked out past the fire, out into the shadows and the night. "Oh, he's a danger; never doubt that. Not to me, though." Stanach raised a brow. She cocked a crooked grin. "Or to you, Sir Ambassador, as long as he sees you're no threat to me."

They said no more that night about it, but Kerian noticed that the dwarf didn't sleep easier.

Three days later, followed and unchallenged, Kerian and Stanach stood on a high place, a granite hill made of boulders flung during the Cataclysm. Elf and dwarf looked down into a dell where once had spread a thriving village. Nothing stood there now, and the land lay black, scarred by fire and destruction. Kerian went down, Stanach following. She knew the village as one sympathetic to her cause—or had known it. Her blood running cold, she saw the head of every villager, man, woman, and child, lining the broad street, piked upon lances. Their cattle lay dead, their horses, their dogs, and the fowl in the yards.

Stanach didn't stand long in the street. He stumbled away, back to the forest, and Kerian let him go. She knew the look on his face, the greening of his cheeks. She stood alone, smelling burning, smelling death, and thinking that she had not been gone from the kingdom long, hardly a scant month, but something had changed.

Something had happened to bring Lord Thagol's Knights out in full rampage.

Stanach gagged in the brush, the sound of his retching loud in the stillness. Kerian looked north and south, then east and west. She stood waiting.

Softly, a voice at her back said, "Kerianseray of Qualinesti."

She turned and though it had been only since summer that last she'd seen him, she hardly recognized Jeratt, so changed was he. He was not the man she'd left only weeks before, the cocky half-elf who'd led Night People beside her, who had planned raids, strategies and victories. His hair had turned white. His cheeks thin, his eyes glittering, this was not a face she knew. His voice, that she knew.

"Y'never should have left us, Kerian." He scrubbed the side of his face with his hand. "He knew it when y'left. He took advantage when y'were gone."

Stanach came out from the brush. Jeratt turned, arrow nocked to bow in the instant. The dwarf's good hand flashed to his side and clasped the throwing axe before Jeratt could draw breath or arrow.

"Hold!" Kerian shouted. She put a hand on Jeratt's shoulder, felt the muscles quivering with tension. She nodded to Stanach, and the dwarf dropped his arm. "Jeratt, he's a friend of the king."

They stood in heart-hammered silence until Kerian said, "Jeratt, tell me what has happened."

"You can see it." He looked around. "This is what they do now, Kerian. Up and down the land, they do this. Maybe they used to think it would teach us some kind of lesson. Now—now it's Thagol himself doing it and not caring what we learn, past hating him." He pulled a bitter smile. "He's waiting for you, Kerian. You've been gone; you haven't killed any of his Knights. He can't find you on the dream-roads, but he's still looking for you, and he's waiting for you to come back." Jeratt glanced around. "Him and Chance Headsman and their Knights and draconians. He's brought in reinforcements from Neraka."

His eyes narrowed. "They've broken us, every band, all the resistance you put together It was you, Kerian, who made it work, you who held us together, who heartened us and gave us a will. Without you—" His arm swept wide. "Y'went away at a bad time, Kerian."

Ah, gods. Yet there had been no choice.

"Elder?"

Jeratt shook his head. "Gone!"

The word ran on her nerves, like lightning. "Gone? Where?"

"Don't know. One night she was there, sittin' at her fire. The next . . . gone. That was only three days after you left. There's been none of her confusions now, nothing to help."

"But you kept on."

Jeratt's chest swelled proudly. "I didn't just keep on. I did what we'd planned, put warriors in the south, and I been back to the dales and roused 'em there, but . . . I couldn't keep it going against Thagol. He's . . . he's like the sea, Kerian. We're all scattered again."

Looking from one to the other, the scruffy half-elf and the woman who had only days before spoke in the Court of Thanes, Stanach whistled low. Softly he said, "First time I saw you, missy, you were tripping over a Knight's corpse on the way out the door. Then you show up in the High King's court. Now . . . " He shook his head. "What in the name of Reorx's forge are you about?"

Kerian looked at him, and the smile she crooked had little to do with humor. "Stanach, I've been too long gone from the forest. I will take you so far as where you are safe. After that . . ."

Jeratt looked at her, his mouth a thin line. In his eyes, though, she saw hope rising.

———◆———

Around the basin, men and women stood. Most Kerian knew, a few faces she didn't. Some were gone: Rhyl, who had not proved trusty; Ayensha, about whom Jeratt said they would later speak; and Elder, who had vanished one day between midnight and dawn.

Old comrades regarded Kerian variously, some pleased to see her, some angry for her sudden departure and return. Newcomers stood with shuttered eyes, waiting. Bueren Rose looked upon her warmly, but a group of strangers eyed her with thinly veiled suspicion. Each of them, four men and the two women, looked to Jeratt to reckon the mood of the occasion. These were the leaders of other bands, other outcasts, highwaymen and robbers. These Jeratt had collected in Kerian's absence, and no one knew her. News of her, tales of her, these things they knew. In their world, that mattered nothing at all. The deed done at your side, the back watched, the Knight killed who would have killed you—these things mattered. Of these things, they had no experience with Kerian.

She stepped past Jeratt, past Stanach Hammerfell, the dwarf uneasy among all these rough, suspicious elves.

Kerian looked around at them all, all of them cautious. Out the corner of her eye, she noted Stanach. The dwarf stood watching, blue-flecked dark eyes on her. He had come to speak with her king, and he intended to do his errand then return to his thane, that doubting uncle of his who sat upon the throne of the Hylar. In his eyes she saw how far from Thorbardin he felt, and he stood very still in the face of this unwelcoming elven silence, a careful man trying to know whether the ground had suddenly shifted under his boot heels.

Kerian laughed, suddenly and sounding like a crow. "You!" She pointed to an elf woman standing apart from the others on the other side of the fires. This one, a woman with hair like chestnut, seemed to be the one to whom others deferred. "I am Kerianseray of Qualinesti. I don't know you. Who are you?"

The woman's eyes narrowed. Her hand drifted toward the sword at her belt then stilled. "Feather's Flight, and I don't know you either."

"I don't care. In time maybe you will. Till then, declare yourself, Feather's Flight, here in my place, with Lightning—" a glance toward the dwarf— "and Thunder to witness: Are you here to join me, you and all of yours to take up arms in my cause?"

"Well, I don't know—"

"You don't know my cause? You lie! If you have run with Jeratt, you know it. You know my cause is a king's, and you know—" she reckoned the woman's age, she counted on old alliances, and she gambled with her next statement—"and you know that the king's cause is not far different from the cause of the prince whose name is honored by our elders."

Feather's Flight cocked her head, her lips crooked a smile. "I've run with Jeratt, true. What if I now choose to run away?"

Kerian laughed. "If you gave me your word to go and go in peace, I would let you go."

The woman hadn't expected that. She stood like a deer with her head to the wind, trying to understand a sudden, complicated scent. "You'd let me go! I come and go as I please, Kagonesti."

Kerian shrugged. "There used to be a man named Rhyl with us. He isn't now. He didn't turn out to be as trusty as we like our friends to be. If I thought for even an instant you were untrustworthy, Feather's Flight, you'd be an hour dead, and I'd be talking to someone else."

Someone laughed, one of those beside Feather's Flight. Someone else murmured, and Bueren Rose breathed a small sigh of relief as the outlaw stepped forward and stood before Kerian.

"We are six bands," said Feather's Flight. Kerian withheld a satisfied smile as she realized she'd calculated correctly and called out the woman who best represented the others. "We are from the mountains in the western part of the kingdom, past the dales. Even there heads grow on pikes like evil fruit. Some of us did know the lost prince, Porthios, whom some say perished in dragon-fire." She stood taller. "I came from Silvanesti with him, and we cleaned the green dragons out of the Sylvan Land. I don't know his nephew, I haven't heard good of him, but I see you, Kerianseray. I have heard good of you. In the name of the dead, we will join you."

The others nodded silently. Bueren thumped her shoulder, and Jeratt grinned wide. Beside the half-elf, Stanach Hammerfell had the look of a dwarf who wasn't quite ready to relax. Kerian caught his eye and winked.

"Ay, Jeratt," she said. "The dwarf looks like he could use a meal. Me too, for that matter. Anyone been hunting lately, or is it all bone and stone soup?"

On the hills, elves kept watch. No one counted on magic now, for with her going it seemed Elder had taken all her useful confusions. The dwarf Stanach volunteered to take his own turn at watch, and Kerian didn't refuse him.

What will he say to his thane about all this? Kerian

wondered. How will I get him to Gil so he can form some kind of opinion?

Ah, well, that was for another day's thinking. She looked at Jeratt. Firelight made him seem older; shadows sculpted his face till Kerian might have imagined him twice his age.

"You know," Jeratt said, "no matter how well you plan our raids, Kerian, Thagol's going to find you the first time you kill someone. He's like a dog sniffing down the road."

She remembered. Absently, she rubbed the bridge of her nose. There was the old pain forming. From old habit, she gauged the headache, trying to know it for what it was. Not Thagol, hunting. Not yet. This time the throbbing behind her eyes was weariness.

"Before we fell apart, we were all over the place, several bands striking at will and no one for him to grab or follow." He shook his head grimly. "It's why he started this slash and burn campaign. Figured he'd cut us off from the villagers and the farmers. He did that right. No one was going to risk his life to feed us, no one would shelter us or even give us news for fear of their own lives. Let me tell you, Kerian, it all fell apart fast."

Kerian nodded, thinking.

"The first time you kill, though," Jeratt continued, "he'll catch up with us, Kerian. The first time you kill, he'll know it."

Yes, he would. She'd thought of that. She was considering it very carefully. Her outlaw bands would begin a stealthy campaign. At dawn they would scatter through the forest, making a noose around the capital. They would continue Jeratt's plan of random strikes, each band falling on targets as they would, in no discernible pattern. Tribute wagons, supply wagons, these were of no moment now.

Now the struggle would intensify. Bridges would be thrown down, roads would be blocked with fallen trees.

Streams and rivers would be clogged. "We will not go so far as to fire the woods," Kerian said. "That is forbidden, but we will fall on his work details as he rebuilds the bridges and clears the roads, we will kill all the Knights who guard those details. We will give the bastard no quarter!"

They would strike hard and strike without mercy. Slowly, in no obvious way, they would move farther out from the city, farther out into the forest, drawing Thagol's forces into the deeper woods.

"Jeratt," she said, still rubbing the bridge of her nose. "I'm not going to be at any one of those raids. I'm not going to kill any of the enemy. When I next come to kill, I'll kill Eamutt Thagol. If I join a raid, it will be to lop the head off Headsman Chance."

She paused, gave him a moment to digest that, then said, "Jeratt, where is my brother?"

The question surprised him; she saw it on his face. "I don't know."

Kerian shook her head. "Yes, you do. Ayensha isn't here, and you know where she is, so you know where my brother is. Where is Dar?"

She watched him thinking and watched him choose. He'd held faithful to her trust after she'd gone, without notice, to Thorbardin. He'd done better than that: He'd tried to build the core of what would now become—if all gone gods were good!—the terror of Thagol's Knights. Yet she saw it now, again as she had a year ago. Jeratt had a deeper allegiance to her brother, to Iydahar who did not trust her or like her king.

"Who is he to you, Jeratt?"

The question surprised him. "Dar? He's my friend."

She snorted, unbelieving. "He's more than that. I've seen how you are when he's around—all of you. It's like he's a . . . I don't know, priest or shaman."

Jeratt sat a long time quiet, poking at the fire, chasing

bright orange cinders up to the sky. Kerian watched him; she looked at the guards on the hill, then at Jeratt again.

"He's none of those, Kerian. He's—he was a man of the prince. He fought beside Porthios, and when the prince vanished and most of Dar's folk went away into the forest, Dar stayed. You don't know, Kerian. Maybe you don't remember how hard the winter was that year, you in your towers at Qualinost. Maybe you looked out your window and saw the snow falling and you thought it was pretty." He stopped, his eyes gone suddenly hard. "Maybe you scurried out from the silks and the satins of your lover's bed and thought how cold the floor was when your little foot missed the carpet."

Kerian drew a breath, sharp and swift.

"Dar is the one who gathered up all of the prince's broken men and found us shelter in a winter that would have killed us. Broken bones, broken hearts, broken spirits. He took us all as his, when he could have gone away with his kin, with your father and mother and the White Osprey tribe. He healed us and helped us, and when the spring came and he did go away to be with Ayensha and her folk, he never forgot us. He brought us news, just like in that terrible winter he brought us food and healing. In all the years, though we fought for no cause but our own anger and greed, your brother never let us go afoul of the Knights we hate if he could help it, and one day he brought us Elder to keep and care for. . . ."

In silence, he poked at the fire again. In silence, he watched the embers, light flowing across them, like fire breathing.

"He was our brother in arms, Kerian. We were sworn to the prince, and that's like we were born of the same kin. Dar never forgot that. We owe him everything, and though we've sworn to your cause — I'm sorry to say it, we don't owe you him. Dar wants no part of you, your cause, or your king, and there's no persuading him. I ain't going to be the one to go against him. Now, Ayensha will be back in the morning, so you go get some sleep now. We got a bit of work ahead of us, eh?"

Ayensha would be back, so he'd said, but in the morning she didn't come. Neither did she on the morning after, or the one after that, and on the fourth morning, Jeratt said no more than that the girl must have come to her senses.

"She learned she is childing in the time you were gone. She's come to her senses now and will not be following you to war."

———◆◆◆———

He lay upon a bed of bracken, the Skull Knight among his men. They'd made camp in the forest, out of sight of the Qualinost Road heading west. Watch had been posted and turned twice before he'd finally settled to sleep. The forest smelled of fern and earth, and down a thin wind, distantly of draconian. He never let those creatures camp near his Knights. They disgusted most humans, and black-armored Knights were no exception.

Thagol closed his eyes. His disciplined mind let go of the thoughts and concerns of the day. He had plotted his next strike, scouted the village, and deployed his men. It would be a fiery morning, this he trusted. In Gilianost lived a taverner who had given shelter to one of the outlaws, a half-elf on the run from two of Thagol's Knights. The taverner would find that offense costly.

Thagol settled, and though he had not lain upon a true bed in a month, still he settled easily. He didn't miss Qualinost, that warren of elves, the very scent of whom turned his stomach. He lay upon the forest floor, the hard earth that hated the very touch of his body, that loathed the sound of his voice. As willingly as he hated Qualinesti, so did Sir Eamutt Thagol imagine the forest hated him.

In the deepest part of his sleep, then, he went out walking. Sir Thagol went out from his body and traveled on the roads of dreaming and through the deep places of sleeping minds. It was no unusual journey for him, and he found no unusual thing. When he woke, the soft gray light before the dawn in his eyes, Sir Thagol had the feeling that something had changed in the forest.

It was a feeling he knew, akin to the air of a barracks when warriors are called to muster.

———————◆◆◆———————

Sorrow drifted like ghosts through the forest. Villages lay in ash and ruin. Heads were posted everywhere as warnings. In the little towns untouched by Lord Thagol and Chance Headsman's blighting hands, people shunned the rebels now. Kerian's name was known in every quarter of the forest now, as was the price for her head. The Skull Knight did not offer steel, gems, or precious metals. He offered nothing. He promised death to all he looked upon until she was brought to him, alive for killing.

At farms where once they had been welcomed, no one dared open a door to Kerian, Jeratt, or any of the Night People. In this forest now, all strangers were suspect, any traveler going by could be one of the resistance fighters Lord Thagol hunted. Anyone could lose his head on the mere suspicion that he'd given aid to one of them.

"He doesn't know where I am," Kerian reminded Jeratt. They had hunted well, and thanks to Stanach's deft hand with a snare, they had five fat rabbits to spit. A clear cool stream ran nearby. "Right now, this moment, he can't even guess."

Stanach said he wondered how she knew that. Kerian and Jeratt exchanged wry grins as she tapped her forehead.

"I know." She pulled the bloodstone out of her shirt. "This hides me from him, but if I kill, it doesn't keep him from knowing I'm around. I haven't killed. I don't feel him in my head. He doesn't know where I am."

The dwarf grunted skeptically, then sat in silence for a while. Then, "When are you taking me to Qualinost?"

Kerian leaned close to the fire, to the warmth, for the night was chill.

"You've seen this place," she said. "You've seen what Thagol and Chance Headsman are doing. Do you think I could get you as far as Qualinost?"

Stanach snorted. He was a long time quiet, his face, his eyes above his black beard gone still as he cradled his ruined right hand in the palm of his left.

"In good time," said Kerian.

Jeratt grinned. "And we'll get you there with your head still sitting on your shoulders."

Stanach turned his head this way and that, as though trying to loosen a kink in his neck. "I'd appreciate that."

The fingers of his left hand curled round the haft of his keen-edged throwing axe as he stood to take the first watch. Beyond the fire, he looked at Kerian, a long, considering moment. He thought about the serving girl he'd met in the forest, perhaps not far from here, two years ago. She had been a tender creature then, soft hands, perfumed hair. Now here she sat, a leader of a shadowy force of warriors known as Night People. She crouched before her forest hearth, in leather boots and woolen trews, a shirt a man might wear. Her tattoos shone in the light, and it seemed to Stanach she had as much of the forest about her as the owl now sailing the night between the trees.

❖

The elf woman screamed. Her voice soared high above all the rest; her face shone white in the night as she clutched her child to her breast. Howling, five Dark Knights ringed her round, circling, swords high, laughing. One howled higher than all, and one kept starkly silent. She fell to her knees, bent over the child, the little creature wailing in her arms against her breast. A voice shouted "Erathia!" A sword screamed through the air, and the voice did not shout more. Erathia wailed, knowing her husband dead, knowing his head would join the heads of other murdered elves.

Horses thundered round her, Knights yelling madly.

Erathia prayed to a goddess long fled the world, she prayed to Mishakal, the giver of mercy elves named Quenesti-Pah.

"Merciful goddess, lady of light, spare my child, oh spare—"

Beside her face, so close the iron shoe ran red with fire-light, a tall war-horse stamped and grew still. Around her, the others did the same. Erathia had heard no command, but these Knights had a Skull Knight for a lord. There had been a command.

Trembling, she hunched lower over her child and realized she heard nothing of elf voices. No villager wept, howled, or pleaded.

Gods, she was the last.

"Merciful Lady . . ."

She looked up, and two Knights departed from the circle around her; two came close, one on either side. They wore their helms closed, and that didn't matter. Erathia knew which was the Skull Knight. From him, his very being, flowed the coldness of death, like a wind out of winter, belling in the forest, howling in her heart. He flung back the visor of his helm. The other mirrored the gesture.

"Headsman," he simply said.

She looked to them, to one and the other, the agents of her death. In the eyes of the Skull Knight she saw nothing, not a killing lust, not hatred, not even determination to get the job done. Nothing, as though she looked into the windows of an empty building, into blackness. In the eyes of the other, Chance Headsman, she saw fire. Flames leaping, consuming, bloodlust and killing-need.

In his eyes she saw her death, the raising of his blade before he lifted it, the fell swing before he caused it. She screamed, flung herself aside, and there was nowhere to go. A horse jostled her, and the child fell from her arms, wailing.

Whistling, the sword of Chance Headsman swooped low. She looked into the eyes of the Skull Knight, perhaps to plead. In the moment of her death, the moment the blade kissed her neck, she saw a thing happen in those eyes. They kindled with sudden savage joy.

CHAPTER

21

The season of Autumn Harvest began in woe, and grief ran through it like a river of blood. Sorrow rained upon the forest in that season once known for joy, and the fires lighting the night were not the traditional harvest bonfires. No one danced round these, laughing girls and lusty lads. No one shouted for the joy of the harvest; no one cried out thanks.

They wept before these fires, elves pared to bone by their grief, their voices fit only to keen and moan.

A pall of smoke hung over the land, drifted like the ghosts of the dead between the trees. Looking, a person would have thought all the forest had been put to the flame. It had not been, but villages burned. Farmhouses, barns and byres, and the neat stacks of hay in the fields—these all burned.

For two weeks, the Speaker of the Sun watched from the highest point in the city, from the gardens on the roof of the Tower of the Sun. He stood alone on some nights, watching, and thinking, It is she. Kerian is back!

Once he said this to his mother, Laurana standing beside him and tracking the fires. She asked him how he knew this, and he said, "Mother, think like a general. Before, Thagol went here, and then he went there. You could imagine his next blow only looking at a map. Look now—over the last nights we've seen no pattern at all. He is chasing someone. He's chasing Kerian."

Laurana considered this, looking out past the bridges, the eastern one bristling with the skulls that marked Thagol's rage. They gleamed now in the moonlight, bleached by the seasons.

"What is she doing, my son?" she asked, her voice heavy with sadness.

Gilthas didn't know, and he said so. "I do know Kerian, and so I think she's engaging him, Mother. I think she's jerking him wherever she wants him to be. I would guess that she's drawing him north and eastward."

"Toward the Stonelands."

"Yes. Thorbardin, beyond."

"Thorbardin." Laurana stood a moment quiet, and at last she gave voice to the question between them. "If Kerian is back, why hasn't she come here to tell us how her mission to the dwarves fared?"

Gilthas pointed to the fires by which they tracked her. "I don't think she's had time to, Mother."

Wind shifted, smoke stung their eyes, and in the stinging Gil's sudden bravado shivered. With startling suddenness, he recalled the nightmares that lately haunted him. In those dark dreams he sent his lover to her death. He put a hand upon the parapet to steady himself. Had he doomed her in reality?

Soft, his mother's hand touched his shoulder, an old gesture, a steadying one. She said nothing, not she who felt the deaths of those in the forest, she who had raised up a son whose nights were often savaged by dreams that looked sometimes like prescience.

Gilthas shook his head, swallowing to steady his voice.

"There is reason to hope, Mother. I don't know why she hasn't come here. There are ways to reach her, but I won't try those now. Whatever Kerian is doing, she does for a reason. The wrong move from me, and I might cause it all to fall in ruin."

Warm breezes, smoky and thick, tugged at Laurana's hair as she leaned out over the marble wall framing the little garden. She leaned out to see. Gilthas knew her and knew she did not strain only her eyes to see. She looked with her heart, with all her mind. What was happening in the kingdom? How many more would have to die?

"Mother," said the elf king. He took her hand and put it in the crook of his arm. "Come away now. We'll trust her. Whatever Kerian is doing, she is doing her best. As for Thorbardin, we must trust about that, too. She spoke well there and was heard, or she spoke well and wasn't. We must wait and see."

For she will not forget. She will come to me, he thought, looking out to the smoky night.

For another fortnight, the king went up to the roof to watch the forest. On almost every night, he saw the signs of burning, smoke hanging. To his city came news that the winter to come would be a hard one. Sir Thagol did not know the meaning of mercy, and he seemed to hate the crops of farmers as much as he hated farmers themselves. In the halls of elven power, Senator Rashas looked around at his fellows nervously, hearing their unease, their fear, and he grew afraid they would recall that he had been the greatest champion of the idea of Beryl's Dark Knights doing all they could to bring order to an uruly kingdom.

"An orderly kingdom," he'd argued, "will produce all the tribute the dragon wants. She will thrive, and we will survive. It is the only way!"

Now as his fellows looked out into the forest and

marked the smoke, they heard the cries of the people who feared that the winter would be a hungry one, and they began to look at Senator Rashas with narrowed eyes.

"This had better end soon," said Lady Sunstrike, who held lands out by the eastern part of the kingdom, in sight of the Stonelands. She had received her governorship from the hand of the young king. She had spoken with him lately, the king who sat upon his throne with his usual air of disinterest. To see him, anyone would think he was half asleep. Lady Sunstrike believed otherwise. "If it doesn't end, we will be wondering what to do with the hungry when the snow comes."

Rashas looked right and left, trying to think how he could rein in the Skull Knight.

As he thought, Lady Sunstrike cast another glance at the king. He seemed to rouse, his lids lifted. He held the lady's glance, only a moment. She did not nod, and he did not look again her way, but in the morning a rider went out from the city, naught but a lad with a saddlebag full of missives from his mistress to her steward.

In two days time, Kerian of Qualinesti received from Jeratt the startling news that they had not fought alone in their last battle with Knights. Outnumbered, certain to be killed, Jeratt had looked up to find a dozen fresh, armed men and women at their backs. Rabble, ragged outlaws like themselves, or so they thought until, the last Knight dead, they learned that these were not men and women of the forest at all. They were farmers, two of them villagers, three from the estates of Lady Sunstrike who governed this stony eastern province, all dressed to appear the most disreputable of citizens.

They had little to say, but one, as the others drifted away into the forest, suggested to Jeratt that they would not again fight alone.

"Call on us," he said. "I'm a stable boy on Lady Sunstrike's estate. We hear she's here, the lady who fights like a lioness. We know who she fights. If you call for help, we will come."

Kerian had lost the faith of farmers who feared to lose their heads. She'd seen her network of trusty villagers fall to ruin. Here, unlooked for, she found a strand with which to reweave her rebellion of elves. Fighters at need, carriers of news, granters of shelter, these would support her and her warriors in her battle.

———◆———

Kerian watched as Stanach came out of the passage through Lightning—Thunder, as he insisted on naming the falls—his hair and beard glistening with moisture, his clothing damp. The dwarf had been a patient prisoner—his word, not hers—and had done his duty at watch whenever required. He had never offered to go on raids, and no one asked. He was a king's ambassador and Kerian made it clear from the start that Stanach had no part in this work.

Stanach stood watch, hunted with the others, in all ways did his duty in camp, but he was not a genial ambassador. He kept to himself, told no tales around the fire, and made no friends among the resistance. What he did was watch Kerian. He watched her plan, he watched her lure Thagol this way and that, like a rough handler jerking a hound's chain. He saw her make maps for her warriors when she planned, he saw her pacing all the while a band of them was gone, on her feet almost every moment till they returned.

When she mourned the dead, she did so feeling the eyes of the dwarf on her. They were not unkindly, but they were always on her.

Damn, she thought, he watches me eat!

For all she knew, he watched her sleep.

There he stood, wet from the falls, his eyes on her again.
"What?" she said.

Usually he shook his head and sometimes he muttered,
"Nothing." This time he nodded to her once, a jerk of his
head, up and then down.

"Got company. Looks like a farmer to me."

Curious, Kerian rose and bade Stanach show the farmer
through. The dwarf was gone but a few moments before he
returned with a wide-eyed, soaking lad. The boy's name
was Aran Leafglow, he said, and he was no farmer but a
village lad. He jerked his head in a kind of bow, tugging at
his forelock.

"Lady Lioness," he said. "I come with news for you."

Lady Lioness. Kerian caught Stanach's grim smile out
the corner of her eye. Her warriors liked the spreading
name, so did the villagers and farmers. Thagol, from what
she had learned, hated it, for the people rallied to it.

Thagol had made a mistake. He'd punished the elves
widely for crimes they did not commit. In rage he'd fallen
on them with the fierceness of a dragon, unleashing his
Knights and his draconians, trying to cow the countryside.
He had pushed too hard.

"Give me your news," Kerian said. "Sit and talk."

The boy shook his head. "No'm. I can't sit, for I have to
get back and there's all the gorge to travel. I come to tell
you—there's a pack of Knights near. You said you'd want
to know. They're not but beyond Kellian Ridge."

Kerian drew a breath, long and slow and satisfied. "A
pack. How many?"

"Five, no more. Armed to the teeth, though, and they
have three draconians with them."

Eight. She thanked the boy and sent him out through
the falls. She called six outlaws to her, three down from
the hills, and sent them out with word to gather in all the
leaders of her scattered bands. Last she turned to Stanach,

and she said, "It's time now, Stanach Hammerfell. I'm going out to kill some Knights."

His eyes grew wide. "You're mad. You said yourself that the next time you kill you'll draw Thagol to you like steel to a lodestone."

"Yes," she said, "and I'm going to do just that. He's going to chase me right to the place where I will kill him."

"Ach, lass, you're mad."

She smiled and took up the sword she liked to wear. She sighted along the edge, decided it needed honing, and sat down to work. He watched her, and she let him. When she was finished with the sword, she took out the knife he'd given her long ago at the Hare and Hound. This, too, she honed with long singing strokes.

As she did, her eye on steel and stone, she said, "Of course there'll always be a safe place for you here, Stanach. I'll keep men back to ward you. When it's over, and Thagol is dead—"

He snorted. "You're a cocky one, aren't you Mistress Lioness?"

She smiled, stroking the steel with the stone. "When it's over and Thagol is dead, I will take you to Qualinost myself, and you can let my king know what you think about his chances for a treaty."

The dwarf shook his head and merely said again, "You're mad."

When she finished with the stone, he took it up and sat to work on the edge of his axe's blade. He set the axe head on his knee, the edge out, bracing with his right forearm while he worked with his left hand.

"What are you doing?"

"Going with you."

"No. You're not."

"Yes." He didn't look up, good at her own game. "I am. I'm here on my thane's business, Mistress Lioness, and

283

that means I go where I think he is best served." He looked up then, his blue-flecked black eyes hard and bright. "Will you be trying to stop me?"

She drew a slow, wry smiled. "If you're killed, there will be two kings I'll have to answer to."

Stanach returned to his work. "In that case, you won't be the one many people envy, will you?"

She said nothing more, seeing he wouldn't be moved. He kept quiet, listening to the voices of stone and steel with the air of one who hears a long forgotten song.

———◆◆◆———

They did not go quietly through the forest, the Knights and the draconians. They went as though they were lords of the place, crashing through the brush, the broad-chested horses tearing up the little road across the top of Kellian Ridge. A drover's path, the way a farmer took his sheep or cattle to market, it wandered up through the trees, over the stony crest, and down again. They went laughing, and one bore a sack of heads dangling from his saddlebag.

Kerian smelled the blood, and she knew this one at last was Headsman Chance. So did the nine men and women concealed in ambush. Beside her, Stanach balanced his throwing axe, testing. In the shadows, his teeth shone white in a hard grin. Kerian shook her head, pointing to the two draconians. Scales the color of greening copper, the creatures marched behind. One spat. The stone his spittle hit sizzled then melted. Another, as though challenged, imitated his companion. The acrid stink of acid stung Kerian's nostrils.

She gestured to her warriors, her fingers speaking her mind: Draconians first, then Knights.

That meant Stanach held back, for he'd lose that weapon if it killed a draconian. The creature would turn to steel-eating acid as it died. He lifted his lip in an impatient snarl. Kerian glared. He stilled.

One Knight went by, then another. The third passed, and nothing moved in the brush on either side of the path. If she had not placed them there herself, Kerian wouldn't have known her outlaws waited.

A crow called, high. The fourth Knight rode by, and then Chance Headsman with his sack banging on the shoulder of his tall steed. Kerian's hands itched, her fingers curled around the grip of her sword. Stanach poked her ribs. She smiled wryly and settled.

The first draconian came, a little ahead of the second. Kerian counted three beats and then heard the high whistle of one, two, then three arrows. The first caught the lagging draconian in the eye, right through. The second missed both, and the third fell useless into a hissing pool of acid just as Sir Chance turned.

Kerian shouted, "Go!" and the forest erupted in battle cries, in flashing steel, in wasping arrows. Half her warriors attacked the horses, and the beasts screamed, dying. Knights cursed, falling. The other half went after the last two draconians. Among those, Kerian fought. They fell upon the beast-men with stone from above, heaving crushing boulders from the hilltop, the stone breaking bone. One creature died howling, while the other leaped aside from the path of a stone half its size. Leathery wings rustled, Stanach shouted, and Kerian saw the draconian's leap turn into a swift glide.

Two arrows flew. One took the creature in the throat, its flight staggered now. Another arrow sped to the draconian's eye. Screaming, it fell.

Kerian shouted warning to the elves below. Two scrambled, one fell. Stanach leaped to pull the elf up—and Kerian caught him by the back of his shirt as the draconian fell, dead upon the unlucky elf.

NANCY VARIAN BERBERICK

Hideous screams rent the forest air as the elf died, his flesh melting from him, his bones rendered to slag.

Kerian cried, "Kill them!" but all around her that work was being done as her warriors gutted the war-horses, toppled the riders, getting the armored Knights down and helpless. Two fell into the road, one fell under his horse. The third slashed about him with singing steel. Another elf died, screaming. Hacking, slashing at the downed Knights, Kerian's warriors killed three. One remained on horseback, one on foot. Kerian leaped for the unhorsed man, sword high, her steel clashing against his, sparks flying. She fought snarling, she fought cursing, and it had been a long time since she'd killed, but now she longed for blood.

She shoved at the Knight hard, her weight no proof against his. Nimble-footed, she leaped a little aside, got around him, and tangled her feet in his legs. He fell. She stamped on his neck, her boot heel crushing his larynx through gorget and mail. She jerked off his helm and threw it into the brush. With one swift stab, Kerian killed, pinning him to the earth with her sword.

Panting, sweat running on her, she stood with arms trembling from the effort, hearing the cries of her wounded and a sudden thunder.

Someone shouted, "Kerian!"

She turned, saw the sword of Chance Headsman flashing high, the blood-red nostrils of his war-horse, the Knight's visored face, the face of death. She saw the hand gripping the sword fly out, fly off the man's arm, fingers still clutching, the sword tumbling, and Stanach's throwing axe landed on the ground, nearly at her feet.

They fell on the Headsman like wolves, the surviving Night People. They tore him from his horse and flung him to the ground. They held him, ripped his helm from him and one—a young woman with fierce green eyes, picked up his own sword, prying the dead hand from the grip.

The glances of warrior and Lioness met like steel sparking.

Kerian nodded.

In the dust, in the forest he had terrorized, Chance Headsman lost his head, and out near the Stonelands, Lord Thagol felt a jolt and knew he had found his prey, his enemy, at last.

———◆———

Eamutt Thagol gathered all his forces, every Knight he could spare. He marched them into the forest, he marched them after the Lioness. He flanked his column with blood-lusting draconians, and these he let range out into the forest, searching for outlaw prey. They went like a bludgeon tearing down the roads, ripping through the villages, and they never got very far.

Kerian had all she needed, a canny force of warriors and farmers who knew their territory well. Sometimes they surrounded a column, hitting hard, killing mostly horses in the first wave, then retreating. "Until six breaths after they think we are gone," she'd say, then the elves would fall upon them again, this time from the rear.

In this way, for Kerian's well-planned strikes seeming random as lightning, the Night People wreaked havoc upon the Knights. They fought a battle of harassment, Kerian's forces splitting when she needed them to, coalescing again, and harrying again. She came at the Knights from behind, killing the rearguard. She fell upon them on every side, savaging the flanks, and there was not a bridge for them to use between Qualinost and the Stonelands, not before or behind. The roads were blocked with felled trees.

Kerian drove her enemy deep into the thickest part of the forest, but Thagol would not turn back. He would not give up. He smelled her, he tasted her thoughts, he knew what her blood would feel like on his hands. He hated her with a passion as strong as fire. He dreamed of killing her, waking and sleeping, he had the thousand images of her thousand deaths in his mind.

He would not give up. All around him Knights died, elves died, and Sir Thagol would not give up. Fierce, furious, he drove his men, and one night he saw Kerian's plan. He looked into her mind and read it as though it were a book. He saw not as a Skull Knight, for she had the ward of an ancient elf woman's ancient magic on her. He saw as a general. He realized what she would do because he knew what he would do in her place. She wanted to drive him to the eastern edge of the forest, and he thought that was a good idea. A little at a time, he let his men bleed away from him in numbers she wouldn't notice. He sent them with orders, he ranged them in careful position. He let Kerian harry him on. He didn't make it too easy for her, but he was eager to put the Stonelands at his back. From there, he would fight her back into the forest and—by vanished Takhisis!—he would drive her into the arms of his waiting reserves.

He would return to Qualinost with the head of a Lioness to hang.

———◆•◆———

Kerian gathered her warriors, Jeratt, Feather's Flight, all of them. They came one by one to her fire, rough and bloodied, hard-eyed and weary. They came, and the leader of each band of Night People told their weapons, each speaking the count of sword and dagger, of bows and arrows, of axes, of mail shirts and helms. Each told the names of the men and women in their bands.

Jeratt, who went last, said, "That bastard Knight has the border at his back, and he isn't going to flee now. Once out of the forest, he's lost. He won't get past the border and into the kingdom again. He'll fight and be trapped, just like you want."

She thought so, too. Across the fire, near Feather's Flight, the dwarf Stanach stood, his eyes on her. To him, Kerian said, "You can go now. Thagol's not guarding the roads to Qualinost. I'll send warriors to guide you to a safe place."

He shook his head. "No need to."

"If you go into battle—"

Stanach laughed, a harsh, bitter bark. He lifted his hand, his right, ruined and the fingers twisted. "Nay, no need to tell me what can happen, Mistress Lioness. I'm with you."

She looked around at them all, the dwarven ambassador, the half-elf who was her friend and her second. She looked at her captains and her good and trusty outlaws. Their numbers had grown while, by last count, Thagol had lost a good part of his force, run off or killed.

"Remember Jeratt," she said, "Thagol's mine. No one else gets him, and no one else tries. Now post watch, get some sleep, and we go at him—" She grinned to match Jeratt's own. "We go at him when the moon sets."

She watched them go, each of her Night People back to his or her own band. She watched until they became part of the night. Beside her, Stanach said he thought she would do well to sleep. She looked at him long in the firelight and shadows.

"Do you know," she said, musing, "I used to sleep in silk and satin. I used to sleep in a high bedroom and my lover would wake me gently with kisses and whisper to ask if he could send for my breakfast."

He is a king, she thought.

"I used to sleep above a tavern," Stanach said, "with the clatter of the cooks in the kitchen below. Getting hard to remember that, eh?"

"A little."

"Go," he said. "Get some sleep. After, I will, then we fight."

She curled up, her arms wrapped tightly around herself for warmth, the bloodstone amulet in her hand, but she didn't sleep. This night, her plan was nearly ready to spring, and she dared not dream for fear Lord Thagol would be listening.

———————◆———————

A storm roared out of the forest, falling upon the Knights like lightning from the night sky, thunder screaming. Blades shrieking, elf warriors howling for the deaths of their enemies overwhelmed the watch, tearing through them. The Knights leaped up from their bedrolls, naked of their armor, scrambling for weapons, and Lord Thagol's voice roared over all, cursing. His draconians came in from the outer parts of the camp and met a wall of arrows, a hail of swords, and the forest reeked with their deaths, rang with the shrieks of elves who had fallen to their talons, their fangs, their poison.

All the forest smelled of blood and poisonous acid, all the forest echoed with the clang and clash of steel. Kerian threw all her forces at the Knights, believing them helpless. She flung herself furuiously into the fray. She strode the slaughter field and spilled the blood of her enemies. All around her, her warriors gave good accounting, no more than the good and simple folk who had come to fight beside them. The outrages of the seasons past carried them—the killings, the burnings, the savageries of Thagol's Knights.

They had their cause; they had their fierce Lioness. She had her king's need. All this carried them, surging into slaughter, made them redden the earth with blood, made them forget they ever knew the word mercy as the din of battle filled their ears. The sound was so loud it pressed the air from their lungs, and their eyes saw such sights as another day would make their stomachs turn.

Through it all, Kerian ran fighting and searching for Thagol, for the Knight who had unleashed the butchery of the past year. She ran killing, and even before she saw him, sword high and about to plunge it into the breast of an elf, she knew she had him. He withdrew, blood dripping, and she ran at him, roaring. He laughed over the corpse and pointed, somewhere behind her, somewhere over her shoulder. Laughing still, he reached for her.

She ducked, sword staggered, her swing broken. She turned and saw what made the Skull Knight laugh.

From out of the forest, like lightning, like thunder, a band of horsemen, all armored in black, all howling for death. Her warriors fell before them, trampled beneath iron-shod hoofs, slashed, beheaded, speared upon lances and flung aside.

His face like a burn-scar, terrible eyes dark as death, Thagol lunged for her, his sword high. He screamed in her head, and it was the sound he imagined she would make, dying one of the thousand deaths he finally chose for her. Kerian turned and tried to defend. She lifted her own sword and knew the gesture for no more than that. His sword hung, right at the arc of his swing and came down—

—hard upon the skull of a young elf leaping between the Lioness and Dark Knight. She saw the boy's face— Ander! Blood spurted, white shards of skull tumbling through the air, and in the ruin of his face Kerian she saw the terrible surprise in his eyes as he fell. On the face of the Skull Knight there was fury as he lunged again. Kerian dropped back, hoping his thrust would overbalance him. It did not, and she moved swiftly, brought up her own blade, met his and held. Thagol, the heavier, pressed. Kerian, the lighter, let him. He thrust again, she moved as though to counter, then ducked hard aside. He lost his footing on the blood-slick earth. In the instant that bought her, she turned and screamed, *Retreat! Retreat!* With all the air in her lungs, every second the boy's life bought her, she shouted her warriors off the field.

They did not hear her; they did not have to. The farmers and townsmen, never trained to fight, were the first to die. The outlaws, her good warriors, knew a losing fight when they saw one. They ran, leaping over the corpses of foes and friends alike, into the forest, deep into the woods and high up the granite slopes where, maybe, horses would find it hard to follow.

Kerian ran after, cursing, and hearing Lord Thagol's laughter ringing not in her ears but bellowing through her mind.

CHAPTER
22

Kerian counted her dead. She counted them by reckoning those who did not make it out, who fell in the forest to Knights, to the trampling hoofs of war horses, to swords, to maces, to Thagol's evil. She counted them in tears and wasn't ashamed of that. She wept, Jeratt did, and Feather's Flight did not, for she was among the dead. She lay among the farmers, the villagers, beside Ander the miller's son who had refused to hand her over to Thagol's Knights. He'd been in love with her, so said Jeratt

"When I close my eyes, I see it on him still, Jeratt. The look on him, dying for me." The flash of madness, of glory as he flung himself between her and the killing steel.

They sat on a high, boulder-topped hill of the kind she first saw an age ago, in another autumn, as she climbed endlessly behind Stanach to avoid Knights on the road to the Hare and Hound. Stubborn, that day she'd climbed in ill-chosen boots until her feet bled. She thought, now, that her heart bled. When she looked down the hill, Kerian saw the dwarf coming up. He'd fought well—for a one-handed man, Jeratt had said.

"What are you going to do about the dwarf, Kerian?"

Kerian shrugged. "What's to do? He's here, and I can't get him safely to Qualinost. He should have stayed behind. Damn, maybe he should have stayed in Thorbardin."

Kerian watched Stanach labor up the hill, weary as she, sweat running on him, a filthy bandage wrapped around his head.

"Are you all right?" she asked when he came close.

He looked up at her in moonlight, his eyes fierce as a blade's edge. He said, "No, I'm bleeding. I'm hungry. I am in this gods damned forest, Mistress Lioness. I am not all right." He looked around, behind, to the sides. "I don't think any of us are."

She frowned. Jeratt lifted his head.

"There's something in the forest," the dwarf said.

Jeratt rose, his hand on his sword.

"No." Stanach dropped to a seat beside Kerian, his breathing a weary groaning. Kerian touched his shoulder lightly. He shook his head. "I'm all right. By Reorx's beard, though, I am *tired*."

"In the forest," he said, returning to what he'd started to say. "Not Knights. Not the rest of our folk straggling back or away. Something else. Something sly and quiet."

Kerian nodded to Jeratt, who went off down the hill to gather a few of those still standing. They went out into the forest, cat-footed. A young woman ran up the hill—where did she get the strength?—to whisper in Kerian's ear.

"Yes, and quickly. Keep an eye out for friends."

Down she went, bounding, and in moments, one by one, guards took stands around the hill, setting a perimeter. Stanach put his arms on his drawn-up knees, his head on his forearms. He did not take four breaths before Kerian heard him gently snoring. She sat alone beside the sleeping emissary from Thorbardin, a dwarf far from home. When he wavered, she helped him lie down. He hardly woke, never missed a breath. Neither did he stir when Jeratt came back to say he'd found nothing and no one in the forest.

"I don't know what the dwarf heard, but we didn't see sign of anything. Just his imagination?"

Kerian glanced at Stanach, sleeping, then back. "Doesn't usually have a very active imagination, does he?"

Jeratt agreed that he didn't. "What dwarf does? There's nothing there, Kerian. Just the night, the forest and our doom, eh?"

Just those things. Jeratt sat down. He'd found a good stream and offered her his leather water bottle, fat and dripping. "That's supper, I'm afraid, and I'm thinking breakfast won't be much better."

After a time, he went away to watch at the edge of the camp, and Kerian saw him walking among the warriors, bending low to speak to one, slapping the shoulder of another. In the morning they would break their fast on a bitter bread. In the morning, Thagol would come through the forest with steel.

She sat a long time thinking, gazing into the forest. After a time, she saw a fire spring up, then another. The blood in her veins was cold, and her heart weighed like stone as one after another fires of Thagol's encampments glowed, out in the distance, out between the trees. One and one and one . . . they made a circle, wide and strong.

"They ring us in," she said to the night.

She closed her eyes, and when she opened them again her heart stood suddenly still. Upon the forest night, the trees, the darkness, the little bits of light from campfires, something moved between her camp and that of the Knights. Hair rose up prickling on her arms, the back of her neck. Kerian's breath caught, and she let it go silently. Whatever it was drifted, then stopped, then drifted again. It moved like smoke, like shadow, and as Kerian watched, trying to make out shape and substance, the thing vanished.

295

Beside her, Stanach stirred. He groaned, cursed, and shoved himself up to sitting. He saw the water and drank deeply. He offered her some, and she drank more.

Kerian pointed to the lights, the real gleams of real fires. Stanach sighed.

"I tell you, Mistress Lioness, I don't like being away from Thorbardin. It's never good. I'm meant to be there, I'm supposed to be there. All this . . . " He swept his arm wide, taking in the sleeping elves, the distant Knights and draconians. "All this, damn, I don't even know why I'm here anymore—where I am or what I'm fighting for."

"You're north of Reanlea Gorge, not far from Lighting—"

"—Thunder."

"Lightning and Thunder. You aren't even all that far from Thorbardin. Closer than you'd be if you were sleeping in a bed of goose down in the best chamber King Gilthas could offer."

A small breeze wandered around the top of the hill, smelling like earth and stone, like the water in the rill below. "Ah, your king. And you, his own, dear outlaw."

She looked at him sideways. He did not smile, but he slid her a look of knowing.

"His own, dear outlaw, that's you. What are you going to do in the morning, Mistress Lioness?"

"Fight."

He shook his head. "You won't make it through. The Skull Knight is set up to crush you."

"Us," she murmured, her eyes on the fires.

He grunted. "You'll die."

"We probably will."

The first howling of wolves wound through the night. One to another, they called out, *Brother! Where are you? Brother! There is food! Brother!*

Kerian winced, thinking of the corpses to be stripped, the bodies of friends who could not be decently buried.

Softly Stanach said, "How will we die, Mistress Lioness?"

Kerian drew a breath, a long one, and on it she felt again the quiver of tears she'd shed for a boy who had flung himself between Thagol's sword and her breast.

"We will die well. If anyone knows about it, if anyone of us gets out of here to tell, they will be singing the song of us in every tavern in Qualinesti and all the best bars in Thorbardin."

"Our kings would be proud."

Now tears did prick behind her eyes. "Yes, they would be proud."

They stood a moment longer, silent and watching the wood. Once, Stanach peered a little closer into the darkness. Kerian followed his line of sight and thought she saw a darker darkness moving. She glanced at the dwarf, he at her. They looked again and saw only fires winking, out there in the darkness, like bloodshot stars. Wolves howled, and Stanach said they'd better get some more sleep.

"Goodnight, missy," he said, his voice low and fond.

Kerian, however, did not sleep. She sat long awake, watching the fires of her foe, watching over her warriors.

Now and then she saw flitting shadows in the woods, swift out of the corner of her eye and gone. No more than that and certainly nothing of the odd shape she'd seen earlier.

***

The risen sun set the morning haze afire, gilding the tops of the trees, staining the stones with ghostly blood-paint. In the sky, crows hung. Ravens burdened the trees, and Kerian stood upon the hill, high on the top of the lichened boulder. Below, her warriors made ready. They had slept cold, not lighting fires. Now they sat proving their weapons, honing bright edges, attending to bow strings, to fletching.

"Do we wait?" Jeratt asked, his eye on the distance, his mind already in the field.

Kerian didn't think there was anything else to do. "Get them all to high ground," she said, with one gesture sweeping the hollow below. "If Thagol's going to get us, he's going to work for it."

Jeratt whistled. Every head turned, faces lifted. He gestured, and Kerian counted them, coming. There weren't more than a hundred of them, with weakened weapons. Some had stolen swords, lifted from corpses. Out in the forest, there had to be half as many draconians and twice as many Knights. She gathered her warriors around her.

"Find cover wherever you can, make them find you. We don't rush; we don't attack. We hold this hill until we've killed all we can."

Until they have killed us.

Beside her, Stanach made his axe sing to a whetstone. Little sparks flew up from the blade. It amazed her he still had it. The weapon was made to fly, to kill at a distance. It was easily the first weapon lost in any battle.

"Are you fond of it?" she asked, her eyes on the forest, watching for her foe.

"The axe. Pretty much. I made it."

She turned, surprised. "You?"

From lowering brows, he looked at her. He held up his hand, the one with the broken fingers. He turned the hand over, as though to study it. "Surprising, isn't it? Fight pretty good for a one-handed man. Imagine what I could do with two."

The color mounted to her cheeks as she watched him study his hand. He didn't move those fingers, he couldn't, but sight of them reminded her of the sign above his tavern door, a broken hammer on an anvil's breast. Stanach's Curse.

"Look," said the dwarf, with his axe pointing down to the forest. "Time has come, Mistress Lioness."

Time had come. The Knights came through the forest on foot, their steeds abandoned. They did not come clanking in armor. They came lightly, in mail and some wearing breastplates. They came behind a vanguard of draconians, the lizard-men their shield and decisive weapon all at once. The wind came from behind, carrying the reptile stench of them, the reek of their foul breath.

"Archers," Kerian said, surprised by the coolness of her voice. "Draconians first. Go after them the way they used to go after dragons in the days before dragonlances—aim for the eyes, send your shaft right through to their tiny brains and drop them where they stand. Let the Knights wade through the poison."

Jeratt laughed, liking the picture of that.

"We never leave this hill," Kerian said. "We make them come up."

Closer, the draconians slashed through the underbrush, and now Kerian heard their voices, growling curses in a language whose every word seemed like a curse. She put a hand on Jeratt's arm. She knew this was the moment to steady him or he'd leap too soon.

"Easy," she said. "Let them see us. Let them come to us."

He quivered under her hand, but he held. Because he did, the rest did. Arrows whispered from quivers. By the handful each archer took them, one to nock to the bowstring, four to hold between clenched teeth.

"Not till you see the first of them among the ashes of our fires," Kerian warned.

Below the crest, on either side, men and women with swords and war-axes stood ready to fall upon whatever enemy made it up the hill.

"Soft," Kerian said, "now patient, patient."

The first draconian stepped into the empty campsite, stopped and looked around. His fellows came after, and they slowed, then stopped, looking around for prey.

Stanach stood and tucked his whetstone into the little pouch at his belt. Jeratt took a careful breath around the shafts of his arrows. He lifted his bow. Every archer had an eye on Kerian, and every one of them saw her lift her hand, drew breath as she did, and let fly when she dropped her fist.

The arrow-storm whistled down the hill, shrieking in the morning silence. One draconian fell, and another. A third, and one after that. Four in the first volley! It was not enough. Came the second volley, and two more fell. One stumbled into the decomposing corpse of his fellow and died screaming. Three fell wounded, and it needed another volley to kill those.

Kerian shouted, "Archers!" and the fourth volley flew.

Beyond the hissing, reeking corpses of draconians, the Knights stopped. Some stumbled into the acid, others pulled away in time, and those saw their prey atop the hill.

"Go!" shouted Thagol, pointing. "Charge them!"

The Skull Knight drove them hard, howled at them, cursed them, and sent them around the deadly draconian corpses. They split and regrouped to come up the hill from the sides.

Heart hammering, her sword in her right hand, the dwarf-made knife in her left, Kerian looked at Jeratt, looked at Stanach.

"Now," she said, as the first of Thagol's men came up the hill. "For the song!"

For the song, she cried, and even as she did, her battle cry changed to a baffled shout as the line of Knights wavered at the sides and in the rear. From the crest, she saw them falter and fall out, one after another staggering from the line. Some cried out, others fell in silence, as death came suddenly.

"Look!" Jeratt shouted. "What is that?"

He pointed. Something moved like a shadow behind the Knights, dark and swift and silent.

"By the gods," Jeratt whispered. "It's him."

Kerian's heart lifted. "It's Dar," she said, for she recognized the tactic, the swift charge with filled bows and the equally swift retreat. The foray out from shadows with cudgel to smash a skull, with sword to gut a foe, then slipping away. The newcomers flashed in and out of shadows, striking swiftly, sometimes in silence so that they seemed like ghosts, sometimes howling to chill the blood of their enemies.

"Look!" Stanach cried, even as the confused Knights turned in on themselves, back to the ground they'd tried to flee. The dwarf laughed. "They're being herded like cattle!"

As they watched, the Kagonesti shifted ground, surrounding the Knights, and indeed, herding them. Hurt, confused, their numbers falling away before their eyes, the Knights tried to break out, tried to find their lord or hear his commands. Kerian didn't doubt the Lord Knight shouted or tried to direct his men, but no one could hear him above the blood-chilling war cries of Dar and his warriors. A little at a time, though they fought hard and sometimes bravely, the Knights were driven toward the bottom of the hill, forced to mass—in many instances weaponless—to the place Kerian defended.

"Will we just stand here?" Jeratt said.

Kerian flashed him a bright and sudden grin. "I don't think we'd better or we'll be overrun by fleeing Knights."

Shouting, Jeratt waved their warriors down. Behind Kerian the archers filled their bows again.

The Knights, beset from behind, driven from the sides, heard at last the voice of their lord. Thagol's command ripped through the melee, rallying his men until they formed three forces, one at point, two flanking. One of the flanks turned into the forest eastward, the other westward. The point of the spear, the draconians and the Knights, no longer driven, charged the hill again.

In the wood the air filled with war cries and death-screams as the Kagonesti and the Knights came together. Kerian saw them, the Wilder Elves outflanked, the Knights and draconians rampaging among them, savaging Dar's band from two sides.

"Go!" she shouted to her warriors. "To the Kagonesti! Go!"

First down the hill was Jeratt, eyes alight, face shining with a warrior's half-mad laughter. He ran to help an old comrade, the friend who had never forgotten him, and whooped a high and joyous battle cry.

Before her eyes, Jeratt staggered. He stumbled, turned, upon his face the same expression she'd seen on Ander— the utter shock of the dying. He fell, his hands clutching his chest, blood spilling out over his fingers, out around the steel of a Knight's flung dagger.

Kerian shouted, "No!" and bellowed orders to her warriors to fight on. Someone yelled, "For Jeratt!"

For Ander! For Felan!

For Qualinesti!

They went, and as they did the two flanks of Knights and draconians turned again, wheeling to meet the charge. Outnumbered, still Kerian's warriors fought, for it was Jeratt at their head, Jeratt, somehow still stumbling forward, unwilling to turn from embattled friends until death stole his last breath. From the hill, commanding her archers, Kerian saw the Wilder Elves and her own warriors falling before the draconians and the Knights like hay before the scythe.

Furious, Kerian turned to the archers. Every one of them stood drained of color, the blood run out of their faces, leaving the flesh ashen. Stanach, halfway down the hill, stood like stone, while blood and battle lapped up the hill. Eyes on the forest where Kerian's warriors had gone to fight for the Wilder Elves, he shouted:

"There! By Reorx! There!"

The forest trembled. The trees shook. Darkness came, and darkness went as though the wood itself possessed eyes to blink. Shadow and light ran together, not in dappling but in a great whirling force as though they rushed to each other like live beings, long parted and longing for one another's embrace.

Screams arose from all around, and these were not the shrieks of the dying. These were screams of terror, cries in elven voices and human voices. Somewhere, draconians raged, but their voices sounded small.

The ground heaved, and the trees danced. They lifted root, raised branches like revelers. The earth gaped wide, in places swallowing combatants. Not one of the fallen was an elf, Qualinesti or Wilder, however. Kerian drew breath to call back her warriors and let the breath go. A great howling filled the world, as though from the throat of the earth itself.

It rose from ground, from stone, a beast with arms like enormous trees, legs like hewn stone. Stanach cursed and prayed. Beside him, Kerian felt as though she were falling, falling into a vortex. She had seen this in Elder's fires! Listening to the whisper of the ancient's magic, she had listened to the distant thoughts of Elementals. This beast she had dreamed in smoke and firelight, with a woman so old no one knew her name. It rose before her now, a misshapen thing, with a head like hills, eyes like forest fire, and hands like slabs of stone. A creature made of the elements of air and earth walking among them.

A voice like thunder's clap roared.

The first to fall before the thing were the creatures no nature had ever envisioned, the draconians bred of sorcery and the eggs of dragons. They died under the massive feet of the beast. They died of the fire of its eyes. Their poison became as mist and vanished. Upon the forest air ran rage, a fury like fire. Before that the Knights cowered. Some fell dead of hearts burst in terror. Others fled, and those who did not died on the swords of their enemies or the swords of their battle companions, enraged by cowardice. One who did not run, one who beat his own men with the flat of his sword, who cursed them screaming, was the Knight Kerian most longed to see.

Sword in hand, she ran down the hill, into the violence of the forest and the killing. Eamutt Thagol, his back to her, felt her coming.

Roaring, Thagol turned. His eyes took and held her. In her mind, she heard him, like a wolf howling, she heard him, and she felt him as she had in nightmare, hunting her. She lifted her sword high in the killing arc. As though a hand gripped her wrist, she halted. As though commanded, she stayed, and she could not take her eyes from his, could not look away. While all around her the earth rioted at the will of a shadowy beast born of Elemental magic, she stood arrested, frozen in the grip of the Skull Knight's mind.

In her brain, she felt a roaring, like storm, like thunder. Behind her eyes, she saw the bright flash of his sword, like lightning. She felt something, a pull, a tug toward him, like a cold hand on her heart. He wanted to taste something, to taste her dying.

Blinded by the light of his sword, deafened by his voice in her mind, she cried out. She wrenched away and lost her balance. Stumbling, she fell, and he was upon her, the weight of him bearing her all the way to the ground. She thrashed beneath him, his mail biting into the flesh of her neck, his elbows pinning her at the shoulders. His breath on her face was icy, a dead man's breath.

Kerian fought, thrashing harder. She got a knee up, got a foot on the ground. Weaponless, her sword flung far from her, she snarled and lunged at him, biting his face, his cheek. She tore flesh and pushed up hard. He lifted, and she brought up her knee to advantage. Howling, he cursed her, falling away, doubling over as she grabbed his own sword.

All the forest stood still, as though even the beast made of Elemental fury held its breath.

Kerian played the headsman's part. Hard she lifted and hard she let fall her sword. Even then, his voice was howling in her head, like a wolf's. When he died, his head fallen from his shoulders, even then she heard him.

Though all the forest had fallen still, the howling didn't stop in Kerian's head. It never stopped, until she'd finished counting her dead, until she found one over whom she must howl herself.

On the killing ground, the forest floor running with blood, Kerian found her brother, Iydahar, for whom she had come out of Qualinost, a long, long time ago last year. He was dead of an axe, the blade sunk keep in his chest, the haft running with his blood.

She said, "Dar," as though he could answer. Wind off the battleground ruffled his hair. She touched his cheek and felt sweat cooling on his lifeless skin. She traced the planes of his face, a face known to her all her life, the face of a man she had hardly known.

Again, she said, "Dar . . ."

Beside him knelt his wife, Ayensha, with her arms wrapped round herself. She did not keen or make any sound until she looked up and saw Kerian.

"Is he dead?" she said. "Thagol?"

"He is dead."

Ayensha nodded, then bent low to put her cheek upon her husband's chest. "He didn't want to come. I begged him. Elder begged him."

Kerian looked up, the stilling breeze cool on her cheeks. "Elder."

"You saw her."

"Her . . ."

"The shape of her magic, the shape of her rage."

She'd spoken with Elementals, the ancient woman whose magic could make the forest a confusion for her enemies.

"Dar came," said Ayensha, "because of Elder, because I had promised and pledged to you and your cause. You killed my rapist and saved me from worse. You tried to drive the alien Knights from an elf kingdom. We told him—I told him—you were owed that much."

In her eyes shone the terrible light of one who had paid far more than she thought she owed. Together they sat in silence, each beside the man they had loved, brother and husband. For a long while no one came to disturb them, the two women in the wreckage of the forest, one in the ruin of her life.

CHAPTER 23

"Tell me," said the king, Gilthas with his hand on her cheek. "Kerian, my Lioness, tell me."

She'd dreamed of the wolf again, but she would not tell him. Instead, she covered his hand with her own, and she brought his hand to her lips to gently kiss. He took her in his arms, held her, and when she nestled against him, her head on his shoulder, she smelled the old familiar scent of exotic spices, the fragrance of far Tarsis, of an older time when she was a laughing servant who spied upon her master for the sake of her lover. Now she wore that girl's clothing, her silk bed gown, her perfumes and her lotions, but she was not that girl. She would never be again.

"Gil, tell me what your mother has learned from Thorbardin."

He sat up, and he drew her to sit beside him. From the window a chill breeze came wandering. He wrapped her in the sheets when she shivered. "Only hopeful things. In Thorbardin, they may soon be laying plans to create a safe passage out of here if and when we need it. As soon as he returns home, Stanach Hammerfell will speak to the

Council of Thanes in our behalf. He doesn't imagine anyone will gainsay us now.

"The dragon will not hold her patience much longer, and that hasn't to do with us. It has to do with the politics of her own greed and lust for power."

She moved to slip under the covers again.

"Kerian." He brushed her hair from her cheek, breathing the scent of it, the scent of her skin when he kissed her. "Kerian, my own outlaw. You're soon gone."

She was. Plans had already been made for her return to the forest. Her force of Night People had been severely damaged in the battle with the Skull Knight and his draconians and Knights. No one imagined that a new Lord Knight would not swiftly be sent to oversee green Beryl's kingdom. Kerian planned that this one, whoever he might be, would come into the kingdom thinking Eamutt Thagol had died putting down a rebellion that hadn't the least spark left in it or thinking that he'd left behind a population so cowed by the fighting that they would not, could not, lift a hand to defend themselves.

She smiled, a predatory smile. That was fine with her if the new lord protector thought so. Those in Qualinesti who needed to know otherwise, did know otherwise.

Gilthas sighed. "You're soon gone," he said. "I know. Before you go, I will do what I am certain no king in Krynn has had to do as often as I."

Kerian looked up at him, knowing what he'd say. In the silence before he did, she saw again all the dreamless nights of the year gone past, the hard days without him, the long roads away from him. She saw loneliness, and still, she did not know how she could answer him as he wished.

"Kerian," he said, "you have risked your life to fight the enemy of my embattled kingdom. My love, my Lioness of Qualinesti, I ask you again: Be my wife, be the queen my people need. We can wed in secrecy but go on as before for now. Kerian, you have loved me, you have fought in my cause, you have—in the name of all gods, woman, why will you not marry me?"

"In the name of all gods," she said, "how can I? How can I risk what would be said, how this marriage would be used against you? Gil, you don't know what you're asking."

His eyes narrowed; she saw a sudden flash of royal impatience. He took her by the shoulders, gently, and he turned her to face him. He leaned close, kissed her, and held her a little away again.

"I know what I'm asking. I'm asking you to marry me. I'm asking you to trust the future. I have asked you to be my outlaw, now I ask you to be my queen."

Trust the future. Who could ask her to do a harder thing? Yet, what else had she been doing all this year past?

"Today I have to leave," she said. "I am taking Stanach to the border. Your mother will have an escort for him from there." She smiled grimly. "He'd rather trudge through the Stonelands than use the emerald's magic again, but we can wait a bit. Meet me at Giliean's Oak at day's end."

She said only that, and the king took her into his arms again.

———◆———

In the evening of the day, with the sky purpling and the light dimming, the last of the year's fireflies danced in the gloom beneath the oaks, four people gathered: a king, his lover, the queen mother, and a dwarf far from home. This should have been a marriage of golden splendor, of feasts the month before, feasts all the month after. There should have been balls and wine pouring from fountains. There should have been masques, visitations from every lord and lady in the land, felicitations from each member of the Thalas-Enthia.

None of these would happen. In the little oak grove, the elf king was not splendid. He dressed in gear as rough as that of any hunter in the forest, any one of his own outlaws. His lover stood as rustic as he, and the only thing to betray a softer life was the last fragrance of a soap made with Tarsian spices lingering on her skin.

"Who will wed you?" asked the dwarf. He looked askance at the king. "The woman deserves a true marriage, honest and fair."

Gilthas smiled. "We wed each other, and ceremony isn't necessary, though half our history is writ by ceremony. Only a witness, friend dwarf." A witness, and stars for company, fireflies for light. "Do you witness?"

Stanach bowed with sincerity and grace. "I witness, Your Majesty."

A queen, once a general, Laurana stepped forward. The hem of her russet woolen gown swept across a fragrant carpet of fallen leaves. Resplendent in simple wool, legend said she had been splendid in war regalia, in battle leathers and blood. She took Kerian's hand in hers and turned toward her son.

The king looked at her long and said to her softly, "Kerianseray of Qualinesti, my Lioness, will you put your hand in mine?"

"My hand is in yours, my lord king."

"Kerianseray of Qualinesti, my Lioness, will you weave your fate with mine, take my kingdom as you take me?"

Her heart beating hard, her throat closing up with a sweet sadness, she said that she would do these things. "I am your wife, my king. Together we will make such a light that it will stand always against the darkness."

He let go her hands and took a ring from his finger, the old one she knew; the hands joined round the topaz. "We are joined, heart and heart, hand and hand, fate and fate. We are one, wife." Solemnly, he repeated her vow.

"Together we will make such a light that it will stand always against the darkness."

They were one, wed before a dwarf and before the queen mother joined in law as they had been in body and spirit. Alone in the forest, they were wed, soon to be parted, one to return to his city, the other to take the long road away.

Yet they knew it, all of them, that dark forces pressed against their kingdom, a dragon's greed, fate's iron fist. They knew it, and still they rejoiced.

The Dhamon Saga
Jean Rabe

The sensational conclusion to the trilogy!

Redemption
Volume Three

Dhamon's dragon-scale curse forces him deep into evil territory,
where he must follow the orders of an unknown entity. Time
is running out for him and his motley companions—a mad
Solamnic Knight, a wingless draconian, and a treacherous ogre
mage. Is it too late for Dhamon to redeem his nefarious past?

July 2002

Now available in paperback

Betrayal
Volume Two

Haunted by the past, Dhamon Grimwulf suffers daily torture
from the dragon scale attached to his leg. As he searches for a
cure, he must venture into a treacherous black dragon's swamp.
The swamp is filled with terrors bent on destroying him, but
the true danger to Dhamon is much closer than he thinks.

Tales that span the length and breadth of Krynn's history

The Golden Orb
Icewall Trilogy, Volume Two • Douglas Niles

The Arktos prosper in their fortress community, while the ogre king and queen seethe and plot revenge. Humans and highlanders must band together to defend against an onslaught that threatens mass destruction.

Sister of the Sword
The Barbarians, Volume Three • Paul B. Thompson & Tonya C. Cook

The village of the dragon is under siege. Riding hard to the rescue is the great nomad chief Karada. Can her warrior tribe overcome a raider horde, mighty ogres, and the curse of the green dragon?

Divine hammer
The Kingpriest Trilogy, Volume Two • Chris Pierson

Twenty years have passed since Beldinas the Kingpriest took the throne, and his is a realm of unsurpassed glory. But evil threatens, so Beldinas must turn to a loyal lieutenant to extinguish the darkness of foul sorcery.

October 2002

The Dragon Isles
Crossroads Series • Stephen D. Sullivan

Legendary home of metallic dragons, the Dragon Isles attract seafaring adventurers determined to exploit the wealth of the archipelago, despite the evil sea dragon that blocks their success.

December 2002

Revisit Krynn with these great collections!

An all-new anthology of classic
DRAGONLANCE® stories

The Best of Tales, Volume II

Edited by Margaret Weis & Tracy Hickman

This new collection contains a selection of classic DRAGONLANCE tales and an all-new roleplaying adventure by Tracy Hickman. This "best of" includes favorites by well-known DRAGONLANCE authors Douglas Niles, Richard A. Knaak, Paul B. Thompson & Tonya C. Cook, Dan Parkinson, Roger Moore, and others.

Available now!

The great modern fantasy epic —
now available in paperback

The Annotated Chronicles

Margaret Weis & Tracy Hickman

Margaret Weis & Tracy Hickman return to the Chronicles, adding notes and commentary in this annotated paperback edition of the three books that began the epic saga.

October 2002